*The*
# DIAMOND
*of* # LONDON

*The*
# DIAMOND
*of* # LONDON

## Andrea
# PENROSE

KENSINGTON
PUBLISHING CORP.
www.kensingtonbooks.com

KENSINGTON BOOKS are published by

Kensington Publishing Corp.
119 West 40th Street
New York, NY 10018

ISBN: 978-1-4967-4421-0 (ebook)

ISBN: 978-1-4967-4420-3

First Kensington Trade Paperback Printing: February 2024

10 9 8 7 6 5 4 3 2 1

Printed in the United States of America

For my Mother,
who was a rebel herself when it came to the conventional rules
of what women could and could not do.

I'm forever grateful to her for being such a great role model
and encouraging me to believe that a girl could be
anything she wanted to be.

*Fortes fortuna juva*

# *Historical Figures Appearing in*
# The Diamond of London

## Lady Hester's Family

- William Pitt the Younger, British Prime Minister: *Lady Hester's uncle*
- John Pitt, Lord Chatham, government official and Pitt the Younger's older brother: *Lady Hester's uncle*
- The dowager Countess Chatham: *Pitt the Younger's mother, Lady Hester's grandmother*
- Charles Stanhope, 3rd Earl Stanhope: *Lady Hester's father*
- Philip "Mahon" Stanhope: *Lady Hester's half brother*
- Charles Stanhope: *Lady Hester's half brother*
- James Stanhope: *Lady Hester's half brother*
- Thomas Pitt, 2nd Lord Camelford: *Lady Hester's cousin*
- Sir Sidney Smith, naval officer and war hero: *Lady Hester's cousin*
- William Grenville: government official and British Prime minister after Pitt: *Pitt the Younger's cousin*

## London Society

- The Prince of Wales: *eldest son and heir of King George III; Pitt the Younger's political enemy*
- George "Beau" Brummell: *confidant of the Prince of Wales and London's leading arbiter of fashion and style*
- Granville Leveson Gower: *diplomat in Pitt's cabinet*
- George Canning: *member of Pitt's cabinet*

- William Dacres Adams: *Pitt's private secretary*
- Georgiana, Duchess of Devonshire: *Society hostess and supporter of Pitt the Younger's political rival*
- Henrietta "Harriet," Countess of Bessborough: *Georgiana's sister*
- Lieutenant-General Sir John Moore: *one of Britain's top military commanders*
- Thomas Lawrence: *famous artist and leading portrait painter of the beau monde*
- William and Caroline Herschel: *brother and sister; astronomers to King George III and well-known figures in London's scientific community*

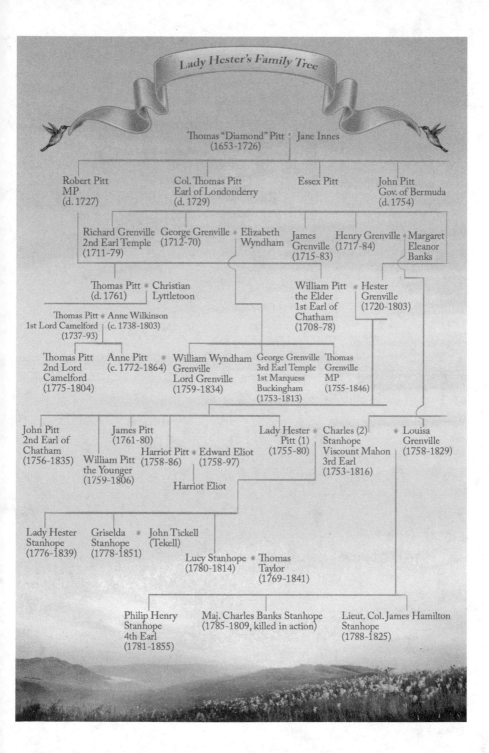

Lady Hester's Family Tree

Thomas "Diamond" Pitt • Jane Innes
(1653-1726)

Robert Pitt
MP
(d. 1727)

Col. Thomas Pitt
Earl of Londonderry
(d. 1729)

Essex Pitt

John Pitt
Gov. of Bermuda
(d. 1754)

Richard Grenville
2nd Earl Temple
(1711-79)

George Grenville
(1712-70)

Elizabeth
Wyndham

James
Grenville
(1715-83)

Henry Grenville
(1717-84)

Margaret
Eleanor
Banks

Thomas Pitt
(d. 1761)

Christian
Lyttletoon

William Pitt
the Elder
1st Earl of
Chatham
(1708-78)

Hester
Grenville
(1720-1803)

Thomas Pitt
1st Lord Camelford
(1737-93)

Anne Wilkinson
(c. 1738-1803)

Thomas Pitt
2nd Lord
Camelford
(1775-1804)

Anne Pitt
(c. 1772-1864)

William Wyndham
Grenville
Lord Grenville
(1759-1834)

George Grenville
3rd Earl Temple
1st Marquess
Buckingham
(1753-1813)

Thomas
Grenville
MP
(1755-1846)

John Pitt
2nd Earl of
Chatham
(1756-1835)

James Pitt
(1761-80)

William Pitt
the Younger
(1759-1806)

Harriot Pitt
(1758-86)

Edward Eliot
(1758-97)

Lady Hester
Pitt (1)
(1755-80)

Charles (2)
Stanhope
Viscount Mahon
3rd Earl
(1753-1816)

Louisa
Grenville
(1758-1829)

Harriot Eliot

Lady Hester
Stanhope
(1776-1839)

Griselda
Stanhope
(1778-1851)

John Tickell
(Tekell)

Lucy Stanhope
(1780-1814)

Thomas
Taylor
(1769-1841)

Philip Henry
Stanhope
4th Earl
(1781-1855)

Maj. Charles Banks Stanhope
(1785-1809, killed in action)

Lieut. Col. James Hamilton
Stanhope
(1788-1825)

# *Prologue*

~~~~

To understand me, and the forces of nature that have shaped my family, you need to know about The Diamond.

The story began in 1687 when the gem was discovered in the famous Kollur Mine of Golconda, an independent sultanate located in the heart of exotic India. Legend has it that the enslaved soul who found the treasure cut a slash in his thigh and hid it in the wound, and then with yet another show of boldness and bravery, he escaped during the Mughal siege of the sultan's fort and made his way to the coast. There he encountered an English sea captain and offered to split the proceeds of The Diamond's sale in return for safe passage out of India.

Alas, his courage was no substitute for cunning. The poor fellow paid for his naïveté in blood. The captain, who had a far more profitable deal in mind, murdered him and sold the stone—at 410 carats it was the largest diamond ever found—to a gem merchant named Jamchand. It changed hands again in 1701 when Jamchand sold it to my great-great-grandfather, Thomas Pitt, a raffish adventurer turned nabob of the formidable East India Company, which had established a lucrative trading monopoly between Britain and the vast subcontinent.

There were rumors that Pitt's acquisition of the magnificent gem was less than legal. But then, the actions of those who are clever and daring are often shadowed in whispers of skullduggery. The truth is Pitt and The Diamond were made for each other. Both were bigger than life and glittered with a hard-edged fire, a fire lit by an inner ice-blue flame that seemed to burn both hot and cold, casting a mesmerizing glow.

In 1702, my great-great-grandfather—now known as "Diamond Pitt"—sent the precious stone back to England, concealed in the heel of his son's boot. It was entrusted to the London firm of Long & Steele to shape into a polished gem. The cutting took over two years and cost the extravagant sum of £6,000. But when Pitt saw its final form on his return to England, he knew that Fate and Fortune had smiled kindly on him.

The Diamond, now a 140-carat white cushion-cut brilliant featuring lozenge and triangle facets that glittered with pale blue highlights, was truly extraordinary. Two of the smaller stones from the cuttings were sold to Peter the Great of Russia—the third one now graces my finger in a ring passed down from my mother—but the real treasure was brokered to the French regent, Phillipe II, Duke of Orléans, in 1717. Dubbed the "Regent Diamond," it adorned the coronation crown of King Louis XV in 1723. Later in the century, the blue beauty cast its spell over Queen Marie Antoinette, who fell in love with it at first sight and often wore it sewn onto her favorite black velvet hat.

The gem survived the French Revolution and then fell into the hands of Napoleon, who had it set into his coronation sword when he had himself crowned Emperor of France in 1804. In 1812, Marie-Étienne Nitot, official jeweler to the Emperor, recrafted it into the hilt of Napoleon's military sword. However, just as it had for the poor beheaded queen, it proved an unlucky talisman. Napoleon was defeated in battle by the British and their Allies, who forced him to abdicate the throne—but not before his wife, the Empress Marie Louise I, fled with the gem to her family in Austria. I have heard that it has since been returned to France, though my present circumstances don't allow for me to say so for sure.

Luck, however, continued to shine on Thomas Pitt. The sale of

The Diamond made my great-great-grandfather—already a wealthy man—fabulously rich, and his fortune gave the Pitt family entrée to the highest circles of power and privilege. Destiny continued to favor them as they gained increasing influence in Britain through marriage with the illustrious Grenville and Stanhope clans, as well as through their own scintillating talents. I can't help but wonder whether that singular gem sparked some indefinable inner fire in the family blood, for the descendants of Diamond Pitt have more than their fair share of luminaries.

My grandfather, the legendary orator and politician William Pitt the Elder, served as prime minister of Britain during the epic Seven Years' War with France to determine global supremacy . . . his son, my uncle William Pitt the Younger, made history when he was chosen as our country's leader at age twenty-four—the youngest prime minister ever handed the royal seals . . . my cousin, Sir Sydney Smith, was a swashbuckling war hero, who through sheer bravado held the citadel of Acre against Napoleon and his army, forcing the Little Corsican to abandon his dream of conquering Jerusalem and the East.

Then there was my other cousin, Thomas Pitt—1st Lord Camelford—a rakehell rogue and sometimes spy . . . William Grenville—1st Baron Grenville—Pitt the Younger's cousin and yet another British prime minister . . . my own father, Charles Stanhope, an eminent man of science who along with his good friend Benjamin Franklin was renowned for his experiments with electricity . . .

So you see, we of The Diamond's blood seem impelled by some elemental force to live large and follow our fire-kissed passions, no matter that passions are rife with danger.

Especially for a lady.

I have just paused to sharpen my pen and reflect on what I've just written. I'm old now, and see things much more clearly. Here in the deserts of Syria and Palestine, the searing sunlight and scouring sand strip away all artifice and illusion. One of my present passions—a tamer one compared to my youthful follies—is to excavate the region's ancient ruins, carefully exposing the hidden layers in search of subtle secrets from the past. History has much to teach us.

Some of which are lessons I should have learned long ago.

Do I regret my life and the choices I have made? It's a question that I am often asked.

*Ah.* How to answer . . .

Like Icarus, I've soared impossibly close to the Sun, lifted on wings made of hubris and a refusal to be bound by the earthly strictures that seek to keep those of my sex locked in a cage. From such glorious heights, the view is intoxicating.

One feels invincible.

*A foolish thought.* The Heavens are not made for mere mortals.

So, of course, each time I dared to fly—I am stubborn to a fault—I fell back to *terra firma*, leaving me battered and bruised in both body and spirit. I don't deny that it hurt. *Loss, grief, betrayal, the bitter taste of ashes after all hope goes up in flames.*

I have heard what people say of me now. Strangers whisper that I am a wit-addled eccentric, living alone and unloved in my mountain fortress. A cautionary tale for any woman who wonders whether daring to shuck off the corset of conventional behavior is worth it.

Which again begs the question—do I regret my life and the choices I have made?

Yes, regret has been part of the journey. As has disappointment. But so has triumph. I lived—*truly lived*—unyielding to any voice, save for the whisper of my own heart. And in refusing to let the cacophony of voices around me drown out that fragile sound, I have, against all odds, achieved things that men said couldn't be done by the weaker sex.

But I suppose that my deepest satisfaction has come from the fact that I stayed true to my heart, rising phoenix-like from the ashes of my most egregious mistakes, each time reforming into a new and stronger self.

Tomorrow I shall pick up my pen again. There are so many stories told about me. *Lies, conjectures, exaggerations.* Fear is an elemental human emotion—I frightened people and their preconceptions.

Time is slipping away. The truth will blur over the coming years and so I find myself compelled to write my own narrative. I shall leave it for future readers to decide whether I am truly mad . . . or merely a woman who refused to be defined by all the naysayers.

*Ha! A truly scary thought to those who don't dare to stray off the straight and narrow road.*

A story must have a beginning. So perhaps the best place for me to start is the night my father put a knife to my throat, cutting away the last, lingering illusions that my life was ever meant to follow a conventional path.

# *Chapter* 1

*Summer 1800*

The steel was cold as ice against my throat, and yet I wasn't afraid.

"Put the knife away, Papa," I said calmly. "One little slip and you might accidentally prick your finger." I could always govern my father better than anybody because I could bear his oddities and understood how to use humor to coax him back to reason when plain sense and argument would have failed.

The flame from his desk lamp shivered, casting a flicker of light over his face. I saw the spasm of conflicting emotions—razor-sharp logic warring with his increasing eccentric ideas about power and privilege, and how our family should live within the rarified world of the British aristocracy.

"I am like King Lear! My daughters have abandoned me!" His voice was plaintive, as if he couldn't comprehend how such a thing had come to pass. "And all the noble principles upon which I raised them."

I felt more sorrow than anger. The truth, noble or otherwise, was that his unorthodox method of raising us had been a cause of consternation among all our relatives.

Papa was an ardent admirer of the eminent Enlightenment philosopher Jean-Jacques Rousseau, who believed that mankind was born innocent and it was Society's rules and hierarchies that corrupted our natural state. Thus, while he taught us the rudiments of reading, mathematics, and a smattering of French, we were forbidden to have any intercourse with books, even the Bible, until he deemed that we had learned our primary life lessons from Nature. My younger half brothers—my own mother, a very charming and well-educated lady, a member of the illustrious Pitt family, had died when I was three and Papa quickly remarried—had found themselves apprenticed to the local blacksmith in order to learn the moral rewards of manual labor, despite being the sons of an earl.

"Clearly I haven't abandoned you, Papa," I replied. "Here I am, and the basic laws of physics say that I can't be in two places at once."

My quip make him smile.

The night breeze rattled the windowpanes. Moonlight fluttered over the library's bookshelves, illuminating shelf after shelf of Papa's leatherbound books. His scientific instruments and journals cluttered the worktables, his cabinet of curiosities rose up from the gloom, its wondrous collection of strange and exotic things coming to life for just an instant as a quicksilver gleam danced over the glass.

Genius and madness, blurred in the shadows.

My father's intellect was unquestioned. His interest in electricity led him to form a fast friendship with the American luminary, Benjamin Franklin, as the two of them become the leading experimenters in the field. His other scientific inventions drew accolades, including an innovative printing press and the Stanhope lens, which allowed microscopes to create a greater magnification. It was his emotional stability that descended into the netherworld of darkness.

"Ah, Hester . . ."

Feeling his muscles relax, I dared to slowly ease away his arm, which was pressed against my chest, pinning me to the wall. I didn't really think he was planning to slice through my windpipe, but the blade was making me uncomfortable.

"Clever, clever, Hester." He patted my cheek. "I have missed our little games of logic."

At a young age, I sensed that my father thought me the cleverest of all his six children. On the whole, he paid little attention to any of us. However, he seemed to enjoy devising philosophical puzzles for me to reason out.

"Think, think, Hester," I recall him saying when I was twelve years old. "You are the best logician I've ever seen. Why, when you put your mind to it, you can talk through a problem and bring Truth to the point of a needle."

Staring at the knife in his hand, as if seeing it for the first time, he blew out a sigh and set it aside. "Come, let us sit by the fire and talk about philosophy. I have a theoretical question that will test whether your reasoning is as sharp as ever."

*Oh, yes, I am sharp*, I thought. Sharp enough to see that his increasing eccentricities, both personal and political, were fast alienating him from all his family and friends.

Including me.

The French Revolution and its ideals had been the catalyst for my father's transformation from august aristocrat to radical republican. "Citizen Stanhope" was now the laughingstock of London, fodder for the pens of London's satirical artists, who dissected his foibles with surgical skill. His scathing criticism of his own country alienated his close friend, my uncle William Pitt the Younger—who was serving as the prime minister of Britain—and turned him into a lifelong enemy.

As for his family, there was a terrible irony to his ideas. His reverence for liberty, equality, and fraternity was in confounding contradiction to his despotic rule over our household. My stepmother soon wearied of his quirks and turned distant. She spent less and less time at Chevening, our ancestral estate, leaving all of us children to fend for ourselves.

*Decisions, decisions.*

It was at that precise moment, with the chill of the blade still lingering on my throat, that I finally resolved to make an emotional and physical escape from the tyranny of his misguided genius. Though in truth, I suppose the rumblings of my discontent had been growing ever louder over the past year. An opportunity to spend time in London with my relatives had allowed me tantalizing glimpses of the world beyond the confining gates of Chevening.

And the experience of the last twelve months had kindled a spark in my Pitt blood and given me a yearning for adventures.

*Spring 1799*

"Lady Hester, do come here and allow me to introduce you to Lord Robert Ashton and his cousin, the Honorable Frederick Thornwood," called Georgiana, Duchess of Devonshire.

The magnificent drawing room of Devonshire House, a grand residence known for its opulent glitter and scintillating parties, was ablaze with light from a trio of ornate chandeliers, their candle flames reflecting off the intricate cut-crystal baubles and casting flickers of fire over the crème de la crème of London Society.

I dutifully crossed the carpet, taking pleasure in the sensuous swoosh of fine-spun silk frothing around my ankles.

Fearing the corrupting influences of aristocratic entertainments, my father had forbidden me and my sisters to dress in pretty clothes once we were old enough to mingle in Society. Sack-like gowns made of drab muslin—another of his peculiar rules—were meant to trumpet a disgust of the rich and their frivolous indulgences, as well as discourage a gentleman's attention on the rare occasions when we were permitted to accept invitations.

No wonder my youngest sister had eloped at age sixteen with the local apothecary three years ago.

As I approached the duchess, I saw a momentary spark in the eyes of the two gentlemen. *Curiosity, perhaps?* Wondering, no doubt, whether the eldest daughter of the eccentric Earl Stanhope also had an odd kick to her gait.

My chin came up a fraction as Georgiana began the formal ritual of introducing members of the ton to one another. She had been quick to befriend me when, pressured by the Pitt side of the family, my father had reluctantly allowed me and my sister Griselda to visit London and begin circulating in Society. I wasn't quite sure why, given that my uncle—known as William Pitt the Younger to distinguish him from his father, the legendary politician William Pitt the Elder—was currently prime minister of Great Britain and Georgiana was an ardent supporter of Charles James Fox, Pitt's greatest political rival. Maybe she had heard that I was headstrong and opinionated, and was hoping that I would embarrass Pitt by making a cake of myself.

"Lady Hester, how delightful to make your acquaintance." Lord Ashton performed an exaggerated bow over my hand. "You look the very picture of feminine beauty in that particular shade of blue."

*What a tarradiddle!* I was too tall and too thin for such an inane compliment.

"Do you consider yourself an expert on female beauty, milord?" I shot back, challenging his platitude. I had always been forthright, and was determined not to be intimidated by London Society.

He hesitated, looking confused on how to respond. However, he was saved by his friend, who smoothly replied, "One need not be an expert to recognize beauty when one sees it."

Mr. Thornwood appeared to possess a modicum of wit and cleverness. Ignoring Lord Ashton, I turned my attention to him. "Are you equally good in recognizing the fine points of horseflesh, sir?" I was a neck-and-leather rider and, as most gentlemen of the ton paid attention to horse racing, I was eager to discuss the upcoming races at Royal Ascot.

A cough. "I consider myself to have some skill in all things equestrian, milady."

His understated response further piqued my interest.

"Excellent." I waved for one of the passing footmen to bring me a glass of champagne, a gesture that drew disapproving titters from the Duchesse de Gontaut and her trio of sycophants. I had heard through friends that the haughty French emigree thought I was not *comme il faut*.

*Tant pis.*

I responded with a challenging stare before looking back to Thornwood with a smile. "I should very much like to hear your opinion on which horses you think are the favorites for winning the Queen Anne's Plate."

"Come, Lord Ashton." As Georgianna hooked the baron's arm, I thought I detected a smirk. "I see Marquess of Downdell's daughter has arrived. She's a charming and polished young lady. I'm sure you will find *her* to be *amiable* company."

Games within games were being played. Though inexperienced in Society, I knew that feminine wiles had a feline quality. Ladies moved gracefully around on soft little cat paws, purring quietly until the moment when they saw an opportunity to unsheathe their claws.

Alas, my temperament was not one of subtlety. No wonder I preferred the company of men.

To his credit, Thornwood didn't shy away from my request. We spent a pleasant interlude discussing the merits of the entries in the prestigious Plate race as well as their jockeys—his knowledge was impressive—before one of his cronies beckoned for him to join a discussion on politics and the latest measures my uncle was seeking to push through Parliament.

For an instant, I was tempted to follow. I far preferred talking about politics with the gentlemen to joining the ladies in their pea-brained chatter on the latest fashions for flounces and furbelows. However, I recognized the group as prominent Whigs and decided that we would only end up in a shouting match.

And naturally, I would be the only one accused of scandalous behavior. Unfair, but that was the way of the world. A lady had few weapons with which to fight back. Especially as our hands were, metaphorically speaking, tied behind our backs.

I handed my empty goblet to one of the footmen serving champagne and took up a full one before wandering into one of the side salons in search of my uncle, who had kindly offered to chaperone me for the evening despite his less than cordial relationship with Fox and the Devonshire crowd.

I smiled. Despite all the pressure of his political office, my uncle had been remarkably supportive of me and my sister, and our desire to partake in the normal pleasures of aristocratic Society. I think that my youngest sister's elopement had made the Pitt family painfully aware that Griselda and I were past the age when most highborn ladies should have been passed from patriarch to husband.

Marriage was considered an elemental duty for those of our sex—not for our own happiness, of course, which was considered irrelevant, but for the advantage of our family, whether it be for money, joining aristocratic bloodlines, or forming alliances for power and prestige. My sense was that my uncle felt honorbound to the memory of my mother—his beloved favorite sister—to free us from our father's tyranny and see that we did not suffer the stigma of sliding into the pitiable state of spinsterhood.

I paused to take a sip of my sparkling wine, listening to the trill of feminine laughter and buzz of masculine voices twining with the clink of crystal and discreet serenade of a string quartet playing Haydn's Opus 54, No. 1.

*The symphony of privilege and pleasure.*

The bare flesh on my arms began to prickle.

A quick inhale. The lush tickle of Parisian perfumes filled my nostrils as I looked around me. The jewel-bright colors of the ladies in their sumptuous gowns punctuated the black-and-white elegance of the gentlemen in their evening attire . . . Velvet draperies, marble collonading, gilded furnishings—all the sights and sounds were a feast for the senses.

The night was young and there was a thrumming of heady anticipation swirling through the air. The promise of flirtations and assignations beckoned from the shadows . . . smiles gleamed in the candlelight, innuendo whispered from the walls . . . one could almost see the silvery strands undulating through the crowd, weaving a shimmering web . . . alliances formed, deals brokered, secrets betrayed . . .

A shiver of excitement danced down my spine. In truth, I was in no hurry to shackle myself to a husband. The taste of freedom was sweet on my lips and I wanted to enjoy—

"Hetty." My uncle came up beside me and offered his arm. "Come sit with me for a bit." He looked with longing at the small sofa set in an alcove shadowed by a Roman-style plinth topped with a classical urn filled with flowers. "I confess, my foot is aching like the devil."

Dark smudges accentuated the hollows beneath his eyes, and fatigue had pulled his sallow skin taut over his cheekbones, making the famous Pitt nose look even more prominent. I felt a stab of guilt. Work was his only mistress—he had never married—and she rode him hard. His health, always delicate, had suffered of late under the strain of steering the country through difficult times. Gout caused him much discomfort these days.

And yet, he here was, limping through hostile territory so that I might have an evening of fun.

"You dear, dear man." I placed my glove on his sleeve and helped him take a seat. "Let me fetch you a glass of port."

"Port," he said, "would be most welcome."

I quickly returned, on impulse bringing along one for myself as well.

Three gentlemen—two prominent aristocrats who were acquaintances of my father and an exquisitely elegant fellow who I did not recognize—had come over to converse with my uncle. Noting the two glasses in my hands, Pitt thought for an instant, and then smiled. "Thank you, my dear. You have, I see, anticipated that my thirst won't be satisfied with just one libation."

*Clever man.* No wonder he was such a good politician. Clearly he sensed what I was planning and was discreetly nudging me to seek safer ground.

But emboldened by the invisible current of high-spirited devilry humming through the gathering—or perhaps it was the two glasses of fizzy wine that I had just drunk—I threw caution to the wind.

"Oh, I shall fetch you a second glass when you have finished the first, Uncle," I replied with a saucy grin. "As all you gentlemen are so exceedingly fond of port, I would very much like to try it for myself."

Pitt's brows arched up a notch but he refrained from comment. His companions did not. A series of inarticulate male huffs and snorts from my father's two acquaintances, Lord Cullworth and Lord Farnham, articulated their shock.

Though I'm not sure whether the stricture actually appeared in any written set of rules, every lady knew that she was strictly forbidden to drink port. Indeed, in my admittedly limited experience with the world at large, I had noticed that gentlemen were loath to share a great many interesting things with those of my sex.

Which of course made them all the more alluring. *Wearing trousers, riding astride, wielding a cavalry saber* . . .

My mental list was interrupted by a low chuckle from Elegance Personified. As I looked up to meet his eyes, he gave me a wink.

"Now see here, Pitt, you must do something!" sputtered Cullworth.

"Indeed?" Pitt took a meditative swallow of his port. "What would you suggest?"

Cullworth's lordly jaw opened and closed several times in succession but no words came forth.

"This is a very fine vintage, Hester," added my uncle, cocking a small salute to me with his glass.

Stifling a laugh, I gave the garnet-red fortified wine a taste. Sweet, rich, the velvety port filled my mouth with a myriad of sensations.

All of them delicious.

As I swallowed, allowing the liquid to make a sensuous slide down my throat, Lord Cullworth and Lord Farnham turned and stalked away.

"Trouble," murmured Elegance Personified, his dark eyes subjecting me to an intense scrutiny.

Unflinching, I met his gaze and lifted my chin.

Another chuckle. Even his low-pitched laugh seemed to fit him to perfection. "Pitt, why is it that I sense your niece is Trouble?"

My uncle hesitated. A careful man, he was known for taking his time to analyze the ramifications before making a decision.

The string quartet was now playing Mozart's String Quartet No. 20 in D Major.

"Hester," he said softly, his voice hard to hear over the notes of the violins. "Allow me to introduce you to George Brummell."

# Chapter 2

*B*rummell.

I should have guessed. Unlike most young ladies, I regularly read the newspapers and scandal sheets, and made a point of perusing the latest satirical drawings by London's great gadfly artists, James Gillray, Thomas Rowlandson, and George Cruikshank. Despite his youth, George Brummell had become something of a celebrity in Town.

"Ah, the Paragon of Fashion and supreme arbiter of gentlemanly style," I responded.

His casual shrug didn't cause so much as a miniscule crease to mar the shoulders of his impeccably cut coat.

After allowing a mock grimace to hover between us for an instant, I added, "Thank heavens you haven't yet turned your discerning eye and caustic comments to the state of feminine fashion." My fingers smoothed at the folds of my gown. "I fear that my attire would be found sadly lacking in panache."

His gaze flitted over me and came to rest on my diamond ring. "Style is about far more than clothing, Lady Hester."

I smiled and took another sip of port. "Then perhaps there is hope for me yet?"

A glint of amusement lit in Brummell's eyes. "Do you care what others think about you?"

"Probably not as much as I should," I admitted.

"She is way too clever for her own good," added Pitt, though he said it with a fond smile. "You were right to call her Trouble."

"I would rather be called Trouble than be called a Bore," I said under my breath.

Brummell fingered his chin, fixing me with another assessing look. "Even better is to be called Interesting."

"Interesting?" I repeated uncertainly. There were a great many nuances to that word. My father was often called "interesting" as a euphemism for "blathering idiot."

"Give me your glass," said Brummell abruptly.

"Why?" I demanded. I was only half finished with my port and very much enjoying it.

"Because, Lady Hester, you're about to get your first lesson in the meaning of style."

Curious, I handed it over without further protest.

"I'll take yours as well, Pitt, and refill it."

My uncle flashed him a grateful look. "Consider yourself lucky, my dear," he said once Brummell had moved off. "He's quite discriminating when it comes to dispensing his favors."

*Why me?* I wondered. According to the scribblers of London, the Prince of Wales and his Carlton House cronies all fawned over George Brummell, seeking his approval on dress and deportment.

Brummell was back before I had much time to mull over the matter and gave Pitt the same cut crystal glass, now refilled, its facets throwing off sparks of red. To me, he offered . . .

A frown pinched between my brows. "Why—"

An exasperated sigh cut me off. "You must trust me, Lady Hester." Brummell spun the stem between his elegant fingers. "Otherwise this experiment will be an utter waste of effort."

The word "experiment" raised my hackles. My father's obsession with science and the scientific method had led him to conduct a grand experiment with me and my siblings to test his theory on education. And in my opinion, the result had proved disastrous.

But I was curious, and so I grudgingly accepted his offering.

"Is she always this difficult?"

Pitt cleared his throat with a cough. Or perhaps it was a laugh.

"Hold up the glass, Lady Hester," commanded Brummell.

This time there was no hesitation.

He muttered something under his breath—something rather uncomplimentary—and pursed his lips.

The glass he had given me was a stemmed wineglass, but rather than rise in a tall, conical flute as was the current fashion, it was shaped like a shallow bowl, the wine a pool of shimmering deep red.

Brummell reached out and adjusted the angle of my elbow. "Grace, Lady Hester. You must hold it with grace." He gave a tiny wince. "And an air of confidence."

"I—"

He plucked the glass from me and assumed a pose. "Like so."

*How did a mere mortal contrive to appear so elegant and assured?* He looked like one of those classical marble sculptures in the British Museum come to life. Only one tiny flaw, a small bump betraying a broken nose from some past mishap, kept him from appearing a paragon of heavenly perfection.

"I'm afraid that I don't possess the art of making myself look like a Greek god or goddess."

"Then pay attention and learn it." Brummell softened the retort with a quick smile. "Attitude is everything. Use it as armor."

It took me a moment to grasp the metaphorical message of his statement. Armor was forged to protect a person's vulnerable parts . . .

He took hold of my right hand, curled my fingers around the stem, and slid them down to within an inch of the base.

"Relax," he encouraged, once again positioning my elbow just so. "Now, thrust your hip out just a touch." A smile blossomed on his lips as he stepped back and observed me. However, a critical squint quickly chased it away. "It's a decent beginning, but you have much to learn."

"Why this particular glass?" I responded.

"Because it is distinctive," he shot back. "It is called a coupe, and it is the favored shape for champagne in France, while we here in Britain prefer the flute. Yet most wealthy and fashionable households possess them, so you may request your libation to be served in one."

Brummell paused. "More importantly, it has a story. Legend has it that the shape is based on the left breast of Madame de Pompadour, mistress to the French King Louis XV." An airy wave. "Though others claim it was the breast of Marie Antoinette. What matters is, you will have a titillating response to give when someone asks. And that will make you *interesting*."

I lifted the glass a little higher, studying the way candlelight danced around its curve,

"From now on, at fashionable gatherings such as this one, you will drink nothing but port out of a coupe. The fact that you are drinking forbidden libation out of a slightly scandalous glass will make you distinctive. More importantly, it makes you *intriguing*," he added after glancing around the room. "As you pointed out, most people are bores."

"You have a very sardonic view of life, Mr. Brummell."

"I prefer to think the worst of people. That way I am rarely disappointed."

I bit back a laugh.

"Now come," he said gruffly, "show me again how to stand so as to draw the eye of every man and woman in the room . . ."

He had me practice a few more times before inclining a brusque nod. "That will do." A pause. "For now."

"Zeus has made his pronouncement." I looked up at the frescoed ceiling, with was painted with a profusion of classical deities. "Are thunderbolts about to rain down from Mount Olympus?"

A flash of amusement from Brummell. "Given your father's expertise with lightning, I imagine you know how to avoid being burned to a crisp."

"Ah, so you don't think me completely lacking in the skills necessary for survival?"

Brummell looked at Pitt, who had finished his second glass of port and was sitting with his eyes closed. "We shall see, Lady Hester." His voice held a challenge. "If you wish to test yourself further, meet me at Lady Hillhouse's soiree tomorrow night."

"You may count on it." I drained the coupe in one long swallow and set it down atop the plinth.

Ignoring my bravado, he flicked a mote of dust from his coat cuff. "It's late and your uncle is exhausted. Take him home."

It *was* late. The moonlight was fading, ceding its place in the night sky to the first hint of dawn's rosy glow.

The clatter of the ironshod carriage wheels on the cobblestones had roused my uncle. Leaning back against the squabs, he stifled a yawn. "Whatever his other egregious faults—and they are legion—the Duke of Devonshire possesses a very fine wine cellar."

My stomach wasn't inclined to agree, but my queasiness likely had more to do with my indiscriminate mixing of champagne and port than any fault with the duke's choice of vintages.

"Tell me more about George Brummell," I asked. "How did you come to be friends with him?"

"I'm not sure 'friend' is the precise word I would use to describe our relationship." Like his father, Pitt the Elder, my uncle was much admired for his command of the English language. "Brummell has a certain magnetism—he's used his wit, charm and sense of style to make himself welcome within the very highest circles of Society—"

"Is he not an aristocrat himself?"

"No, but through a combination of luck and patronage, his father secured the plum position of private secretary to our former prime minister, Lord North," replied Pitt. "That allowed him to send his son to Eton, where young George began his forays into fashion by redesigning the traditional white tie required to be worn by students."

"So, Brummell was a strong personality, even at an early age," I observed.

A soft chuckle. "Yes, as were you, Jockey Girl."

"You exaggerate," I drawled, though the truth was that, as a child, I did indeed indulge in a number of unladylike rebellions. Riding like a demon was one of them.

"I do not." His mouth twitched. "I seem to recall a family outing to the seashore at Hastings when you were eight years old. Intrigued by your father's admiration of France, you spotted a small boat pulled up on the beach, and decided to sneak off and row yourself across the Channel to visit Paris."

Another chuckle. "Thank God your governess spotted you bobbing away on the waves."

"My stepmother rang a peal over the poor woman's head, though it wasn't Miss Cotter's fault that she couldn't control my impulses," I replied. "I concede that I was ungovernable as a child." Perhaps that was because I had so little loving guidance. Neither my father nor his second wife had any interest in offering any emotional nurturing to their children.

"Your mother . . ." My uncle closed his eyes for an instant and sighed.

I knew from my Pitt relatives that she had been his favorite sister and her early death had cut him to the quick.

"Your mother was a paragon of grace and intelligence," he said. "She filled your household with good cheer and convivial company, and was the one person who could keep your father on an even keel. Her early death was a great loss to us all. Had she lived—"

"Enough about me and my family," I said quickly, the talk of such memories making me uncomfortable. My mother had died when I was three and I couldn't remember her. "Let us return to George Brummell. I would like to know more about him."

Pitt hesitated. "Very well. But only because I wish to offer some caveats once I finish with his curriculum vitae."

"You are going to warn me not to be seduced by his charm and aura of magnetism?"

Rather than answer, Pitt picked up the thread of his narrative. "From Eton, Brummell went to Oxford for a year, but then asked his father to buy him his colors in the Tenth Royal Hussars."

That drew a murmur of surprise from me. It was standard practice for wealthy and influential gentlemen to buy their sons an officer's commission in the British Army. But the 10th Royal Hussars was the personal regiment of the Prince of Wales, a very elite and exclusive group of young bucks from the most prominent families in Britain. That it opened its ranks to a commoner was highly unusual. Expense was one reason. Officers in such regiments were required to buy their own uniforms—they were permitted to add their own personal embellishments—and horses, as well as to pay for the regiment's lavish dining and entertainments.

"Brummell immediately captured the prince's fancy," continued Pitt. "You know how vain the prince is. Brummell soon became one of his confidants, advising him on style and fashion. However, when it was announced that the regiment was being transferred out of London, he sold his army commission."

A pause. "Brummell was smart enough to realize that staying close to the prince, whose goodwill provided him entrée into the beau monde, was key to his aspirations."

"And yet a London lifestyle within the highest circles of Society does not come cheaply," I mused.

"Yes, but Brummell's wit and style make him welcome within that world. He's invited to the most exclusive soirees and parties, he has entrée to the best clubs, where he has an opportunity to expand his circle of influential friends. And that in turn makes him a sought-after guest in the grandest homes and estates in Britain."

I considered what I had just heard. "So you're saying that his position in Society depends on his connections to powerful people—and his ability to keep them entertained."

"Yes, that's an accurate summation of George Brummell's situation," said Pitt. "Getting back to my original comment, I have no doubt that he is an exceedingly astute fellow and understands his position. So I imagine that friendship is not as important to him as survival. I assume he seeks out my company and takes pains to be pleasant because of my position." He smiled. "One can't have too many friends in high places."

As the carriage jolted through a turn, a glittery blur of diamond-bright lights from one of the elegant Mayfair mansions flashed against the windowpane. It was, I mused, a seductive world . . .

"I, in turn, enjoy his wit and his commentary on the foibles of Society. He makes me laugh. But I don't make the mistake of thinking his bonhomie means he is truly my friend. If it suited his purposes, I daresay he would turn on me in a flash."

I was not so naïve as to think expediency didn't play a part in the workings of the world. Still . . .

"That doesn't bother you?"

"I am a politician, Hester. It would be the height of hypocrisy for me to criticize such choices."

"But I know how fiercely loyal you are to your true friends!" I protested.

He gave me a kindly look. "There are times when pragmatism must overcome passion. You have to choose your battles carefully."

I let my eyes slide away.

"And always weigh the consequences of your choices."

# Chapter 3

The next evening, my uncle and I passed through the entrance portico of the Hillhouse mansion on Half Moon Street at the appointed hour and made our way up the grand curved staircase to the formal drawing room. The earl—Hillhouse was a Tory and thus a great admirer of my uncle—and his wife graced us with a very handsome greeting. Adding an apology to Lady Hillhouse, her husband then left her to greet the arriving guests on her own and hurried my uncle to one of the side salons, where by the sounds emanating from within it, a gaggle of gentlemen were already engaged in heated political discourse.

As Lady Hillhouse turned to welcome new arrivals, I made my way to the refreshment table. After drawing a deep breath, I mustered my resolve and asked for a glass of port, adding that I wished to have it served in a coupe.

The footman made me repeat the request, which provoked a round of disapproving mutters from the gentlemen around me. It was considered unladylike for me to seek my own libation, rather than ask my escort to do so for me.

However, I refused to be cowed, unwilling to have Brummell think that I didn't have the courage to be Interesting.

"A glass of port," I said for the third time, raising my voice a notch. "Surely the earl's wine cellar contains a decent vintage, as well as a decent selection of elegant glassware."

The butler appeared from the shadows. "If you will follow me, milady, I will be happy to assist you." He led the way to a foyer between the cardroom and the supper room. "Please wait here while I consult with your uncle."

"My uncle is discussing affairs of state," I replied in my haughtiest voice. "And I am not a child. Kindly fetch me my drink."

He hesitated.

I drew myself up to my full height, which was considerable for a lady. I was now looking him straight in the eye. "And don't forget that I wish to have it served in a coupe . . . unless your household does not possess one."

The butler appeared shocked by my manners—or lack of them. But I didn't care. My blood was up. He must have sensed it, for although his jaw clenched so tightly that I expected to hear his molars crack, he retreated.

*The skirmish appeared won. But what of the battle?*

I waited impatiently, annoyed that Brummell had not yet arrived to serve as an ally. A minute passed, and then another. My scowl deepened. What if my strategy failed? Then what?

However, I didn't have to face that question. The butler returned and with an aggrieved huff, gave me my port.

I confess, it tasted even sweeter than I remembered.

Flush with my victory, I wandered off in search of Brummell. *Still no luck.* Perhaps, on second thought, he had decided I didn't merit his attention. After all, what did I, a lady past the first bloom of youth, have to offer a man who—according to my uncle's gentle warning—valued access to influence and power above all other considerations?

He already had a connection to Pitt, and given that my father was now a virtual outcast from Polite Society, I had nothing to offer him.

With that lowering thought in mind, I drifted over to where one of my Grenville relatives, a widowed baroness, was holding court with a group of middle-aged ladies.

One of them, a plump, prune-faced matron sporting a peacock-blue turban with ostrich feather plumes, gave an audible sniff at my approach. "I assume it is your father who has encouraged you to drink that vile stuff. He seems inordinately fond of the color *red*."

A titter ran through the ladies at the reference to my father's admiration for the radical Republicans of France, who wore red knitted caps as a badge of their beliefs.

"Have you ever tried port?" I took a sip and flashed a cat-in-the-creampot smile. "You might be surprised at how tasty it is."

*Silence*. And then the baroness let out a low laugh. "Actually, I can vouch for the fact that it *is* tasty, far more so than sherry or insipid ratafia punch." She regarded me as if trying to decide whether Pitt's approval of me made me acceptable to her side of our family tree.

"How clever of you to request it," she added, a tacit acknowledgment that she deigned to consider me an ally.

"B-but isn't it forbidden—" began a lady with mouse-brown hair.

"That's because it is men who come up with the rules," I responded. "Though I don't think the one forbidding port is actually etched in stone."

The ladies shuffled uncomfortably, as if my small rebellion might somehow spill over and taint their pristine reputations.

Before anyone verbally responded, Brummell appeared in the archway and inclined a graceful bow. "Good evening, ladies. If you are plotting some naughty mischief, I do hope you'll allow me to be a part of it."

More titters, though these were more girlish than the ones that had greeted me. Brummell was a very handsome gentleman, his lithe height and physique set off to perfection by the exquisite fit of his clothing. Rumor had it that he often spent five hours each day dressing for his evening engagement, and judging by the knife-sharp symmetry in the intricate folds of his starched linen cravat, I could well believe it.

"Mr. Brummell, as Society's leading arbiter of taste and style, what is your opinion of Lady Hester drinking port in public?" asked the turbaned matron.

The ladies all looked to him expectantly.

"Hmmph." His eyes narrowed and such was the intensity of his gaze that I felt myself blush under his scrutiny. For a moment, I wondered whether he might have been toying with me all along and now, for the sake of his own amusement, was going to throw me to the wolves.

But then he smiled. "The darkest shade of ruby red is not the easiest color to complement, so I would, of course, be horrified if she was wearing a gown that clashed with it. However, as that particular shade of smoky emerald green is the perfect match of two complementary gemstone colors . . ." He mimed raising a glass in toast. "I highly applaud your taste, milady."

All of a sudden, the temperature around me was decidedly less frosty.

"And now, might I steal Lady Hester away from you?"

"But of course," replied the baroness. "However, in return, I shall expect you to attend my Venetian breakfast next Thursday."

"I would be delighted to do so."

As I turned to join him, I caught the looks of jealousy cast my way. It felt odd—and a bit titillating.

Brummell waited until we had had passed the cardroom and found a quiet nook just outside the music room before speaking. "You have just learned lesson number two—perception is everything. Having someone influential applaud your behavior is another way of ensuring that you are considered stylish rather than eccentric."

A pause. "Or you must make yourself important enough in the eyes of others that they will be loath to find fault with your behavior. Something you were well on the way to doing."

"I reacted mostly on impulse," I admitted.

"I saw from the first that you have good instincts, Hetty." He took the liberty of calling me the pet name used only by my family and I didn't object.

"Now, as we would with a diamond in the rough, we just have to shape the facets." His mouth curled up at the corners. "And give them a final polish."

*A diamond in the rough?* The words touched off a sudden longing. I twisted at my ring, the smooth coolness of my great-great-grandfather's gem setting off sparks of ice and fire against my flesh as I wondered whether some of "Diamond" Pitt's spirit of devil-may-care adventure pulsed through my blood.

I hoped so. My great-great-grandfather hadn't settled for an ordinary life. He had wanted something more.

*More.*

I couldn't articulate what that was, but I somehow felt that I would know it when it beckoned.

Brummell stopped my fiddling by taking my hand and placing it in the crook of his arm. "Come, we have work to do."

The next week brought a blur of entertainments—musicales, soirees, a reception honoring a diplomatic delegation from Saxe-Gotha. Brummell and I were constant companions. His dark humor and razor-sharp wit made me laugh and for some reason I seemed to keep him amused. We spent much of the time in secluded corners with heads bent together and mirth on our lips as we observed the foibles of the other guests and played the game of making me into a Person of Interest.

I learned much simply by watching the nuances of Brummell's behavior, which changed with chameleon-like artfulness depending on his companions. What struck me most was his iron-willed self-control.

Such discipline was beyond my understanding.

"How can you be so polite to such a self-important prig?" I asked after one particular interaction with an insufferably pompous aristocrat.

"Because," answered Brummell coolly, "I am looking at the chessboard of life, and how each move affects another. Yes, I could have easily been rude to him, as I have nothing personally to gain from having his goodwill. But I happen to know he controls the votes in a certain parliamentary district, and I have an acquaintance who dearly wishes to run for the seat. If I can be the go-between, and help broker the arrangement, my acquaintance will feel himself in my debt."

I sighed. "Are you saying that you always know what you want to achieve from an interaction and are willing to make yourself act accordingly?"

He shrugged. "Favors are extremely important to collect. You never know when they will be needed."

"I would rather be true to my feelings than toady up to someone I don't respect," I muttered.

"Then you are a fool," he replied sharply. "Lofty principles are all very well in the abstract. If you are unwilling to allow some compromises to your ideals, you will find the real world a very cruel place."

I thought he was wrong, but I exercised some restraint and didn't say so. Perhaps his situation—he didn't have a formidable family for support and seemed dependent on his own skills and savvy for survival—demanded such an attitude. But for me, idealism mattered. Never mind that my father's example showed the pitfalls of such unyielding resolve.

Or was it merely the hubris of youth that had me sure I could make the world bend to my liking?

My face was deliberately turned to the shadows. Still, Brummell seemed to see exactly what I was thinking.

"You disagree."

"I have a different view of things," I said carefully. A number of thoughts were spinning in my head. Trying to make sense of ideas and put them into words wasn't easy.

"Idealism, that is, a sense of self—of who you are and what you believe—is one of the few things that a female can control. Most aspects of our lives are ruled by men. We have little voice in our destiny and few legal rights. So perhaps that is why my sentiments on staying true to my heart are important to me."

He eyed me thoughtfully. "I think you have more courage and conviction than you realize. And I applaud you for it."

I heard the hint of hesitation in his voice. "But you think me daft?" I pressed.

A sudden brassy tinkling of bells interrupted our tête-à-tête.

"The supper room is open," intoned a trio of liveried footmen as they moved through the drawing room and side salons, summoning the guests to the midnight refreshments. "Come eat, drink, and be merry."

"We shall continue our discussion of philosophical questions at some later date," drawled Brummell. "But for now, the call to partake in fleshly pleasures is too tempting to resist."

A clever quip, I thought, allowing myself to be led toward the sumptuous feast of delicacies waiting for us. Already the sounds of convivial good cheer were punctuating the popping of champagne corks.

My father had often commented that the well-fed were rarely revolutionaries.

So why did I hunger for more than caviar and *foie gras*?

By some unspoken accord, we never returned to the subject of our differing philosophies. I had half expected him to grow bored and drift away to new challenges, but our friendship seemed to please him as much as it did me. So with him as my mentor, I continued to learn about the art of having people see what I wanted them to see. Brummell likened it to the theater and the great actors and actresses who could play a role so convincingly that the audience believed they were royalty on Monday night and beggars on Tuesday night.

I also saw how he used ridicule—or the prospect of it—as a finely honed weapon in his extensive arsenal. Everyone feared to look foolish, and Brummell was so exquisitely clever with his humor that he could use it with devastating effect. An adroit prick here, a droll comment there . . .

After observing him deflate a pompous windbag who came up to brag about the costly fabric of his new brocade waistcoat, I said, "I see it's no coincidence that you've named your favorite horse 'Stiletto.'"

A smile played on his lips.

"I can see that there is a certain secret thrill of donning a second—or sixth—skin," I added a little wistfully. "But I will never be as good at it as you are." A sigh. "You seem so at peace with the world of artifice and illusion."

"I am a cynic at heart," replied Brummell. "It is my opinion that most people are playing a multitude of roles, whether they know it or not—husband, lover, hero, saint . . ."

I, on the other hand, struggled with my conscience. I hated the need to hide my real self. It was ironic, really. Girls were taught from a very young age to do just that, so it should be second nature. The trouble is, I had always rebelled against hiding my light beneath the itchy cloth of convention. Maybe the Almighty wasn't perfect and had erred in trapping my spirit in a female form. I felt that I had been born to do great things, not simply serve as a brood mare and glorified housemaid to whatever man my father deemed a suitable match.

A gentleman was admired for his accomplishments. Why should the same not be true for a lady?

Brummell laughed when I asked him that question the following evening. "Surely that is a rhetorical query. Of course there is no rational explanation, although men will pontificate until they are blue in the face that women are the weaker sex—in everything."

"And yet Queen Elizabeth was one of Britain's greatest monarchs."

He made a wry grimace. "The politicians will all argue that it was really the men behind the throne who were doing the real ruling."

"What fustian," I retorted.

"Yes, but it's men who get to pen the fustian." His brows waggled. "And if it's written on paper or printed in books, then it must be true."

I allowed a reluctant chuckle though I really wanted to curse.

The look of humor flickered and disappeared from his face, his expression suddenly inscrutable. "If you want things to change, you must force men to see that they are wrong."

"How?" I demanded.

His insouciance was back in a flash. "Damned if I know. It's not my fight, Hetty."

We were attending a soiree at the Earl of Shrewsbury's townhouse, with informal dancing as part of the evening's entertainment. The first tentative notes of the musicians tuning their instruments drifted out from the ballroom, the dulcet tones of the pianoforte harmonizing with the violins and cello.

Laughter bubbled up all around us. The swoosh of silk and the soft patter of evening shoes fluttered through the corridor as the guests hurried to take their places on the dance floor. The mansions of Mayfair cared naught for serious thoughts—people were here to partake of the pleasures that wealth and privilege served to them on a silver platter.

"Shall we join the mindless merriment?" asked Brummell.

The practice scales died away and then suddenly the melody of a familiar country gavotte burst into life in the ballroom.

*Hop to the left, spin to the right . . .*

I realized that I knew the steps by heart. *Ah, if only all the twists and twirls of Life's dance were choreographed so clearly.*

"You think too much, Hetty," he said. "And take the world too seriously."

The comment stung. "Perhaps you don't take it seriously enough."

Emotion seemed to flicker in his eyes. Or maybe it was just a quirk of the candlelight.

"Don't you have hopes and dreams?" I asked.

A smile. "If wishes were silver-winged unicorns, then we would all fly to the Moon and back."

That wasn't an answer.

We stared at each other, neither of us willing to look away.

Several moments slid by. The music was quickening to a crescendo. Brummell leaned in until we were nearly nose to nose. "I have what I need to satisfy my wants and desires." His whisper tickled against my cheeks. "What about you, Hetty? Do you even know your deepest longing?"

"I—" I couldn't begin to put it into words.

He gently tucked an errant curl behind my ear. "Lord, what fools these mortals be!"

I recognized the quote from Shakespeare's *A Midsummer Night's Dream* as it was one of my father's favorite sayings.

"And be assured that I include myself at the top of the heap."

His self-deprecating sense of humor drew a grudging laugh from me. "You are incorrigible," I added.

Without warning, he swept me off my feet and spun me round and round in a dizzying circle.

"The night is still young . . ."

Breathless, I found myself fighting for balance as he put me down.

"Let us go watch our fellow fools make cakes of themselves on the polished parquet." For some reason known only to himself, Brummell refused to set foot on the dance floor. "It is always much easier to laugh at the follies of others than to admit to our own shortcomings."

# Chapter 4

*My poor uncle.* I was feeling guilty as I could see that the whirl of my nightly social engagements was exhausting him. And so I took it upon myself to approach Lady Clarendon, an acquaintance of my stepmother, and ask if she would consent to take on the duties of being my chaperone through the autumn months. The countess, a plump, amiable matron, was a well-known hostess of Society and her sterling reputation ensured that her guardianship would meet with approval from the beau monde.

The arrangement pleased all of us. Lady Clarendon was envied by her friends for the connection to me and the supremely fashionable George Brummell while Pitt was relieved to be finally allowed a proper night's rest. And knowing that the countess had a fondness for tippling sherry and playing whist with her lady friends, I was certain that her attention would be on her cards, not on what Brummell and I were doing together in the secluded shadows of Mayfair's mansions.

There was, I knew, a growing speculation among the ton about just what our relationship was.

"You know, Hetty, you are garnering much admiration for your beauty," remarked Pitt, after I gave him the happy news that he no longer had to attend the nightly soirees of the ton. "I have heard that a great many gentlemen are waxing poetic on your dark hair, flawless complexion, and sapphirine eyes."

Thanks to Brummell's polishing of my rough edges, I was getting better at the art of flirtation and was aware that I was attracting more and more attention from the opposite sex.

All of which stirred the inevitable pressure that an unmarried aristocratic lady faces.

"Has anyone in particular caught your fancy?" he added.

*In other words, when the devil are you going to say yes to a legshackle?*

"It is still unfamiliar terrain, Uncle," I replied, using a riding metaphor. "I should not wish to rush my fences."

Ever the diplomat, Pitt smiled and did not badger me. But still, his message was clear: The family was impatient for me to make up my mind and settle down to domestic life.

The utter unfairness of Society's expectations stuck in my craw. After several casual twirls around the dance floor with a gentleman—heaven forfend that a lady spend any time in private getting to know the character of a prospective husband—she was supposed to make a decision that chained her to a regimented existence for the rest of her life.

Was it any wonder that I was in no hurry to be rushed?

And so I was determined to dance to my own tune, at least until I was sure the prick of Cupid's arrow was more than skin deep.

I never lacked for partners at the lavish balls. Brummell adamantly refused to dance—he would not explain why, though I guessed that it was a deliberately chosen quirk to add to his aura of mysterious allure. He watched me caper with the crème de la crème of Society until I tired of the exertion and retreated to join him.

Which of course provoked questions of whether he and I were romantically involved.

It was clear there was a chemistry between us, although neither of us seemed certain of what the exact ingredients were.

*Was I in love?*

The idea appealed to my elemental emotions. I wanted very

much to feel the rapture of my heart beating with unfettered happiness.

And yet . . .

I think the defining moment of what we were to each other occurred at the gala ball at Carlton House given by the Prince of Wales to celebrate the official unveiling of the magnificent portrait of him painted by Sir William Beechey.

"Are you ready to enter the Belly of the Beast?" drawled Brummell, as we passed through the magnificent entrance portico of the prince's London mansion.

I repressed a smile. The caustic comment referred, of course, to the fact that the prince was a fierce supporter of the Whigs and thus a leading political enemy of my uncle. It was also a sly reference to the prince's expanding girth, though the portrait was said to be highly flattering.

"What a disloyal comment," I remarked. "I thought the prince was a dear friend, which should temper your sarcasm." I remembered from my initial conversation with Pitt that Brummell owed his acceptance into the highest circles of Society because the prince had made him a royal favorite.

"I appreciate Prinny's patronage," replied Brummell coolly. "Prinny" was the informal name for the prince, though it was never said to his face. "That does not mean I don't see his many faults."

A liveried servant pointed the way to the West Ante Room. The prince was welcoming his guests there before moving to the main reception room, where Beechey's painting would be revealed with a show of pomp and pageantry.

"He is shallow and vain," continued Brummell, "caring for naught but his own selfish pleasures."

I was surprised by the venom in his voice. "So why do you spend so much time with him, attending his parties and advising him on the fine points of fashion?" I had heard that the prince was a frequent visitor to Brummell's residence in order to observe the art of tying a faultless cravat.

"Why do you think?" he shot back. "Being part of Prinny's inner circle is useful. It opens opportunities that might otherwise be closed to me."

After glancing my way he raised his brows. "Have I disillusioned you?"

"No," I replied after giving the question a long moment of thought. I considered my father and how his unyielding refusal to budge from his beliefs had alienated his wife, his family, and his friends. "I understand that there are situations in life where one must be pragmatic."

Brummell's expression softened. "But as a lady of strong passions, you don't like it."

"There are a great deal of things I don't like about the world as it is, starting with all the strictures on what a lady can and cannot do," I said. "However, in these few short weeks since we met, I have learned some invaluable lessons from you about the difference between a public and private persona."

My answer seemed to affect him. His lashes fluttered but couldn't quite hide the flash of emotion in his eyes. "I'm touched to hear that you feel I've been a good influence." The sardonic tone that usually edged his voice had given way to a hint of vulnerability. "That means . . ."

As if suddenly aware that he was revealing too much to me, Brummell cleared his throat with a brusque cough. "Perhaps that means we should consider having you drink whisky as well as port."

I laughed, although I wished I knew what had really been on the tip of his tongue. "That may be crossing the line of acceptability."

"If you don't occasionally cross the line, Hetty, then how do you know if you're truly testing the boundaries?"

I wondered whether his words were meant for me or for himself. However, as we joined the crowd waiting to pass through the prince's receiving line, my attention was quickly diverted by the hum of voices and the flash of jewel-bright colors.

Despite the swirl of sounds and splendor, it was impossible to miss the imposing presence of the prince. George Augustus Frederick, eldest son of King George III and Queen Charlotte of Mecklenburg-

Strelitz, and heir to the throne, stood alone on the center of a crimson carpet, resplendent in a military uniform festooned with yards of gold and a weighty amount of decorative detailing. His lidded gaze swept the room, and on spotting Brummell, he gave a languid wave for his friend to cut to the head of the line.

Taking my arm, Brummell was quick to respond. "Your Royal Highness," he said, inclining a graceful bow. "Allow me to present Lady Hester Stanhope."

I dropped into a requisite curtsey.

"Ah, Lady Hester." The princely eyes moved from my face to my bosom and then back again, a smile slowly curling on his fleshy lips. "I see that the talk around Town of your beauty has not been exaggerated."

I forced an answering smile, even though his naked scrutiny made my skin crawl.

"What a magnificent ring," I said admiringly. "Your exquisite taste in art and fashion is, of course, well known throughout the land."

Brummell was standing quite close to me and I could feel him quivering with silent laughter. It was true, Prinny did have an excellent eye for art and fashion, but his profligate spending on such personal pleasures had put him greatly in debt, much to the dismay of the king and Parliament.

"Ho, ho." Oblivious to anything but my flattery, the prince raised his hand and gave it a little waggle, setting off the glitter of the massive ruby on his ring finger. "I'm well aware that your family has an excellent eye for precious gems, milady."

At the reference to my great-great-grandfather's diamond, I smiled again, hoping we could now move on.

"We mustn't keep you from greeting your other guests, sir," said Brummell.

"Yes, yes. But you must come and join me when it's time to pull the drapery off the portrait." Prinny gave me a lecherous wink. "I'm sure you will be very impressed."

"How could I not be?" I responded, fluttering my lashes at him. "I have heard it is a perfect likeness."

As the prince simpered, Brummell guided me into the Crimson Drawing Room. The mood was even more effervescent here, fueled, no doubt, by copious amounts of sparkling wine. A footman hurried over with a tray of champagne. Brummell took a glass—he sent the fellow scurrying to fetch a glass of port for me—and then we began to circulate through the crowd.

Brummell stopped often to greet his friends. I, too, had admirers who wished to pay their respects and we passed a very convivial hour enjoying the pleasures of fine wine and scintillating company.

A trumpet blast from the main reception room then summoned us for the unveiling of the portrait.

"Must we?" I asked as Brummell edged through the milling guests, making his way to where the prince and his entourage were standing.

"Yes," he answered firmly. "Prinny's words were not a request, they were a command."

"How can you tell the difference?"

"Because I understand him better than he understands himself." A subtle frown then warned me to silence.

Several dignitaries stepped forward to give effusive speeches on the prince's character and his charitable works. A bevy of servants moved in to take up the silken ropes attached to the drapery.

*Heaven help the poor fellow who fumbles his assignment*, I thought.

But the ceremony went off without a hitch. The prince lifted a finger, the servants tugged as one, and with a sinuous slither, the velvet fell to the floor.

Oohs and ahhhs filled the room, my voice added to them.

It was a marvelous portrait. The prince was depicted as a paragon of manly grace and virtue. His pose radiated confidence, and his handsome face was alight with determination undimmed by whatever challenges lay ahead.

What a pity that it bore precious little resemblance to the flesh-and-blood Prinny.

"Do you like it?" asked the prince, tearing his eyes away from the canvas to look at me.

"It's a work of artistic genius," I answered with complete honesty. Beechey had used a few of Prinny's features, but then with a skilled sleight of hand he had somehow transformed an indolent, overweight sybarite into a heroic figure for the ages.

"Majestic," added Brummell. "Truly majestic."

Prinny returned to staring at his self-likeness, a look of rapture spreading over his features. "Yes, it is."

As others crowded in to offer their compliments, Brummell and I slipped away. Already the corridor leading to the ballroom was crowded with guests eager to begin playing the nightly games that kept boredom at bay. Laughter echoed off the wainscoting, gazes bright with anticipation and a surfeit of champagne darted from face to face.

*Looking for a thrill of pleasure?* I wondered. *Or perhaps a frisson of danger?*

Brummell was hailed by one of his former regimental comrades in arms, and a moment later, one of my Grenville cousins rushed over to request my hand for the opening dance.

I finished a cotillion with him only to be claimed by one of my recent admirers for the following lively gavotte . . . For the next hour I was in much demand, spinning through the steps with a variety of partners, who filled my ears with effusive flummeries.

A part of me was flattered. And yet, there was something hollow to their charm.

Flush with thirst and fatigue, I begged off from further capering and retreated from the dance floor to find Brummell. He was in one of the anterooms, standing alone in a niche created by the collonading. He looked lost in thought. I took a tentative step toward him, unsure whether he wished for company. The movement must have caught his eye, for he looked up . . .

And smiled.

My heart gave an odd little lurch.

"Have you tired of dancing?" he asked.

"For now." I slipped in beside him, my hip grazing against his for just a moment, and let out a sigh. The heat and the exertion seemed to have me in a strange state of mind. The music in the ballroom suddenly sounded louder and a little off-key.

I drew in a breath, trying to cool the flush on my cheeks. "Do you think Prinny sensed that my compliments weren't sincere?"

"Prinny is too narcissistic to imagine that the people around him don't share his self-adoration." Brummell paused, his gaze growing more shuttered. "Even when my needling turns sharp, he takes it as a compliment."

"You don't fear that you might lose his goodwill?" For all his faults, the prince was a powerful patron. It would not be wise to offend him.

"I am important to him. My reputation as the leading arbiter of wit, taste, and style in London makes me an invaluable member of his inner circle. It reflects well on him." A sardonic smile. "I make him look good in every sense of the word."

*Ah, but styles and taste are notoriously mercurial.*

Somewhere off to our right, a lady let out a sultry laugh. Silk rustled as a low-pitched masculine reply danced through the flitting shadows.

I was suddenly tired of it all. *Flirtations, innuendo, gossip, betrayals*—the games within games that the aristocracy played to keep themselves amused for the moment. It had been a thrill at first, but now . . .

"It's all such a superficial charade," I said. "Do you not ever wish for something more meaningful? A kindred soul whose heart beats in tune with yours?"

His expression turned even more inscrutable.

"Someone whose sense of loyalty is woven into the fabric of their being," I added. "Not based on expediency."

"Your sentiments are too noble for your own good." Brummell leaned closer.

My pulse quickened. A spark of heat rose in my belly. Closing my eyes, I softened my mouth.

A kiss would surely ignite that tiny ember into a red-gold flame.

His breath caressed against my face. His fingers touched my cheek . . . and gently brushed back a loose strand of hair into its proper place. "Artifice is the way of the world, Hetty. You are the rare soul who feels your passions deeply and honestly."

I opened my eyes and smiled as the realization struck me that whatever our bond, it was not true love.

And I would not settle for less.

"Yes, you have warned me that passions are dangerous. I shall try to take your words to heart."

"A wise decision." Brummell took my hands in his and gave them a squeeze. "You are very dear to me. I should hate to see you hurt."

So far in my life, love had been elusive. My mother, who was no more than a ghost of memory, had died when I was very young . . . my father cared more for his abstract ideas than he did for his flesh-and-blood children . . . my stepmother had grown disillusioned with our family and spent little time at Chevening.

But I was determined to have it, no matter how long the search took.

"Oh, I am tougher than you might think," I replied.

"I have never doubted your strength," he said. "Or your courage."

"There is just one thing I do lack," I replied. "A glass of port! Dancing works up a terrible thirst."

"Then let us go fetch you some wine. There is still much revelry to be had before the night is over."

As summer slipped into autumn, Brummell and I continued to meet frequently and share our caustic comments on the frivolity of the ton. However, our friendship was never quite the same. I heard rumors that his heart was engaged elsewhere, though I saw no signs of it. As for me, I continued to enjoy the parties, and the attention of my admirers. Their flatteries were intoxicating after the dreariness of life at Chevening. I drank it all in, though none of the gentlemen sparked the sort of flame I yearned to feel in my heart.

It remained cool, and calmly pulsing . . .

And then, at a family dinner held just before the Yuletide holidays, I met the Half-Mad Lord.

# Chapter 5

I was expecting naught but an uneventful family supper when my uncle and I entered the London residence of Lord Grenville, who served as foreign secretary in Pitt's cabinet. The Grenvilles, Pitts, and Stanhopes had intermarried over several generations, so it was hard to keep the exact relationships straight. I was related to Lord Grenville through my maternal grandmother, who married my uncle's father, Pitt the Elder. A more recent connection was added when my father married my late mother's cousin, Louisa Grenville.

Garlands of decorative holly festooned the banister of the curved staircase leading up to the drawing room, the flames of the candle sconces flickering over the glossy midnight-green leaves and scarlet berries. A hint of pine scented the air as we ascended and passed through the open double doors.

"Hetty, come and allow me to introduce you to your cousin, Lord Camelford," called Lord Grenville after his wife had finished welcoming me and Pitt.

Thomas Pitt, 2nd Lord Camelford was some sort of cousin—his grandfather was the brother of my grandfather—but as he had gone to sea at an early age and spent years abroad in the Royal Navy, I had actually never met him.

However, I had heard of his exploits. Indeed, most of London had.

And the gossips had taken to calling him the Half-Mad Lord.

Curious, I studied the gentleman standing next to Grenville as I approached them. Camelford was tall—an inch or two over six feet—with the sun-bronzed face and muscular physique of a sailor long exposed to the harsh rigors of the elements. His curling hair was brown, his eyes an arresting shade of ocean blue.

Up close I saw they were currently lit with a mischievous spark.

"Perhaps Lady Hester would prefer not to make my acquaintance," said Camelford.

"And why would that be?" I countered.

"Because I have a *very* bad reputation." He flashed an unrepentant grin.

"Is it deserved?" I asked. I had heard all the rumors, but my own father's experience with the press had taught me how the scribblers exaggerated and twisted the truth in order to sell their scandal sheets. So I preferred to hear his side of the story before I formed my own opinion.

"That depends," said Camelford. He gave me a challenging stare. "What have you heard?"

"That on your first voyage with the Royal Navy, your ship struck a mountainous iceberg in the southern seas below the Cape of Good Hope and was on the verge of foundering," I replied. "Your captain allowed most of the crew to take the lifeboats and abandon ship. You stayed behind with him, and by some miracle and acts of great courage, the remaining crew managed to keep the hull afloat and brought the ship to safety."

He shrugged. "For a boy, it was a grand adventure."

"I've also heard that you killed a fellow officer with a pistol shot to the heart—"

Grenville interrupted with a forced smile and gestured for one of the servants to bring me some champagne. "Come, let us talk of more pleasant subjects—"

"In a moment," I replied. "First I would like to hear my cousin's answer."

Camelford bobbed a nod. "As you wish."

I noticed that he carried his head at an odd angle and wondered whether it was the result of some physical injury. He was, it seemed, no stranger to rough-and-tumble violence.

"What you have heard is true," he continued. "However, the naval board of inquiry handling the incident deemed me innocent of any wrongdoing. The other fellow had refused to obey my direct orders, and as I was the senior officer in charge, that made him guilty of mutiny."

He turned slightly, throwing his eyes into shadow. "Our harbor had been warned of an imminent attack by the French, so I had no choice but to pull the trigger."

"My dear Thomas." Lady Anne Grenville—who was also Camelford's sister—hurried over to take her brother's arm. "Please, this is meant to be a festive party, full of good cheer for our present happy circumstances, rather than dredging up fraught memories from the past."

She smiled at me. "Do you intend to spend Christmas at Chevening, Lady Hester?"

"I have been invited to spend the holiday with my Pitt relatives. The dowager Countess of Chatham is hosting a family gathering at Burton Pynsent," I replied politely, following her lead.

"How delightful!" Lady Grenville called to my uncle, who was by the hearth conversing with several Grenville cousins. "Pitt, we must come join you for a few days . . ."

The talk quickly turned to a lighthearted discussion of the guest list and what activities would keep us all entertained.

Camelford watched his sister with a beatific smile. I had heard that he was exceedingly fond of her, and that her steady good sense helped mellow his mercurial moods.

I had mentioned only two of the numerous rumors that swirled around my enigmatic cousin. I confess that I was intrigued by the conflicting stories. To some he was a misunderstood angel, a gentleman of moral integrity as well as a loyal, steadfast friend. While others whispered that he was the Devil Incarnate, a hellfire Lucifer disguised in lordly attire whose volatile, unpredictable temper made him dangerous.

*Where did the truth lie?* I wondered. Human nature was rarely black and white. But by all accounts, Camelford was deemed to be Trouble.

As a rule, a highborn lady shouldn't find that interesting.

Perhaps that explained why I was intrigued.

My musings were cut short by Lady Grenville's announcement that it was time to proceed to the dining room.

I was hoping that I might be seated next to Camelford, but found that we had been placed at opposite ends of the table. My supper companions were two amiable gray-haired Grenvilles whose interest in horses and horse racing provided fodder for conversation through the five-course meal. My eyes, however, kept straying to my cousin. It wasn't because of his looks. While his face was pleasant enough, it had been coarsened by the sea—and perhaps a fist or two, as his nose appeared to have been broken at some point.

Rather it felt as if I was caught in the current of some inexplicable magnetic force.

After lemon ices had been passed around to clear the palate and a delicate raspberry custard served as pudding, Lady Grenville stood, a signal that we ladies were to withdraw so the gentlemen could enjoy their postprandial port and cigars.

I was tempted to remain in my seat, but a discreet waggle of Pitt's brows warned me that such a rebellion would not be welcome. Given all he had done for me, it would have been churlish to ignore him.

I rose and dutifully followed our hostess and the other ladies of our party to the music room, where two servants were waiting to serve tea by the sideboard. But instead of joining the others, I paused by the hearth and watched the flames lick up from the blazing chunks of coal.

\* \* \*

"I was under the impression that you preferred port above all other libations, Lady Hester."

For a big man, my cousin moved with light-footed stealth.

"Ah, so I'm not the only one listening to the beau monde's gossip," I replied. "I do on occasion imbibe other drinks, Lord Camelford." A hiss and crackle rose from the fire. "Isn't it often said that variety is the spice of life?"

A chuckle, low and husky, rumbled in his throat.

It felt as if a finger dipped in cool ocean water was teasing down my spine.

"An astute observation," he said. "In so many ways."

The statement was a simple one, and yet he made it sound seductive. Suddenly feeling off-balance, I covered my confusion by turning the conversation back to him.

"What about you, sir? You did not wish to stay with the gentlemen and drink port? Or do you prefer brandy?"

"I greatly enjoy both, but I had no desire to swallow a long and boring exchange on the state of politics," answered Camelford. "I would much rather talk with you."

Uncertain of how to reply, I gazed into the flames.

Camelford stepped closer, the heat of his body making me uncomfortably warm. "Do I frighten you, Lady Hester?"

"Not at all." The coals crackled. "Though perhaps I should be afraid."

He said nothing in reply.

I twisted at the ring on my right hand that held the Pitt diamond, a habit of mine when I was faced with making a difficult decision. "I must ask you about a very unsettling incident from several years ago, sir. According to Gillray, you accosted your former commanding officer in the middle of Conduit Street without provocation and beat him with your cane."

James Gillray, one of London's leading satirical artists, had published a large and colorful print of the confrontation, and for days, the drawing rooms of Mayfair had been abuzz with the scandal.

"Might I ask why?" I added. "There are some who claim you have a hair-trigger temper and are unable to control it." Actually, there were some who claimed his sanity had given way to madness.

Camelford's blue eyes darkened. But when he spoke, his voice was calm. "I am, on the whole, an amiable fellow who is slow to take offense. However, the one thing I will not tolerate is an attack on my honor or integrity," he replied. "Captain Vancouver had me flogged before the entire ship's company when I was a young midshipman for a trivial offense. I felt it to be a terrible injustice, one that humiliated me in front of my fellow officers and the men I commanded."

The cause of the dispute had of course not been mentioned in the satirical prints. The more outrageous the scandal, the more prints would be sold.

"My postings then took me to another ship, and it was some time before I finally returned to England, Vancouver had retired, and I went to visit him and demand satisfaction for his personal insult to my honor," continued Camelford. "He refused, claiming his acts as an officer were not subject to a gentleman's code of honor."

"Clearly you didn't take that explanation to heart," I responded.

"I did not," he agreed. "I made several more requests for him to do the right thing as a gentleman, but the craven coward refused. So, when I happened to run into him on Conduit Street—he was in the company of his brother—I called him out publicly for his dishonorable behavior. Push came to shove . . ." Camelford shrugged. "I don't regret what happened, as I feel that moral right was on my side."

I fell to fingering my ring again, watching the candle flames set off sparks within the faceted diamond.

"You think I did wrong?"

A reasonable answer might have been "yes." Physical violence was not something that ought to be condoned. And yet, I found myself in perfect sympathy with his emotions. "On the contrary," I replied. "I applaud your refusal to compromise your sense of right and wrong."

"You surprise me. Most highborn ladies don't understand the principle of being true to your personal principles of honor."

"That's because most highborn ladies are taught to be docile and not to think for themselves," I responded. My blood was hot. "We have no legal rights to control our own destiny. The only thing a lady cannot be stripped of is her personal principles of honor. So be assured that I completely understand your emotions."

We were both facing the fire. The other gentlemen had not yet joined us and I could hear the soft flutter of feminine voices behind me, like rose petals stirring in a gentle breeze.

Camelford shifted, and took my hand and placed it in his upturned palm. His knuckles were thick and his fingers scarred, the weather-beaten flesh several shades darker than the creamy paleness of my skin.

"You have the hands of a pugilist, Lord Camelford."

That made him smile. "I've thrown my fair share of punches. And taken them, too. I'm not ashamed to stand up for my beliefs. Right ought never back down from Wrong."

His thumb caressed the diamond. "I sense that you are a fighter, too, Lady Hester. Perhaps it's something elemental in our blood. Only see how your uncle battles bravely against his political opponents, even though he is outnumbered."

He lifted my hand for a better look at the ring on my finger. "I've heard that you possess a fragment of the original Pitt Diamond, an heirloom from your mother." His gaze sharpened. "Is this it?"

"Yes."

"Beautiful," he whispered. "Fire and ice."

A shiver skated across my palm. "It is indeed a remarkable ring, Lord Camelford," I responded.

"I wasn't just remarking on the ring." He looked up. "Do call me Tom. All my friends do."

"Among my close acquaintances, I'm known as Hetty." I allowed a small pause. "Though in truth, it strikes me as a rather drab name."

"I agree, it doesn't do you justice," said Camelford. He touched the stone again, as if it were some sort of talisman, and then looked up with a grin. "I prefer to call you 'Diamond.' It's a far better reflection of who you are."

*Diamond.*

I liked that. Very much, in fact.

"Halloo, there." My uncle stopped short on entering the music room, his gaze coming to rest on the two of us standing before the dancing flames. The other gentlemen continued on to join the ladies, but he came over to join us.

"For what reason are you two sequestered over here?" It was said lightly but I didn't miss the concern in his eyes.

"Merely discussing family history," answered Camelford with a smile. "I daresay ours is more interesting than most."

"Be that as it may," replied Pitt coolly, "it would be unfair of you to keep Hetty all to yourself. She has yet to have a chance to converse with her Grenville cousins."

Camelford acknowledged the statement with a polite nod, and Pitt left us without further word.

"I would much rather stay and talk with you," I said. "You have traveled the world and experienced so many adventures. While I have never been farther from home than Somerset." A sigh. "But Pitt has been so kind to me that I must not appear ungrateful."

"You wish to hear about adventures?"

In truth, I wished to experience them. But that was a fanciful longing. And as aristocratic ladies were not encouraged to use their imaginations, I kept the thought to myself.

But it seemed that my cousin read my mind. "Well, vicarious pleasures are better than none at all, my dear Diamond, so I would be happy to regale you with the stories of my peregrinations," he responded. "Are you perchance attending Lady Davenport's soiree with your uncle?"

"I am, sir."

"Tom," he corrected, allowing a long and lazy rakehell smile. "Surely we now count ourselves as friends as well as family."

I smiled back at him. "I don't see why not."

"Excellent. Then we shall continue our conversation tomorrow evening." A wink. "Over a glass of port."

I turned to rejoin the others. One of the lady guests had taken a seat at the pianoforte and began to play a traditional Christmas carol.

"Or perhaps two," he added.

# Chapter 6

A bright blaze of light lit the leaded glass windows of the Davenport residence, the glow softening the black-as-Hades gloom of the December night. A footman took our wraps, and then my uncle and I headed up to the drawing room, where he was quickly whisked away by our host to join a group of politicians gathered in one of the side salons.

After exchanging pleasantries with Lady Davenport, I spotted an elderly Stanhope relative holding court with several other turbaned matrons and moved away to pay my respects. The room had more than the usual color and glitter of a Mayfair soiree as there were a number of military officers among the guests. *The scarlet of the Army tunics, the deep blue of the Navy's coats*—all of them dripping with gold braid and gaudy medals.

"I do so love a gentleman in uniform," remarked one of the matrons, surveying the room through her quizzing glass as I joined them. "The others in their black evening clothes look like a flock of crows pecking among peacocks."

A chortle sounded from the ladies.

"Not only that, they are far more interesting than most of the beau monde gentlemen, who always prose on with boring details of their horses and hounds!" The Countess of Malden sidled over to add her voice to the conversation. "I just had the most intriguing conversation with Lord Camelford, who only recently resigned his naval commission. Such fascinating tales and enchanting manners! He is the very paragon of manly perfection."

The countess fluttered her fan. "So well-bred, so charming. I swear if I were ten years younger . . ."

"Make that thirty," whispered my relative, just loud enough for me to hear.

I managed to swallow a very unladylike snort. "Oh, has Camelford arrived?"

"You are acquainted with the baron?" responded Lady Malden.

"He is my cousin," I answered. "And yes, he certainly has led a very adventurous life."

Looking slightly miffed that someone had stolen her thunder by having a more intimate acquaintance with Camelford, she gave a glance around the room. "Oh, look—there is Captain Quincy. He's just returned from Egypt, where his ship was part of our glorious victory against the French fleet at the Battle of the Nile. I must go have a word with him and learn all the details."

The remaining ladies then began to talk of the latest fashions, so I drifted away, intent on finding Camelford.

He was in the Blue Parlor, standing by the window overlooking Curzon Street. The whisper of my evening shoes crossing the Aubusson carpet alerted him to my presence—the room was deserted save for us—and he turned, a meditative look shading his features.

"Thank God you have arrived. Throw me a lifeline, Diamond. I feel that I am drowning in a sea of superficiality."

I came to stand next to him. "After the spartan rigors of naval life, I would have thought that you would welcome the frivolous pleasures of Society."

He frowned. "These people here—" Camelford gestured toward the drawing room. "They take their wealth and privilege for granted. Precious few of them have done anything to earn it."

He let out a harried sigh. "I envy our cousin, Sir Sidney Smith. Through great acts of personal courage and bold leadership, he has won glory for our country and the admiration of all of Britain."

Earlier in the year, Sir Sidney had been ordered to sail the war frigates and gunboats under his command into the harbor of Acre in a desperate attempt to break the French siege of the beleaguered fort, which was the only obstacle standing in the way of Napoleon's march on Jerusalem and his dream of conquering the East. Risking his own life on countless occasions, Sir Sidney had devised a daring plan of maneuvering his gunboats dangerously close to the French army and pounding them to flinders. His bravery in forcing Napoleon to give up his grand plan and retreat had won him the sobriquet "Hero of Acre."

"Honor and glory is something that can't be bought or begged for," added Camelford. "One must do something worthy of acclaim."

The yearning in his voice touched me in a visceral way. I understood the passion behind it. So many members of our family had done something extraordinary to distinguish themselves from the crowd. Pitt the Elder and Younger had helped to shape the destiny of an empire, our Grenville relatives had steered Britain through the turbulent waters of politics, Smith had proved himself a war hero. And, despite his eccentricities, my father was, along with his good friend Benjamin Franklin, considered one of the leading experimenters in electricity, and had contributed other scientific discoveries that had made life better for a great many people.

To challenge oneself to rise above the ordinary . . . to have one's name and accomplishments remembered long after one had gone to the grave . . . It was a lofty goal, open to Camelford if he wished to pursue it.

But not to me.

Ladies were not considered the stuff of legends.

I reached out to touch Camelford's hand.

"You are but twenty-four, Tom. There will be plenty of opportunities to prove yourself."

"Your uncle Pitt was appointed prime minister at age twenty-four," he pointed out.

"Destiny works in unfathomable ways." I hesitated. "You, at least, have a myriad of different ways to test your skills, to achieve your dreams." I watched the lights of a carriage bounce by on the street below and then disappear into the night's gloom. "While I must be content with watching the world from inside my gilded cage, rather than experiencing it."

Sympathy flared in his eyes, along with a look that I couldn't quite fathom. "You wish to have adventures, Diamond?"

"Yes," I replied without hesitation. "Why shouldn't ladies have dreams, and the same chance to sparkle and shine as gentlemen?"

"Why, indeed?" replied Camelford. "The world is rife with unfairness. And trying to fight against it is sometimes the greatest battle of all."

Pressing his palms against the night-chilled glass, he stood very still, his breath misting the windowpanes. "But don't ever, ever surrender."

His words reminded me of his explanation on why he had come to blows on Conduit Street with his former commanding officer. "How did you contrive to get away from the tyranny of Captain Vancouver's ship? I imagine that took some courage and cleverness."

Camelford shrugged, and for a long moment I thought that he wasn't going to answer. However, as our eyes met, he decided to satisfy my curiosity.

"I was persistent in my wish to return to England and be reassigned by the Admiralty, no matter that we were half a world away from home, sailing the Pacific Ocean. Finally, after putting into port at one of the Sandwich Islands—which is now known as the Kingdom of Hawaii—Vancouver agreed to a discharge and put me on the *Daedalus*, a Royal Navy supply ship that was on its way back to Southampton."

He paused. "When we reached the Antipodes, a letter finally caught up with me at one of our naval stations informing me of my father's death, and the fact that I was now Lord Camelford. It also included an order from the Admiralty that I was to be released from naval service and return home as quickly as possible to take up my title."

For a moment he looked to be lost in the past. "Vancouver's unfair flogging had ruined my chances of advancing up the ranks of the Royal Navy, and I wished to prove he was wrong about my abilities. So I struck out on my own and set out for India, where I hoped to find a berth on one of our warships fighting against the French in the Bay of Bengal. It was a long and interesting journey, up through vast archipelago to Cathay."

The thought of such exotic travels sent a shiver of longing through me.

"In the Dutch port of Malacca, I had the good fortune to encounter a British frigate commanded by Captain Pakenham. He took a shine to me, and I joined his ship." Camelford paused, as if savoring the memory. "Pakenham thought me a fine officer and three weeks later, he promoted me to acting lieutenant. But after a year of service, he counseled me to return to England as there was little chance of advancement and winning any sort of glory in India. And so, once again I set out on a journey for home . . ."

I listened in rapt silence as he recounted his enthralling adventures. *Purchasing his own ship to sail across the Bay of Bengal . . . the vessel breaking up off the island of Ceylon with the loss of all his official papers documenting his promotion . . . joining forces with the Scottish adventurer Hugh Cleghorn, who was on a secret mission for the British government to undermine Dutch control of Ceylon and have the island surrender to Britain . . . sailing with Cleghorn to Arabia and crossing the desert by camel to reach Alexandria . . .*

"Ye heavens, what an exciting time!" I exclaimed as he finished his account of returning to London via Venice and the Continent.

Camelford shook his head. "Without my official papers from Pakenham, which were lost at sea, I was forced to return to the Navy as a midshipman—"

"But you need not have continued in military service—" I began.

"The military is where a man of action may prove himself," replied Camelford. "But after shooting the mutinous officer, I was dispatched back to England to wait a reassignment. And then . . ." Another pause. "A misunderstanding resulted in my being asked to resign my officer's commission."

"Is that really such a terrible thing, Tom?" I asked. "It seems to me that with your talents and tenacity, you can make a name for yourself in a great many endeavors."

"The Navy has been my life."

"Yes, but think of how lucky you are! Unlike me, you have a world of opportunities to make a new one for yourself," I answered.

His brow creased in thought. After another moment of pensive silence, Camelford turned abruptly. "I must go."

The announcement took me by surprise. "I-I thought that we might continue talking—" I made myself stop. "But it seems that I have said something to offend you." The fact that I spoke my mind was a mark against me with most gentlemen.

"What? . . . Good God, no! You are the one bright spot in my life since my recent return to London."

I felt a measure of relief, but still—

"Forgive me," he continued in a rush. "I find my mood is such that I simply can't bear to remain among this gaggle of strutting peacocks and feather-headed widgeons." A smile. "Present company excepted, of course."

He grabbed my hand and pressed a kiss to my knuckles. "I feel the need to walk the streets and clear my head, but I promise that at our next meeting, I shall regale you with any of my other adventures that you care to hear."

My heart told me that he was being sincere. I understood the urge. I often found escape from my frustrations by riding neck and leather through the countryside surrounding Chevening, often not returning until I was physically spent.

Outracing one's demons demanded every ounce of strength and willpower.

"Go, Tom," I said. "And Godspeed."

Another fleeting kiss touched my flesh, then Camelford turned and hurried away.

I stood for an interlude, lost in thought. After his cynical comment, the sounds drifting in from the drawing room—laughter, clinking crystal, voices twined in conversation—seemed to take on a slight shrillness. Feeling unsettled, I went in search of Pitt, thinking he would be delighted that for once I was ready to leave a party before the wee hours of the morning had arrived.

But some perverse force must have been at play, for my uncle requested that I wait while he enjoyed one more round of drinks with his friends as they were engaged in a lively political discussion.

I wandered off, seeking solace with a coupe of garnet-red port. Several gentlemen sought to draw me into conversation, but I sent them away, claiming fatigue and a headache. My thoughts, however, were no better company. If Camelford, a man of action, wealth, and powerful aristocratic connections, felt discouraged about his chances of rising above the ordinary, what hope did I have? I had used the gilded cage as a metaphor but in truth, it was all too real.

"Hetty." Pitt's voice finally drew me out of my brooding. He stopped short as I looked up. "Are you unwell?"

I was loath to admit my mental distress. "Simply fatigued, dear uncle." I feigned a yawn. "I rose very early to ride in the park."

He smiled. "Then come, Jockey Girl, let me take you home."

Once we were in the carriage, however, my uncle turned to me with a searching look. "I heard someone mention that you were with Camelford earlier."

"I was," I answered. "But he seemed in a rather odd mood and decided to quit the party early."

"Mercurial would be a more accurate word." He pursed his lips, as if uncertain to go on. An irony, given that he was one of the greatest orators of his generation.

"Far be it for me to lecture you, I have too much respect for your intellect. However, given your father's withdrawal into his own little world of interests, I feel it would be remiss of me to not offer some counsel."

"I am listening, sir."

"I like Tom," began Pitt. "Nobody can doubt his courage and

resolve. But I fear that his volatile temper makes him unpredictable. And that makes him dangerous to those around him."

"Is that an oblique way of telling me that I should avoid forming a friendship with him?" I demanded.

He pinched at the bridge of his long nose. "Call it a warning, Hetty, one born out of concern for your well-being. I do not wish to see you hurt."

"I think perhaps you exaggerate his faults," I replied. "From what I have observed, Tom is thoughtful, clever, and possesses a wry sense of humor."

"Allow me to remind you that you've barely met your cousin. Yes, he can be gracious, charming, and witty. And yet, he's also capable of being reckless, impulsive, and erratic. His behavior over the last few years has given cause to question his ability to control his emotions."

"It seems to me that he has reason to be frustrated with his treatment by the Royal Navy."

"Personal frustration does not give one the right to attack another man and beat him with a cane."

I could not in good conscience argue the point.

"As for killing his fellow officer, Tom was technically correct in enforcing the exact wording of naval regulations—which is the only reason he escaped punishment," explained Pitt. "The fact is, he showed a grave lack of judgment in using lethal force. The situation could easily have resolved without violence."

The clatter of ironshod hooves on the paving stone sounded unnaturally loud in the sliver of silence that came between us.

"It was not the only alarming indication that his thinking is not always sound," pressed Pitt. "Allow me to remind you of his attempt earlier this year to smuggle himself across the Channel to France, despite the fact that an Act of Parliament made it a capital offense for any man to travel to enemy soil from our shores."

"Tom mentioned that there was a misunderstanding—"

"It was far more than a misunderstanding," said Pitt. "Your cousin was apprehended in a boat about to set off for Calais. In his possession was some money, a pair of pistols, and two letters assuring the authorities that the bearer of the letter was an ardent friend of the French Republic."

"W-why was he going to France?"

Pitt let out a mirthless laugh. "He claimed he was traveling as a tourist, and simply wished to visit Paris and see the sights."

I looked away, unable to deny the absurdity of the claim.

"Speculation is that he was planning to assassinate Napoleon—"

I gasped. "You are jesting."

He shook his head. "There is nothing remotely funny about the incident. Your cousin, Sir Sidney Smith, had just been given command of an eighty-gun ship of the line and ordered to head to the Mediterranean on a special mission. Tom's friends testified that he seemed obsessed with outshining Sir Sidney, and so concocted a plan to make himself a national hero."

"One can't help but admire such audacity," I responded.

"Hetty," growled my uncle.

"No, wait," I interrupted. "Perhaps he deserves some credit for being willing to undertake such a daring plan. Granted, it was very risky, but isn't it said that with great risk comes great reward?"

"It was more than risky," retorted Pitt. "A great many senior government officials are of the opinion that Tom's head is deranged."

"He's not crazy!" I protested.

"No—just half mad." My uncle sighed. "The point is, once again Tom put himself—and his family—in hot water. It was, to say the least, highly embarrassing to the government. Here I am the prime minister, my brother is the president of the Privy Council, and Tom's brother-in-law is the foreign secretary."

Pitt cleared his throat. "We couldn't overlook the fact that he had broken a law that should have consigned him to the gallows. The only solution was to ask the king to grant him a royal pardon—which His Majesty graciously did. However, the Privy Council ordered that Tom never be entrusted with command of a Royal Navy ship."

I reluctantly admitted that the decision was probably a wise one. Leadership demanded more than raw courage and daring.

"Perhaps Tom hasn't been quite as disciplined as he should be," I said. "But I still think he has sterling qualities and can excel if he finds the right endeavor."

"You are a steadfast and loyal friend, Hetty. I have always admired that about you. Your recent appeals to me concerning the welfare of your three young half brothers speak volumes about your heart."

"My father has grown unpleasantly self-absorbed, and my stepmother has turned her back on her family, preferring to indulge in her own amusements in London. My brothers have no one else to battle for their welfare."

"Few sisters would trouble themselves to pick up the proverbial sword," replied my uncle.

"You know me—I never back down from a fight." The fizz of carefree gaiety in the drawing room suddenly had me feeling very much alone. "I am determined to see that they have a chance to flourish and choose their own path in life. I vow that I will find a way."

He smiled, and when he spoke again, his voice had a gentler tone. "I'm not suggesting that you cut off all contact with your cousin. By all means, enjoy his company. But I fear it would be a mistake to allow yourself to become emotionally entangled."

Ah, an adroit reminder that a lady of my age had better get on with the task of making a suitable match. However kindly meant, it made me bristle.

"Because a lady's mind is not capable of making such a nuanced decision about her own future?"

Pitt had the grace to flush. "I meant no insult to your intellect, Hetty." He allowed a long silence before adding, "Surely among all your many admirers, there is a fellow who is capable of winning your regard."

Not one I could think of. But it felt churlish to say as much, so I chose to prevaricate. "Give me time," I forced a smile. "As my father would say, one never knows when lightning might strike."

# Chapter 7

Winter–Spring 1800

The new century stirred a new sense of urgency within me to escape from all things ordinary—ordinary routines, ordinary expectations, ordinary dreams. I was soon to turn twenty-four, an age when most unmarried aristocratic ladies began to fear that they were fated to become a spinster.

The truth was, I had no such worries. I was reveling in my freedom, however limited. So while I appreciated my uncle's expression of concern for my welfare, I didn't find the idea of conformity as comforting as he did.

Brummell, who had recently earned the flattering sobriquet "Beau" from Polite Society for his faultless deportment and style of dress, added his chidings to those of Pitt. He didn't like my cousin, though that didn't surprise me. The two men were opposites. Brummell's outward appearance mirrored his iron-willed self-control and coolly calculated willingness to tailor his scruples in order to achieve his goals.

He wished to be accepted and admired within the highest circles of power and privilege. While Camelford didn't give a rat's arse about what people thought of him.

My cousin paid little attention to details of dress. *Hair uncombed,*

*wrinkled jacket with pockets pulled out of shape by the bits and bobs col-
lected throughout the course of his day, boots spattered with mud* . . . He
looked more like a street sweeper than a wealthy lord.

To my eye, he radiated a restless energy, a crackling current of
unseen electricity. And I couldn't help feeling drawn to him, like a
moth to a flame.

A confrontation with the Beau came at a soiree held in one of
the imposing mansions surrounding Berkeley Square. I had just
moved into the vestibule connecting the main drawing room to a
series of side salons, when a familiar drawl halted my steps.

"Hetty, might I have a private word with you?"

Repressing a sigh—I was in no mood for yet another lecture
concerning my cousin—I turned as Brummell moved from out of
the shadows. "But of course."

Brummell offered me his arm and escorted me to the picture
gallery, which was deserted. "I see you've dispensed with drinking
port," he commented, eyeing my empty hands.

I had. Camelford had said that I had no need for posturing or
props to draw attention to myself. And over the past few months, I
had gained enough self-confidence to agree with him.

"You once said to me that it's best to abandon a mannerism before it becomes tiresome to others."

"Did I say that?" he quipped. "How clever of me."

I didn't reply.

"Might I offer some words of advice?"

"I always value your opinion."

"Lord Camelford is an unusual and engaging fellow, which
gives him an undeniable allure. But you might wish to consider
spending less time in his company."

I felt my spine stiffen, but forced a smile. "Oh? For what
reason?"

A flicker of irritation passed over his face. "I think you know why."

When I remained silent, the Beau raised his brows. "You wish
for me to say it? Very well then, in the eyes of Polite Society he's
simply not *comme il faut.*"

"Perhaps he prefers to be guided by his own heart rather than follow a rigid set of arbitrary rules."

Some unreadable reaction seemed to ripple through his gaze, and for an instant I wondered whether he regretted choosing a life of hiding his innermost thoughts behind a polished veneer of charm and civility. But perhaps it was just a quirk of light for it was gone in a flash and all I saw in his eyes were two flat, opaque pools of steely gray.

"The heart," he said slowly, "is a terribly unreliable organ. Passion and emotion can so easily throw off its inner compass and lead you astray."

"And yet, staying true to yourself might actually bring you to true happiness and fulfillment."

"If that is what you truly believe, then I shall refrain from further comment." Brummell inclined a graceful bow and stepped back, throwing his face into shadow.

"But don't say I didn't warn you."

Unsettled by the encounter, I went in search of Camelford, hoping his devil-may-care comments would help chase away my uncertainties. I found him in a small parlor off the cardroom. He was sitting at one of the board game tables arranged by the hearth, his profile limned in the glow of the fire as he contemplated the chess figures arrayed on the ebony and ivory checkered tiles.

He looked up at my approach. "The origins of chess are said to lie in a game called *chaturanga*, which developed in India during the sixth century. It then spread to Persia, where it became popular with the nobility."

"Fascinating," I said, taking a seat in the chair facing him.

"Do you play, Diamond?"

"A little. Games have never captured my fancy."

"Chess is more than a game." He took a moment to study the board, where the previous players had abandoned their match before it was finished. "It teaches you to think about strategy and how to look ahead and anticipate your opponent's moves."

A smile touched his lips. "Though I confess that I've never learned those lessons terribly well."

"Chess requires patience." I grimaced. "Alas, a quality I sadly lack."

Camelford laughed. "Patience is vastly overrated. Or so I tell myself, as I have none to speak of." He moved an ebony bishop on the diagonal until it was threatening an ivory knight.

*A challenge?*

Narrowing my eyes, I assessed my options, determined to show my mettle. A moment ticked by. I tapped a finger to my chin, and then made my move.

"Check."

A frown creased his brow, but gave way to a laugh. Rather than move my knight, I had spotted an opening and moved a lowly pawn to force his king to react.

"Clever." He pushed his king forward to capture my piece and banish it from the board.

Whereupon, I moved my knight, taking one of his ebony pawns and putting his king back in check.

"You're bold, my dear Diamond, and play with no fear."

"Since I have so little control of my own moves in life, I suppose that I find the freedom to be bold is exhilarating."

To my surprise, Camelford suddenly swept all the pieces off the board.

"How would you like to play another sort of game?" He leaned in closer. "You said that you wished to have adventures. Have you ever attended a prizefight?"

I swallowed a burble of excitement. "You need ask?"

"It's not for the faint of heart." A pause. "It's raw and raucous. The smell of sweat and unwashed bodies . . . grunts and curses . . . bloody knuckles and bleeding faces, the crowd in a primal frenzy . . ."

It sounded absolutely mesmerizing.

"Yes," I said. "Yes, yes, yes."

Leaning back, Camelford pressed his palms together and nodded in satisfaction.

"So, when do we go?" *And how do we go?* I added to myself.

"Tomorrow."

I felt a prickle of disappointment. It seemed he was merely teasing me. "Impossible."

"Not at all, Diamond," he responded. "You did tell me that your personal maid is devoted to you, did you not?"

"Utterly so," I replied. I had saved Susan, a young parlormaid, from being unfairly dismissed from Chevening by my stepmother for some imaginary transgression. Knowing the girl to be both clever and bright, I had asked if she would like to switch from her household duties and become my lady's maid. Needless to say, she jumped at the chance, and from that moment on, Susan had assured me that I had her undying loyalty.

"Excellent," said Camelford. "That makes everything easy to arrange. Your relatives appear to have accepted that you come and go as you please from the family townhouse."

"They have." My paternal grandmother, the dowager Countess Stanhope, and my stepmother were busy with their own interests as well as hosting frequent visits from other extended family members, leaving little room for any fretting over my affairs.

My curiosity piqued, I quickly added, "So, what is your plan?"

"A simple one," he replied. "Slip away unobserved from your townhouse at the hour of five tomorrow afternoon. If your maid is questioned as to your whereabouts, have her say that your Grenville cousins invited you to accompany them to a supper party and soiree."

"Where shall I go—" I began.

"Dress in an old gown and a hooded cloak," he said. "Walk down Montague Street. I shall meet you at Great Russell Street and we'll take a hackney to my residence. It's there that we'll prepare for the prizefight."

"How—"

"You'll see soon enough," interjected Camelford with a teasing laugh. "Just be sure that your maid ensures that the scullery door is unlocked for you to sneak back into the house in the wee hours of the morning."

\*    \*    \*

Unsure of what to expect, I felt a strange fluttering inside my rib cage as I exited the family townhouse through the side portico the following afternoon.

Camelford was waiting at the corner of Great Russell Street. He, too, seemed gripped by an air of anticipation. He took my arm and we strolled to one of the quieter side streets, where he had a hackney waiting. We traveled the short distance in silence. A myriad of questions were on the tip of my tongue, but I refrained from voicing them, not wanting him to think me frightened, rather than simply curious.

Answers would come soon enough.

"Keep your hood up," he cautioned, once we had reached our destination. "And your head down." An oblique warning that we were crossing the line of propriety and treading on dangerous ground.

After entering his lodging, Camelford led me up a back stairwell to his bedchambers. A shiver danced down my spine as we entered the sitting room and I caught sight of a carved four-poster bed in the adjoining room, though in truth my body had been experiencing all sorts of odd little hot and cold flashes ever since I had left the family residence. I had never been in a gentleman's intimate living space—my younger brothers didn't count—so I couldn't help but be curious and darted a look around.

The furnishings were surprisingly spartan for a man of Camelford's wealth.

"As a naval officer, one gets used to life without luxuries," he said, looking amused as he read my reaction. "Though I do enjoy the comforts of a very large and very soft bed after years of a narrow bunk or swinging hammock."

I felt myself blush at the mention of "bed."

"Come, let us not dawdle." Without waiting for a reply, Camelford marched me through the half-open door.

*Oh, surely he didn't mean . . .*

My steps faltered, which drew a chuckle.

"Yes, Diamond, my intention is to seduce you out of your cloth-

ing, but not for the reason you think." He gestured to the bed coverlet. Upon it lay a collection of rumpled clothing—breeches, shirt,
jacket, waistcoat, hat. "Thank God you're taller than most men."

"You mean for me to disguise myself as a man!"

Camelford arched a brow. "How else did you think you were
going to attend a prizefight?"

"I . . ." I considered myself clever, but clearly I had much to
learn. "I assumed that you would pass me off as your doxie."

"Men do *not* bring their doxies to prizefights. The ritual of bare-
knuckle fighting embodies the very essence of our primitive nature. We honor and respect those who excel at it. When the two
pugilists are in the ring, the hearts and minds of the spectators are
on them. Nothing else matters."

I thought about that. Men relished conflict. And they were encouraged to be good at it. While a show of strength by a woman
was considered unnatural.

"On the other hand, Society expects women to be passive, to
accept pain without complaint, rather than fighting back," I mused.
"All their infernal rules are meant to keep us chained in such conventional thinking."

"I'm all too aware of that. Challenge convention and Society
calls you mad," said Camelford. "Oh, yes, I'm aware of the whispers concerning my sanity." A grin. "I say to hell with them."

He pointed again to the clothing. "Make up your mind. Are you
coming or not?"

I unfastened my cloak and let it fall to the floor. "Turn around,
please. I'm not used to undressing in front of anyone other than
my lady's maid."

"That is an issue to be addressed at some other time," he
replied, his gaze lingering on me.

Pretending not to notice, I turned. "Before you do, I'll need you
to untie the tabs of my gown."

"With pleasure." His fingers grazed against the nape of my neck
as he performed the task.

The muslin slid a little lower on my shoulders. I felt quite wanton as I gave a tug and let it slither down over my legs. Kicking it

aside, I took a quick peek to make sure he wasn't watching and then stripped off my shift.

*Ye gods, I was nearly naked.*

I snatched up the shirt and pulled it on, then grabbed the breeches. I wasn't a total stranger to men's clothing. With three younger brothers, I had of course noticed the freedom of movement that their garb gave them, especially for riding. And so, I had bargained with Philip—we all called him Mahon as he was my father's heir and thus possessed the courtesy title of Lord Mahon—for some of his garments.

It took me little time to deal with all the buttons and make myself presentable. "You may turn around now, Tom."

Camelford gave an appreciative glance at my bare calves. "You have very shapely legs, Diamond." A grin. "I imagine that your other facets are just as lovely."

"Do stop teasing," I replied, trying to repress the flare of heat tickling in my belly.

He stepped closer. "Trust me, I'm not teasing. But again, we'll deal with that some other time."

Another lick of heat. There was an undeniable chemistry between us, though I dared not give it a name.

His fingertips lingered for a moment on the sensitive flesh at the base of my jaw before shifting to adjust my shirt collar. "Naughty girl. You've done this before, haven't you?"

"Skirts and petticoats are a cursed nuisance," I muttered, grabbing up the waistcoat and doing up the buttons.

"I couldn't agree more," he said with the devil's own smile.

"I trust you have stockings and boots for me. I can hardly go out wearing my satin slippers with this attire."

A sigh. "You're right. Much as I'm tempted to linger here, I promised you a prizefight." He went to his dressing room and returned with a pair of high-top Hessian boots and several other items.

"They fit," I remarked, after pulling them on over the knitted stockings he provided.

"I have a good eye for measurements."

"Do you always flirt so outrageously?"

His look of amusement turned into something more inscrutable. "I do not, Diamond."

Before I could react to his statement, he reached into the small sack he was holding and pulled out what looked to be a handful of ashes. "We need to make your face look a little less feminine. Take a seat on the bed."

His touch was light as he dabbed and rubbed the substance into my skin, shading my jaw, deepening the shadows under my eyes. "Now hold out your hands."

I did as he ordered, giving an inward wince as Camelford worked grit under my nails. Once he finished, he took two strips of ragged linen from his pocket and one by one wrapped them around my palms.

Crinkling my nose in dismay—they were none too clean—I asked, "What's that for?"

"We need to disguise your hands as well as the rest of you. They're too feminine, even with a layer of dirt." He finished tying off the ends. "This will hide enough," he added, stepping back to observe the effect.

I flexed my fingers, feeling like a stranger within my own body. It was unsettling . . . and exciting.

*Who am I?* Perhaps I was about to find out.

Camelford quickly turned up my shirtpoints and knotted the requisite cravat around my neck. I smoothed the folds in place and put on my coat.

"Your head covering, sir," he said, handing me a flat-crown, wide-brim round hat that had seen better days.

I put it on and pulled it to a rakish angle. "The mill had better be a good 'un, Tom," I said, lowering my voice to a husky rumble and using the cant for "prizefight" that I had overheard from my brothers.

Camelford let out a peal of laughter. "Excellent. But as a precaution, let me do all the talking. I'll introduce you as a cousin fresh from the country, and a little intimidated by the hustle and bustle of city life."

"Oiy," I uttered.

After another critical squint, he nodded. "Use the looking glass on the dressing table to make the final adjustments to pinning up your hair."

A single candle, its flame undulating in a draft seeping in through the window casement, beckoned.

Light flickered over my face. I smiled, my teeth a flash of pearl white in the gloom. Although my bandaged hands made it awkward to maneuver the hairpins, I secured the coil of tresses hidden under the crown of my hat, and gave a last-minute primping to the cropped curls falling over my forehead and ears before hurrying back to join.

He handed me an ebony walking stick. "I do hope that you don't puke at the sight of blood."

# Chapter 8

The hackney let us out in a narrow lane deep within the slums of St. Giles. The stench of rotting cabbage assaulted my nostrils as I descended and God only knew what filth squelched beneath my boots.

"From here we continue on foot," said Camelford.

I swallowed hard, a foul taste coating my throat. A leaden silence hung heavy in the night, broken only by the rusty creaking of a loose shutter in the wind and a feral scrabbling from a nearby alley.

"Couldn't a more salubrious location have been chosen?" I asked.

"The venue adds an aura of danger to the evening, which makes the rich and bored aristocrats who come to rub shoulders with the violence-loving crowd feel that they are alive," he replied. "And as a practical matter, it makes the authorities less inclined to rush in and harass the participants." A pause. "If they do, stick to me like a cocklebur and run like the devil. Pitt will have my guts for garters if I allow you to create an embarrassing scandal for him."

I hunched down deeper into the collar of my coat and followed without further comment.

The way twisted through several turns and suddenly we were

treading through a maze of alleys. Crumbling warehouses, all sagging slants and filthy brick, were squeezed along the crooked turns, while the boarded-up rookeries rose up at drunken angles, blocking out all but the smallest slivers of sky.

The murk grew darker, the stench stronger.

I was now breathing through my mouth.

"Ah, here we are." Camelford came to a halt and drew me into a narrow gap between two windowless buildings. Feeling his way along the wall, he found an iron door and rapped out a series of knocks.

After a moment, it opened just enough to allow us entry.

A man with a lantern led us deeper into the bowels of the building. The greasy beam showed another weighty door. Grabbing hold of a rusting lever, he heaved it open.

After the silence of stews outside, the sudden rush of noise was deafening. *Shouts, laughter, curses. The cries of vendors hawking mugs of ale and cheap blue ruin.*

"Oiy! Look, lads! The Prince o' Pugilists has arrived." A big, hairy, oxlike fellow with a misshapen nose and fists as large as ham hocks gave Camelford a welcoming thump to the shoulder. He squinted at me. "Who's the puppy?"

"A young cousin, fresh from the country, Joe," replied Camelford, countering with his own friendly punch. "He's still a trifle shy, so he's not fair game for you lot."

"Well, Pup," called one of the Ox's cronies, "ye couldn't have a better guide te introduce ye to the pleasures of Town."

"Take 'im te Covent Garden te tup a whore!" cried another. "That'll loosen the Puppy's tongue. Woof, woof, woof!"

Howls of laughter greeted the comment.

Camelford laughed with them. As did I.

One of the ale sellers rushed over to offer two tankards of ale. Camelford thanked the fellow and then pushed his way forward.

The crowd made way for him, as if he really were royalty. Greetings were called out, caps doffed in respect.

"Who's yer money on, milord?" called someone.

Camelford pursed his lips and then took a slug of his ale. "Hervey has brute bulk and a right cross that can fell a bull. However, I learned that's never wise to underestimate a protégé of Gentleman Jackson, no matter if he appears to be a scrawny runt."

Rumblings of agreement rose up from around us.

"So, it promises to be an interesting match," he finished.

Staying close to his side, as ordered, I made a show of swigging my ale while observing the scene around me. The air was thick with the mingled scents of sweat, tobacco, and an indefinable masculine musk of arousal. They were here to see two opponents punching and thrashing at each other until only one was left standing.

After trading more quips with the men around him—he was clearly at home with the rough-and-tumble camaraderie of the crowd—Camelford steered me toward the center of the cavernous space, where a high wooden platform stood. A chalked square had been drawn on the rough planking, indicating the area for the fight. Ringing the platform's perimeter was a double set of ropes held in place by sturdy posts at each of its corners. I assumed the arrangement was meant to keep the pugilists from being knocked arse over teakettle into the scrum of spectators.

The men already standing in the prime view spot crowded together, making room for Camelford and me.

I leaned in close to his ear. "You appear to be a welcome member of this primal fraternity."

A chuckle. "Who do you think pays for the ale?" He flexed a fist. "They also know I'm one of them."

As I stared at his scarred and swollen knuckles I realized that he meant it literally. "You fight in the ring?"

"Occasionally." The cacophony suddenly quieted and his eyes moved to the far end of the room. "Enough talking for now," he said. "Pay attention. You're about to get an important lesson in life."

The light in the spectating area was dim, as there was only a smattering of lanterns dotting the space. At first I saw only a shift-ing of shadows. But then I caught the faint movement of a door. A bare-chested man materialized from the gloom, his oiled flesh gleaming white against the blackness behind him.

*It must be Hervey,* I thought. Even from this distance, the breadth of granitelike shoulders and rippling of corded muscles was im-pressive.

Sure enough, the crowd broke into a rhythmic chanting and stomping.

*Her-vey, Her-vey.*

The air was thrumming with electricity. I could feel it crackling against my skin.

Hervey passed close to us—he was big as a bull—and threw a wink at Camelford as he grasped the ladder and climbed up to the boxing ring.

The space quieted, all heads turning to watch for Hervey's op-ponent.

I shifted from foot to foot, feeling hot all over.

Leaning close, Camelford whispered, "Fire in your blood burns away the sense of ennui. You'll get used to the rush of heat." A pause. "In fact, you'll come to revel in it."

My mouth went dry.

A new chant rose up. *Bur-nett, Bur-nett!* Both Camelford and I strained to catch sight of the second pugilist. For a moment I couldn't pick him out from the raucous spectators. And then . . .

The slender fellow marching down the corridor created by the crowd was stripped to the waist, his torso sheened with a coating of oil to make the blows skid off his skin. But I found it hard to be-lieve that this was not some sort of jest before the real opponent made his entrance.

"Surely that's not Burnett."

"Don't let his looks deceive you," counseled Camelford. "Pugilism is an artform. If executed properly, agility and quickness can count for more than muscle."

I didn't see how that could be true, but refrained from saying it.

With a lithe grace, Burnett climbed up to meet his opponent, followed by his second. Hervey lumbered to the center of the ring, while Burnett danced from side to side on the balls of his feet.

The man overseeing the bout took his stance between the two pugilists and gave a stentorian shout to get the crowd's attention. "Oiy! Oiy!"

The noise dropped to a low rumbling.

"The fight will be governed by Broughton's Rules," he bellowed.

"A rudimentary list. No grabbing your opponent's balls, or any part of his breeches," explained Camelford. "And no hitting him when he is down."

The overseer stepped back, his only job now to stop any gross infractions of the basic rules and to count off the allotted time allowed for a man to recover from being knocked down by a punch.

"You may begin!"

Fists flailing, Hervey charged forward, looking to end the fight before it had a chance to begin. Burnett, however, anticipated the attack and deftly spun away, but not before landing a hard punch to his opponent's kidneys.

Shouts and groans sounded from the crowd.

Hervey pivoted and came at Burnett more slowly. The two of them traded jabs as they turned in a slow circle with carefully gauged steps, neither landing a telling blow.

More shouts and exhortations. The spectators had come to see blood, not a display of ballroom dancing.

Mirroring the frustration of the crowd, Hervey threw himself into another furious attack. He managed to grab hold of Burnett and lifted him off the boards before throwing him down with a shuddering thud.

The overseer waved Hervey back to his second, allowing the allotted thirty seconds for recovery. Burnett, however, was back on his feet in a flash, taunting the bigger man to come at him again.

With a bull-like snort, Hervey charged. This time Burnett dodged the grab with a lightning-fast pivot and slammed his fist into his opponent's face. Blood spurted from the broken nose, spraying both the fighters.

A roar went up from the crowd, followed by a frenzied chant that seemed to shake the very walls. *"Blood, blood, blood!"*

From there, everything became a blur. Pushing, shoving, the spectators all around us had lost any semblance of civilized beings. A primal madness seemed to possess them as they howled, urging the pugilists to pound each other to a pulp. And to my surprise, I was as guilty as the next man.

"Have a care, Diamond," warned Camelford as he steadied my shoulders. "Your high-pitched screams are in danger of giving you away."

*Was I screaming?*

I sucked in a breath, suddenly aware that my throat was raw and my face was drenched in sweat. As our eyes met in the swirl of light and shadow, Camelford gave a wolfish grin. "I knew you would like this," he whispered. "You're different from other ladies. You have an elemental fire in your belly. You just needed the right spark to ignite it."

It did feel like flames were licking through my blood as it fizzed through my veins. I looked back to the fighters, whose bruised flesh was spattered in scarlet.

Hervey's brawn now seemed to be working against him. His arms appeared heavy; his movements had slowed. Burnett was still quick as a cobra, his fists snaking in to thump away at the bigger man. A hard hit had opened up a cut on Hervey's forehead, and with blood streaming into his eyes, he was now half blind.

"This will soon be over," observed Camelford. And sure enough, Burnett spotted an opening and swung with a vicious uppercut that caught Hervey flush on the jaw and knocked him to the boards.

His legs spasmed as he attempted to rise, and try as he might, Hervey couldn't lever himself to his knees.

His second gave a brusque wave, signaling surrender.

Cheers rung out as Burnett lifted arms in victory. There were a few disgruntled shouts, but for the most part, the crowd was well satisfied by the spectacle.

The mood turned more raucous as the ale sellers opened more barrels.

"Come," said Camelford. "Time for us to go."

"Leaving already, m'lord?" called one of Camelford's cronies.

"I need to take the puppy home. It's his bedtime," came the laughing response. "If you're all headed to the Jolly Brewer on Wardour Street, I shall meet up with you there later."

A number of others shouted good-natured jibes at me as Camelford took my arm and hustled me toward the exit.

The chill air hit me like a punch as we stepped into the alleyway. Too many emotions were bubbling through me to attempt to put them into words, so I simply let Camelford keep hold of my arm and followed along in silence.

It wasn't until we had flagged down a hackney on one of the narrow side streets near the church of St. Giles-in-the-Fields, that my thoughts were settled enough for speech.

"I *loved* it, Tom—the raucous noise, the raw energy, the unfettered emotions."

The squabs creaked as Camelford shifted against the stiff leather and a whispery laugh. "I thought you would."

"Promise me that we'll do this again, and soon."

"Prizefights don't happen every day," he replied coyly.

"I'm talking about feeling that fizz of excitement. Surely there are other ways to experience it."

He spun his walking stick back and forth between his palms. "That can be arranged, Diamond."

It was at that precise moment when I realized my life had irrevocably changed and that I would never be the same.

I had read in my father's French edition of *One Thousand and One Nights*, a collection of Arabic folk tales, so I knew that once a *djinn* had been allowed to escape from a sealed bottle, it was impossible to recapture it and force it back into its prison.

The hackney came to halt by the alley running behind my family's townhouse.

"Sweet dreams, Diamond." Camelford took my hand and pressed a kiss to the inside of my wrist.

I doubted that I would sleep at all.

"Thank you." I slipped out of the hackney. "For everything."

True to her word, my maid Susan had left the scullery door unlocked. I slid the bolt home after entering, then quietly picked my way up the servants' staircase to my bedchamber, where I peeled off my male clothing, stuffed the items into the burlap sack that Susan had left beneath my bedcovers, and hid it in the back of my armoire.

After scrubbing the dirt from my face and shaking out my tightly pinned hair, I donned my nightrail and slipped into bed, still feeling giddy with the thrill of having discovered a new world.

*A new life.*

One filled with all sorts of forbidden freedoms.

I had just experienced my first real adventure . . .

And was already craving more.

# Chapter 9

My appetite whetted for the pleasures that came from breaking the rules. I became more reckless over the next few weeks. Thumbing our noses at propriety, Camelford and I enjoyed carriage rides together alone, rode in Hyde Park unaccompanied by a groom, and I took the liberty of appearing at parties unchaperoned. Perhaps there were whispers, but as none of them reached the ears of Pitt or the rest of my family, I reveled in my boldness.

That Camelford favored me above all others flattered my vanity. His aura of danger, along with his wealth and title, made him irresistibly alluring to the ladies of the ton. I felt their envy, and as someone who had been allowed precious little opportunity to indulge in the pleasures of Polite Society I confess that it puffed up my self-esteem. That a devil-may-care man of such worldly experience appeared to find me fascinating was rather thrilling. As to where it might lead . . .

I was too busy enjoying the moment to think of the future.

And so I continued to flaunt propriety, and for a time it truly appeared that there would be no consequences. Camelford continued to be extremely attentive, and our forays out to Houndslow Heath, a wild stretch of deserted moorland just outside of Town, proved particularly seductive.

"The boxing match has made me think about how I ought to

know something about fending off an attack," I said to him one afternoon as we reached a secluded swath of meadowland.

"You wish to learn a few tricks for self-defense?" Camelford sounded amused.

"You told me that quickness and agility can triumph over brawn," I challenged.

"So I did, Diamond." He stopped and shrugged out of his coat. "Take off your bonnet and shawl."

I quickly tossed them aside. "What—"

Camelford was already moving and before I could go on, he seized me from behind in a bear hug.

"Now what would you do?"

I hesitated, acutely aware of his body pressed up against mine and the musky heat of his scent.

A rough laugh. "Are you a pigeon, just waiting to be plucked?"

I began to struggle, which only made him laugh. He tightened his hold, nearly squeezing all the breath out of my lungs. "Wrong choice."

"Then show me the right one," I wheezed. "I hate feeling helpless!"

"There's always a way to fight back. The key is not giving in to fear," he answered. "Let us switch places."

Once my arms were around him, Camelford continued, "Every man, no matter how strong, has a few vulnerable spots. A well-placed blow, be it with your foot, elbow, or knee will work wonders."

He demonstrated how to stomp on an assailant's instep at the same time as throwing his head back to smash the fellow's nose. "Surprise will work in your favor, so you need to react without hesitation."

We practiced a few times, my confidence growing.

"This time, when I grab you, react as if I were a real attacker."

"But—"

"No 'buts,' Diamond. We both need to know that with your life or your virtue on the line, you can defend yourself."

I drew a deep breath . . .

And did what I was told.

A grunt, and in the next instant, Camelford was on his knees, a trickle of blood flowing out of his squashed nostrils. "Well done!" he cried, waving off my apologies. "You have the heart of a tiger, Diamond. Don't ever count yourself out of a fight."

He got gingerly to his feet, wincing as he put weight on his injured foot. "Now let me show how to deal with an assailant who comes at you from the front. A hard knee to the bollocks will drop him like a stone . . ."

We spent the next interlude in practice, limbs intimately entangling, breath heaving, sweat dampening our clothing.

"That's enough for now," said Camelford, catching me in his arms. "God help the miscreant who challenges you."

He brushed a loosened lock of hair from my flushed cheek and suddenly captured my lips in a hard, demanding kiss.

The physical exertion already had my senses aroused. Heat spiraling through me, I returned the embrace with equal intensity.

A chill breeze stirred through the trees, the fluttery light warning that the sun was sinking in the sky.

"We had better return to Town." Camelford released me and picked up his coat.

I heard the muffled *chink* of a well-filled purse jingle in his pocket, which reminded me of something that Camelford's sister had told me recently. His public image was that of a dangerously hot-tempered gentleman prone to physical violence. In private, however, it seemed that Camelford often dressed in shabby clothes, his pockets stuffed with money, and walked the streets in the slums of Seven Dials, Southwark, and Wapping, conversing with the residents and handing out large sums to those in need.

"Anne has told me about your generosity to the poor," I said as I gathered my own garments from the grass. "It does you great credit. Most aristocrats couldn't care less about those in need."

Camelford shrugged. "That's because they know nothing of life outside their gilded world. I've spent most of my life cheek to jowl with ordinary sailors on naval ships who come from grinding poverty. Life is hard for most people."

Perhaps, I mused, he felt a deep sympathy for the plight of those who struggled in life, perhaps because he had experienced an unhappy childhood, with little parental love or encouragement.

"And yet, Anne says you insist on keeping your generosity a secret, even though such kindness would help burnish your reputation."

His expression hardened. "I don't give a rat's arse what people think of me. What matters to me is staying true to my own moral compass."

I couldn't muster any argument to that, so I simply accepted his arm and allowed him to lead back down to where our carriage was waiting.

To my delight, during the drive back he agreed to teach me the fine points of marksmanship with a pistol on our next visit to Houndslow Heath.

And several weeks later, Camelford gifted me with a lethally sharp jeweled dagger that he had brought back from the Levant, and showed me how to use it to defend myself. These clandestine adventures kept my blood thrumming . . .

However, my alluring life of careless freedom came crashing down around my ears at the end of February.

I told myself it was through no fault of my own, but that, of course, was just wishful thinking, as quickly became clear when Pitt summoned me to a private meeting at the family's townhouse in London. Camelford had created an ugly scandal and as I was the cause of it, I had to face the consequences.

My uncle's taut expression immediately betrayed the seriousness with which he viewed the situation, and I felt a niggling of remorse as I took a seat in the chair by his desk.

"I assume you know that Camelford challenged an acquaintance of his to a duel over a remark the fellow made about your less-than-proper behavior with men," he began.

"Yes, but the duel never took place—"

Pitt signaled me to silence. "It is true that swords were not crossed, but the scandal is still a threat to you—and to all of our family."

I hung my head.

"The fellow refused to fight and explaining that his words had been misinterpreted. But Camelford could not control his temper, and instead of accepting the apology, he assaulted the fellow with his fists. The fellow's friends promptly hired a Bow Street Runner to apprehend Camelford on charges of assault."

A gasp slipped from my lips. I hadn't realized that things had gotten so out of hand.

"Aware that a public trial would likely reveal the cause of the bad blood, Grenville and I negotiated with Camelford's victim to drop the complaint to spare our family a highly embarrassing scandal." He paused and blew out his breath. "The current political situation is extremely fraught, Hetty. My opponents are frothing at the bit to find the slightest reason to question my leadership."

Tears welled up in my eyes. He had shown me nothing but love and fatherly kindness. That I had repaid him with such blindly selfish behavior cut me to the quick.

"I'm so ashamed of myself for causing you trouble," I mumbled. "You must think me horribly ungrateful." A sob. "And unforgivably d-disloyal."

Pitt reached out and patted my hand. "I know how deeply you feel loyalty to family and friends, Hetty," he replied. "It is only because of you and your concern for the welfare of your younger brothers that the rest of the family is aware of how bad things are for them under your father's increasingly eccentric views of the world."

I felt another stab of guilt. Caught up in my relationship with Camelford, I had let the worry about my brothers slip into the shadows.

"I will be more careful here in Town," I promised, "and give you no further concern for worry."

My uncle shook his head. "I'm afraid it's not that simple, Hetty. There will be no trial, but rumors are still circulating. Grenville and I have decided that the best way to ensure that they die away quickly is for you to leave London."

"And go where?" I asked, though the answer was obvious.

Pitt's expression was sympathetic, but he didn't hesitate in replying.

"Home."

My father's estate had long since ceased to feel like home to me. But it wasn't as if there was any other option.

And so, without further ado, I had no choice but to pack my trunks and return to Chevening.

Living at home was a rude reminder of how little real control I had over my life. My father had become even more erratic in his moods and he was determined to exert an iron-fisted control over me and my three brothers. We were permitted no social intercourse with the surrounding families, and each night we were locked in our quarters to enforce his dictates. But if he thought to break my will, he should have known better. My childhood stubbornness had matured to an unbending resolve when I was confronted with an injustice. The more I learned of the situation with my brothers, the more I was determined to see that they were freed from his tyranny and given the freedom to chart their own course in Life.

Isolated in the dreary splendor of our ancestral estate, the poor boys had been allowed little contact with the outside world. My father had refused to send them away to school, their only education being the occasional haphazard efforts of Mr. Joyce, my father's private secretary, to teach them history and mathematics. However, that ended several years ago when Joyce was tried for high treason because of his support for the radical French government. It was no wonder that they found life at Chevening unbearably odious and oppressive.

Mahon, the eldest, felt it most deeply.

"I am a grown man!" he exclaimed to me as he jabbed a poker into the coals of the hearth, stirring up a flame.

The four of us had taken to gathering each evening in the parlor of the west wing, where our bedchambers were located, while my father toiled away at his various experiments in his workroom.

I nodded in sympathy. He had just turned nineteen and though he still had the gangly limbs of a youth not fully formed into adult-hood, I knew he was acutely aware of all that he was missing in life. "If you had your choice, what would you choose to do?" I prompted.

"I wish to travel!" Mahon clenched his jaw, the firelight accentuating his look of frustration. "And attend university! When Father's friends come to visit, they talk of foreign countries, and how the experience of studying abroad gives a gentleman poise and polish."

His words resonated with me. I, too, wished that I could experience such freedoms. "Perhaps there is a way that can be arranged."

"Ha! And pigs might fly." A note of despair shaded Mahon's reply. "Papa controls the purse strings, and trust me, he has no intention of loosening them. Without money, I am a prisoner here."

I thought for a moment, watching the red-gold sparks glimmer within the darkness of the coals. "Our extended family has both the influence and funds to help. I shall write to Pitt and his cousin, Lord Grenville, and inform them of the sorry state of affairs here."

"They are busy with their own grand affairs. Why should they care?" he demanded.

"Because I shall *make* them care."

"Huzzah for Hetty!" exclaimed Charles, the middle of the three boys. "She always stands up for us."

"Oiy." James, the youngest, was cuddled next to me on the sofa. He sidled closer and looked up at me with a smile. "Don't worry, Mahon. Unlike Mama, Hetty won't forget about us."

My hand found his and gave it a fierce squeeze. "Of that you may all be sure."

My stepmother had dutifully provided my father with an heir and two spares, but had grown increasingly disenchanted with life at Chevening. Resentful of my father's eccentricities and the colorless existence they created, she had taken to spending most of her time in London with her Grenville relatives, pursuing her own interests amid the pleasures of Town.

I couldn't fathom how she could abandon her own flesh and blood, and though I only shared one parent with the boys, I vowed there and then that as long as I had a breath in my body, I would fight for their well-being.

"I appreciate the sentiment." Mahon jabbed at the coals again. "But I fear it's hopeless. Papa will never relent, and I'll be trapped here for the rest of my days."

*Ah, the histrionics of youth.* However, I took care not to make light of his fears. I knew all too well what it felt like to have no control of one's life.

"No matter how dark things may look, there is always hope," I said stoutly. "You simply have to believe that the future is there, just waiting for you to make it your own."

Mahon made a rude sound and went back to his brooding. But Charles caught my eye and grinned. The two of us had always been close despite the difference in age. Unlike his older brother, who was rather serious by nature, he possessed an outgoing exuberance that aligned with mine. We had made much mischief together growing up together—much of it at my instigation—which had only strengthened our bond. As for James, he was hardly more than a child, which stirred a certain sense of protectiveness in me.

"Shall we play a game of cards to pass the time?" suggested Charles, drawing me back from my reveries.

"Perhaps the time would be better spent reading aloud," I suggested. I had been shocked to discover that he and James barely knew their letters or rudimentary arithmetic.

Charles made a face. "Books are boring!"

"That's because you can't figure out the words," needled Mahon.

Taking up the copy of *Robinson Crusoe* that I had brought from the library, I opened the pages to the first chapter and passed it to Charles. "Come, I've chosen a novel which is all about a shipwreck and exotic adventures. Why don't you begin . . ."

Over the next few days I dispatched a flurry of letters to Pitt and my Grenville relatives, as well as to several longtime friends of my father who might help to convince him of the unreasonableness of his behavior toward his heir. I also set aside some time each afternoon in which to tutor Charles and James. They were not happy about it, but as I was wise enough to use a stick-and-carrot teaching method, rewarding them with a rousing gallop through the estate lands after the lessons were done, we settled into a comfortable routine. Had he known what I was doing, my father would have raised holy hell. But as all his time and interest was devoted to his own arcane endeavors, life at Chevening was at least free from overt conflict.

However, that soon changed when a distraught Mahon sought me out one afternoon to tell me about my father's latest eccentricity.

"Surely you must have misunderstood him!" I exclaimed, after listening to my brother's agitated account.

"I am not!" he responded. "Papa is pressing me to sign documents that will have me give up my claim to our family's hereditary title when I reach my majority."

For a moment, I was too stunned to speak. It was a radical and shocking demand, one that was all but unheard of within our aristocratic world. If Mahon acceded to the demand, the entail that passed all ancestral property from father to son would be broken, allowing my father to sell off the family's property and assets, which would utterly ruin Mahon's future, and that of subsequent generations. The Stanhope earldom would disappear . . .

"Did he give any explanation for this outrageous idea?" I asked.

"He claims that he needs the money for his scientific experiments," answered my brother. "Apparently, they have become quite expensive."

"How expensive?" I pressed.

Mahon mumbled a number.

I was aghast to learn that my father was spending tens of thousands of pounds for such dabbling, while for years he had been refusing to fund any of the most basic expenses for his sons.

"He's offering me a sizable amount of money if I do so," added Mahon. "Enough that would allow me to escape Chevening—"

Appalled, I silenced him with an unladylike oath. "Absolutely not! You must not make such a devil-damned bargain and renounce your birthright." I drew in a breath, taking a moment to cool my anger. "Put off making any decision. I will write to Pitt this instant."

Seeing his stricken expression, I pulled Mahon into a hug. "Take heart, I promise you that your future will not be destroyed in order to win your freedom."

Pitt was just as shocked as I was by the news, and assured me that he had rallied our extended family to hammer out a solution for Mahon's dilemma. While he worked with our relatives to deal with financial matters, I continued to write to family friends concerning educational opportunities for my brother.

So, with the gears set in motion, we simply had to wait.

I, however, found it impossible to keep quiet about the unfair demand and began broaching the subject with my father. At first he was embarrassed. But he quickly turned aggressive, berating me and my sisters for being unnatural daughters and failing in our duties to see to his comforts.

And so came the fateful night that he pressed a dagger against my throat.

When it happened, I knew that my life had inexorably changed for the second time. The first had been meeting Brummell and Camelford, which had given me the confidence to believe in myself as an independent-minded individual, with ideas and emotions that need not conform to the traditional strictures imposed upon ladies of my social standing.

*Be damned with rules.*

The cold steel cutting against my flesh was a visceral reminder that men bent the rules when it suited their purposes. But rather than submit meekly to such tyranny, I was determined to live life on my own terms.

I fled Chevening shortly after the knife incident, assuring my brothers that I wouldn't abandon their interests. And once again I had to find a way to fit into the world without compromising my principles.

# Chapter 10

*Autumn 1800*

Pitt refused my request to return to London and stay with Lord and Lady Chatham, his older brother and sister-in-law who resided at Chatham House. Though he was sympathetic and supported my flight from my father's tyranny, the prospect of scandal still worried him. However, it was quickly arranged for me to live with my maternal grandmother, Hester, dowager Countess Chatham, who was currently living at Burton Pynsent, the Pitt family estate in Somerset.

My grandmother, a widow with the freedom to shape her life as she wished, may have sensed my need for independence, for she allowed me to do pretty much as I pleased. I continued to write letters to family and friends on Mahon's behalf, and kept in frequent communication with Pitt to make sure progress was being made.

And I also threw myself back into riding, and would often gallop from twenty to forty miles through the surrounding countryside over the course of a day. The sense of unfettered freedom was exhilarating—perhaps too much so.

I was out riding with my grandmother's head groom one afternoon and we were discussing the various challenges offered by the local bridle trails when he pointed out a particularly evil-looking stone wall bordering one of the pastures of the neighboring estate, its jagged rocks bristling with a tangle of thorny vines.

"Not even the most skilled riders of the local hunt dare to challenge that beast," he said. "It's deemed to be too dangerous."

"Is that so?" I reined to a halt and studied the approach.

"Good Lord, m'lady, I didn't mean to suggest—"

I was already maneuvering my horse for a run at it.

"M'lady!"

"Don't worry!" I cried. Spurring forward, I leaned low, reveling in the thunder of pounding hooves. I had chosen the perfect angle, and urged the muscled stallion airborne at just the right moment. Up, up, we soared, clearing the top with ease—

And then my horse's trailing leg caught in a tangle of thorns, throwing us off-balance. *No, no, no!* We hit the ground off stride, and as the stallion fought to regain its footing, I was thrown from the saddle, a thrashing hoof missing my skull by mere inches.

"M'lady, m'lady!" The groom dismounted and scrambled over the wall.

With the breath knocked out of me, I couldn't move for a moment, and then when I did, pain lanced through my bruised back and shoulders. "I'm fine," I wheezed. I could tell that nothing was broken, but no doubt I would be black and blue for a while. "See to Ajax."

Thank heavens the horse was uninjured, but the groom appeared unnerved by the brush with disaster when he came and helped me to my feet. "Ye have more courage than a Death's Head Hussar, milady. But if ye don't learn when te rein it in, I fear it will land you in the suds."

He was right, of course. Next time I might not be so lucky. Still, I found it hard to take the warning to heart. After all, even the best of riders took an occasional tumble.

Notwithstanding my reckless tumble, my riding skills were noted by our neighbors and I soon found myself being asked to break their vicious or unruly horses for them.

The challenge brought a bloom back to my cheeks. As did the local entertainments. Though not as sophisticated or sparkling as parties in London, they offered pleasant company and casual flirtations. After my temporary banishment to Chevening, living at Burton Pynsent was like a breath of fresh air.

Thankfully, the dowager had a soft spot for Camelford—I have noted that ladies of a certain age tend to enjoy the company of charming rogues with exotic stories—and when he began to appear frequently as a guest of various friends in the area, she raised no objections to my rekindling the relationship. The question of whether we were adhering to the strict rules of propriety was not one she ever asked.

"Your namesake seems to have a great fondness for you, Diamond," observed Camelford as he escorted me to the barns, where a groom was saddling my horse for a ride out into the surrounding countryside. He glanced down at my legs. "Our grandmama doesn't mind that you've taken to riding astride?"

"The local gentry have all encouraged me to do so. Word passed from the grooms here to others in the area concerning my expertise in training difficult mounts," I answered. "The gentry take their horseflesh seriously, so pragmatism takes precedence over rules of feminine dress and deportment. They heartily approve of my breeches."

"Wise fellows," said Camelford with a wry smile.

Our boots crunched over the gravel walkway as he gazed off at the distant hills where the trees were just beginning to show a hint of their autumn colors. He had not visited in a fortnight. No explanation was given, and I didn't ask.

"Here I go away for a bit," added Camelford, "and come back to the news from my friend Radley that you are engaged."

"Yes, gods, Tom, according to the gossips, I have been engaged fifty times in my life—and have been said to be married half as often." I huffed a laugh. "But provided I have control over such decisions, people may say what they please."

In truth, I *had* received a proposal of marriage. More than one, in fact. And while there were benefits to the state of matrimony—

as a wife I would have certain freedoms—I was in no hurry to take such a momentous step, despite Pitt's subtle pressure.

For there was no going back.

Camelford's expression turned thoughtful. "I was under the impression that all ladies aspired to marriage."

"For most, spinsterhood is more frightening than a life of wedded servitude." I drew in a sharp breath. "Men have their elemental freedom, so I daresay you all take it for granted."

"Not I," said he softly. "Naval life taught me early on how precious freedom is."

*Precious, indeed.*

He looked about to add something more, but as the breeze stirred the leaves, throwing shadows over our faces, he dropped his gaze to the pebbles beneath our feet.

After we had walked on for another few moments, he asked, "And what about adventures? Do you still crave them? Or did your banishment from London knock the wind out of your sails?"

The question sparked a flare of anger. "As you damn well know, a lady is merely a pawn, to be moved around on life's chess board by the gentlemen of her family." I drew in a sharp breath. "Until they pass her off to a husband, who will do much the same."

He took my hand and placed it in the crook of his arm. "Unless her husband is the sort of fellow who understands that she could never be happy within a cage, however gilded, and would allow her to spread her wings and fly."

"And pigs might sprout feathers and soar through the heavens."

Camelford turned his gaze to meet mine, his eyes bright with an indecipherable fire. "Stranger things have happened."

Was he in love with me? My heart skipped a beat. Was he about to make a declaration?

I looked away, uncertain whether it was hope or dread swirling around in my belly.

"I understand your frustrations," he said softly. "I know you long to explore the world and all the myriad experiences it has to offer. I have some ideas."

Our steps had brought us to the barn, where a groom was waiting with our horses. Thrusting my boot into the stirrup, I swung myself up into my saddle.

Camelford did the same and gathered his reins. "Follow me," he called and spurred his stallion into a gallop.

I urged my spirited filly to meet the challenge, reveling in the thunder of pounding hooves and the slap of the wind against my cheeks. *Faster, Faster*—the rush of sensations was exhilarating and made me feel gloriously alive.

Tightening my reins, I bent low. What my horse lacked in muscle, she made up in grace and speed. We were soon matching Camelford and his stallion stride for stride.

As the grove of trees edging the rolling meadows came closer, we slowed to a walk, allowing our sweating and snorting mounts to catch their wind.

"*Brava!*" exclaimed Camelford, touching a quick salute to the brim of his hat. "You ride like a princess of the Amazons."

I replied with a mock bow. "I wouldn't like to have been one of those ancient Greek warriors. As I recall, they were required to chop off their left breast so it didn't interfere with their archery prowess."

His gaze came to rest on my bosom. "I agree. That would be a sin." He continued to stare, and despite my frogged jacket I felt naked to his eyes. "One doesn't mar absolute perfection."

"What fustion," I chided. "You have no idea of whether I am . . . perfect or not."

"Trust me, I know perfection when I see it." A smile. "You forget that I've seen your lovely breasts in naught but a linen shirt."

"How ungentlemanly of you to remind me of that."

"Ah, I'm no gentleman."

That was likely true. No true gentleman could possess the devil's own smile. Aware that I was blushing like a schoolgirl, I looked away.

"Racing works up a thirst," he said. "I'm in need of some ale."

Disappointment pinched at the corners of my mouth. I had hoped we might ride for the rest of the day. "Must we return to the manor house so soon?"

"Who said anything about returning to the manor house? I know a snug tavern that makes surprisingly good brew."

A lady did not frequent taverns. Especially not one dressed in breeches. "But—"

"Trust me," he repeated.

And so I did.

On we rode through hill and dale, the air turning crisp with the scent of ripening apples, fresh-cut hay, and the tang of salt from the sea. The farms grew sparser, the hills more rugged as the trail brought us to a remote area of the shire.

"Where are we?" I asked, when Camelford paused to look down at a narrow valley with a river winding along its far edge.

"Somewhere on the River Parrett near the ancient ferry crossing at Combwich," he replied. "As far as I know, the hamlet doesn't have a name."

Squinting into the sun, I could just make out a few stone-and-thatch dwellings among the hardscrabble fields bordering the water's edge. But before I could ask any further questions, he spurred his horse down the rocky descent.

After winding through a cluster of houses—or rather hovels—we came to a larger building, where he indicated that we should dismount. Other than a few scrawny chickens scratching in the dirt, we appeared to be the only living souls around. The impression didn't change as he knocked three times on the age-dark oak door and pushed it open halfway. Then the sounds of hurried scrabbling escaped from inside—a flurry of bootsteps punctuated by loud thumps and muttered curses.

A big, bearlike man appeared from the gloom, his fierce scowl fading at the sight of Camelford.

"Thought ye wuz the revenue cullies," he said, his hands dropping away from the thick brass-buckled belt around his middle. The movement revealed the butt of an ancient-looking flintlock pistol sticking up from the leather.

"Try wiping the shite off your windows, Isaiah. My horseflesh is far superior to theirs," drawled Camelford. "By the by, do you perchance have a cask of your good stuff open?"

"Fer you, Cap—always." A gap-toothed grin. "Ye always pay right 'andsomely fer it." Turning, Isaiah barked out a few orders before giving a wave.

"Come in, come in, an' bring yer friend—" He stopped short as I came closer. "Well, I'll be buggered." His gaze lingering on my face, and the plumed shako set at a jaunty angle atop my curls, and then dropped to my legs. "That's a wummun wiv ye! And she wearing breeches."

"How observant," replied Camelford.

Isaiah's scowl was back. "As a rule, we don't allow wummen in here."

"S'right," chorused his unseen companions from the depths of the murky taproom.

"She's not a woman, she's a crown princess," corrected Camelford, flashing me a wink. "Visiting from Amazonia, a grand country on the far side of the world."

"Oiy?" Isaiah narrowed his eyes, looking as if he had just been told that the Man in the Moon's daughter had descended from the heavens on a silver unicorn. "Wot's a princess doing here?"

"Hoping to wet her whistle with a mug of decent ale," answered Camelford. "But we can always ride on to Combwich."

Isaiah appeared deeply offended. "My ale is a match for any in England."

"So you say," I countered, placing a hand on my hip. It was one thing to masquerade as a man, the act of rebellion against the rules tempered by the fact that nobody knew the truth. To flaunt my femininity for all to see felt even more daring.

"And yet you're not willing to prove it." With an imperious sniff, I added, "Come, Captain, let us go somewhere that will offer us a more cordial welcome."

"She speaks English!"

"Of course I do. King George is my third cousin." I accentuated the blatant lie with an airy wave. "You know royalty. We're all related."

A sudden flash lit in Isaiah's eyes. The realization, no doubt, that a goodly number of coins were about to slip through his fingers. "Wait!" He scratched at his grizzled cheek. "I s'ppose a princess doesn't count as a wummun."

"Indeed not—she's a *lady*," offered Camelford.

"Oiy, well in that case, she's welcome to enter!"

I paused after crossing the threshold. It was dark as the devil's lair and the air was thick with the scents of spilled ale, stale onions, and unwashed males. Somebody struck flint and steel to the wick of a lantern, and an oily flame danced to life, illuminating a half dozen rough-planked tables and stools arranged on the stone flaggings.

Camelford gestured to one in the far corner. "Bring us two tankards," he said to Isaiah. "And feel free to continue going about your business."

The ale was quickly thumped down on the scarred wood. Isaiah then gestured at the four wide-eyed men standing still as statues—perhaps the sight of me had turned them into stone—and spat out a string of oaths that would have singed the ears of a stevedore.

I laughed, which seemed to break the spell.

Punctuated by a rumble of lewd replies, the men tore their eyes away from me and got back to work, wrestling the few remaining barrels down through a well-disguised hatchway in the flooring that gave access to a cellar.

Emboldened by my breeches—and a bellyful of ale—I called out to them once the grunting and shoving was done. "Come join us and wash the dust from your throats." A wink at Camelford. "The captain is paying, of course."

The floodgates were now opened. The whole cask was shimmied closer to our table, and Camelford was handed refilled tankards as quickly as they could be drained. Tongues loosened by the brew, the men began to pepper me with questions about Amazonia.

Perhaps a gift for oratory as well as a taste for adventure ran in my Pitt blood because my words seemed to keep them enthralled. I'm not quite sure what prompted the moment, but somehow a fiddle appeared and I was dancing atop the table with Camelford, demonstrating the Amazon Gavotte to thunderous applause.

"Lud, that was fun!" I exclaimed, as he finally hustled me out of the tavern. A blade of sunlight slashed across my eyes, causing me to stumble. "Why must we leave so soon?"

"Because you need to stay upright in the saddle," drawled Camelford. "And be sober by the time we arrive back at Burton Pynsent."

"I'm sick to death of being sober!" I announced.

A bark of laughter. "That's the spirit, Diamond!" He steadied my step. "But rebellion is a two-edged sword. The trick is to make sure it only cuts one way."

I needed a few moments to parse through his meaning. "So you are saying . . . that one still needs to be careful?"

"I'm simply being pragmatic." A mischievous glint flashed in his eyes. "If you wish to keep breaking the rules, then you have to be careful not to get caught."

"In other words, when I choose to dance along a blade's razor-sharp edge I must be sure-footed enough not to fall off."

"Precisely."

"Because," I added, "a gentleman is allowed a slip or two. And a lady is not."

"The most important lesson that I've learned from my many adventures is that life is not fair, my dear Diamond. The sooner you accept that, the better."

We had reached the spot where our horses were tethered. The cool breeze had helped to clear my head, and as I untied my reins, I thought about what he had just said.

"I suppose that I should thank you. Those are wise words."

"I have been called a great many things in the course of my short existence," said Camelford as he swung himself into his saddle. "Wise is not one of them."

I mounted as well and spurred my filly to keep up with Camelford's stallion, deciding that whatever the risks I faced in an unfair world, they were worth it in order to feel the fizzy elation that was bubbling through my veins.

Camelford slowed as the trail led into a grove of trees and halted to allow me to come up beside him. "Having second thoughts about the path you are on?" His expression was inscrutable. "Even though it may be the road to perdition?"

"Not a one," I answered with a challenging stare. "I could ask the same question of you, Tom."

"My answer would be the same." Leaning toward me, he reached out, twining his fingers in the loosened curls beneath my shako and drawing my lips to within a hairsbreadth of his. The spicy scent of ale was on his breath . . .

It was, I realized a moment later, also on his tongue.

Camelford kissed me, but not in a way that I had ever experienced before. His lips touched mine, and with a sensual flick, his tongue teased its way into a more intimate embrace. I froze and then let out a little moan as the sensations sent shivers of fire and ice down my spine.

Our horses stilled. My hands were on his shoulders, urging him closer. He deepened the kiss, and I thought for an instant that I might faint with pleasure.

One of my boots slipped from the stirrup. I was half out of the saddle, when Camelford slowly withdrew.

"Damnation, this is a well-traveled trail," he rasped. "I can't . . . I won't . . ."

I kept hold of his coat. "But—"

He touched a finger to my lips, silencing my protest. "For now, Diamond, we must be patient."

The sound of an approaching rider rose above the rustling of the leaves.

"But not for long."

# Chapter 11

True to his word, Camelford wasted no time in coming up with an idea, and by the following week he informed me of his plan. Pitt had relented and allowed me to make occasional visits to London, where I stayed with various relatives or family friends. As my grandmother paid little attention to my coming and going, he suggested that I should merely inform her that a carriage would call for me and that my hosts would provide a lady's maid, so there was no need for Susan to accompany me.

When the appointed morning came, a footman carried my luggage out to a waiting vehicle, the driver cracked his whip, and off we drove. About a mile down the road, Camelford appeared from the woods skirting the lane and climbed in beside me.

"Where are we going?" I pressed, as he had still not revealed any of the details about our clandestine trip.

A laugh. "All in good time, Diamond. For now, let us just enjoy the journey."

The carriage soon moved from the smaller lanes onto the main road heading southwest. The driver—a former pugilist and crony from Camelford's boxing circle—was skilled in handling the reins and kept us moving at a fast clip.

"He's also the soul of discretion," assured Camelford when we made our first stop at a coaching house to change horses and partake of some refreshments. "Our privacy is safe with him. If any-one inquires, we're simply Mr. and Mrs. Smythe from Manchester on our way to visit relatives in Falmouth—"

"We're going to Falmouth?" I interrupted.

His mouth quirked. "I didn't say that."

"Do stop teasing, Tom." I finished my cup of fresh-pressed cider, the tart sweetness reminding me of how much I loved the autumn season. "When do we arrive at this oh-so secret place? An hour? Two?"

"Actually, not until tomorrow."

My face must have betrayed my surprise, for Camelford gave me an encouraging smile. "Yes, that means we will be stopping for the night at an inn, but be assured that all the rules of propriety will be respected and your honor will not be compromised. I shall inform the innkeeper that my wife is feeling unwell from traveling and needs her own room in order to get a restful sleep."

I wasn't sure whether to feel relieved or disappointed. Some-how, I had assumed . . .

"Let us wait for the perfect moment." He leaned in closer, his whisper caressing my ear. "Besides, anticipation is a powerful aphrodisiac."

*Was that why my body was suddenly thrumming with all manner of un-known sensations?*

As he promised, we passed an uneventful night at an out-of-the-way inn and were on the road again by early light. The carriage made its way from Devonshire into Cornwall, a wild and mysteri-ous part of England known for its aura of enchantment. We headed inland after skirting Plymouth, and I noted that Camelford was watching the passing landscape with an air of growing expectancy. After turning from a secondary road and bumping down a country lane, we passed through a set of wrought-iron gates—and he fi-nally revealed our destination.

"Welcome to Boconnoc."

*Boconnoc.*

My heartbeat kicked up a notch. The estate was part of the Pitt family's lore. My great-great-grandfather, "Diamond" Pitt, had

bought it with the proceeds of his famous gemstone, and the estate
had a storied history, beginning with its mention in the Domesday
tax roll of 1086.

"The place has witnessed much over the centuries," mused
Camelford. "It was purchased in 1579 by Sir William Mohun. In
1644, King Charles I used it as his headquarters during his battle
with the Parliamentarians. After the king's defeat and beheading
by Cromwell, Mohun's great-grandson was forced to pay a princely
sum to retain the estate, and it stayed in the family until the fourth
Baron Mohun was killed in a duel with the Duke of Hamilton in
1712. His wife then sold it to our illustrious forebearer."

My flesh began to tingle. I could almost feel the powerful presence of Diamond Pitt within the shadows of the carriage.

"My father, the first Lord Camelford, laid out the parkland,"
continued Camelford, gazing out the carriage window at splendid
woodland gardens filled with magnificent rhododendrons, azaleas,
and magnolias.

"It's beautiful!" I exclaimed.

"He also brought in Sir John Soane to redesign elements of the
stableyard and decorative touches to Boconnoc House itself . . ."
He hesitated, a spasm of emotion seeming to tighten his throat.
"It's quite impressive."

The coolness that had crept into his tone hinted that like the
grand manor of my childhood, Boconnoc House had been naught
but a fancy pile of stone and woodwork to him, devoid of any
warmth that would have made it a true home.

"And now it is yours," I said softly. He had, I recalled, inherited
the estate at the age of sixteen while halfway around the world
with the Royal Navy. "To shape as you see fit."

His answer was a gruff sigh.

"It's beautiful," I repeated, watching the sunlight play hide-
and-seek through the leaves of the majestic oaks.

The carriageway broke free of the trees and as it rounded a
bend, the manor Boconnoc House came into view.

The stark simplicity of the building, unsoftened by any ornate
details, struck me as being in perfect harmony with its current

owner. The weathered stone, the straight lines and solid corners reflected Camelford's chiseled and scarred body. It was a place that had endured all that Nature could hurl at it without flinching.

"I love it."

His expression lightened. "I hoped you would."

We were met in the courtyard by the elderly housekeeper and several servants. The two footmen took charge of our luggage, and after greeting Camelford, the housekeeper offered to escort me to my quarters so that I might refresh myself after the rigors of travel.

"I shall come fetch you in a bit and give you a tour of the place," said Camelford, as I turned to go. "And then we shall enjoy a quiet evening together, blessedly free of the pomp and artifice of London Society."

After a delicious supper of roast pheasant and other local delicacies, Camelford took me upstairs. But rather than turn into one of the parlors overlooking the courtyard, he continued on to his own set of rooms. A large sitting room, imposing with its age-dark oak furniture, was alight with a blaze of candles.

"King Charles I is said to have slept in this suite during his stay," he said. "Indeed, my bedchamber is called the King's Bedroom." A pause. "The king was famous for taking his pleasures with beautiful women."

My face grew warm, and not merely from the flames licking up from the burning logs in the hearth.

"Come, let us get comfortable." Taking my hand, Camelford led me through the half-open door to the connecting room.

A grand four-poster bed—clearly fit for a king—dominated one side of the room. Facing it was a massive stone fireplace, the marble mantel carved with a graceful twining of acanthus leaves.

He moved to a bureau and struck steel and flint to an ornate lantern-like object made of brass. Sparks flared from the thin sticks poking up from its middle, and an exotic scent—a mixture of sweet and earthy spices that I couldn't begin to put a name to—teased through the air.

I shifted my stance, and on spotting the muted swirls of a Persian carpet beneath my feet, I was reminded of all the many adventures Camelford had experienced.

While this current journey was the farthest I had ever been from the place of my birth.

A sigh of longing escaped from my lips as I took a seat on the bed. "Tell me about the Levant," I begged.

Coals crackled in the hearth, sending up a tongue of red-gold fire. Smoke swirled with shadows.

"The sunlight is dazzling," began Camelford, "teasing and tantalizing the senses . . ."

I listened, enchanted, as he went on to describe the colorful souks, the dark-skinned Bedouin warriors, the musical lilt of Arabic, the sweetly languorous scent of hashish . . .

He was a colorful storyteller, bringing the exotic settings to life. And his words were like a drug, drawing me into a magical world far beyond the boundaries of my ordinary existence.

"I want to travel," I whispered as he paused to remove his coat. "And experience the world and all its wonders."

He smiled. "You're a true Pitt. You have an adventurous spirit." He traced the line of my jaw with his forefinger. "You're not afraid of the unknown?"

"On the contrary." I drew in a quick breath. "I embrace it."

"Life should always be embraced." He untied his cravat and let it slip through his hands to fall to the carpet. "To the fullest."

I shrugged off my shawl, feeling the woven silk slither off, baring my shoulders. "Half measures are for the half-hearted."

One by one, the pins holding my coiled tresses in place yielded to his deft touch. "Shall I regale you with further explorations into the wonders of the world?"

His words were like liquid fire, bringing my blood to a boil.

"Yes, please!" I begged.

"Then close your eyes, my dear Diamond, and allow me to take you on a special journey."

My lashes fluttered, blurring the flames in the hearth to a swirl of color as I surrendered to the moment . . .

And let myself be swept away.

## Chapter 12

*Winter–Spring 1801*

The new year quickly brought yet more changes to my life.

In February, Pitt resigned as prime minister over the question of Catholic Emancipation. Having shepherded the Acts of Union through Parliament the previous year, which united the Kingdom of Britain with the Kingdom of Ireland, he believed that it was imperative to abolish the political restrictions on Catholics. King George III, however, was adamantly opposed. And so, Pitt handed the seals of office over to his friend, Lord Henry Addington.

I confess, the news shocked me. He had been prime minister for seventeen years, and I suppose that I had come to think that he would always be there as Britain's leader. But he, alas, was a mere mortal, not a God-anointed king, and the stresses of the last few years had taken their toll on his health. Ailing and in debt, Pitt left London.

He still held the appointment of Lord Warden of the Cinque Ports, an ancient title—and a mostly ceremonial one—and went to live at Walmer Castle, the lord warden's official residence on the coast of Kent, which was a place he had often used as a refuge from pressures of Downing Street. Convinced that France intended to eventually invade Britain by landing along the Channel coast, he began organizing volunteer militias in the area, as well as overseeing the coastal defenses.

Closer to home, the simmering conflict between my father and his heir was coming to a boil.

Poor Mahon! His most recent letter informed me that my father was ratcheting up the pressure on him to sign over his hereditary rights. I quickly informed Pitt, and with his blessing, I redoubled my efforts with our network of influential relatives and acquaintances to arrange for letters of credit—provided by my father's former friends Sir Frances Burdett and William Lowther—and a passport for Mahon to travel abroad. As he longed to engage in academic life, I also managed to procure recommendations to ensure his acceptance at Erlangen University in Bavaria.

With all this in place, I drew up a plan of escape . . .

With the help of the gatekeeper at Chevening, I managed to set up a clandestine meeting with Mahon at one of the outbuildings on the estate.

"Thank God you have come!" he cried, dismounting and hurrying to join me inside the shadows beneath the eaves.

"I told you I wouldn't abandon you." I gave a quick kiss to his cheek.

"Papa is growing desperate." He blew out a shaky breath. "I fear that his knife will soon be at *my* throat."

"It won't come to that." I smiled. "Tonight is the night that you'll take your first steps toward independence."

His eyes widened, and then he seized me in a hug. "I can't thank you enough, Hetty—"

"Love needs no words. Come, listen closely while I explain what you must do—"

"Papa has the place locked up even tighter than before," warned Mahon.

"I've thought of that, "I interjected, and went on to explain my plan.

He stared at me for an instant and then let out a peal of laughter. "Ye heavens, that's brilliant!"

"You can tell Charles and James that reading is a very useful skill to have in life." Putting aside all humor, I added, "The three of you must be careful not to betray that anything is afoot. When midnight comes, keep watch at your bedchamber window, I will flash a lantern when all is in place for you to make your move."

I hesitated. "Your brothers are too young to leave the nest, but assure them that when the time comes, I shall see to it that they have the chance to spread their wings."

Night fell, and using a ploy straight out of a gothic novel, Mahon tied his bedsheets together and lowered himself from his upper story room to the gardens. From there, I gave him a packet with money and all his official papers, then led him to where a carriage was waiting to whisk him to Dover and the ship that would carry him to freedom.

My father was furious, and my actions resulted in a final break between us. And to my dismay, my maternal grandmother sided with him, saying that I had brought unwanted scandal upon the family by bringing private quarrels to the public's attention. I was hurt, yet I did not rue my banishment from Chevening, even though I felt terrible about leaving my two younger brothers without an ally. However, I vowed to them that I wouldn't forget their plight, a promise I didn't take lightly. They deserved my loyalty.

Besides, I had a soft spot in my heart for underdogs.


*Summer–Autumn 1801*

The family strife complicated my relationship with Camelford. We had managed a few more dalliances since our visit to Boconnoc, but with Pitt out of London and my focus on the turmoil at Chevening, we saw less of each other as winter segued into spring. I had noted early on in our relationship that Camelford's moods were mercurial. He was easily distracted, and of late, something within the world of boxing appeared to have caught his fancy. His trips out to Burton Pynsent became less frequent, and as Pitt's older brother, Lord Chatham, was caught up in politics, it wasn't as easy for me to spend time in London as it used to be.

If only those of our sex were permitted to possess property and funds—and the independence to control them . . .

Bored by the quiet life with my grandmother at Burton Pynsent, I arranged to spend some weeks with family friends in Bath, just as the spring social season came into full swirl. It was a pleasant interlude. The town was the most fashionable spa in Britain and the Upper Assembly Rooms, which catered to the visiting aristocrats and local gentry, offered a lively array of balls and informal dances. I greatly enjoyed the opportunity to re-sharpen my skills at flirting.

They must not have been too dull, for I received yet another proposal of marriage.

"What a marvelous dancer you are!" My partner paused for a moment to catch his breath as the notes of a rollicking country dance ended with a flourish. "I have never met a lady with your . . . verve and sparkle!"

I laughed. "Life should be embraced to the fullest, don't you think?"

"Indeed, indeed." He cleared his throat. "As to that, umm, might I fetch us some champagne and suggest a stroll out to the terrace . . . ?"

Mr. Methuen of Corsham was a pleasant enough fellow, possessing wealth and good looks. But I knew in my heart that I could never settle for a quiet, traditional life as a country gentleman's wife.

I should go mad within a week.

As for other options, I told myself not to fret on the future. I was still young and had not yet come close to drinking my fill of life's pleasures.

And there was, of course, my relationship with Camelford . . .

But in October, I learned the news that Camelford—without saying a word to me or anyone else—had left Britain. And nobody had a clue as to where or why he had gone.

*Winter 1802*

Come January, I had another invitation to visit old friends—one that I seized with great enthusiasm.

"Hester! Ye gods, is that really you?" In response to the footman's announcement of my name as I entered the drawing room on the evening of my arrival, a tall sun-bronzed naval officer broke away from a group of ladies and gentlemen and rushed to greet me.

Even if the uniform hadn't given away his identity, the distinctive Pitt nose would have told me that I was meeting my war hero cousin, Sir Sidney Smith.

"You've grown since I last saw you," he said with a chuckle, after pressing a kiss to my cheek. "Which was, I believe, when you were an imp of nine years old and trying like the devil to run me over with your monstrous horse."

"Actually, I was endeavoring to have Bucephalus jump *over* you," I replied. "However, you refused to stand still."

Sir Sidney gave a mock shudder. "The sheer fright of it caused me to run away to sea!"

"Ha! From what I've heard, nothing frightens you, Sidney," I countered with a smile. "It is so good to have you back in England. I was delighted to receive the invitation to be part of your house party."

With peace about to be announced between Britain and France, the Royal Navy had sent a number of its officers back to shore on half pay. Sir Sidney was among them, and with the backing of our influential relatives, he was seeking election to Parliament from Rochester in Kent. In the meantime, he had rented a grand house in Weymouth right after the New Year and I was among the various friends and relatives that he had invited for a visit.

Princess Caroline, the estranged wife of the Prince of Wales, had also come to the charming coastal town to escape the smoke and gloom of London, so it had become a popular gathering place for the beau monde, a pleasant spot in which to partake of the healthful sea air—and to break the boredom of winter with a swirl of entertainments.

I had arrived in late afternoon and been taken to my appointed quarters while Sir Sidney had been out promenading in town. Apprised of the evening soiree taking place in the house, I dressed for the occasion and made my way downstairs to join the festivities, so this was our first meeting since childhood.

"I'm delighted you were able to come," said my cousin.

"How does it feel to be back on *terra firma*?" I asked.

"I confess, it's rather nice to be able to stretch my legs without the worry of crashing cannonballs and flying bullets." Sir Sidney gave me a peck on the cheek. "Perhaps I'll settle down to a quiet life as a country squire and grow fat by the fireplace with a charming wife and a brood of offspring."

"Be careful what you wish for." I eyed him thoughtfully. "You would likely be bored to flinders within a fortnight."

A grin. "I daresay you're right. The progeny of Diamond Pitt seem to be fated to . . ." He paused as if searching for words.

"Make waves?" I suggested.

That made him laugh. "An apt metaphor, Hetty. And not only did your uncle Pitt make his own waves, but he also managed to navigate through the tricky shoals and currents of government for many years—which was no small feat."

"Yes, but the last political storm forced him to shore," I mused. "Do you think the peace with France will last?"

"No," he said without hesitation. Taking my arm, he drew me into a small side salon where we might converse with added privacy. "Napoleon is merely rebuilding his forces. As soon as it suits him, the world will once again explode into flames."

I twisted at the diamond ring on my finger. "That's what Pitt believes. As does our cousin Camelford." Lowering my voice to a near whisper, I added, "He's disappeared, you know. Have you any idea what he's up to?"

"Ah. Tom." Sir Sidney sighed. "If only our cousin could trade a bit of his courage for a grain of common sense."

"He was apprehended trying to cross to France a while back. And rumor had it that—"

"Yes, I've heard the rumors." Sir Sidney's expression took on a grim set. "I don't doubt that they were true."

"He yearns to be a hero," I responded. "Your exploits, and the accolades you've received for your valorous actions, have made him even more desperate to do something that will earn him the undying gratitude of king and country."

"Like assassinating Napoleon," growled Sir Sidney. "Bloody fool."

"Lord Grenville has also made some discreet inquiries. He says there is no sign that Tom is in Paris."

"Let us hope that is true. Joseph Fouché, France's Minister of Police, is the Devil Incarnate, and trust me, a stay in Paris's notorious Temple Prison is not something I would recommend."

Fear caused my throat to tighten. During a daring attempt to sneak into the harbor of Le Havre and sail away with a French ship, Sir Sidney had been captured by the French and imprisoned for two years in the infamous Parisian hellhole before managing to escape with the help of French Royalists.

Sir Sidney patted my hand. "As you see, I survived," he said lightly. "But given Tom's volatile temperament, I'm not sure he would fare so well."

"Nor am I," I whispered.

Sir Sidney cocked his head. "You, too, have a reputation for fiery behavior, Hetty. But you're also pragmatic and possess common sense. I have heard that you and Tom are . . . close." A pause. "And are perhaps contemplating matrimony. Can't you rein in some of his more reckless impulses?"

"Tom is not the sort of gentleman who responds well to bit and bridle, no matter who tugs on the reins," I replied. "As for any formal understanding between him and me for the future . . ."

Much as I was drawn to Camelford—I admired his adventurous spirit, sense of honor, generosity, and courage—I was coming to recognize that our strong-willed temperaments were too similar to bode well for a happy marriage.

"There is none," I finished.

"Ah."

"But I care deeply for him and worry about his present predicament."

"I shall make inquiries through my military friends," said Sir Sidney. "Though I daresay the diplomatic members of our family will likely be the best ones to handle the situation."

"And pull Tom's cods out of the fire yet again," I said.

Speaking of which, Sir Sidney was also known for getting into trouble because of his swashbuckling attitude. He had made an enemy of Admiral Nelson by acting on his own in the Mediterranean. According to my uncle, that was one of the reasons Sir Sidney was now in drydock.

My cousin laughed again, but before he could add anything, a flurry of rustling silk just outside the doorway warned that we were no longer alone.

"La, Commodore, here you are!" A lady dressed in a scarlet velvet evening gown, its décolletage cut just a little too low for strict propriety, gave an airy wave. "I trust you have not forgotten your promise to tell me about some of your seafaring adventures."

"Indeed not, Your Royal Highness."

*Ah, so this must be the Prince of Wales's estranged wife, Princess Caroline.* She was no raving beauty but there was a prettiness to her features—fair, curling hair gave a winsomeness to her blue-gray eyes, rosy cheeks, and Cupid's bow mouth. Rumor had it that Prinny had taken a loathing to her at first sight. But that, I mused, might well be because he was already secretly—and illegally—married to Maria Fitzherbert.

However, given the way Sir Sidney eyed her, Princess Caroline seemed to have no trouble attracting other gentlemen admirers.

His manners still polished despite his years at sea, Sir Sidney immediately introduced us.

Unlike my father, I respected royalty and acknowledged the princess with a deep curtsey.

"Lady Hester Stanhope," said Princess Caroline. "I've heard a great deal about you."

"And my family, no doubt," I responded.

A peal of laughter. "I like your cousin already," she said to Sir

Sidney, before turning her gaze back to me. "Do come call on me
tomorrow, Lady Hester. I should like to get to know you better."

"With pleasure, Your Royal Highness."

The princess was already back to batting her lashes at Sir Sidney. "The commodore knows where I'm residing. He will show
you the way."

"Your wish is my command," answered Sir Sidney.

"Then might I ask for your escort to the refreshment room? I
suddenly feel a thirst for some champagne."

Sir Sidney hesitated, darting a look at me.

"Of course he will," I said quickly.

Princess Caroline fluttered a wave of thanks my way as she took
Sir Sidney's arm and steered him out to the corridor.


"A wise decision," came a purring voice from the shadows outside the doorway. A moment later, Georgiana, Duchess of Devonshire, padded into the salon on silent little cat paws. "It's always
best to be in royalty's good graces."

I took umbrage at the inference that I was a toadeater. "Do you
believe that everyone puts pragmatism above personal principle?"

"If they don't then they are fools," she answered without batting an eye.

"So you choose to speak with a sugar-coated tongue to those
you despise?" I challenged.

"When it suits my purposes."

Our gazes locked. Georgiana was nearly twenty years older than
I was, and had been a leading lady of the beau monde for much of
her life. Her marriage to the Duke of Devonshire, one of the rich-
est and most powerful men in Britain, assured her a position of
prominence and influence—and she embraced it to the hilt, setting the trends in fashion and style for Society. Unlike other ladies,
however, she had also become active in politics. She was a tireless
campaigner for Charles Fox and the Whigs, who were my uncle's
chief enemies and political rivals.

Was it any wonder that I disliked her on principle?

The duchess seemed to sense my feelings and find them amusing. She smiled. "Perhaps when you are older and the passions of youth have cooled, you'll understand what I mean."

My chin rose a notch. "I like to think that the things about which I am passionate are not merely childish games."

*As for the games within games of the rich and powerful . . .*

Georgiana's scandalous personal life was an ill-kept secret among the beau monde. Devonshire was said to be a cold, unfeeling man with a taste for philandering, and the duchess, who possessed a warm and outgoing nature, had sought solace in her friendship with Lady Elizabeth Foster. When the duke seduced Lady Elizabeth, the household became a *ménage à trois*.

*Smoke and mirrors. Artifice and betrayal.*

Georgiana and her circle of highborn friends contrived to create an elaborate set of unwritten rules, which allowed them to appear daring and independent as they lived their own lives within the confines of their marriages. But in truth, it was mere illusion. Their husbands held all the power. With a flick of a finger, they could bring their wives to heel . . . like a well-trained hound.

I made a vow to myself then and there that I would never submit to such tyranny. If I was ever to legshackle myself to a man, I would be sure that he respected me in mind and spirit.

Georgiana was watching me intently. Age was beginning to show on her face. An illness had left one of her eyes scarred, dimming her youthful beauty. But what I noted was the rippling of shrewd intelligence in her gaze. Only a fool would fail to recognize that she was still a formidable presence.

"I suppose only time will tell, Lady Hester," she remarked.

I said nothing in reply.

"Georgiana—" A tall, elegant lady paused in the doorway. "Forgive me, I didn't realize I was interrupting a tête-à-tête."

"Do come in. Lady Hester and I were just becoming acquainted." To me, she added, "Allow me to introduce my sister, Henrietta, Lady Bessborough."

*Ah, yet another unhappy wife.* The Earl of Bessborough was known to be an abusive husband who apparently beat her whenever the mood struck him.

"It's a pleasure to make your acquaintance, Lady Hester," said Georgiana's sister with a gracious nod. Despite the travails of her personal life, I knew that she was much admired by the beau monde for her intelligence, wit, and kindness.

"Is it?" A rude reply, but her sister had put my back up.

Georgiana smiled. "I fear Lady Hester is offended by my politics and support of Charles Fox. We are a thorn in the derriere of her uncle, William Pitt."

Harriet—she was called Harriet rather than Henrietta by her family and friends—let out a trill of cheerful laughter. "Be assured I have no interest in politics, Lady Hester. Indeed, let us talk about a less fraught topic. I've heard that you are a superb rider. There are a number of excellent bridle paths in the area and Georgiana and I have brought some fine horses from Chatsworth. If you would care to ride out with our party tomorrow, you are welcome to join us."

It was a handsome invitation and it would have been churlish of me to refuse. Besides, the duke, for all his faults, was known to keep a magnificent stable.

"Thank you. I should like that very much."

A time was arranged, and to my surprise, she drew me into an engaging conversation about the upcoming races at Newmarket. Her charms were hard to deny. Unlike her sister, she seemed to possess an unfeigned warmth, and I found my intention to dislike her begin to melt.

More guests were arriving, and the sounds of festive cheer were growing louder. After exchanging a few more pleasantries, the three of us returned to the main drawing room, where my attention was quickly claimed by several distant Pitt cousins.

# *Chapter* 13

*Spring 1802*

The next few weeks of my stay in Weymouth passed in a whirl-wind of activity. Riding and rounds of morning calls occupied the days, while soirees, musicales, and dancing until dawn took up the evenings. Princess Caroline invited me to her residence so frequently that people began to ask if I had been appointed as one of her ladies-in-waiting. It took me a while to realize that it wasn't my charms—such as they were—that had captured Caroline's fancy. My presence was an excuse for Sir Sidney to serve as my escort, allowing him to engage in an affair with the all-too-willing princess.

Indeed, dalliances were de rigueur and marriage vows were naught but a sham for both the gentlemen and ladies, though the ladies were only allowed to stray after they had produced a male child to serve as heir of the family name.

It reminded me of Brummell's cold calculations to curry favor among the beau monde, and I found that the hypocrisy of it all weighed heavily on my spirits.

That there was still no word about Camelford, despite all the letters Sir Sidney and I dispatched to influential friends of the family, also darkened my mood. As did another concern that continued to weigh on my mind. I had not forgotten about Charles and James, my two younger brothers who were still trapped at Chevening. They were growing up fast and I needed to think of how to secure their freedom.

And so, a gleam of light within the shadows surrounding me was the arrival of Princess Caroline's brother-in-law, Prince Frederick Augustus, Duke of York and Albany, who was spending some time at Weymouth as he inspected the military defenses along the Channel coast. I had met him at a number of Pitt's receptions and our dealings had always been cordial. And as we renewed our acquaintance, it occurred to me that he might be the answer to my prayers concerning a brighter future for the boys.

I managed to draw him into private conversation at one of his sister-in-law's soirees.

"I commend you on the important reforms you are making within the military, sir." Though Pitt was out of office, I continued to closely follow politics, so was aware of his good work. "Establishing better living conditions for soldiers, founding a military college at Sandhurst to train professional officers, allowing advancement through the ranks due to merit," I recited. "Thanks to you, we shall have a fighting chance if war with France resumes."

The duke—who had been named commander-in-chief of the British Army by his father, the king—smiled. "As always, Lady Hester, you are well informed and have a keen grasp of the challenges that face our country."

"It must run in the blood," I replied.

That made him chuckle. "Let us hope your father's ardent support of Republican France is an aberration."

"Indeed it is, sir. The rest of our family are ardent supporters of Pitt and the Tories."

The duke looked thoughtful. "I miss having your uncle in office. He is a man of great principle and intelligence."

"He has always been devoted to Britain and its best interests." That the duke was in a position to arrange commissions as officers in the military gave me an opening.

I batted my lashes. "As it so happens, I have two brothers coming of age who wish nothing more than to serve our country in uniform."

"Is that so?" he mused.

Both Charles and James loved action and adventure rather than book-learning. They were perfectly suited to military careers.

"They talk of nothing else," I assured him, deciding a little stretching of the truth was all for the common good. "Might I ask a favor . . . ?"

To my elation, the duke proved amenable to the idea of aiding me, and after exchanging a flurry of letters with Pitt and Lord Grenville, money was raised among our family and friends to equip the boys for serving their king and country. Through the good graces of the duke, Charles was to join the 25th Foot Regiment, based in Gibraltar, and James was to enter the Navy as a midshipman.

Once all that was negotiated, the only task left was to arrange another clandestine escape from my father's clutches. It was decided to employ the same method as before. A nocturnal flight employing knotted bedsheets lowered from the upper windows allowed the boys to shimmy down to the ground and creep away to a carriage waiting just outside the gates. The plan went off without a hitch, and I could finally breathe a sigh of relief knowing that all three of my brothers were now free to shape their own lives.

As for my own future, I was growing more and more unhappy with my situation. The rift with my father was now irreparable, so I was completely dependent on the generosity of my relatives for a place to live and financial support. There was, of course, a remedy to ensure my future if only I would knuckle under to convention. However, the more I saw of what lay beneath the polished veneer of Polite Society, the less I was willing to compromise my principles.

A cage, however gilded, was still a cage.

Brooding over Camelford and his whereabouts got me to thinking about the world beyond my limited horizons. I had gotten in the habit of rising early each day and taking a solitary walk down to the wharves of Weymouth harbor. One morning, I stood staring out over the wind-whipped sea and was suddenly reminded of that long-ago day when, as a curious child, I had set off in a rowboat to cross the Channel and land in France, impelled by my father's glorious descriptions and wanting to see Paris for myself—

"A penny for your thoughts, dear cousin."

"I fear you would be wasting your money," I replied lightly as Sir Sidney, his naval cloak flapping in the gusts, moved through the mist to join me. "They are of no earthly interest to someone like you who has traveled the world, tasting its pleasures and braving its dangers."

With peace now reigning over the Continent, travel abroad was once again possible . . .

Sir Sidney seemed to read my mind. "There is a certain thrill to testing yourself against challenges of the unknown," he said. "It makes you feel . . . alive." His gaze followed mine out to the horizon. "I take it that you wish to see what lies beyond the familiar boundaries."

"I do," I admitted. "Indeed, I am determined to find a way to fulfill such dreams."

"Then my money is on you to succeed, Hetty. I've heard from your uncle Pitt that when you set your mind to something, your determination is as hard-edged and unyielding as your great-great-grandfather's diamond."

"I'll take that as a compliment," I replied, "no matter that ladies are expected to be soft and fragile."

"It was meant as one." He took my arm and we began to stroll along the breakwater in companionable silence, the frigid salt spray stinging our cheeks.

As I watched the gulls soaring overhead, the sounds of the waves breaking against the rocks was like a siren song to my ears.

"Come, your lips are turning blue with cold," observed Sir Sidney. "Let us head for home."

Encouraged by his words, I began to think seriously about how to make my dream of foreign travel a reality. I was not so unrealistic as to imagine that I could travel around the Continent unchaperoned. And so I began to make discreet inquiries among my extended family's acquaintances and learned that the Egertons, a well-respected elderly couple, were planning a European sojourn. It turned out that they were pleased with the idea of a companion, and as their placid temperament suited my needs, it was arranged that I would travel with them. I sent letters to my brother Mahon, who was happily studying at Erlangen University in Bavaria, and arranged a rendezvous. Now, all I had to do was wait—with great impatience—for the Egertons to name a date for our departure.

It was in mid-April when I finally received news about Camelford. After a series of peregrinations through Italy and Switzerland that also took him in and out of France, he was arrested in Paris, having entered the city under a false name and with false papers. Armed with such incriminating evidence, Fouché, the French Minister of Police, accused him of conspiring to assassinate Napoleon.

However, my cousin once again managed to talk his way out of dire trouble, claiming that he was a great friend of revolutionary France. Ironically enough, he bolstered his argument by pointing out that he was a great supporter in Parliament of my father, Citizen Stanhope, whose radical Republican ideals were well known to the French. Aware of Camelford's other connections to the prominent Pitt and Grenville families, the French decided not to create any ill will that might threaten the peace between our two countries and released him. He was put on a boat back to England and warned never to set foot on French soil again.

Camelford arrived back in London at the end of the month. I wasn't sure whether to feel impressed or exasperated by his secret sojourn. He confided to me that of course he intended to kill Napoleon—and claimed that he would have been successful if only the experimental multi-shot pistol that he had brought with him hadn't proved to be temperamental.

Granted, his charm was as magnetic as ever, and despite my pique with his disappearance, I felt a flame of my old infatuation spark to life. Marrying him would solve a number of practical problems for me, and given his unconventional thoughts on Society in general, I believed that he wouldn't seek to keep me under his thumb.

However, honesty compelled me to admit that the fire was kindled more by self-interest than by love. By now I was fully aware of his many faults. He drank, he philandered, he was prone to uncontrollable violence—and I suspected that those weren't the most dangerous urges hidden within the shadows of his soul. As I, too, could be volatile and impetuous, I feared that one of us might burn the other to a cinder.

And besides, despite my tendency to be reckless and flaunt the rules of Society, at heart I was a romantic. I believed in love, and would settle for no less.

Camelford's interest in me seemed just as intense as before—thank heavens he was experienced enough to know the ways of taking precautions—but trysts were not as easy to arrange as in the past, and given my own unsettled thoughts, I went to stay in London with Lord Chatham and his wife, hoping to nudge the Egertons into readying themselves for the journey.

At last a date was set, though there was a further delay after I went to take my leave of Pitt at Walmer Castle and found him alarmingly ill. I stayed to nurse him back to health, an interlude that only deepened the bonds of our special friendship.

And then at last, as September segued into October, I was finally able to spread my wings and head to Dover . . .

And my first taste of freedom and adventure beyond my familiar little world.

# *Chapter* 14

*Winter 1802–Spring 1803*

The Egertons proved to be inoffensive but boring companions, with little curiosity about the local sights, the culture, or the storied history of the places we visited. I soon began to wonder why they had bothered to travel at all.

After landing in France, our first destination was the city of Lyon. The ancient capital of the Gauls during Roman times and an influential economic hub with Italy during the Renaissance, it was known for its gastronomic delicacies—though the Egertons quailed at eating such oddities as *fois gras* and pined for their familiar roast beef.

It was also where we had arranged to meet up with my brother Mahon, who had finished his university studies and left Bavaria for good in order to travel on with us to Italy. The reunion was a joyous occasion for both of us.

"I can't help remarking yet again on how you have changed," I said, slanting a smile at him as we were strolling along the city ramparts one afternoon shortly after our reunion.

"Of course I have." Mahon paused to admire the view. "Spending the last two years with other gentlemen of refined intellect has allowed me to throw off the shackles of Papa's absurd ideas and fully develop my own mind and opinions."

"It does you credit," I replied. He had clearly thrived at the university, the experience transforming him from a frustrated, introverted adolescent to a happy, confident young gentleman. "Pitt has promised to think of what next step in life might be best for you and advise—"

"I'm perfectly capable of deciding that for myself, Hetty. I've decided that a diplomatic position would suit me and shall pursue the opportunity through my own connections."

"If I might counsel you to—"

His mouth set in a patronizing smile. "I'm not a child anymore, Hetty. I hardly think a female can offer me any advice in the ways of the world."

Perhaps Mahon had become *too* confident. However, I let the comment pass without making a tart reply. We resumed walking and the talk turned to pleasantries about our route into Italy and what sights we wished to see.

Our steps soon brought us to the stairs leading down into the charming cobbled main square of the town. "Shall we stop at one of the cafés for a pot of coffee and pastries?" I said. "Having read our guidebook, I suggest we should try the Golden Gryphon."

"Why don't you let me be the judge of what establishment is a suitable place for us."

Again I held my tongue and dutifully acquiesced. However, I confess that I was a little disappointed to sense an arrogance shading his attitude, and it soon became clear that he thought himself far too sophisticated to accept any sisterly advice.

The friction grew greater as we headed for Italy—though I was distracted from sibling worries by our crossing of Mount Cenis in the French Alps by mule. For me, it was a chance to challenge the natural elements and experience a frisson of danger, for the steep and narrow trails were known to be treacherous in places. I chose my own mule and muleteer, then set off on my own, leaving the others—including Mahon, who was not nearly as good a rider as I was—to dither with their doubts and fears. It was exhilarating! The day dawned crisp and clear, and I came upon a regiment of horse soldiers crossing over the pass, which greatly enlivened the scene.

I rode without a break until dusk, guiding my mount without a misstep. And in truth, the day of freedom from my brother's pontifications was a breath of fresh air.

In Florence, the simmering tension between Mahon and me came to a head, though not for the lack of me trying to forge the close brother-sister bond that I wished to have with him.

It occurred to me that perhaps if I confided some of my most intimate vulnerabilities to him it would encourage him to do the same. *Trust and love*—we had both had so little of it from our father and his second wife. Mahon had already asked a few oblique questions as to why I was not married yet, but I had chosen to ignore them. And so one evening after supper in our lodgings, I visited his room for a private tête-à-tête, intent on opening my heart to him.

As he looked up from the book he was reading, his brows slowly drew together. "I'm not sure it's entirely proper for you to be here."

"I think even the highest sticklers would have no objection to a sister visiting her brother." I took a seat in the facing armchair, and for a moment the only sound in the room was the soft crackling of the coals in the hearth. "I would value your thoughts on . . ." I hesitated, seeking the right words with which to broach the subject. "On my future."

He closed the book and folded his hands atop the cover. "It is wise of you to come to me rather than Papa."

I wished that he might have added a touch of warmth to his voice, but nonetheless, I made myself continue. "You asked me about marriage, and I have to confess that the idea is unsettling. I would be giving up all rights to make decisions about my life—"

"Of course you would," he interjected. "That is the natural order of things."

"But you were miserable being under the iron-fisted control of Papa," I pointed out.

Mahon moved uncomfortably in his chair. "It's different for ladies."

"And yet you know very well that my intellect is no less sharp than yours."

Finally a smile, though it, too, was devoid of any real feeling. "I think you overestimate your abilities, Hetty. Unlike me, you've never had a chance to test them in the real world."

"And yet I orchestrated the actions of a great many influential gentlemen to ensure that you had the money and means to escape from Chevening."

He had the grace to flush. "I am grateful for your efforts, and of course will offer my support to you." He cleared his throat. "What precisely do you wish to ask me about marriage?"

Even though I feared my honesty would not be as welcomed as I hoped, I made myself go on and explain about my relationship with Camelford.

"So you see," I finished, "while we have a physical chemistry, I fear our temperaments are too volatile to mix."

Mahon leaned forward. "Are you saying that you have *kissed* him?"

"Ye heavens!" I could no longer hide my disappointment in his refusal to try to understand my feelings. I had hoped that foreign travels and his time at university would have broadened his outlook. Instead, he seemed to have become as rigid in his thinking as his father. "Gentlemen are allowed far more liberties than that to explore what it is that will make them happy in life. Why should it be any different for ladies?"

"Because . . ." His jaw tightened. "Because that is just how it is." He sat back, a look of censure darkening his gaze. "It seems to me you have no choice. You must marry Camelford or be considered a wanton woman."

"I . . . I was hoping that you might show some sympathy for my situation."

"I will do so when your behavior deserves it," he said with a pompous tone that set my teeth on edge.

The discussion didn't stop there. Emotions flared, and we both said intemperate things in the heat of the moment.

I left his room feeling shocked and saddened. I had sacrificed—gladly!—all ties with my father so that Mahon could have his freedom. I had hoped that my love and loyalty would have created an unbreakable bond between us, and that he might feel some sympathy and support for the challenges that confronted me. His rejection hurt—thank heavens I had not revealed the most intimate details of my relationship with Camelford—and with a heavy heart, I realized I would have to look elsewhere for the acceptance and support that I so desperately craved.

Mahon left shortly after that to take a ship to Gibraltar in order to visit with Charles, who was stationed there with his regiment. And from there, he would be heading home to England. Despite my disappointment, I penned a letter to Pitt asking him to discreetly arrange for a government position to be offered to my brother on his return. He may have abandoned me, but I wished for him to have every opportunity to forge a fulfilling life for himself.

The Egertons and I passed the winter in Naples and Venice. But then, after we had made our way into the German principalities, Mrs. Egerton—I had come to think of her as a fidget married to a fool—had second thoughts about making the promised sojourn to Vienna and Berlin. Fed up with their dithering, I, too, decided to return to England. The timing proved prescient. I joined a group of British aristocrats who were also intent on making the journey home, and while at sea, we learned that just as my cousin Sir Sidney Smith had predicted, the peace with France had come to an end on May 18, 1803.

Britain was now once against at war with Napoleon and his fearsome armies.

The trip had not been the exciting adventure I had yearned to experience. As the ship dropped anchor in Portsmouth harbor, I realized that there were few truly memorable moments to savor from the nine long months of travel. But perhaps my reflections were colored by the dark news that awaited me as soon as I arrived in London.

Reckless as ever, Camelford had chanced another clandestine trip to France and had once again been arrested. This time, Fouché had shown no mercy and incarcerated him in the infamous Temple Prison, a fate that a great many prisoners did not survive. Pitt and Lord Grenville had been required to exercise the full range of their diplomatic skills in order to secure his release.

But that was not the worst of the revelations. Pitt had also sent word from Walmer Castle that his mother—my beloved grandmother—the dowager Countess Chatham had died and that Burton Pynsent, the family estate, had passed as prescribed by the laws of primogeniture to his older brother, Lord Chatham.

It had taken a moment for the initial wave of shock and grief to subside . . . and then the truth of my current situation washed over me.

I now had no home where I was welcome, as well as no money and no means of supporting myself . . .

*How the devil was I going to survive?*

After drawing in a shaky breath, I conceded that my first reaction was a trifle melodramatic. It wasn't as if I was entirely alone in the world. My influential relatives were not about to let me starve in the streets.

But in truth, that only heightened my frustrations.

Unlike Mahon or my younger brothers Charles and James, I could not aspire to a career in politics or the military. Or, for that matter, any other occupation that would offer me intellectual and financial freedom.

However, my first encounter with Camelford in nearly a year reminded me that Mahon had been right. There *was* a way out of my dilemma, however fraught my feelings were about considering it . . .

"Diamond."

The low, rough-cut voice sent a shiver spiraling down through my belly. I turned to meet Camelford's lidded gaze. His face was thinner and more angular. He had lost weight during his time in prison, though the experience didn't seem to have snuffed out the devil-may-care gleam in his eyes.

"You are looking even more beautiful than I remember," he added, taking my arm and leading me to a less crowded part of the drawing room. I was staying with Lord Chatham at his London townhouse and the evening's entertainment was an informal dinner for family and friends. "Your recent foreign travel appears to have suited you."

"I can't say the same for you," I replied. "What in the name of Satan were you thinking?"

"You know me, thinking isn't my strong suit."

I smiled in spite of myself. "You're incorrigible, Tom."

"Guilty as charged," said Camelford with an unrepentant grin.

Such cheerful thumbing his nose at authority rekindled a sudden fierce flame of attraction. Perhaps a match with such an unconventional gentleman wouldn't be so bad. I would likely never be bored.

But the fire died quickly as I reviewed a mental ledger of his charms and faults—and didn't like how things added up.

"Yes, well, thank heavens you have relatives," I replied coolly. "Otherwise you might have been rotting in that Parisian hellhole for the foreseeable future."

A careless shrug. "I would have found a way out of trouble." His grin grew more pronounced. "I usually do."

"Arse," I muttered.

Camelford chuckled. "Admit it, that's part of the reason you find me alluring." He moved closer. I could feel the tantalizing heat of him radiating against my bare arms.

"I know you feel it, too, Diamond. We have a special spark," he whispered.

I hesitated, recalling the sensual, sweat-sheened undulations of our naked bodies entwining in the flickering candlelight. "We do, Tom. But alas, you find that a great many flashes of fire captivate your attention, and so you are constantly flitting from here to there."

"Like you, I am not made to walk the straight and narrow path," replied Camelford. "Is that a fatal flaw?"

I had no answer to the question. Turning away, I gazed at our blurred reflection in the mullioned window as rain pelted against the glass.

"Hetty, might I have a word with you?"

Giving silent thanks for Pitt's timely intervention, I drew in a steadying breath. "But of course."

"If you will excuse us, Tom," added my uncle, when Camelford gave no sign of leaving us. It was said lightly, but the meaning was clear.

A spasm of emotion—like a thundercloud scudding across a squall-dark sky—passed over Camelford's face, but he merely nodded and walked away.

Pitt waited until my cousin passed into one of the side salons before releasing a sigh. "There is much to admire in Tom, but I fear that his darker impulses are in danger of eclipsing the better side of his nature."

Unlike Camelford, I had some sense of self-preservation. Not knowing the reason for Pitt's request to speak, I decided it was wise to hold my tongue.

He waited a moment, and then allowed a hint of a smile. "You have the instincts of a good diplomat."

"I do," I responded. "Indeed, I would be an exemplary diplomat, if only I, like a gentleman, was allowed the opportunity to exercise my talents."

"As to that . . ." Pursing his lips, Pitt fixed me with a searching stare, as if he was trying to see into the very depths of my soul.

I lifted my chin, willing myself not to flinch. *Judge me as you would a man, and you'll find nothing about which I should be ashamed.*

His expression softened. "I have a proposition for you, Hetty."

"Go on, sir."

"The political winds have begun to shift, now that war once

again grips our nation. My sense is that Addington won't last long as prime minister, and given the other choices—Fox is an anathema to the king—there is a chance that I will be asked to take on the seals of the office again and form a government."

"Why, that is wonderful news, Uncle!" I exclaimed, though I failed to see how it could have anything to do with me. "You are, by far, the best man for the job."

He smiled, though the flickering of the candlelight caught the lines of fatigue etched around his eyes. "It will be a daunting challenge. Napoleon is a formidable enemy. It would be a mistake for anyone to think otherwise."

I nodded, and waited for him to continue.

"I shall need help to sail the ship of state, assuming that I am asked to take the tiller once again," said Pitt. "Trusted advisors, clever and competent help to manage the demands on my personal household."

His gaze met mine. "A hostess to make sure the many dinners and receptions with colleagues and foreign diplomats run smoothly. You would be an ideal choice, Hetty—"

"Yes." My heart was suddenly thumping against my rib cage. "Yes!"

He held up a forefinger. "Wait—you haven't yet heard my requirements for the job."

I laughed. "I'm sure we'll be able to negotiate a deal."

"I've only one demand, and it is nonnegotiable." Pitt's expression turned solemn. "If you accept my offer, you must agree to stop seeing Tom. We both know that his volatile temperament makes him unpredictable, and I can't afford to have any further scandals caused by his mad behavior damage my reputation at this critical time. If gossip links you with him, it will reflect badly on my judgment."

I couldn't argue with his reasoning. "I understand, sir."

"I don't expect an answer at this moment. Please think on it tonight, and give me your decision in the morning," said Pitt. "You must be certain of your feelings."

He was offering a home, interesting responsibilities, and a seat at the table where momentous decisions for the world would be made . . .

And my doubts about Camelford were already growing stronger.

I didn't need to think twice before making up my mind. "I don't require time to mull it over, Uncle. I accept your offer."

A pause. "With all of my heart."

A smile blossomed on his lips. "I am very glad of that, Hetty. Now, let me explain the details . . ."

# *Chapter* 15

*August 1803*

I stepped down from the carriage, filling my lungs with the salty tang of the sea as I gazed around the grounds of Walmer Castle. *Home*. Tears prickled in my eyes. I hardly dared to believe my good fortune.

I had visited a number of times before, but with my new perspective, everything looked different. In the past, I had seen it as an aging fortress, rich in heritage, but well past its prime. Now, the ancient stone and menacing cannons took on a new stature as Britain faced a fearsome threat from across the Channel.

"Welcome, my dear!"

I turned to see Pitt hurrying down from the ramparts to greet me.

"Once again, this glorious castle is called upon to defend England's honor." He kissed my cheek. "It has a storied history, you know. In 1539, Henry VIII first built an artillery fortress on this spot in response to the Pope's call for the French King and the Holy Emperor to invade England because of his divorce." His gaze turned to the sea beyond the battlements. "No attack came, but Walmer's guns continued to defend the shores over the centuries of conflict with Spain, Holland, and France."

His enthusiasm made me smile. "And under your leadership as

Lord Warden of the Cinque Ports they will do so against the present threat," I replied, giving his arm an affectionate squeeze.

Walmer Castle anchored an ancient confederation of coastal towns known as Cinque Ports—Five Harbors—which had their own set of arcane laws, granted in the 1100s in return for guaranteeing ships and men to defend the coast. The post of Lord Warden of Cinque Ports was established at the same time, with the castle as its official residence. Pitt had been appointed to the position in 1792, and after he resigned as prime minister, King George III, who greatly admired Pitt personally, allowed him to keep the prestigious appointment.

"I am so glad you have arrived, Hetty." He made a grand gesture that encompassed the castle and its surroundings. "We have much work to do!"

I brushed back a lock of hair that the wind had blown over my cheek. "Give me my marching orders."

"Let me show you the new additions to our arsenal and the—" He stopped short, looking a little sheepish as he watched two of the footmen begin unloading my trunks. "Er, perhaps you wish to settle yourself in your quarters and partake of some refreshments before beginning a tour."

"Nonsense!" My muscles were cramped with fatigue but I would have chewed on nails rather than disappoint him. "Let's get to work."

"Ah, Hester. Thank heavens for your indomitable spirit."

Seeing his beatific smile was well worth any discomfort.

"This way," he added, with a wave at the stairs leading to the armory.

For the next few hours, we walked from the cellars to the top of the tower behind the central bastions, making a full inspection of the castle's state of readiness. I pulled a small notebook and pencil from my reticule and began scribbling madly to keep up with Pitt's comments.

As we turned into the residential section of the castle, we encountered a young woman inspecting the work of the two parlor-maids who were applying a coat of beeswax to the wood paneling of the corridor.

"Hetty, you remember Elizabeth Williams," said Pitt as he waved for the woman to come join us. 'She kindly agreed to accompany me here and take charge of overseeing the domestic staff."

"Of course," I replied, greeting her with a smile. I had met her several times before at Pitt's London residence, and she had struck me as both intelligent and competent.

"I don't know what I would do without her managing the household," he added. "From the way I take my tea to the perfect amount of starch in my cravats, she knows exactly how I like everything."

Elizabeth seemed a little uncomfortable with his praise. "I do my best, sir. Your comfort is of great importance to all of us." She turned and dropped a small curtsey to me. "As is yours, Lady Hester. Please let me know if there is anything you need as you settle in."

"That's very kind of you," I replied. "I am here to help my uncle with his correspondence and his hosting of political guests, so between the two of us, we shall do our best to see that he has the support he needs to concentrate on defending Britain from its enemies."

"Indeed we shall." Elizabeth nodded, her eyes lighting with fierce admiration as she slanted a look at Pitt's profile.

I had once inadvertently overheard my late grandmother and Pitt's older brother discussing Elizabeth and her sister, who was also employed in the Pitt household. There was apparently speculation within the family as to whether the two of them were Pitt's illegitimate daughters, for he seemed to treat them quite differently from his other servants. Whether it was true or not, I chose to ignore such talk. My own experience with the salacious gossip about my father had given me a dislike of rumor and innuendo.

"Speaking of duty to king and country . . ." Pitt shuffled his feet, clearly impatient to continue our tour. "Come, Hester, let me finish showing you the outdoor changes that have been made since your last visit."

I looked around as we stepped outside, happy to see the improvements. The walled kitchen garden was thriving, and much to my special delight, the stables had received some recent renovations.

"The grounds have been expanded through the purchase of some neighboring property," explained Pitt as he led me down a new graveled pathway. "It will allow the creation of a private park around the castle." He paused to look around at the flat, featureless ground and sighed. "Though it will take some major landscaping to transform it into a place of natural peace and tranquility."

My time at Burton Pynsent had given me an appreciation of how Nature was indeed soothing for the soul. And given the responsibilities weighing on Pitt's frail shoulders, I realized how important it was to create a place where he could find an escape from the daily pressures.

"Let me consult with the head gardener," I responded, adding another entry to the list in my notebook. "And see how we might begin such a project."

Pitt smiled. "It is good to have you here, Hetty." He took my arm. "Let me show you the abandoned chalk pit. Granted, it looks a bit barren now, but with the right plantings it could become a lovely secluded glade in which to stroll . . ."

A mizzling rain finally forced us back indoors, but Pitt continued to wax poetic about the possibilities of making the castle and its grounds a comfortable residence. He clearly had come to love the place. I understood his enthusiasm—I could already feel in my bones that it was a special property—and resolved to help bring his ideas to fruition.

He ordered tea to be served in his study, and brought me to a very pleasant room overlooking the sea. The squall had blown over, and as I turned to the tall bank of mullioned windows, a sudden shimmering of sunlight danced over the water—

"Good heavens, what is that?" My gaze had come to rest on a large odd-looking mahogany-and-brass apparatus attached to a complex wooden stand that was set in front of the middle case-ment.

"My telescope." Pitt unlatched the casement and pushed it open, then rotated the long barrel—it was nearly seven feet long—down from its vertical position and angled it to point out to distant foam-flecked waves. "It was made specially for me by William Herschel, court astronomer to our king, and a Fellow of the Royal Society." He gave the polished casing a fond pat and smiled. "Who used the concept behind the Stanhope lens to help create his com-plex system of optics, I might add."

Along with the Stanhope printing press, my father's innovations in magnification were some of his most useful scientific accom-plishments.

"William Herschel," I repeated. "Didn't he discover the planet Uranus hiding within the constellation of Gemini?"

"Yes. He's one of the leading men of science in Britain," an-swered my uncle. "I've hosted him and his sister here several times, as I find his company, and that of artists and writers, to be inspiring." A pause. "They keep me from becoming too melan-choly over the state of the world."

I knew that Pitt battled with inner demons—the dreaded blue devils that could drag a person down into the darkest recesses of the mind. "Imagination is a marvelous thing," I responded. "It al-lows one to soar free of conventional expectations and see beyond the horizon."

My words brought a thoughtful gleam to his gaze. "Herschel gifted it to me, saying he had created it so that I could spot a com-ing French invasion and raise the alarm along the coast." Hunch-ing down, he squinted through the eyepiece and spun a set of dials to adjust the focus. "I enjoy searching for sails in the distance, but I confess that I've also grown fascinated by the night sky. Seeing the stars and planets in that vast expanse of space gives me some perspective on how very small our earthly concerns are in the grand scheme of things."

He stepped aside. "Would you care to have a look?"

"Very much so." My father rarely shared his brilliance with his children, so I had never actually looked through a telescope or microscope.

Pitt explained how to work the levers and gears, and as the complex lenses inside the brass barrel brought the distance into focus, my eyes widened. "How wonderful!"

With a twist of my fingers, the whole world had suddenly changed.

"Yes," mused my uncle. "It reminds us that we are surrounded by an infinite array of marvels. We just have to learn how to see them."

Before I could respond, the door opened and one of the parlor-maids carried in the tea tray. Our attention was quickly drawn to the fragrant plume of steam rising from the silver pot and a platter of pastries. I was famished from my travels and happily heaped my plate with an assortment of cakes and savories. Punctuated by the genteel click of our forks, the talk then turned to family and other mundane matters.

But as I enjoyed the excellent refreshments and pithy observations of my uncle regarding our relatives, I was also chewing over a more fundamental question . . . just how was I going to fit into life at Walmer Castle?

# Chapter 16

September 1803

The next few weeks proved to be a revelation. Intent on lightening the demands on my uncle, I took it upon myself to assume a variety of duties and was soon waking up every morning with a strong sense of purpose, the likes of which I had never experienced before. *Oversee arrangements for the constant stream of prominent visitors, preside over the formal dinners and help create an aura of convivial camaraderie, consult with the gardener on landscape plans for the grounds, along with a myriad of smaller items . . .*

I loved it all.

Rather than feel intimidated, I reveled in the responsibilities. Pitt must have approved of my handling of things for he responded by asking me to help him with even more essential matters. Each day, the mail deliveries brought a stack of letters, and to help keep him from drowning in a sea of paper, I began reading through them and sorting each piece of correspondence into a separate pile according to its importance.

Occasionally Pitt would ask me to summarize the contents of a certain stack, and then we would discuss whether the matters touched in the papers needed his attention. He soon came to trust my judgment and I was permitted to write responses in his name.

It gave me a great satisfaction to pen a note to a leading politician and see my initials lettered in copperplate script below Pitt's name to indicate who had actually written it.

Even more rewarding was the night I went down to the library at a late hour to fetch a book of engravings on Capability Brown's garden designs. Pitt and his political ally George Canning—a brilliant but abrasive gentleman, though fiercely loyal to my uncle—were settled by the hearth enjoying a glass of ruby-red port.

"Hetty, do come join us." There was a mischievous gleam in his eyes as he indicated the empty armchair beside him. To his friend, he added, "My niece appreciates an excellent vintage."

Seeing that they were on their third bottle, I assumed that my uncle was intent on teasing the stiff-rumped Canning. Few people realized that beneath his reserved demeanor, Pitt possessed a very sly sense of humor.

Canning's brows waggled in disapproval, but he refrained from comment.

After pouring me a glass, Pitt waited for me to take a sip before asking, "You've read the recent reports from Addington's secretary—what is your opinion of our readiness to repel a French invasion?"

Canning nearly choked on a swallow of his wine. "She read the reports?" he sputtered. "Do you really think that wise, Pitt?"

My uncle responded with a basilisk stare, then gestured for me to answer his query.

"As to that, sir, our navy, the heart and soul of our defense, is stretched a bit thin because of its actions in the Mediterranean," I began. "And if Spain joins with France, and its fleet augments our enemy, I believe there is cause for concern, sir. Though it does seem that Billy Cornwallis is doing an excellent job guarding the approaches to the English and Irish Channels. It seems to me that the key is keeping a strong blockade on the French port of Brest . . ."

I paused for a breath and then went on to give a summary of the logistics to support my opinion.

"I fear you don't entirely understand the nuances of the mili-

tary, Lady Hester," said Canning with an insufferable air of condescension.

"Oh?" I challenged. "Kindly point out where I have erred in assessing our strategies. Does it concern our blockade of Brest? Or is
it my thoughts on Sir John Orde's watch on Cádiz, or Nelson's activities around Toulon?"

A fraught silence, and then a hiss of smoke rose from the sudden crackling of the red-hot coals.

Pitt chuckled. "I have to say, I find no fault with my niece's
analysis."

Canning glowered but could summon no retort.

Not wishing to make a mortal enemy of him—nobody liked to
be made to feel a fool—I quickly asked him a question about a
complicated issue being debated in Parliament. And after listening
intently to his grudging answer, I made a point of asking him more
questions, and appearing impressed with his explanation.

Pitt caught my eye as he refilled his friend's glass and gave me a
subtle smile.

Perhaps I was learning the subtle art of tact.

There was just one fly in the ointment . . .

Camelford appeared at Walmer Castle several days later and put
me in an awkward situation that would test my nascent diplomatic
skills.

"Shall we take a walk through the grounds?" After handling the
reins of his stallion to one of the grooms, Camelford offered me his
arm. "A pity there aren't more trees around to provide some privacy," he added, once we were out of earshot of the stables. "I'm
dying to kiss you."

"Control yourself, Tom," I warned.

"*Moi?*" He waggled his brows. "*C'est impossible.*"

His choice of speaking in French was not amusing. "Life may
be one long joke to you, but it's not to me."

"Egad." He gave me a mocking smile. "Here I thought a trip to
the Continent would encourage your sense of adventure. Instead,
I fear that it's turned you into a prig."

An angry flush heated my cheeks. "How easy that is for you to say! A title and a fortune shield you from Life's slings and arrows. A lady has no such defenses." I took a moment to steady my emotions. "I haven't the luxury of casting all caution to the wind."

A look of remorse pinched between his brows. "Forgive me. I know that I am often mercurial, and self-absorbed. But my heart is not quite so black as people think."

I expelled a sigh. "I know that, but—"

"You and I were made for each other."

*Only if the Almighty was seeking to perform the unholy experiment of throwing two volatile substances into a red-hot cauldron and seeing how long the pairing took to explode,* I thought wryly.

"That may be," I replied. "However, you have no desire to be a conventional husband."

He laughed. "And you have no desire to be a conventional wife."

*Touché.*

"So as I said, that makes us a perfect pair."

*How to explain?*

"Tom, I am very much enjoying my present life. I am engaged in interesting work, I am helping my uncle, whom I greatly admire, with affairs of state, and influential gentlemen are beginning to listen to my opinion." I drew in a breath. "I have a voice."

"You've always had a voice, Diamond," he reasoned. "You're known for your sharp tongue and outspoken opinions."

"That's my point, Tom." I felt impatience rising in my gorge. "I've always been seen as an unnatural lady for daring to think for myself. While now, I have a chance to be taken seriously!"

He shrugged. "Seriousness is vastly overrated. I daresay you'll grow bored with it all in a month or two."

I said nothing, my gaze angling up to watch a solitary hawk circling high overhead, a lone speck against the cerulean sky. For all our similarities, how little he truly understood me or my desires. My passions were more than a sudden incandescent spark, here and then gone in the blink of an eye.

I sought to find meaning and purpose in my life, not fritter it away in frenzied distractions.

"In the meantime, come have some fun with me. There's a mill taking place next week in Wootton," continued Camelford. "Tell Pitt that you've been invited to visit a childhood friend in Kent. I'll send my coachman to fetch you . . ." A grin. "I know an out-of-the-way tavern where we can enjoy ourselves without anyone being the wiser."

"I think not, Tom." To soften the rejection, I added, "There is a good chance that Pitt will be asked to serve as prime minister again. I can't—I won't—take a chance of causing a scandal that might harm his prospects."

"So, you choose to let your head overrule your heart?"

I thought for a moment before answering. Perhaps my experiences the last two years were teaching me some valuable lessons . . .

"The heart," I replied, "isn't always right."

Before he could respond, I turned and began walking back toward the castle. "Let us go find Pitt," I called over my shoulder. "He'll be delighted to see you and will wish to show you the improvements that he has made to the battlements."

Camelford left the next day without a word of goodbye.

Though I felt a small pinch of disappointment, for the most part I was relieved to see him go.

# *Chapter* 17

*October 1803*

Though I had been at Walmer Castle for only a few months, I felt more at home there than I ever had at Chevening or Burton Pynsent. My room was enchanting. It overlooked the ancient moat and gardens, where a stately magnolia tree stood sentinel among the plantings, its rich scent perfuming the air. I thought of its essence as Hope, for the future felt full of promise. And just outside my door were stone steps leading to the battlements. I was free to make my way up to their heights whenever I chose. The solitude was pleasant, and I often stood watching the night guard on patrol as I thought through the events of the day.

Pitt's quarters were right above me, and occasionally late at night I could hear his soft shufflings when sleep wouldn't come to him, along with the faint chink of glass against glass as he poured himself a measure of port. Sometimes I would go up and see if he wished to have company. Both his sisters—my mother had been his favorite—and his mother had passed away, and my presence seemed to lift his spirits. I felt our bond growing closer. We talked of many things, often until well past midnight—family, friends, the present political maneuverings—which gave me an inside understanding of how power within the highest echelons of government worked.

By day, every waking moment was taken up with some engaging task. I surprised myself by how interested I became in gardening. I collected the books on landscape design from the library and pored over the pages before bedtime, making notes on the types of trees and hedges that captured my fancy. Sir Joseph Banks, the legendary botanist and one of the founders of the Royal Botanic Gardens at Kew, was an old friend of my father and welcomed my appeal for advice. We corresponded frequently and he was kind enough to have some of the Kew gardeners draw up sample designs and send specimen seeds and cuttings.

However, the real highlight of autumn and early winter was riding out with Pitt to review the local volunteer regiments that had been raised in readiness for a French invasion.

To my delight, Pitt invited me to serve as his unofficial aide-de-camp, saying that I was a far better equestrian than any of the men on his staff. My presence, however, seemed to take Lieutenant-Colonel Harris, the local commander of the Kingsdown militia, by surprise when he came to escort my uncle to his first ceremony.

"Don't worry, Colonel," Pitt said in response to the officer's startled expression as he settled his magnificent gilt-trimmed bicorn hat on his head—symbol of his rank of Colonel Commandant of the Cinque Port Volunteers—and pulled himself into the saddle. "My niece will give no cause for complaint."

We all started forward and I took great care to maintain a respectful silence as my uncle and the colonel began to discuss recruitment efforts and the frustrations of trying to wrest military supplies from the Home Office.

It was only a short ride along the road skirting the sea to the parade grounds. The wind was rising as we arrived, blowing in off the foam-flecked sea in fitful gusts as the regiment's drummers began to beat a welcoming tattoo.

All at once a sudden swirl caught Pitt's hat and lifted it from his head. He snatched at it, but it had already spun out of reach.

Without thinking, I spurred forward. The hat looked in danger of being swept out to sea.

Leaning low, I urged my mount to a gallop, keeping us on course with the zigzagging bicorn with a firm grip on my reins.

The hat rose and then the gust seemed to give out and it began to fall—

With a last burst of speed, I reached it just in time to unhook my leg from the sidesaddle pommel and swing down to pluck it from the air just inches from the muddy ground.

As I gathered my skirts and began to trot back to rejoin Pitt and the colonel, I was suddenly aware of a thunderous cheer rising above the sound of the surf.

"Well, Pitt, you and your, er, aide-de-camp certainly know how to make a grand first impression," quipped the colonel. To me, he added, "That was a very impressive show of horsemanship, Lady Hester."

Pitt smiled as I handed him his hat.

"I'm so sorry," I apologized, mortified at my actions. "I—"

"You were splendid," he assured me. "In one fell swoop, you've won me their allegiance."

Indeed, the troops performed their maneuvers with great enthusiasm and gave Pitt a rousing ovation after his speech.

The colonel snapped Pitt a salute as we took our leave—and then added one to me.

"I do hope that Lady Hester will accompany you on all your reviews, sir," he said to my uncle.

"Oh, you may count on it," replied Pitt.

*The thud of hooves, the scent of leather and sweat, the slap of the wind against my cheeks*—a powerful rush of exhilaration pulsed through my blood as we started back to the castle. I was born to gallop neck and leather . . .

However, most of the time, I tempered my pace. Pitt was not nearly as comfortable in the saddle as I was, and as he was Lord Warden of the Cinque Ports, I was very aware of not dulling the shine of his stature.

"That is the last of the reviews," he said a fortnight later, as we finished with yet another long and boring interlude of watching the men perform parade ground maneuvers for their commander. "Shall we head home?"

It was a glorious autumn day, the weather unseasonably warm for early November. But much as I yearned to ride out along the cliffs overlooking the sea, I saw the lines of fatigue etched around the corners of his eyes and readily agreed.

"An excellent suggestion," I agreed, massaging the back of my neck. "I fear that I've overexerted myself today."

A chuckle. "What fustian! You could ride from here to Hades and back again without batting an eye." He smiled. "But I appreciate your stalwart support, my dear Amazon. Your dashing presence inspires not only me but our soldiers as well."

The militias in the area had named me the Amazon because of my riding skills. I suppose the fact that I had commissioned a special riding habit to be made for me—a scarlet military-style jacket with gold braid, high black nankeen riding boots, and jaunty plumed military shako to complement Pitt's impressive uniform—made me all the more noticeable.

"If you think me too colorful and distracting—"

"God knows, with war threatening our shores, we all need a little dash and color to lift our spirits."

"If you are certain . . ."

"I am," assured Pitt as we crested a hill and paused to survey the surroundings. There was a lone rider—a military officer—coming toward us, moving in harmony with his cantering stallion with a centaur-like grace.

"Ah—it's Moore." Pitt whipped off his hat and waved a vigorous greeting.

The rider acknowledged the gesture by spurring forward.

"A bracing day, is it not, Pitt?" he called, reining to a halt beside us.

"Indeed, indeed!" answered my uncle. "Allow me to present my niece, Lady Hester Stanhope." His smile broadened. "Now that she has come to stay with me, you may be only the *second* best rider in Kent."

"Is that so?"

Most gentlemen would have voiced that reply with an unmistakable edge of condescension. Heaven forfend that a lady might ever be their equal at anything—especially riding. And yet, I detected naught but a friendly note in his tone.

"Hetty, this is Major-General John Moore."

"A pleasure to make your acquaintance, Lady Hester."

*Major-General Moore.* I had, of course, read about his military exploits. Unlike most high-ranking officers, he had earned acclaim for his battlefield heroics, leading his men from the front, not the rear. But even as a number of his exploits popped to mind, the first thing that struck me was he had a very nice smile.

"The pleasure is all mine, sir," I replied. "Your valorous reputation in braving the perils of the battlefield precedes you."

His smile stretched a touch wider. He was hatless and the wind-tangled hair gave him a boyish look despite the nicks and fissures carved into his features. "There is nothing valorous about being clumsy enough to stumble into the path of a bullet."

*Oh, yes there is,* I thought, recalling some of the stories I had read in the newspaper about his bravery in battle.

Moore must have caught me staring at the scar near his eye, for he added a shrug. "An officer who won't take the same risks as his troops is, in my opinion, not a real leader."

"You, sir, are the best bloody leader we have!" exclaimed Pitt. "It's said that your men revere you and would follow you to the deepest pit of Hell if you so asked."

"Every battlefield is Hell, Mr. Pitt," he replied quietly. "But we all must do our duty."

"Quite right," said my uncle. Hunching deeper into the collar of his coat as a gust blew over us, he regripped his reins.

"Come, Uncle, let us head back to the castle before you catch a chill," I said, knowing his health was more fragile than he cared to admit.

"Moore, will you return with us and allow me to offer you a glass of brandy?" asked Pitt.

"Alas, I'm on my way to a meeting with the engineers concerning the construction of the Royal Military Canal through Kent and Sussex, which will serve as a further defense against a possible French invasion," replied the general.

I knew that Moore, a brilliant strategist, had also been asked by the military to establish a training camp in Shoreditch to teach his innovative new "light" infantry tactics to the 43rd, 52nd, and 95th Rifle brigades.

"But," he added, "I shall be delighted to ride with you part of the way."

As we all set off, I caught a mischievous gleam come alight in Pitt's eyes. "What say you to a challenge, sir? Race my niece to the wooden signs of the crossroads." A pause. "And give her no quarter. She won't need it."

Moore looked at me. "Are you a good rider, Lady Hester?"

"Yes." I met his gaze. "I am."

"Then it seems a fair match." With a subtle command that escaped my eye, Moore maneuvered his horse to come up alongside me. We both drew to a halt.

"Pitt, please do the honors of starting the race," called the general.

"On the count of three," said my uncle.

I gathered my reins, ruing the fact that I had to ride sidesaddle rather than astride.

"One!"

*But no excuses*, I told myself. My mount was a muscular little filly who ran like the wind.

"Two!"

A sidelong glance showed Moore looking utterly at one with his stallion. The animal snorted and coiled like a spring ready to release at the touch of the spur.

"Three!"

We were both off the mark in a cloud of dust and a clattering of ironshod hooves. Leaning low, Moore rode with a quiet concentration—no kicking heels, no shouts, no slap of the reins to urge his horse to greater speed.

I was mesmerized for a moment, as we pounded neck and neck

down the slope of the hill, but then forced my attention back to my own efforts as he started to pull away. A shift in the saddle allowed me to duck lower. Quieting my hands, I gave my filly full rein, willing her to lengthen her stride.

We were gaining on Moore when the ground turned uneven. Spotting a way through the loose stones, I pulled to the right and we shot through the trouble and crested another low rise, having regained a few yards. The crossroads was up ahead, with a low stone wall forcing us to make a looping turn in order to circle around it to reach the wooden signs.

Moore, however, was thundering straight at it. No rules had been specified about the course . . .

Locking my leg tighter around the top pommel of my saddle, I urged my filly to follow the stallion's lead. Like me, she was not intimidated by competing against the opposite sex. Summoning a burst of speed, she charged ahead. I felt her gather herself—and then she rose to the challenge, clearing the wall with room to spare and landing on the upward slope without missing a stride.

The signposts were oh-so close . . .

A gust of wind hit me just before we crested the rise, tangling my skirts and shifting my balance just enough to break my filly's rhythm.

We would have lost anyway—Moore was a superb rider—but I couldn't swallow my frustration with the absurdity of feminine riding clothes.

"Blast it," I muttered, tugging the flapping wool back into place as I slowed to join Moore in circling the signposts to cool our lathered mounts. Then, lest he think I was a poor loser, I quickly added, "A very handsome ride, sir. You were clearly born to the saddle."

"Allow me to return the compliment, milady." Moore snapped a jaunty salute. "Pitt didn't exaggerate. You're a marvelous rider."

"You are kind to say so, sir, though I feel hobbled by feminine convention. Skirts are a cursed encumbrance." A sigh. "I show to better advantage when I wear breeches."

His lips twitched, and I felt a blush rise to my cheeks as I realized how risqué my comment sounded. Thankfully my race-flushed face hid my discomfort.

"You've ridden in breeches?" he inquired.

*Was he shocked at the thought?*

Deciding that I didn't care if he thought I was a hellion, I met his gaze without flinching. "I have brothers, General Moore. Any girl who likes going fast on a horse would be an idiot not to realize that riding astride allows far more freedom than sitting perched on a monstrous sidesaddle, swathed in skirts."

"My sympathies," he responded. "We men make a great many rules on the conduct of women which strike me as quite absurd, as well as quite unfair."

His reply took me by surprise. "H-have you sisters, sir?"

"No, but my mother, who is the daughter of a famous mathematics professor in Glasgow, is an extraordinary lady. Given her druthers, she would have wished to be a physician like my father," answered Moore.

A smile. "So my father trained her himself, and often said she was more skilled than he was. When he was asked by the dowager Duchess of Hamilton to take her sixteen-year-old son on the Grand Tour of Europe that all young aristocrats are expected to make, he agreed, but only because the invitation included me— and his absence would not affect his patients because they all knew my mother would provide excellent medical care."

"Your father sounds like a remarkable man as well for being so open-minded," I said. "Let us hope the future will eventually bring about changes for women."

I blew out my breath. "In the meantime, I would settle for being allowed to wear breeches when I ride."

The twinkle was back in his hazel eyes. "If I grant you a cornet's commission in the cavalry, that should be permission enough. Breeches are part of the uniform."

"You could do that?" I blurted out.

Moore chuckled. "I don't see why not. I'm the commander in chief of the forces in this area. Who is to stop me?"

I was speechless for an instant, and then let out a peal of delighted laughter. "Who, indeed?" I tucked a windblown curl behind my ear. "Thank you, sir. Though I know you are jesting, I greatly appreciate the sentiment."

"I assure you, I never jest about military matters, Lady Hester," he said. "I'll send the official papers to Walmer Castle—along with a pair of regulation breeches."

I stammered another thanks as Pitt trotted up from rounding the wall. "Dare I ask who was the victor?"

"General Moore—" I began.

"By a whisker," injected Moore.

"By a length," I corrected. "He is far too gentlemanly to boast about his impressive equestrian skills."

"Your niece is being far too modest. She rides like the devil," he responded. "And I assure you that's meant as a compliment."

"She's an unusual lady." Pitt smiled. "And that, too, is meant as a compliment, my dear."

He ended with a cough, which renewed my worries about him taking a chill.

"The wind is picking up, Uncle. We really must be getting home."

Moore clearly heard my concern, for he quickly wheeled his stallion. "I must be off as well." He raised a salute. "It was a pleasure to meet you, Lady Hester. Take care, Pitt."

"Come visit soon," replied Pitt. "I would value your advice on our coastal defenses."

Moore acknowledged the invitation with a wave and then spurred his stallion to a canter.

"What a nice man," I remarked, watching him ride away.

"And our brightest hope for crossing swords with Napoleon," said Pitt.

"He's that good a general?" Even his enemies conceded that the Little Corsican was a military genius, and a charismatic man who inspired undying devotion in his troops.

"Yes, Moore possesses the same skills and yet has none of Napoleon's personal vanity," answered my uncle. "As for courage and steadfast dedication to duty, I think he has no equal."

"Indeed?"

Pitt nodded, his eyes narrowing in thought. "For example, in one of his exploits just before the Peace of Amiens, Moore led a charge against Dutch forces allied with the French, only to have a sally from the flank threaten to cut him and his regiment off from the rest of the British army," he recounted. "During the fray, Moore suffered a wound to the thigh and then had his horse shot out from under him. Undaunted by the pain, he had rallied his men and fought on foot through superior numbers, only to suffer a point-blank pistol shot that miraculously passed just under his eye and out by his ear without striking bone or nerves."

"Good God," I uttered.

"But that doesn't begin to give the full measure of the man and the loyalty he inspires in his troops. He's known for treating them with respect and dignity—which in turn has made the men he trains the best soldiers in our army," continued Pitt. "In that particular battle, two of his soldiers fought tooth and nail to reach Moore, who had been stunned by the shot, and formed a protective ring around him until they procured a horse and led him to safety."

"He sounds like a saint," I mused.

"No, simply a thoroughly good and honorable man." Pitt made a wry face. "Which is perhaps even rarer than a saint."

He looked up as the sun disappeared behind an ominous cloud that had scudded in from the sea. "We had better spur for home before it begins to rain."

True to his word, Moore sent over an ornate certificate dripping with red wax seals confirming my ceremonial appointment as a cornet in the 7th Queen's Own Hussars . . . along with a handsome pair of snowy-white military breeches.

Pitt enjoyed a hearty laugh when I explained about Moore's offer, and insisted that from now on, I must wear them with my scarlet jacket when we rode out to review the local militia, seeing as they had the general's approval. I found it amusing, too, but was also moved that Moore considered his casual offer a binding promise. He was, I realized, truly a man of his word.

I had the opportunity to ride again with him the following week. Moore had stopped by to talk with my uncle about progress on the Royal Military Canal, but after they had finished, Pitt had several important letters to dispatch with the afternoon mail heading to London, so he begged off from Moore's invitation to inspect the beach defenses near Kingsdown.

"But perhaps Hester would like to accompany you, sir, "he announced as I came with the portfolio of papers he needed to consult. "And then she could report back to me on any suggestions you have."

Moore caught my eye and raised a brow in question.

"Give me a few minutes to change into my riding garb," I answered without hesitation.

"She looks very fetching in her hussar breeches," said Pitt as I hurried from the room. Thankfully the door fell shut behind me, for I was sure that my ears had turned flame-red.

I felt a little uncomfortable as I approached the stable, feeling oddly worried that the sight of a lady in snug-fitting male garb might shock the general. If it did, Moore gave no indication of it. Greeting me with a pleasant smile, he gave me a leg up to my saddle and then mounted his stallion.

"Shall we give our horses a good gallop?" he asked. "A friendly one."

"Lead the way, sir."

We crossed through a stretch of rolling grassland, riding side by side with the wind in our faces before slowing to crest the sandy dunes overlooking the sea.

I turned in my saddle, looking up and down the coastline, before surveying the land behind us. "I would imagine that the terrain plays a large part in deciding how to design defenses against a possible invasion."

"A very astute observation, milady," Moore replied. "To the casual observer, the weakest points aren't always obvious. In this case, the first things to understand are the local currents, the hidden shoals beneath the tides, and the depths of the bays. If French ships can get close enough to launch a landing of troops, one must figure out if there are good positions to establish a battery of cannons . . ."

He continued to give a very clear and concise picture of how to prevent the enemy from getting a foothold on English soil.

"You sound extremely knowledgeable on all this," I remarked. "I confess, I imagined that generals thought mostly about clashing with enemy armies and fighting glorious battles."

"Glorious battles are a horrendous waste of good lives. Fighting strategically is often more effective—and more humane."

I watched the sunlight play over his weathered profile as he stared out over the water. For a man who spent his life waging war, he radiated a remarkable aura of being at peace with himself and the world.

"Even as a boy, I found the concept of how to attack a target with the greatest efficiency to be an interesting challenge," he said. "When our grand tour of the Continent with the Duke of Hamilton passed through Switzerland, I drew up a plan for my father showing how I would conquer the city of Geneva. During our walk through the city on the previous day, I had noted the weak points of its defenses, and observed where one might place artillery and mass one's troops for a successful attack."

"Did you always want to be a soldier?"

Moore gave the question some thought. "Military matters interested me, and I seemed to have some aptitude for it. During our stay in Berlin, I met Frederick the Great, whose Prussian army was the best-disciplined force in all of Europe. The senior officers there were very kind and encouraging of my questions, and told me that I would made a good officer."

His stallion gave a fretful snort and tossed its head, but the mere touch of Moore's hand quickly calmed its fidgeting.

"The idea of serving my country was appealing, and as a favor to my father, the Duke of Hamilton's stepfather arranged for me to receive an ensign commission in the 51st Regiment of Foot. I had to wait a year, as I was too young to join the regiment. But I found that the life of a soldier seems to suit me."

"Our country is fortunate to have such an able and thoughtful general." I shaded my eyes as I looked out across the dark waters toward France. "Do you believe that we can beat Napoleon?"

He didn't answer right away, and when he did, it was with none of the bluster and pompous predictions that most military men would make to a lady.

"It will be a very long and bloody struggle, with much devastation and horrors for both sides. But I believe our soldiers, as well as our sailors, have hearts of stout English oak. And we fight to defend our principles of government against attack from one who would impose his beliefs on us."

His gaze followed mine in looking across the Channel. "So yes, I think in the end we will triumph. But the sacrifices demanded of us will be great."

His last words were suddenly punctuated by a rumble of thunder. "We ought to head on to the village," he suggested, spotting the bank of black clouds scudding in from the west. "We can take shelter in the local militia headquarters until the coming squall has blown over."

# Chapter 18

*November 1803*

Moore and I rode out together several more times, but he was then called away to take up his duties at the Shorncliffe army training camp. I regretted the loss of his good company—more than I had expected. Not only was he interesting and knowledge-able on a wide range of subjects, but he also possessed a delight-fully pithy sense of humor. However, I had little chance to dwell on it as other more pressing matters intruded on my thoughts.

Camelford came again to Walmer Castle, which created a very awkward situation for me. On one hand, his devil-may-care disre-gard for rules appealed to my natural rebellious streak . . . and hon-esty compelled me to admit to myself that I missed the fire-kissed excitement of physical intimacy with him. And yet, I was enjoying my life with Pitt, and the heady feeling of being part of his inner circle, where the grand ideas that shaped the fate of nations were being discussed. I was loath to put all that in jeopardy.

Especially as I had nowhere else to go.

Pitt was fond of Camelford, and once I explained that I had not broken my promise and arranged the rendezvous, he was a gra-cious host and assured our uninvited guest that he was welcome to stay for a week, after which a gathering of his advisors from London would require the use of all the guest quarters.

"Bloody hell, Diamond, what a boring place this is," announced Camelford, as we were riding along the cliffs several days after his arrival. "How do you bear the tedium?"

"Actually I have a great deal of interesting things to do," I countered.

His brows gave a suggestive waggle. "Not as interesting as things we could be doing with each other."

Ignoring the comment—and the lick of temptation that teased down my spine—I focused my gaze on the trail straight ahead. Yes, there was an allure and excitement to allowing impulse to have free rein. *But it was also dangerous.* Especially for a lady, I reminded myself. Somehow, those of my sex always had more to lose through any misjudgment.

"Be careful," I cautioned. "The path turns a bit treacherous. A slip and your horse may come up lame."

Camelford spurred his mount to come abreast of me, so close that our boots were touching. "You've lost your spirit of adventure, Diamond." He caught my arm and pulled me to him. "Let me help you find it."

His kiss was hard and possessive.

For a long moment, I savored the sensual sensations—the smoke-and-brandy taste of his tongue, the heat pooling in my belly . . .

And then I pulled back. "We are too much alike, Tom. Both of us are so full of fire . . . I fear we will burn each other to a crisp."

He grinned as a gust of wind whistled through the rocks. "But we will be very sated and satisfied cinders."

I couldn't help but laugh. "You can't simply live in the moment."

"Why the devil not?"

"Because," I said, "at some point there will be hell to pay."

"Then pull the coins out of your purse when that moment comes," he responded.

I evaded his efforts to resume the kiss. "And what if your purse is empty?"

"You sound like an old woman, prosing on about the future instead of enjoying the present."

A tiny voice hidden somewhere in the shadows of my consciousness whispered that he was right . . .

But thankfully the sound of an approaching rider cut short our tête-à-tête. I turned to see Pitt had decided to leave off his work and join us.

I saw the flare of annoyance in Camelford's eyes as he raised his hand in a friendly wave. "We haven't finished our discussion, Diamond," he said softly as Pitt approached.

That, I decided, remained to be seen.

A sense of anticipation began stirring through Walmer Castle as the number of important political visitors increased at the end of October. Pitt was constantly sequestered with advisors and allies to discuss the present prime minister's struggle to govern and the possibility of my uncle taking over the reins of the country again. I worried a little that the long days and nights would take a toll on his health, but he seemed invigorated by the activities.

There were other guests as well. Pitt had invited his friend William Herschel, the king's astronomer, to come stay for several days, and Herschel was bringing his sister Caroline with him. The political gentlemen also added to the complicated logistics of running the castle. They were awfully cavalier about making last-minute additions to their party, which often threw Elizabeth Williams into a fit of megrims—though she always managed to come up with a solution.

I awoke one such morning to the sound of rain pelting against my bedchamber windows—and the frantic knocking of a parlor-maid, who informed me that an early morning post from London had brought a message from Lord Grenville announcing that he was bringing an extra guest. Elizabeth had dispatched her to ask if I might help her organize the last-minute arrangements.

The squall passed quickly, giving way to brilliant sunshine and a clear cerulean blue sky, However, the juggling of rooms, discreetly shifting a pair of junior members of Parliament to lesser quarters to make room for Grenville's companions, took us until well after luncheon.

In need of a breath of fresh air and an interlude of quiet, I made my way up to the battlements, intent on enjoying a view of the sea through Pitt's telescope, which, I noted earlier, had been moved outdoors from the study. To my surprise, someone was there ahead of me.

The gentleman turning the dials looked up at the sound of my approach. "Lady Hester, how lovely to see you again."

I smiled and held out a hand in greeting. "Mr. Herschel, I wasn't aware that you had arrived."

"We have, and I've taken the liberty of showing my sister the view toward France through our joint handiwork."

Confused for a moment, I looked around.

With a small cough, Herschel stepped to the left . . .

I swallowed a gasp of surprise on spotting a diminutive figure who had been hidden behind him. I had never seen such a tiny lady—she was barely four feet tall.

"F-forgive me," I stuttered. "I didn't . . ."

"You didn't see me," finished Caroline Herschel, "which is perfectly understandable." Her mouth gave a humorous quirk. "It requires one of my brother's specially-made optic lenses to magnify me to suit the human eye."

"Actually, Caroline makes more precise lenses than I do," drawled Herschel. Recalling his manners, he quickly performed the formal introductions.

"It is a pleasure to meet you, Miss Herschel," I responded, trying not to stare. "Do you enjoy sweeping the stars, too?"

"Caroline has discovered no less than eight comets, and last year the Royal Society published her well-respected catalogue of the heavens, organized on north polar distance, in its prestigious *Philosophical Transactions*," interjected her brother. "Which is no *small* achievement."

"That's not quite accurate, William," pointed out his sister. "The name listed as the creator is yours."

He waved off the correction. "Everyone in the world of astronomy knows that it was you who conceived of the method, and did all the observations to create the reference catalogue."

I liked Herschel all the more for giving his sister the credit she deserved.

"Pitt has been showing me how to use your gift to survey the night sky," I said. "It's a wondrous feeling to explore the unknown and discover new things."

"It is indeed!" exclaimed Herschel, but before he could expound further on the subject, a footman appeared and invited him to join Pitt and the other gentlemen guests for port in the drawing room.

"Of course you must go," I urged, seeing him hesitate. "I am delighted to have the chance to converse with your sister."

Turning back to Caroline after the exchange, I found that she had somehow managed to seat herself atop the battlement wall next to the telescope and was smoothing her skirts into place with an air of unruffled calm.

*It must be a constant challenge to navigate a physical world that was not made to fit a person such as you,* I mused.

"Welcome to Walmer Castle, Miss Herschel." As I ran my fingers along the dark wood of the octagonal barrel, I added, "How fascinating that you have a hand in crafting the lenses that allow us to see beyond our own imagination."

"That is an interesting—and insightful—way of putting it, Lady Hester." Caroline took a moment to reflect. She was a homely-looking woman, I noted, with a plain face . . . save for her brown eyes, which radiated a luminous intelligence.

"The key is curiosity," she continued. "One must have a sense of wonder and willingness to challenge your own preconceptions." A pause. "Most people find that uncomfortable."

I smiled. "Convention is a comfortable corset. Though there are those of us who chafe against it."

"As an eminent man of science, your father is a good example.

His experiments with optics helped to open our eyes to new ways of seeing things."

"Yes, as you undoubtedly know, he is an unconventional thinker about a great many subjects."

Caroline nodded, a glint of amusement in her eyes. "Which is not always easy for family and friends."

"Indeed not." I fingered one of the brass levers before asking her a question about building the telescope, which led to an interesting conversation on the subject of astronomy and the night skies.

After Caroline had answered yet another of my questions on stars and planets, I found myself curious about her personal life. My first impulse on spotting her was to assume that she was a silent, submissive spinster, a mere shadow in her brother's life. But clearly, she was intelligent and engaging, with a sly sense of humor.

"I can't help but wonder," I ventured. "Do you regret serving as your brother's assistant, rather than marrying and being mistress of your own household?"

Caroline appeared bemused by the query. "Good Heavens, why would I want a different life? My brother respects my talents and treats me as an equal, which allows me the freedom to pursue my passions."

She lifted her face to catch the breeze. "I make discoveries, write up papers, and am acknowledged by men of science for being good at what I do."

"But you get no official recognition."

"Granted, there is much prejudice against the intellectual abilities of women." A smile. "I think that is why men fear allowing us to have a decent education, especially the right to attend university—because they know that they will be proved wrong."

I gave a wry laugh. "You'll get no argument from me on that."

"But as to the other choice you suggested," said Caroline. "Why would I want to be confined to a boring existence of household chores, and to a life where my every action is by law controlled by my husband?" She shook her head. "I am quite content with my situation. No man controls me and that is worth more than I can express."

I frowned in thought. "And yet you are still beholden to your brother for your bread and the roof over your head—"

"Actually, I'm not," interrupted Caroline. "In 1787, King George granted me a yearly salary of fifty pounds to serve as my brother's assistant. Of all my accomplishments, that one makes me most proud. I am the first female ever to be granted an official government position here in England."

*What a towering achievement!* If this tiny woman could earn such a position through her skills, perhaps I could dare to dream—

"Since you asked about marriage . . ." Caroline regarded me with a frank stare. "I was under the impression that aristocratic ladies were expected to make a match early in life, based on forging political, social, and financial alliances for the family, rather than for personal reasons."

"That's true," I conceded. "I am fortunate that my family's connections are strong enough in all those areas you mention that I am not being pressed to make a decision quite yet."

"Have you thought about what would make you happy?"

"I . . . I . . ." I felt myself flush. "It is complicated."

"Most things in life are," replied Caroline with a worldly smile. "As a woman of advanced years, I have experienced a great deal, so I hope you won't take offense if I offer some counsel."

She reached out and angled the telescope's lens to aim at the far horizon. "Look at decisions from every perspective." Pressing a hand to her heart, Caroline added, "And then simply trust yourself to see the right course."

"Put that way, it sounds so easy."

Caroline slipped down from her perch. "We are often our own worst enemy, making things more difficult for ourselves than they should be."

Thinking of Camelford's restless soul, I let out a sigh. But was I really any better?

"The breeze is turning chill," said Caroline, pulling her shawl a little tighter around her shoulders. "Shall we retreat to the parlor and ring for a pot of tea?"

*December 1803*

With the castle filled to capacity and bustling with activities that required my attention from morning until midnight and beyond, I had no chance for further private conversation with Caroline Herschel. She and her brother departed after several days, and I regretted the loss of their company, not only because I so rarely encountered interesting, erudite females, but also because their presence had helped Pitt to relax from the pressures of politics. The four of us had spent time stargazing late at night, and discussing the grandeur of the heavens seemed to lift my uncle's spirits.

More politicians arrived to take the place of the Herschels, and my attention was quickly focused on more down-to-earth concerns. With Pitt in constant meetings throughout the day, I found myself taken aside by the gentlemen waiting for an audience with him and asked for my understanding of Pitt's stance on certain issues, along with my advice on how they should present their own advice to him. As word spread that I was both his confidante and private secretary, I noticed a change in the way I was treated. The light mood of the drawing room gatherings—laughter, witty banter, flattery, and flirtations—remained much the same, but I was increasingly invited for quiet conversations on serious matters of state, where I was engaged as an intellectual equal, with my counsel and my opinions respectfully sought.

Like the glasses of port I shared in their company, the sensation was intoxicating.

With the rumblings of discontent growing louder within the inner sanctums of government, it was deemed imperative for Pitt to visit London and confer with the various factions within the Tories and the Whigs about the future. I stayed at Walmer Castle to deal with the routine matters concerning the local militias and coastal defenses, but as the weather remained quite mild for the season, I took advantage of my uncle's absence to put a secret plan in motion.

On the first day of my arrival at the castle, Pitt had commented on the lack of gardens and trees as he gave me a tour of the grounds. His words on how Nature created an oasis of peaceful tranquility from the slings and arrows of everyday life had stuck with me. I had done the botanical research, sketched out a rough plan, and with the help of the head gardener had arranged to visit several local purveyors with an expertise in landscaping to refine my ideas.

The necessary raw materials were all at hand to create what I had in mind. But given the scope of the project, a great deal of manpower was needed. However, I had an idea of how to conquer that obstacle. The morning after Pitt left, I donned my "Amazon" attire—red military jacket, regimental breeches, and plumed shako—and rode out to visit the commanders of the local militias. It took a bit of adroit verbal fencing, but as my tongue had been sharpened and polished by my interaction with Pitt and his political friends, I managed to convince them that keeping the men of the various regiments busy was good for both discipline and developing practical skills for digging defensive positions in case of a French invasion.

The troops were quickly set to work, laying out the grand design with stakes and rope, leveling the ground, bringing in turf, sowing seeds, planting hedges . . .

I was in my element, constantly in motion, checking on each contingent, ordering adjustments when necessary. The main lawn was redesigned, and a series of flowerbeds added to soften the castle's yew hedges. It was exhilarating to see the plan come to life before my eyes, especially when the time came to move wagonloads of mature horse chestnut trees into place.

We were just finishing the last touches when I received word that Pitt was on his way back to Walmer Castle, and having stopped in Canterbury to spend the night with the archbishop, he would be arriving the following day.

\*   \*   \*

I was up at the crack of dawn, my nerves crackling with nervous energy. All was, of course, in perfect readiness for his arrival, though I felt beholden to enter his private study and make yet another check that I had sorted all the papers that had arrived in his absence into separate piles according to subject matter, topped with a note summarizing their contents.

"Stop fidgeting," advised Elizabeth as I walked through the corridors mentally ticking off the minutes.

"What if he doesn't like it?" I replied, not feeling nearly as confident as I had last week.

"Then you will call in the army again," she said wryly, "and order them to blow it to Kingdom Come with their artillery."

I laughed, knowing it was a little late for second thoughts about my grand plan. But I wanted so much to please him. Of all my relatives—including my own father—he was the one who had shown me unwavering kindness and support, arranging for my well-being and offering me a home when I had nowhere else to go.

I feared that my vision of Walmer's grounds might disappoint him.

At last the carriage rolled to a halt in the courtyard. A footman hurried out to carry his work satchels, while Elizabeth ordered the kitchen to begin preparing tea and refreshments.

"Hetty!" He smiled as I gave him a hug and helped him out of his overcoat. "I have missed you."

"And I you, Uncle," I replied, brushing a kiss to his cheek. I took his arm. "Come, I want to show you something."

Pitt pinched at the bridge of his nose. "Might it wait until after I have chased away the travel aches and pains with a glass of port?"

"It will only take a moment."

"Very well," he replied with an indulgent smile, and allowed me to lead him to the stairs. Up we climbed, to a window overlooking the area where I had made the improvements.

"Have a look," I said.

"I know the grounds by heart—" protested my uncle, only to fall silent in mid-sentence as he peered through the glass.

I closed my eyes for an instant, too nervous to watch his reaction.

"Dear me, Hetty, why, this is a miracle!" Pitt leaned in closer, taking a few moments to study the details. "I declare it is quite admirable. I could not have done it half so well myself. How the devil did you manage this?"

"You, sir, may be colonel commandant of the Cinque Port Volunteers"—I gave what I hoped was a nonchalant shrug—"but it seems that I have a modicum of unofficial clout."

Pitt laughed. "When facing the Amazon's artillery, only a fool would fail to realize that he was outgunned." He stepped back from the window. "Shall we retreat to my study and raise a toast to your triumph of Nature?"

"How did the meetings in London go?" I queried as he headed down the corridor.

"Change is in the air, Hetty—I can hear it, I can see it, I can taste it." He rubbed his hands together. "Much as I like Addington personally, he is making a mull of our military preparations to face off against Napoleon and his forces. The consensus is that the country needs a new leader."

He looked younger and more invigorated than when he had left, and I remember my Pitt grandmother telling me that even as a young boy, it was clear that he was born to be a politician.

*Some things are simply in the blood*, she had said. *An elemental part of one's essence.*

I thought about that as we turned into Pitt's private study and he moved to fetch glasses and a decanter of port from the sideboard. And oddly enough, what popped to mind was my garden plan and the decisions of what went where. My uncle needed to be planted in bright sunlight, with a riot of colors and textures all around him. Put him in a quiet spot of shade and he would wither and die on the vine.

*And what about me?*

I had not yet figured out my exact place in the world, or what conditions I needed in order to thrive. There was, however, one thing of which I was quite certain: I was not cut out to lead a traditional domestic life.

"By the by," said Pitt after pouring two glasses of port. "After spending the Christmas holidays at Burton Pynsent with Chatham and his family, we will be returning to London, rather than Walmer Castle."

'What about our duties here?"

"There is no threat from the French for now. The storms and currents at this time of year make it impossible for them to launch an invasion," he replied. "As for the routine duties, Colonel Harris and Colonel Watkins are perfectly capable of drilling the troops on their own." A chuckle. "Though I daresay the men would much rather be reviewed by the Amazon."

Pitt took a long swallow of his port and then put down his glass. "But the truth is, I need you in London. Momentous decisions affecting countless lives will be made over the coming months, and the two of us are destined to be part of them."

# Chapter 19

*January–March 1804*

*L*ondon. Much as I had come to appreciate the quietude of Walmer Castle, I felt a frisson of anticipation as our carriage clattered down Whitehall Street to our rented lodgings. *The politics, the parties, the whispers of gossip and rumors that swirl through the drawing rooms of the beau monde*—like a cauldron filled with volatile chemicals sitting atop an undulating flame, it was mesmerizing. There was a glittering beauty to the spectacle, made even more intense by the thought that it might explode at any moment.

Pitt moved closer to the window, pressing his nose to the glass.

"You are happy to be back in the fray," I observed.

"Guilty as charged," he replied. "The current situation regarding the cabinet is quite unsettled, with a number of complex negotiations going on in private."

"In other words," I drawled, "you are in your element."

A ghost of a smile, which quickly gave way to a serious look. "I shall need your help, Hetty. Your wit and charm are often more powerful weapons than my oratory. Gentlemen enjoy being in your presence."

I reached out to touch his hand. "My skills, such as they are, are always at your command, sir."

His fingers twined with mine. "Your stalwart support is more important to me than you can imagine."

The two of us made an excellent team, I mused, watching the skeins of coal smoke swirl through the air. I knew that he had come to count on me for a great many tasks that allowed him to focus on the grand scope of the country's needs.

"As to that, sir . . ." I cleared my throat. An idea had been simmering in the back of my mind since meeting Caroline Herschel. "If the king asks you to form a government, I should like you to ask . . ."

Bold though I was in most circumstances, I found myself hesitating.

"Ask what, Hetty?" he pressed.

Drawing a deep breath, I continued in a rush. "I would like for you to ask the king to grant me the official title of Private Secretary to the Prime Minister, along with a salary of, say, fifty pounds per annum."

Pitt let out an uncertain laugh. "You are jesting."

"I am not. You have on many occasions said that I perform the duties required of your private secretary better than any gentleman. So why should I not be acknowledged as such, and receive the same salary?"

As he hunched his shoulders and contemplated my question in shocked silence, I realized that I had never seen my uncle rendered speechless.

"You've worked diligently, Hetty," he finally responded, "and I'm impressed by how well you have learned the nuances of negotiations needed to deal with the complexities of governing."

The carriage skidded over the cobblestones as the coachman turned onto Parliament Street.

"So I'm sure you realize that my position is far from secured." Pitt paused. "However, if I do become prime minister, I . . . I will consider your request."

"Thank you." It wasn't the perfect response. But prejudice against those of my sex was woven into the fabric of Society. It would take time to create a whole new cloth.

\*     \*     \*

Pitt hadn't exaggerated the complexity of the current political situation. Lord Grenville, his cousin and good friend, was pressing him to form a cabinet that included their long-time Whig enemy, Charles Fox. The king, however, was refusing to consider such a suggestion. We all knew why. The king and his eldest son, the Prince of Wales, detested each other, and the prince was an ardent supporter of Fox.

Over the next few weeks there was a flurry of meetings between allies, go-betweens, and various factions, all trying to work out a compromise.

Pitt was playing it coy with everyone—including me. Despite his long-running dislike for Fox, he dropped hints that he would consider working with him. But for the most part, he seemed content to keep his distance and watch the others jockey for position. That didn't mean that he avoided holding sumptuous dinners and soirees. On the contrary, we entertained frequently, and I was called upon to charm the guests into a good humor, as well as see that they were served a superb meal.

A gentleman already seduced by flattery, food, and wine was more likely to be swayed by their host's arguments.

I had worked tirelessly from dawn to dusk on a cold and dreary mid-February day for an evening soiree that including a number of diplomats from the Foreign Office who were supporters of Pitt. Thank heavens that Elizabeth Williams was both efficient and good-humored. She and I had come to be good friends and her managing of the domestic staff was much appreciated. Even so, as the time approached for the guests to arrive, I was bone-weary from checking and rechecking that all was ready and in no mood to exert myself in charming the gentlemen with flatteries and flirtations.

But duty called.

Much as I wished to put on my nightrail and curl up under the bedcovers with a book and a cup of tea, I donned my finery, gave a twist to my diamond ring for good luck, and headed downstairs to the drawing room.

"You are looking especially lovely tonight, my dear," greeted Pitt, after gesturing for the footmen to set up the cut-crystal punch bowl in one of the side salons.

"Is there anyone in particular who requires special attention?" I inquired, smoothing a wrinkle from the sash of my gown.

"Actually, Canning is feeling a little out of sorts with me for attending a meeting with Fox arranged by the Duchess of Devonshire."

As I well knew, Georgiana was a fierce supporter of the Whigs and her exuberant personality, along with her prominent position in Society, had made her one of Fox's most trusted confidantes.

Men thought her exceedingly clever. My opinion of her hadn't changed—I still thought her unpleasantly manipulative.

"I will do my best to coax him into a good humor," I replied. "I read his recent report to you on the state of the Channel fleet's readiness, and will compliment him on his insightful analysis." George Canning was perhaps the smartest of Pitt's inner circle, but he was sensitive to any perceived slight to his importance and required occasional flattery to keep his feathers from becoming ruffled.

"Much appreciated," responded Pitt. "I shall spend most of my time with the diplomats from the Foreign Office. Their observations on the state of things in Europe, and what alliances are likely to be made in response to Napoleon's aggression, are important for me to hear as I prepare my next speech to the members of Parliament."

I nodded as the butler escorted the first arrivals into the drawing room. "I had better go welcome our guests. I will find you later and do my best to charm the diplomats into supporting your call for a tougher stance against France."

"A single smile from you will likely be worth a thousand words from me," replied Pitt. He took a glass of sparkling wine from the tray of a passing waiter and lifted it in wry salute. "I probably should be serving good English ale rather than French champagne. But when it comes to the finer things in life, it is my experience that even the highest sticklers will sacrifice only so much personal pleasure for their principles."

"Few people are true idealists," I said, watching another group of well-dressed and well-fed aristocrats enter the room. "Well, I had better get to work."

For the next half hour, I took up a position by the open double doors and assumed my most scintillating smile as I greeted the arriving guests with a patter of *bon mots* and pithy observations on the latest Society gossip to start the evening with a chuckle. Just as importantly, I made sure that the footmen were quick to offer them a libation. Fine wine and strong spirits were key in lubricating the tongue.

And when a gentleman's tongue was well lubricated, discretion tended to float away.

Politics was a game of give and take . . .

Pitt played it better than anyone.

As the room filled, I drifted away from the doorway and meandered through the crowd, stopping to chat with friends, as well as deepen acquaintances with several gentlemen I recognized as past visitors to Walmer Castle.

The buzz thrumming through the room was resonating down to the very marrow of my bones. All around me, deals were brokered, policies debated, compromises coaxed into being. And I was here in the center of it.

No wonder my blood was bubbling with a fizzier effervescence than the French champagne. Precious few ladies—aside from me, Lady Caroline Howe, sister of the famous General Sir William Howe and Richard Admiral Lord Howe, and the Duchess of Devonshire were the only two who came to mind—had the opportunity to converse as equals with the crème de la crème of Britain's politicians—

"Lady Hester." A hand touched my arm. "Do allow me to introduce you to the Honorable Stephen Boynton, who represents the borough of Littlesham in Parliament . . ."

"What a pleasure to meet you, sir," I said, after the introductions were made. "I have heard some *very* interesting things about you." Lowering my voice to a discreet whisper, I added, "Pitt says you have caught his eye as an up-and-coming member of the party."

It was a blatant flattery. In truth, Pitt had mentioned the fellow's name as someone whose loyalty was lukewarm at best. However, Boynton's face betrayed a flush of pleasure.

"I-I shall of course do my best to deserve such notice from the Great Man himself."

I smiled, feeling confident that he was now a solid supporter of my uncle, and after exchanging a few more pleasantries with him, I excused myself to find Pitt and the group of Foreign Office diplomats.

Failing to spot them in the crowded drawing room, I checked the refreshment parlor and then moved to the adjoining side salon, where I caught the red-gold flicker of a fire burning in the hearth as I approached the half-open door.

A group of six gentlemen were gathered close to the warmth of the coals, listening intently to Pitt. I hesitated upon entering, not wishing to interrupt.

"Your uncle's silvery tongue seems to be working its usual magic." George Canning came to join me after refilling his glass with brandy at the sideboard. "He has them eating out of his hand."

"It's your insight on the present political situation on the Continent that helps him to feed them winning arguments for supporting his position."

"Hmmph." Canning said nothing but I could tell by his expression that my comment had put him in a better mood.

I quickly asked a question about Russia, which allowed him to pontificate on a subject he knew well. A lengthy response followed, to which I listened with rapt attention, taking care to nod frequently in agreement.

Engrossed in charming Canning, I didn't notice that the group by the fire was now breaking apart. It was Pitt's voice that finally caught my attention.

"Forgive the interruption, Canning, but might I steal my niece away? There is someone I wish for her to meet."

I looked around, my skirts stirring a gossamer flutter of silk, and assumed a polite smile.

The gentleman with my uncle had just turned his back to reply to something a colleague said to him. The exchange only lasted a moment and then he pivoted to face me.

# *Chapter* 20

I was no stranger to masculine beauty—the aristocracy had more than its fair share of Tulips of the Ton—and yet for an instant, my heart seemed to stop in mid-beat.

"Hetty, allow me to present Granville Leveson Gower," said Pitt.

Shaking off my inexplicable reaction, I reminded myself that I was here to help Pitt forge political alliances, and quickly reviewed what I knew about the gentleman.

He was the subject of much drawing room gossip, for apparently the ladies of London had dubbed him the most handsome man in Britain. My own quick assessment found no flaw in their judgment. His face had a classical symmetry—well-shaped cheekbones, straight nose, strong jaw—and the chiseled features were complemented by sea-green eyes and a sensuous mouth . . .

However, Granville—I knew he was called Granville by his friends and diplomatic colleagues because they considered Leveson Gower to be a mouthful—was also a rising star in the diplomatic ranks, a skilled negotiator who possessed both poise and polished charm. It was said that Pitt was considering him for an important ambassadorship—

"It is a pleasure to make your acquaintance, Lady Hester."

Granville's graceful bow drew me back to the moment. "Your uncle has told me a great deal about you."

By this time, I had my emotions under control and answered with a cool smile. "Don't believe everything you hear, sir."

My reply seemed to surprise him. He hesitated, his dark brows tweaking up just a touch. "Now you have me intrigued, milady."

"I give you fair warning, Granville. Cross verbal swords with my niece at your own risk. Her tongue can be sharper than mine," said my uncle with a note of pride. "I would also be careful about engaging her in any debate about politics or the war efforts."

Pitt paused. "Unless you want your head handed to you on a platter."

Was it merely the crystalline glitter of the overhead chandelier that lit a spark of interest in Granville's gaze?

"That sounds like a challenge, sir," he said slowly, though his eyes remained on me.

"Some gentlemen would find that frightening," I responded.

Another smile. "And some gentlemen would not."

"Granville has recently met with the Russian, Prussian, and Austrian ambassadors to discuss the situation with France—" began Pitt.

"Do you think we can defeat France?" I demanded of Granville, curious as to whether there was really any actual substance beneath his divine looks.

He looked about to reply and then hesitated.

"What?" I pressed.

"I was about to answer with a platitude, because in my experience most ladies wish to be assured that all is well in hand," Granville answered. "Even when it's not."

Before I could retort, he added, "But my understanding is that you are not like most ladies, and so I wish to give the question due consideration."

I was unusually tall for a female—nearly six feet—but I had to look up slightly to meet his gaze. "Surely you have an opinion one way or another."

"The opposing forces are aligned on the chessboard, but as of yet, the opening move has yet to be made," said Granville. "So there are an infinite number of possibilities as to how the game will play out."

"And you don't care to hazard a guess?"

"I have my conjectures, of course, based on my knowledge of the participants and a wide range of practical factors," he continued, then proceeded to give his assessment of how the initial battle lines would be formed.

It appeared that he did possess a brain to go along with his beauty. Unsure whether that gratified or unsettled me, I decided to make a strategic retreat and sort out my feelings.

"Canning looks to be scowling again," I observed to Pitt. "I had better go and coax him into a better mood." With a polite nod to Granville, I turned and moved away.

*Was he watching me?* I wondered.

Keeping my steps slow and adding a sway to my silk-swathed hips, I approached Canning, and in linking my arm with his, I saw that Granville's gaze had indeed followed me across the room. Pleased—perhaps *too* pleased—I drew Canning to a more secluded spot and said something about one of the other guests that made him laugh. We exchanged a few comments about the troubles facing the current prime minister before I drifted away to one of the side salons.

I paused in the shadows of the archway, needing a moment to myself. I had never had such a visceral response to a gentleman before. Yes, Camelford had intrigued me from the moment I met him. But this . . .

This was different, though I couldn't begin to explain why.

Spotting Pitt's older brother, Lord Chatham, standing alone by one of the leaded windows, I went to join him.

"What do you know of Granville Leveson Gower, Uncle?" I asked.

Chatham looked around from contemplating the spatter of raindrops meandering down the glass. "Other than the fact that every lady in London fancies herself in love with him?"

"I had no trouble figuring that out for myself," I said dryly. "Actually, I'm more interested in his diplomatic and political skills. Pitt seems to think highly of him. What is your assessment?"

Chatham considered the question for several long moments before answering. "His rise has been impressive," he said slowly. "Though perhaps not quite as impressive as he and his closest allies seem to think."

"You think he is all charm and no substance?"

"Not precisely. Granville's parents, the Marquess and Marchioness of Stafford, dote on him, and their wealth and aristocratic connections have made life easy for him. However, along with his wit and refined manners, he also has a sharp intellect and is a savvy judge of people."

"He sounds like the perfect politician," I said.

"His career would seem to say the same," agreed Chatham. "Granville was elected as the representative to Parliament from Staffordshire at age twenty-two—no great feat as his father controls the seat. However, he proved to be a surprisingly effective negotiator behind the scenes, and then was given diplomatic posting in both Paris and Lille."

Chatham took a moment to pour himself a brandy from the sideboard. "On his return to London, Granville impressed the Tory leaders enough that Pitt made him Lord of the Treasury in 1800. Of course, he lost that position when Pitt resigned as prime minister the following year. But he has remained in the inner circle of power and influence. Word is, he's ambitious, and I don't doubt that he'll do very well for himself."

He took a sip of his drink. "Indeed, now that I think on it, I believe I recall hearing that Pitt will consider appointing Granville as Ambassador to Russia if he becomes prime minister."

I remained silent, thinking on what I had just heard.

A cough interrupted my musing and I looked to see Chatham was eyeing me in some concern. "You are not some silly schoolgirl, Hetty. Surely you're old enough and wise enough not to be seduced by a handsome face."

I gave a mocking laugh. "Quite right, Uncle. I've experienced enough of the world to understand all that glitters is not gold."

He nodded, although I thought I detected a glimmer of uncertainty lingering in his gaze. My relationship with Camelford had always troubled him, and my sense was that he didn't trust my judgment.

I supposed that I couldn't blame him.

"Then I shall say no more." He put down his empty brandy glass and excused himself with a peck to my cheek. "It's late, and I should be going."

It was close to midnight and the crowd was beginning to thin. I heard Pitt bidding good night to a group of gentlemen from the Foreign Office and decided that I ought to help in performing the social duties. As I passed through the archway into the short connecting corridor, I spotted a lone gentleman in the other side salon. He was lounging in the doorway, shoulder leaned against molding, perusing the pages of a book from one of the shelves.

It was Granville.

He looked up and as our eyes met for a moment, a current of electricity seemed to crackle between us.

I inclined a small nod and kept going.

He said nothing as I passed. And yet, I was quite sure that I hadn't merely imagined the spark.

However, I had little time to ponder on it as the glare from the drawing room chandelier quickly drew me back from my reveries.

"Lord Ambrose," I said, hurrying to make a fuss over one of Pitt's loyal supporters from Yorkshire. "I hope you enjoyed the evening . . ."


Dawn's first light was creeping closer and yet sleep still eluded me. Tired of my fitful tossing and turning, I threw off the bedcovers and slipped my wrapper over my nightrail. Leaving my feet bare, I lit a candle and headed down to the library.

Surely a room filled with knowledge from the greatest minds of the past and present could offer some answers for the unsettling questions that plagued me.

I pushed the oak portal open and filled my lungs with the comforting scent of ink, paper, and leather. But rather than head to the carved acanthus bookshelves, I moved to the bank of windows overlooking the back garden, which allowed a glimpse of the sky above the city's roofs and spires.

Through the haze, I could just make out a glimmer of stars and was suddenly reminded of how much I missed scanning the heavens with Pitt's telescope. As Caroline Herschel had so sagely said, the depth and breadth of the universe at night made one dare to dream, for there were no boundaries.

Just infinite possibilities.

I lingered for an interlude, watching the moon play hide-and-seek in the clouds before heading to the sideboard and pouring myself a glass of port. As I took a sip and savored the wine's lush sweetness, I thought about my unnerving reaction to Granville Leveson Gower.

I had felt an immediate visceral connection to him. He had sparked something inside me, though I couldn't begin to define what it was. It wasn't just physical attraction . . . though his smoldering eyes would melt even the hardest of hearts.

My gaze drifted to the desk by the hearth, where Pitt was working on a speech for an upcoming debate in the House of Commons. Books, pens, fresh paper, and crumpled drafts were piled humble-jumble on the blotter, the disarray a metaphor for all the passionate ideas that were tumbling around in his head.

As I took up flint and steel, intending to light the desk lamp and read what Pitt had written, I suddenly paused.

*Passions.* My famous forebearers—"Diamond" Pitt, Pitt the Elder, Pitt the Younger, Camelford, my father—were all driven by some primal force to follow their own inner fire. They had dared to imagine a life outside the boundaries of convention, and had not been afraid to pursue it.

*What about me?* Quicksilver shadows flitted in and out of the circle of moonlight pooled beneath the windows. I watched the muddled shapes as I contemplated my past, my present—and the way forward.

The soft trill of a nightingale floated in from the garden. Somewhere in the distance, a nightwatchman rang his handbell to signal all was well. And then suddenly a fire-bright spark came alight in my mind's eye . . . and I saw my future with stunning clarity.

*The life of a diplomat's wife.*

I loved being part of the inner circle of power and feeling that my opinions were given the same respect as those voiced by the gentlemen. I yearned to travel and use my wit and charm—assets that Pitt had often lauded—to liaison with the grand courts of Europe.

Granville could offer me entrée into that magical world of politics and power. With him, I could be the savvy, sophisticated hostess that a gentleman of his exalted position required.

And so, I decided then and there that Granville Leveson Gower and I would make the perfect couple.

Fortune was quick to smile on me. The next day Pitt reminded me that we were scheduled to attend a ball at the end of the week given by Granville's mother, Lady Stafford. It was a golden opportunity to begin courting both of them. According to Chatham, the marchioness had great influence with her son, so currying her good opinion could make her a powerful ally.

My family tree worked in my favor, as did the fact Pitt was soon likely to occupy the pinnacle of power in Britain.

However, I was not unaware of the obstacles in my way. I was well past the first bloom of youth and would bring no handsome dowry to the match, for even though Granville's family was wealthy, those things mattered for the aristocracy. And then there was my relationship with the notorious Lord Camelford. Though nothing scandalous had been said, the gossips had noted our closeness. I would have to figure out a way to extract myself from the awkward connection before it proved fatal to my hopes.

One concern that was far easier to address was my wardrobe. Since breaking away from my father's iron-fisted control, I had come to love the sensuous feel of silk and satin, yet I paid little attention to the latest trends in fashion. But that, I decided, would have to change.

To Pitt's bemusement, I suddenly began spending time studying *The Lady's Magazine*, the bible of beau monde style. I explained that I wished to look my best as he intensified his efforts to retake the reins of government, adding that should our official residence become Downing Street, the prime minister's hostess should reflect well on the honor.

My arguments were apparently persuasive, for he gave me free rein to visit the most exclusive modistes and mantua-makers in London to order an array of new gowns and accessories. And so, as I sat at my dressing table on the evening of the ball while my maid finished threading a pearl-studded ribbon through my upswept curls, I felt ready to start my quest.

"You look stunning," exclaimed Pitt, his eyes lightening in admiration as I floated down the stairs in a shimmering of indigo watered silk.

"Thank you, Uncle," I replied, taking his arm to head out to the waiting carriage. I had chosen the dark color to accentuate the alabaster hue of my complexion, which elicited frequent compliments from my gentlemen admirers. "Now, this evening is about business as well as pleasure. Tell me which of Lady Stafford's guests you wish for me to charm."

After a quick laugh, he gave me a few names. "I am quite sure they would be more receptive to your smiles than mine," he added.

"What about Granville?" I asked.

"I already count him as a loyal supporter," replied Pitt. "However, if you wish to enjoy a dance or two with him, I daresay you both would enjoy it."

"I will keep that in mind." *Along with my own desires.*

A crush of carriages was already crowding the way when we arrived at Whitehall Street. The glitter of myriad candles lit the entrance hall of the Stafford townhouse, illuminating the elegant procession of jeweltone colors of the guests winding up the grand staircase. Pitt and I made our way through the reception line, where I lingered for a moment, giving Lady Stafford my most winsome smile and adding a few compliments on her refined taste, which seemed to please her. And then for the next hour I dutifully circulated through the main drawing room, doing my duty for my uncle.

My throat dry from keeping up a patter of pleasantries, I took a glass of champagne from the tray of a passing footman and sought out a quiet spot in which to compose my thoughts before returning to the crowd.

"Lady Hester."

The words raised a tingle of gooseflesh on my bare arms. Granville's voice was just as seductive as his looks.

I turned. "Good evening, Mr. Leveson Gower."

"Oh, please, call me Granville." He came closer. "All my friends do."

"Are we friends, sir?" I inquired coyly. "We hardly know each other."

"That's easily remedied." Granville offered his arm, along with a smile that would melt arctic ice. "Allow me to show you my father's library. Pitt tells me that you have an interest in political philosophy as well as military strategy, and there are a great many rare editions on both subjects in the family collections."

"I would very much like to see them," I answered. "Assuming you don't find my interests too unconventional for a lady."

"On the contrary. Conventional thinking is vastly overrated for both ladies and gentlemen."

An encouraging response. "Our thoughts align."

I spent the next half hour admiring the highlights of Lord Stafford's magnificent collection. Despite Granville's self-deprecating remark on having never finished his education at Oxford, he proved to be quite knowledgeable about the contents of the books.

By the time we finished, I was well and truly smitten. If ever there was a man who was supremely comfortable in his own skin—

*And why should he not be?* I thought. I had never met a gentleman who embodied such poise, grace, charm . . . A sidelong glance. And masculine beauty.

Knowing that Lady Stafford would expect him to mingle, I resigned myself to losing his company once we entered the main drawing room. But to my surprise, Granville stopped short of the doorway and cocked an ear.

"It appears the music is beginning," he said.

I, too, could hear the lilting notes of a country gavotte.

"Might I request a dance?" he added.

"I must give you fair warning, sir—I don't have as much experience on the dance floor as most ladies, so you may suffer a squashed toe."

"Warning acknowledged." Granville winked. "I like to live dangerously."

He led me onto the dance floor, where a number of couples were forming the figures for a cotillion. Our hands came together, his fingers curling around mine. The violins struck up the first notes, and I was quickly swept up in a whirl of sensations—our bodies moving in time to the melody, the swirl of my skirts brushing against his thighs, the beading of sweat beneath my bodice.

The dance called for us to part, and then another intricate spin brought us together again. Granville smiled. Caught up in the moment, I laughed in delight.

The music ended all too soon, and we moved to the perimeter of the room to catch our breath.

"You're an excellent dancer, Lady Hester," said Granville's mother, who was standing close by with several other regal-looking matrons.

"Your son's poise and grace would make any of his dancing partners shine," I replied.

She flashed a fond smile. "Alas, might I steal him away to greet some old family friends?"

"But of course." I made to step back, but Granville took my hand and inclined a bow.

"It was a great pleasure, milady." As he straightened, he added a whisper just loud enough for me to hear. "Until later."

* * *

The next morning, I awoke with thoughts of Granville Leveson Gower still dancing in my head. Though I would never admit it to Chatham or Pitt, I felt like a giddy schoolgirl in the throes of a first crush. My unconventional upbringing had never allowed me to have the normal experiences of a girl growing into womanhood.

Would that be a problem for Granville? I wondered, as I dressed for the coming day. I was under no illusion that he had lived a chaste life. Aristocratic gentlemen were expected, even encouraged, to sow their wild oats. There was, of course, quite a different set of rules for ladies. Not that I had even been shy about disobeying them.

So I couldn't help but wonder how he would react to learning that I was not a virgin—for of course I would tell him before accepting a proposal of marriage.

Thoughts about the rules of propriety brought me to the uncomfortable subject of Camelford. I would have to make a clean break with him, lest his wicked reputation reflect badly on me and the public's perception of a match. Granville's parents were paragons of proper behavior. I couldn't afford to have a whiff of scandal cling to my skirts.

With such solemn thoughts weighing on my mind, I headed downstairs to begin reading Pitt's daily mail. I had worked for a lengthy interlude, sorting the important letters into one pile, while writing replies to the ones that didn't require his attention, when a discreet knock sounded on the parlor door.

Annoyed at the interruption, I put my pen down. "Yes?"

"Your pardon, milady," intoned our butler, "but a gentleman is here seeking your permission for an audience with Mr. Pitt."

Before I could ask the fellow's name, Granville stepped out from the butler's shadow.

"Good heavens, sir!" I exclaimed. "You hardly need to ask—"

"Knowing that you serve as Pitt's personal secretary," he interjected, "I thought only proper that I go through the correct protocol."

My title was, of course, purely unofficial and most of Pitt's fellow politicians went straight to his office to request a meeting. That Granville was according me the same respect as he would give to a man in my position rendered me speechless for an instant. Then, quickly regathering my wits, I rose. "Come with me."

My uncle's study was just down the corridor. As was our established routine, I didn't bother to knock, but simply lifted the latch with a discreet click.

"Granville wishes to have a meeting with you," I announced.

Pitt removed his spectacles and rubbed at the bridge of his nose. "I welcome the excuse to put aside Fox's pompous and long-winded proposal for how we might together form a cabinet."

"It would never work," I muttered.

"I am trying to keep an open mind." He expelled his breath in something between a sigh and a snort. "But I agree with you."

Folding hands together atop his blotter, Pitt then raised his brows at Granville. "To what do I owe the honor of your visit?"

"I would like to get your opinion of Addington's policies toward Russia and whether it will aid our country's efforts to create an alliance with the tsar against Napoleon."

I turned to withdraw, but Pitt signaled for me to stay. "Actually, Hetty has read through the latest cabinet report on that and knows more of the details than I do. I think it would be wise to have her be part of the discussion."

"By all means," agreed Granville without a hint of hesitation. He gestured to one of the pair of chairs facing Pitt's desk. "I am concerned about trade in raw materials for our Navy—pine tar, spruce logs for masts and spars and the like—which are critical for our war efforts against France."

Pitt looked at me.

"As to that . . ." I had just compiled a summary on the subject for my uncle and so the information was fresh in my mind. I gave them an overview and then the three of us spent a lengthy interval discussing options and whether any recommendations should be communicated to Addington.

"Thank you," said Granville, once we were done. He rose. "You are fortunate to have such an excellent secretary to help with the weighty demands of political leadership, Pitt."

"I am indeed. Hetty is a rare diamond."

"So many brilliant facets," replied Granville, with a smile that took my breath away. He rose and bowed. "I shall leave you both to your work."

I spent the rest of the day floating on air.

A week passed before I saw Granville again. I was in Hatchards bookstore picking up a parcel of newly published books on political philosophy for Pitt when I encountered him at the head clerk's desk, making his own purchase.

"Lady Hester, how delightful to see you." He touched the brim of his elegant hat. "It's a lovely day. Might I tempt you to take a short walk in Green Park before we both head back to our daily duties? We can leave our packages here and return for them shortly."

I readily agreed. The park was close by, and we headed down one of the footpaths that circled through a sloping meadow where cows grazed—a popular attraction of the park was a shed where one could purchase mugs of freshly squeezed milk from the maids who ran it.

An unseasonably warm breeze tickled my cheeks, hinting that spring was coming. Granville and I chatted about the weather and laughed over the latest gossip making the rounds of the drawing rooms. The mood was light, and I marveled at how comfortable we were with each other. As we circled back to Piccadilly Street, I felt a stab of urgency about dealing with Camelford.

I knew that I must, in no uncertain terms, put the relationship behind me.

*The sooner, the better.*

After arriving home and delivering the books to Pitt's study, I hurried to my parlor workroom, resolved to act without delay. Taking a seat at my desk, I reached for my pen . . .

Only to notice a letter sitting on my blotter.

I cracked the seal, and read over its contents. And then read it again before letting the paper slip through my fingers.

"Oh, dear God," I whispered, shock and sorrow welling up in a shaky sob.

Camelford had been shot in a duel, said the note from his brother-in-law. And while he had clung to life for three days, the bullet wound had finally proved mortal.

*Dead.*

A wave of conflicting emotions washed over me as I stared down at the scrawled words. The news that the Half-Mad Lord had become a victim of his own ungovernable emotions didn't come as a complete surprise. I knew that the dark side of his being had always waged war with the innate goodness of his nature. Still, grief squeezed at my heart, and I sat for some time in tearful silence, gripped by melancholy and regret that a life so full of talents had come to such a sorry end.

A number of images flashed through my mind's eye—*Camelford at the prizefight, cheering along with his beer-swilling ruffian friends . . . his face in the bedchamber at Boconnoc, tinged fire-gold by the dancing flames in the hearth . . . the two of us dancing a jig atop a rustic tavern table . . .*

I wasn't sure whether I was laughing or crying.

Forcing the memories aside, I finally composed myself enough to wipe the tears from my cheeks, knowing that I must go inform Pitt of the sad news without further delay.

## *Chapter* 21

*March–April 1804*

The next few weeks passed in a flurry of activity. Addington's position as prime minister was becoming more precarious, and a constant stream of politicians flowed through Pitt's study as talks were held and alliances put together. I was kept busy with Uncle's correspondence and scheduling.

I had become a frequent visitor at the Stafford family townhouse, and Granville's mother appeared to enjoy my company. Given my newfound interest in fashion, I hoped she could find no fault with my appearance. As for my manners, I kept a tight rein on my tongue, careful not to appear too clever or too outspoken. Poise and charm were requisites for a diplomat's wife, so I exercised all my skills to appear the perfect patterncard for the position. And though I was loath to admit it, along with my sorrow and regret over Camelford's death, I also felt a tiny shiver of relief that his shadow would not darken my hopes for the future.

As for Granville, he had invited me to accompany him on several outings—a visit to the British Museum, a lecture by the flamboyant chemist and inventor Humphry Davy at the Royal Institution, a taste of the famous iced confections at Gunter's tea shop. I was elated that our casual friendship was deepening into something more profound.

Early in the month of April I received a note from him asking if I could perchance free myself for an entire afternoon later in the week so that we might enjoy a carriage ride out to Primrose Hill in order to explore the scenic views and historic ruins.

I arranged the release from my duties with Pitt, who didn't think to question my vague explanation as to why. When the day came, I dressed with great care, choosing a stylish walking dress in a deep smoke-tinged blue that flattered my coloring.

My Pitt diamond, of course, adorned my hand. I had come to think of it as a good luck charm. Before coming to London, I had kept my mother's precious legacy in my jewel box. But on venturing into Polite Society, I decided that having a touchstone to remind me of the strength and resourcefulness of my extraordinary maternal family would be of great moral support.

Granville gave me an admiring look when I met him in the entrance hall. "You are a vision of loveliness," he said, offering his arm and drawing me perhaps a bit closer than was quite proper.

He gestured to the waiting carriage. "Let us not waste a moment of such a glorious day."

The sun was indeed shining brightly.

The carriage wheels began rolling over the well-worn cobblestones. Granville sidled closer and draped an arm over the back of the squabs, the soft merino wool of his coat sleeve brushing against the nape of my neck.

We talked for a bit about politics and the latest debates in the House of Commons, but as we broke free from the crowded streets of Mayfair and headed north toward the more rural beauty of Primrose Hill, Granville turned the conversation to more personal matters.

"I have never met any lady quite like you, Lady Hester," he said. "You . . ." He paused, seeming to search for words. "You are different. You possess intelligence, insight, strong opinions—"

"And the gall to express them aloud," I said wryly. "Most gentlemen find that appalling."

Granville laughed. "That's likely because most gentlemen are intimidated by your rapier-sharp tongue. They don't dare cross verbal swords with you."

"And what about you, sir? Do my opinions offend you?"

The tip of his forefinger was now tracing a path along the curve of my ear. "On the contrary, I find your fire . . . exciting."

I looked up, just enough to regard him through the fringe of my lashes. Through the flickers of sun and shadow playing over his face, I saw a look in his eyes that made me smile.

"Exquisitely so." Granville leaned in close—so close that I could feel his breath against my cheeks.

His mouth sought mine.

"Forgive me for such ungentlemanly behavior," he said after several long moments had passed. "But I won't say that I'm sorry."

"Neither will I."

"Ah." My response seemed to please him. "I sensed from the start that you are a savvy, sophisticated lady of the world," he murmured, touching his lips to my brow. "Unafraid of exploring life to its fullest."

I heard a crackling as Granville reached inside his coat and pulled out a folded piece of paper. "Have you ever looked at Rowlandson's titillating etchings of men and women enjoying pleasures of the flesh?"

I was quite familiar with the satirical artist and his knife-sharp political prints. Indeed, my father had often been the butt of them. But as for his other work . . .

My eyes widened as Granville unfolded the colored print.

"This one is called *Meditations Among the Tombs*," he said.

I hesitated, and then leaned closer for a better look. The scene depicted a man and woman enjoying an intimate moment of passion in the shadows of an old church and graveyard. The fellow was leaning up against a stone lintel, his breeches tangled down around his knees. His partner—her dress was rucked up to bare her rounded bottom and shapely legs—was straddling his thighs, and the artist had depicted just enough graphic details to make it clear that . . .

*Dear heavens.* My cheeks began to burn.

"Are you shocked?"

Finding my throat too tight for speech, I slowly shook my head. The truth was, the illustration was rather arousing.

Granville laughed and kissed me. "Admit it, Lady Hester. You're no stranger to such delightful intimacies."

"I am not," I conceded. "So many rules of Society are unfair for those of my sex. I see no reason to obey them, especially as I have no voice in writing them."

"I have no argument with your reasoning, sweeting," He kissed me again.

And again.

It was the lurch of the carriage coming to a halt that jolted us apart.

"Ah, we've arrived." He threw open the door and helped me descend to the charming swath of meadowland that bordered the narrow lane. A footpath cut through the wind-ruffled grass and led up a hill where it soon disappeared into a copse of trees.

"It's a short walk up to the ruins of a Norman church," he added. "I trust you'll enjoy it."

"I'm sure I will."

Granville took my hand and we walked in companionable silence. The leaves of the swaying branches were just beginning to unfurl, their tips adding a touch of color to the woodsy shadows. The path turned steeper and through the soft flickers of newborn green I caught a glimpse of the sun-dappled weathered stone.

Granville quickened his steps. "Come, there is a lovely view from the corner of the transept."

My gaze, however, was not on the surrounding scenery once we ducked into the shadowed seclusion of the niche. Smiling, he pulled me into his arms, and teased a series of soft kisses down the line of my jaw.

How was it, I wondered, that a crumbling pile of ancient rocks could be Heaven on earth?

Granville pushed me back a step as he perched his hips on the stone lintel. I was aware of him fumbling with the fastenings of his breeches . . .

And then all rational thinking ceased.

The world around me became a blur as we joined together in the intimacies of mutual pleasure. Time floated away in a swirl of sensations. It could have been a moment . . . or an hour . . . or an eternity before we melted into a languorous stillness, allowing our heartbeats to come back down to earth.

"We had better make our way down to the carriage," he finally said, after glancing up at the cloud-dotted cerulean sky, "and return to Town before the sun dips any lower."

A curl of my hair had come free of its pin and was tickling my cheek. I caught it and tucked it behind my ear. "Yes, of course."

And yet, my world was no longer the same. The city was only several miles away, and the buildings and streets would not have moved from their familiar spots. But my heart knew that it had been transported to a place from which there was no going back.

The political situation was coming to a head, and the unremitting meetings and negotiations, which often lasted until well after midnight, were taking a toll on Pitt's health. Concerned, I roused his inner circle of advisors and together we got him to agree to leave London for a visit to Walmer Castle in order to regain his strength.

As one of his trusted allies, Granville was invited to join the gathering and arrived a few days after we did. As I oversaw the arrangements for our guests, I was able to arrange for him to be quartered in a room that allowed easy access to the outer walkway of the battlements and the various stairs leading down to the courtyards. However, I was not so besotted as to be unaware of the dangers of being caught in a dalliance. I felt confident about Granville's regard—I had, on his advice, procured the necessary intimate items to prevent unwanted consequences—but was not yet sure that I had won over his mother.

So I couldn't afford to stir any whispers of impropriety. By day, we were scrupulously polite—and professional—with each other as I participated in meetings and presided over meals and evening entertainments for the coterie of gentlemen staying with us.

But at night . . .

"Pssst." The sound was nearly lost in the breeze blowing in from the sea. Mist swirled around me as I stopped short.

Granville reached out from the shadows and pulled me from the narrow walkway that ran along the castle battlements and into a niche in the crenellated stone. "It would be a great deal more comfortable to tryst in your bedchamber," he said, after a long and lush kiss.

"And a good deal more dangerous," I whispered.

"Danger adds a certain spice to temptation."

*True.* I wasn't so foolish as to lead him to my bed, but I was powerless to resist him in all else.

His hands were already fisted in my skirts. I found the fall of his breeches and undid the fastenings. This wasn't so wicked, I told myself. We would soon be married and—

All rational thought dissolved in the moment that flesh touched flesh. I was in love, and with my passions aroused, I surrendered myself to him. Moonlight gave the tendrils of fog a silvery glow as they wrapped around us. And as the stars glittered diamond-bright against the black velvet sky, the future felt very far away.

# *Chapter* 22

*May–June 1804*

Pitt was named prime minister on May 10, 1804.

The king had given his blessing, the seals of office were handed over in the formal ritual that marked the transition from one leader to another—and suddenly my uncle was once again the most powerful man in Britain. Ten days later, Napoleon had himself crowned Emperor of France, setting the stage for another epic clash in the centuries-old battle for supremacy between the two countries.

Having served as hostess of Walmer Castle, I thought myself well prepared for the change. However, the new perquisites of such power, while unseen, were unmistakable. One moment I was merely one individual within the crowd of privileged people who made up the highest circle of Society. And then suddenly, as Pitt's hostess and private secretary, I, too, was perceived to hold power, and so I found myself elevated to a whole new different stature. Indeed, Pitt smilingly called me the First Lady of London when we went over his papers each morning. Every door was open to me. People vied for my attention. They flattered me shamelessly and sought my advice.

I loved it.

I had finally found my perfect place in the world. My opinions mattered. I had a voice—granted, a minor one—in helping to make momentous decisions that would help shape events in history.

How many ladies could say that?

Given the scope of Pitt's duties, he hired an additional private secretary to handle the correspondence and communications with Parliament. While his senior advisors on the Privy Council had grown comfortable working with me, both the House of Commons and the House of Lords would kick up a dust over having to acknowledge that a lady was capable of having government duties. His choice was William Dacres Adams, son of the mayor of Totnes and also a Member of Parliament. Like his father, Adams was an ardent political supporter of my uncle and possessed excellent organizational skills, which quickly became apparent.

Even more to his credit, he was a modest, soft-spoken fellow who treated me with great courtesy and professional respect. A friendship quickly formed between us, and we took to having a tea together every day to share our thoughts on the current political climate and how it affected Pitt's agenda.

Social demands added to the flurry of activities. Invitations arrived daily at our new official residence at Downing Street. Every hostess in London wished for us to make an appearance at their evening entertainment. I worried about my uncle and the toll such parties would take on his health, and so convinced him to let me serve as his surrogate for many of the events. He gladly relinquished the responsibilities, happy to remain home at night with a small number of his political associates for company.

As for me, I was delighted with the arrangement. Having grown up in such bleak isolation, deprived of any color and gaiety, I took shameless pleasure in the scintillating entertainments of the beau monde.

Granville was busy as well. The king had refused to let Charles Fox, Pitt's greatest adversary, be part of the cabinet, a crafty move suggested by Pitt to ensure wide support among the various political factions. Instead, my uncle was faced with the difficult task of passing measures through Parliament with a razor-thin majority.

Granville was an important advocate for Pitt with the influential diplomats of the Foreign Office. And given his own ambitions, such wheeling and dealing also gave him a chance to display his own talents.

Power and prestige was a two-edged sword. Being the center of attention meant there was less freedom to tryst with Granville. During the first heady weeks in London, we managed a few private walks in Hyde Park, but the demands of social whirl kept us in the public eye.

And yet, I decided, that could work to my advantage . . .

"What a lovely evening, Lady Stafford," I gushed, still a bit breathless from my exertions on the dance floor.

"I am glad you are enjoying yourself, Lady Hester." Granville's mother eyed my ballgown—a sinfully expensive design created by London's most exclusive modiste—with a tiny nod of approval. "You are looking well. London life appears to agree with you." She watched her son, who had just squired me through a cotillion, move across the room to greet one of his diplomatic colleagues, and then brought her gaze back to me. "How are you enjoying your residence on Downing Street?"

"Pitt is delighted to be back," I responded.

Another nod. "His return makes a great many other people happy. Granville believes your uncle is the best man for the job in these troubled times."

"That is kind of him to say."

She eyed me with a speculative look. "Granville is an astute politician. He doesn't allow personal feelings to cloud his judgment on affairs of state."

"Your son is both wise and pragmatic," I replied. As was his mother, so I added a subtle reminder that I could help in his ascent. "No wonder Pitt sees him as a rising star in the Tory party."

A hint of a smile touched her lips.

"Oh look, Lady Marquand has arrived," said one of Lady Stafford's companions. "We really must go and greet her."

"But of course," I said, dipping a parting nod and retreating several steps. As they moved away, I headed for the refreshments room. Satisfied that I had gained another point in my favor, I deemed myself deserving of some champagne.

"Are you celebrating something special, Lady Hester?" The coy question, asked by a familiar voice, sounded from just behind me as I raised the glass to my lips.

I turned to face Princess Caroline. As her estranged husband, the Prince of Wales, was a political enemy of the Tories, she was a welcome guest at parties given by Pitt's allies. We hadn't seen each other since the weeks I had spent in Weymouth, and I had forgotten that her eyes always seemed to spark with a scheming glint.

"Just the pleasure of enjoying a lovely evening in the company of good friends," I replied, after taking a sip of the wine.

Princess Caroline's sly grin stretched wider. "I have heard that one of the guests is a *very* good friend."

I merely smiled.

Laughing, she took my arm. "I shall not tease you." A pause. "At least, not for the moment." After plucking up a glass of sparkling wine from one of the trays, she steered me toward a side salon. "Tell me, how is your dashing cousin, Sir Sidney Smith? What a pity his duties with the Royal Navy prevent him from spending time here in London."

"Our country is at war, Your Royal Highness. So, alas, much as Sidney would enjoy the pleasure of your company, the choice is not his to make," I said dryly. I was aware—Sidney had admitted as much to me just before I had left Weymouth—that the princess and my cousin had engaged in an affair. "His latest letter reported that he is working with the American inventor Robert Fulton to develop innovative new weapons to destroy any French invasion fleet that might sail from the Belgian coast."

"Such a clever, clever man," observed Princess Caroline. "Don't you adore a man who is constantly looking for ways to improve his performance in whatever he does?"

My lips twitched. "Indeed."

A throaty laugh sounded, and with a flutter of her lashes, she said, "Speaking of clever men, have you heard the latest gossip about your uncle's friend, George Canning . . . ?"

We continued to chat about the peccadilloes of the ton as we made our way to the main drawing room. Spotting a wave from a group of gentlemen demanding her presence, Princess Caroline slowly released my arm.

"I must take my leave and attend to my friends, but we still have much on which to catch up, Lady Hester," she remarked. "I have a sitting at Thomas Lawrence's studio tomorrow at two o'clock for a portrait he is painting of me. Though we usually do our sessions at Montagu House, my residence in Blackheath, as a favor he asked to meet with me at Greek Street. Do promise that you will come and keep me company. Otherwise, I shall be bored to perdition."

My first inclination was to decline. I found the princess best enjoyed in small doses. However, I suddenly recalled hearing Granville mention that he, too, was sitting for a portrait by Lawrence. So her invitation would give me a chance to see the work in progress.

"That sounds delightful," I answered. "I greatly admire Lawrence's work, and it would be a pleasure to see his studio." A prodigy in drawing and painting since childhood, the artist was the darling of London Society and had garnered accolades for his rich colors, exquisite brushwork, and sympathetic likenesses.

But Lawrence was far from a mere flatterer. Like all great portrait artists, he had the uncanny ability to see beneath his subject's skin and capture their essence. He was never cruel, but however subtle, he always depicted the truth of what he saw.

"Excellent!" exclaimed Princess Caroline. "Then I shall see you on the morrow."

A pleasant scent of mingled linseed oil and pine spirits greeted me as I entered the house that Thomas Lawrence had converted into his art studio on the following afternoon. The entrance foyer was in a state of cheerful disarray, with rolls of canvas crammed between wooden stretchers, crates of supplies, and broken easels.

As the young assistant who answered my knock led me through a corridor leading to the back of the house, I had to flatten my skirts around my legs to keep them from brushing against the unfinished paintings popped up along the wall.

Another assistant darted by us with a jar bristling with freshly cleaned brushes. "Hurry!" he barked to my guide. "He needs you to mix up a batch of cadmium red!"

"Is it always this busy?" I inquired.

"Our master is in much demand," answered the young man. He pointed to a set of double doors up ahead. "You're to go through there," he added, before disappearing into a side room.

Bemused—the creative temperament was rarely tidy as I knew from experience with my father—I did as I was told. I was curious to meet Lawrence as it turned out that he and William Adams, my uncle's new private secretary, were good friends. Adams sung the artist's praises, both personally and professionally, and I had come to trust his judgment.

Pressing my palms to the dark-paneled oak, I pushed the doors open and found myself in a large, light-filled room, its walls and woodwork painted in a shade of soft white.

"Lady Hester!"

I looked to my right and saw Princess Caroline perched on a roll-armed settee upholstered in a damask fabric patterned in hues of red and orange. She was wearing a sumptuous red velvet gown with a froth of white ruffling at the neck and an underlayer of white silk peeking out from beneath the puffed short sleeves. On her head was a high-crown hat with a turned-up brim made of matching red velvet, a single white ostrich plume curling down at a jaunty angle from an oval brooch.

"Thank heavens you've arrived," she added, giving a careless flick of the arrow-shaped brass ornament in her hand. "Tommy is getting quite cross with me for fidgeting."

"Not precisely cross, Your Majesty . . ."

I looked around, trying to spot the speaker, but could see only a small flutter of fabric as my view was blocked by the back of a large stretched canvas sitting on a sturdy artist's easel.

"I am merely concerned," continued the male voice. "When a subject is distracted, a bit of inner life fades from the face."

Princess Caroline expelled a martyred sigh. "Lady Hester will sit and chat with me about all the delicious gossip floating through the drawing rooms. That will perk up my emotions." A trill of laughter. "The miseries of others always makes me forget about my own."

A man—I assumed it was Lawrence as he was wearing a paint-spattered smock that reached down to his knees—came around the side table by the easel and inclined a courtly bow.

"Welcome, Lady Hester. I would be grateful for your assistance in keeping Her Majesty amused."

I immediately liked the glint of good-natured humor that flashed in his eyes. He was a rather plain-looking fellow with a bald pate and fringe of dark hair that framed his ordinary features. But his gaze gave him an arresting presence. I could understand why he had a reputation for being a great favorite with the ladies of the beau monde.

"I shall do my best, sir," I replied.

Lawrence called for one of his assistants and had the young man move an armchair close to the raised platform on which Princess Caroline was sitting. I took a moment to admire the backdrop created for the painting before taking my place. A dark brown canvas hung behind the princess, with a marble plinth and classic bust adding a touch of gravitas to the scene. The muted shades were clearly designed to make the red velvet stand out like a flame.

An apt metaphor for her fiery personality.

My admiration for the artist and his understanding of human nature rose another notch.

I dutifully engaged Princess Caroline in parsing through the latest scandals in Society—including one involving her errant husband, which brought a look of unholy delight to her face.

"Perfect, perfect," encouraged Lawrence, and I did my best to draw out the story.

After another short interlude, the princess began to look fatigued from holding her pose, and so Lawrence suggested a break for her to retreat to a curtained area where a chaise longue had been set up for her comfort.

"Would you permit me to have a look at the canvas?" I asked as one of the assistants escorted Princess Caroline to her place of rest.

"Of course." Lawrence began cleaning his brushes as I circled around him and took up a position in front of the work in progress.

Liquid swirled, glass clinked against glass.

I continued to study the portrait. The composition had been sketched out in broad strokes, the dress and background indicated by blocks of color, as yet devoid of detail. All of his attention was currently concentrated on the princess's face . . .

Lawrence continued to fiddle with his art materials, unperturbed by my silence.

Stepping closer, I gazed at the painted eyes, and slowly drew in a deep breath. "Extraordinary!" Turning to look at Lawrence, I added, "You are truly extraordinary, sir. How is it that you can breathe such life into inanimate oil and pigment?"

He shrugged. "I merely look closely and record what I see."

"You do far more than that." I took another moment to look at Princess Caroline and then stepped back. "Might I see some of your other works in progress?" I asked. "I understand you are working on a full-length portrait of Granville Leveson Gower."

"Ah, yes. The modern-day Adonis." Lawrence smiled. "A friend?"

"He and my uncle are close confidants," I answered obliquely.

If he noticed my evasion, he gave no sign of it. "Let us see what you think," he said. "Come this way."

We threaded our way through more jumbled art supplies and into a side room, which was also filled with light from the north-facing windows. The portrait of Granville—it was almost life-sized—was propped up against the far wall and appeared to be nearly finished.

Holding my breath, I moved closer, the likeness so eerily good that it was unnerving. It wasn't just the facial features, which were excellent but not quite perfect. It was the attitude, the aura of supreme confidence in his posture. He was standing with a relaxed nonchalance, one hand fisted on his hip, the other arm resting atop a drapery-covered plinth, legs casually crossed at the knees.

"You've captured Granville's essence," I observed, but in truth, I was a little surprised by the flatness of the painted eyes and the faint look of self-entitlement hovering at the corners of his mouth. "Though perhaps you made his expression a little too haughty."

"Have I?" said Lawrence softly.

"Yes," I answered. "He's kinder and more sensitive than you show."

Lawrence looked about to reply but then seemed to reconsider.

"What?" I pressed.

He allowed a faint smile. "Clearly your perceptions are better than mine, milady."

*Yes, I know him far better*, I told myself. And yet I felt uneasy. Lawrence struck me as someone who saw through flesh and bone to wherever one's soul was hidden.

Turning away from the canvas, I was about to suggest we head back to the main studio when a smaller unfinished portrait sitting on a tabletop easel caught my eye.

"Why, that's General Moore!" I exclaimed, pausing to examine the face. The first thing that struck me was the warmth of Moore's expression and the kindness in his eyes.

"Yes, he was loath to sit for me, but his good friend General Sir Robert Brownrigg wished to have his likeness to hang in their regimental headquarters, so he reluctantly agreed."

Eschewing the peacock splendor worn by many generals, Moore had chosen to appear in a simple red military coat, with modest gold epaulettes and a double row of buttons as its only adornments.

"He has a lovely smile and a kind gaze"—I gave a wry grimace—"which seems at odds with a military man who spends his life killing people."

Lawrence made no reply.

"I do wonder . . ." I leaned in closer. "You chose not to add the scars to his face. They only add to his humanity."

That drew a low laugh from Lawrence. "Yes, Moore protested that I was making him look way too pretty. However, I tried to explain about artistic license, for it is my impression that the public wants to imagine that their heroes are perfect."

"But . . ." I frowned in thought. "But to me, scars are what make you a true hero—they show the courage and suffering it takes to triumph over fear and adversity."

Lawrence looked pensive. We both continued to stare at Moore's likeness until a plaintive feminine voice rose in need from the main studio.

"Where is everyone?"

"Coming, Your Majesty," called Lawrence. He offered me his arm. "Patience," he observed, "is not one of her virtues."

My mouth quirked. Princess Caroline's scandalous behavior was no secret. "I daresay she possesses precious few virtues."

He cleared his throat with a cough—or perhaps it was a laugh.

As we came to the doorway, Lawrence drew me to a halt. "I would very much like to paint your portrait, Lady Hester."

"Absolutely not," I replied without hesitation.

"Why not?"

"You see too much, sir," I said. "My soul—my strengths, my shortcomings—is not something I choose to put on display for the edification of strangers."

"You need not display the painting in public," he replied. "It could simply be hung in your quarters, to be enjoyed in private."

"Thank you for the offer, but again, no. I would rather not be forced to come face-to-face with my flaws on a daily basis."

Princess Caroline called again.

"The arbiters of privilege and power are clamoring for your superb talents, sir," I added. "Don't waste them on me."

# Chapter 23

*July–August 1804*

Much as I liked Mr. Lawrence, my encounter with him had left me unsettled, though I couldn't quite say why. But as the following week passed in another whirl of glamorous gatherings, I managed to push aside my brooding and enjoy being at the center of London's highest circle of Society. It was a heady experience—I truly was feeling at the peak of my powers. Not only was I courted for my opinions by influential politicians but I was also much sought after for casual conversation and as a dance partner.

Indeed, an acquaintance from my earlier days in London had become particularly attentive. Noel Hill, a Member of Parliament from Shrewsbury and rising diplomat, had served as an attaché to the British chargé d'affaires during the Peace of Amiens and barely escaped with his life when war was declared. We had become friendly before my trip to the Continent, and he appeared interested in rekindling the relationship.

A handsome fellow—though he couldn't hold a candle to Granville's masculine beauty—he was a pleasant companion and I did nothing to discourage his attention. It did no harm for Granville and his family to see that I was surrounded by admirers.

The week's festivities ended with a gala ball given by a visiting prince of the Russian Imperial court, and as I spun across the dance floor with one handsome gentleman after another, I felt like a meteor—a bright, shining point of light streaking through the starry heavens.

The next day began with an even warmer glow.

My meetings with Granville were becoming less frequent as we both had pressing political demands. So I was elated when a note arrived from him, arranging a rendezvous in a secluded part of the gardens adjoining St. James's Palace later that afternoon. I dressed with care, and a glance in the cheval glass showed that my looks were at their peak. Happiness had my eyes sparkling and my cheeks flushed with a rosy hue.

*Passionate kisses, intimate pleasures.* I missed him, body and soul.

"Soon," I assured myself as I snatched up my Kashmir shawl and hurried down the stairs. "Soon we shall be together, partners in every way that matters."

My loyal maid Susan—I knew she was utterly trustworthy— met me in the entrance hall and we made our way to St. James's Park. A short stroll brought us to the carriageway leading past Constitution Hill, and as we passed the thick copse of trees at the far end of the palace gardens, I checked that we were alone, and then discreetly melted into the trees to await Granville.

Susan continued on to do a few errands and would return in an hour to escort me back to Downing Street.

Sunlight flickered through the overhead leaves, sparks that spread a golden warmth through every fiber of my being as I reached our rendezvous spot, a secluded place we had used several times before. A breeze ruffled through the trees, its whisper echoing my own anticipation. The minutes slipped by—too slowly for my liking. I began to pace a meandering circle to dispel my impatience, hoping the burn rising to my cheeks wasn't turning them an unflattering shade of red.

*Damnation.*

At some point my impatience turned to annoyance, though I

knew that any number of reasons could have arisen to make Granville late. But after an hour had passed, I had to concede that he wasn't coming.

Though I knew it was irrational, I felt a pinch of humiliation to have been left in the lurch. Gritting my teeth, I returned to the edge of the carriageway, where my maid was dutifully waiting. I rejoined her once I was sure that we were unobserved. Experienced in reading my moods, she remained tactfully silent and kept her head down as I turned and set out for home.

No doubt there would be an effusive note of apology waiting for me back at Downing Street explaining the delay . . .

But to my surprise, there wasn't.

Pleading an indisposition, I asked for a supper tray to be sent up to my quarters. At the top of the stairs, I encountered Elizabeth, who caught my arm with a cluck of concern.

"You look peaked," she said. "Perhaps . . . perhaps you are taking on too much."

She was clever and perceptive, and as we had come to be good friends, I wondered if she suspected my illicit entanglement with Granville.

"I simply have a beastly headache," I replied.

Elizabeth hesitated, but then merely nodded. "Take care of yourself," she responded. "If it lingers, please don't hesitate to consult with me on a remedy."

"I'm quite sure it will pass," I said, and hurried on to my quarters.

As soon as my meal arrived, I sent the servant back downstairs to check whether the butler had neglected to send up any messages.

But no, there was still no word from Granville.

I was no longer simply annoyed, I was fuming. The slow burn in the pit of my belly erupted in flames.

"How dare he!" I muttered.

As I paced by my escritoire, I snatched up my pen, feeling the urge to vent my anger by throwing something against the wall. Instead, I paused and twirled it between my fingers.

A moment later, I was in my chair and slapped a piece of note-paper down on my blotter. After scribbling a message—I was surprised the ink didn't ignite into flames—I hurriedly sealed it and sent it off with a footman.

I then forced myself to sit down and read through some reports on the state of the volunteer militias and coastal defenses near Walmer Castle. Seeing the familiar names of several senior officers who had come to be friends helped to calm my emotions.

In thinking over what I had just penned, I conceded that I was prone to intemperate reactions when I thought myself or my loved ones unfairly used. My father's shameful treatment of my brothers had exacerbated the tendency. I had precious little tolerance for selfish narcissism.

But in all honesty, I think it was simply in my blood to be head-strong—sometimes to a fault.

Nonetheless, I didn't regret it. He had made me feel like a common strumpet, skulking among the trees waiting for an assignation. I had no intention of accepting anything other than an equal partnership with a gentleman, one based on mutual respect. Too many ladies relinquished the right of independent thought in exchange for a life of . . .

"A life of unquestioning servitude," I whispered to myself. "I shall never be one of them."

It was another hour before a note finally arrived from Granville. The apology was not quite as abject as I might have wished. However, I could not argue with his reason. Understanding the inner workings of politics as I did, I knew that the complexities of some meetings were such that any interruption, however small, could destroy the mood.

The next day, Granville invited me for a carriage ride through Hyde Park. My position as Pitt's private secretary allowed me to accept without stirring gossip. Had Society known of Granville's secret penchant for erotic books—he had quite a collection filled with graphic images—they might not have thought him so perfect. To me, they were intriguing rather than shocking. And as Granville found them highly arousing, I had no objection to perusing the pages as a prelude to our pleasures.

"Am I forgiven?" he asked, after we had rearranged our clothing and sat back on the soft leather seat. The carriage curtains were, of course, drawn and only a faint flutter of light danced over the sensuous curl of his lips.

Considering what delicious things that mouth had just been doing—I blushed to recall them even within the privacy of my own thoughts—I found it impossible to remain angry at him.

"You are," I replied, reaching out to fasten a button on his trousers that had been left undone. "But I trust you won't make a habit of forgetting our engagements."

He feathered a kiss down the line of my jaw. "Surely you know that you're in my thoughts night and day."

A purr of pleasure slipped from my lips. "Is your afternoon free tomorrow?"

"Alas, no, sweetening. My time is not my own these days." Another kiss. "I shall send you word of when we can next meet."

Though our trysts were not as frequent as I would have liked, I understood the reasons. I knew from Pitt's endless meetings with his cabinet and my own efforts to handle the flow of his personal correspondence that the government was facing a number of difficulties in meeting the challenges of war with France. William Adams—the two of us made an excellent team in supporting my uncle—corroborated the fraught feelings in Parliament. When Pitt had first come to power in 1783, he had been able to count on the king's stalwart support. These days, however, the monarch's sanity was in question, and the different factions in Parliament, including some within his own Tory party, were opposed to a number of his initiatives.

Both Adams and I could see that the strain of the job was taking its toll on Pitt's health. *Too few hours of sleep and too many bottles of port.* As for Granville, my uncle had recently appointed him a member of his Privy Council. He was now part of Pitt's inner circle of power, a change in stature that reflected well on his skills and his charm. I was exceedingly proud of him—even though it further curtailed our time together.

As July slipped into August, my niggling concerns about our relationship grew sharper. My notes to him were once answered within hours, but now it took longer and longer to wrest a reply.

Though worry was beginning to gnaw at my self-assurance, I continued to attend the nightly parties and entertainments. Dancing, flirting, entertaining the gentlemen with my bon mots—I threw myself wholeheartedly into the glittering world of the beau monde, hoping that word of my popularity would remind Granville not to take me for granted. My diplomat friend Noel Hill continued his attentions. His dry, self-deprecating wit was amusing and a balm for my bruised spirits. So I made no effort to discourage his increasingly effusive admiration.

Still, it took me by surprise when one evening he drew me out to the garden terrace off the grand ballroom of our host's town house and, under the glimmer of starlight, made a proposal of marriage.

I was gentle in my refusal and he took the rejection well, declaring that it would not alter his devotion to me.

Hill's footsteps receded as I lifted my face to the gentle breeze and regarded the full moon, nestled like a pearl in the black velvet sky.

"The heavens move with predictable precision, while we mortals often struggle to find our way."

I whirled around at the sound of the familiar voice.

"You are looking very well," said Brummell. "Life at the pinnacle of power seems to suit you."

We had seen very little of each other since my return from the Continent. I had been living at Walmer Castle until recently and knew from Society gossip that Brummell had been invited to spend much of the summer in Ireland at the governor-general's estate.

"In that we are alike," I replied.

"Indeed." He, too, gazed up at the canopy of stars. As always, his appearance was exquisitely elegant. Not a wrinkle or mote of dust marred the understated perfection. But when he turned to face me, his smile did not quite reach his eyes.

"I hear you've made quite a conquest." A dismissive wave. "Not that puppy Hill, but a far more influential gentleman."

There was an edge to his tone that I didn't like. "Yes. He possesses refined taste and manners to go along with his wealth and intelligence. Surely not even you can find fault with such a paragon."

Brummell gave a small shake of his head. "Another mistake."

"And yet, it was you who taught me that if one wants to be respected and have a place at the pinnacle of Society, one should be wise enough to align oneself with those who hold privilege and power," I retorted. "So kindly explain to me how I have erred."

He hesitated. Laughter floated out through the open doors of the ballroom as the sedate notes of a quadrille gave way to the livelier melody of a country reel.

"I've said enough. I think you've learned all you can from me, so I have no further words of wisdom to offer." Brummell's expression softened. "Do know that I care about your happiness, Hetty."

"And I yours," I replied quickly, happy to seize the olive branch.

"Then all is well."

We stood for a little longer, watching the flames of the terrace torchieres dance with the night shadows.

"I must be off. I've promised my presence at another party." He took my hand and bestowed a gentlemanly kiss. "I'm glad to know that we part as friends."

When I returned home that evening and found no missive from Granville, I confess that for a fleeting moment I wondered whether Brummell's remark had a grain of truth to it. But I quickly shook off the thought.

Granville was meant for me. I would not be denied.

The following week began with a much-desired tryst that left me sure that Granville's ardor had not diminished. And yet, as several days passed with not a word from him, my apprehensions came creeping back. The next morning I woke to the gloom of a rainy day. But despite feeling low, I consoled myself with the fact that I would be attending a ball that evening, and could count on the flattery and flirtations of my other gentlemen admirers to lift my spirits. I rather hoped that Lady Stafford would be in attendance so that she could report back to her son on my popularity.

Politics had taught me to be Machiavellian, so I would be sure to drop a few discreet hints to her that if he didn't declare soon, he might be in danger of losing me.

With that in mind, I took extra care with my appearance, choosing my most sumptuous gown and having my maid style my hair with a winsome arrangement of curls framing my face.

Heads turned as I went through the receiving line—Pitt had cried off, claiming exhaustion—and I was soon surrounded by gentlemen eager to ask my opinion of the upcoming debates in Parliament. I passed a pleasant interlude discussing politics and drinking port—I had returned to the lesson Brummell had taught me about standing out in a crowd—before drifting off to one of the side salons to enjoy a few moments of quiet solitude before heading to the ballroom.

"Congratulations, Lady Hester. It appears you have become the Diamond of London."

I turned and gave the Duchess of Devonshire a cool smile as she joined me in an alcove created by a set of bookshelves. Georgiana's words were flattering but her tone held a caustic edge.

"You, of all people, know that politics has nothing to do with personal feelings," I replied tartly. "Gentlemen cozy up to me because they seek information."

"Not all of them." Georgiana took a step closer and lowered her voice. "It's been observed that you've caught the eye of Granville Leveson Gower." A pause. "The most handsome man in all of Britain."

I couldn't repress a smile. "He is, isn't he?"

"Indeed. Even your uncle equates him to Hadrian's Antinous."

The reference to the ancient Roman emperor's admiration for a

Greek youth of fabled beauty drew a fluttery sigh from me. "I daresay the comparison is apt."

"You're the envy of every lady in London. It would be *most* unfair of you not to feel a tendre in return," pressed Georgiana. "Tell me, is he just as charming in private as he is in public?"

I merely smiled.

"I thought so," said the duchess with a knowing wink. "Will there soon be an announcement?"

The same question had been preying on my thoughts, and despite the fact that I didn't consider Georgiana a friend, I replied with unfettered honesty. "I hope so," I admitted. "Given my interest and experience in politics, I think we would make a perfect pair."

"You would expect to advise him on matters of government and diplomacy?"

"Of course," I said.

She arched her brows. "Granville might not welcome *that* sort of closeness."

Unlike me, Georgiana wielded her political influence in the traditional feminine way. She used her charms and her social connections to curry support for Charles Fox and the Whigs. But the duchess didn't think it her place to advise the gentlemen on actual policies and initiatives. She used her head, I thought a little snidely, merely as a perch for her flamboyant hats.

"I think you misjudge Granville's willingness to recognize a lady's talents and take them seriously," added Georgiana.

She then turned and gave a quick wave to someone lingering just outside the aureole of the candlelight. It was only then that I realized her sister Harriet had approached while I was speaking. "What do *you* think of Lady Hester's assertion that Granville admires ladies for their intellect as well as their charm?"

By the look on her face, Harriet did not approve of her sister's question. "My opinion is irrelevant. As is yours," she said pointedly. "It is not our business to probe Lady Hester's personal feelings or what understanding she might have with a gentleman."

"I merely wish to applaud her if she has managed to win a proposal of marriage from Granville," responded Georgiana.

"Perhaps," said Harriet softly, "she doesn't wish to discuss such intimate matters. One's feelings for a gentleman are something that one discusses with a close friend, not a casual acquaintance."

I appreciated her discretion, but as I had already confided that I thought Granville and I were perfect together, I decided there was no need for prevarication. Besides, a small part of me wanted to impress the duchess, who always seemed to think that she was the most interesting and alluring lady in the room.

"I don't mind answering," I said. "Yes, I am in love with Granville. He is all that is admirable in a gentleman—honorable, kind, intelligent."

Harriet paled, and for an instant I thought I saw her sway.

Concerned, I reached out to steady her—

"F-forgive me," said Harriet, as she braced a hand on the side table and began fanning her face. "It's frightfully warm in here. I fear I am in need of a breath of fresh air."

"Let me help you find a secluded spot where you can sit and recover," said the duchess, offering her sister an arm.

"That would be best," replied Harriet, offering me a wan smile. "Again, my apologies, Lady Hester."

I watched them walk away and disappear into the corridor, feeling a pang of sympathy for Harriet. Trapped in a loveless marriage with a violent brute of a husband, she must be living a very lonely and unhappy life.

The thought made me feel a little guilty for my current happiness. But then I reminded myself that I had weathered a great many storms and rough seas before sailing into a safe harbor.

"You are looking unsettled." Princess Caroline appeared, a flicker of flame-red through the muted shadows. She cast a knowing look at the doorway and shook her head in mute disapproval. "The Duchess of Devonshire takes delight in fomenting Trouble."

"Perhaps because her private life is just as unhappy as that of her sister's," I mused, thinking of how her husband had come to be lovers with Georgiana's best friend, forcing her to live in a *ménage à trois*. "Her current situation cannot be a comfortable one."

"Men make our lives miserable," said the princess. "If you think any differently, then I fear you will be horribly disappointed."

"Surely there are exceptions," I said softly, though it took several moments to think of one. "My maternal grandmother, Lady Chatham, had a long and happy life with Pitt the Elder."

Princess Caroline carefully smoothed at a crease in her skirts. "Are you sure?"

I felt a flutter of doubt. What did I really know of their life together? I had been hardly more than a baby when my grandfather shuffled off this mortal coil.

A mournful sigh filled the silence, which for some reason stirred a prickling of gooseflesh on my bare arms. Like the duchess, the princess had a knack for roiling the waters.

My discomfort became more pronounced as she took my arm and drew me deeper into the shadows. We were now alone in the room as the dancing had started and the other guests had drifted off to join in the gaiety of the ballroom. I could hear the faint notes of a country reel, the capering melody at odds with the fraught mood that now gripped me.

"I dislike being the bearer of unpleasant news," said Princess Caroline. "Truly I do. But it pains me deeply to know that you are in the dark about certain things." Her eyes pooled with sympathy. "You have a right to know the truth. Hurtful as it may feel at this moment, I think it will save you from even more grievous pain later."

My throat was suddenly so tight that even had I wished to do so, I couldn't have uttered a sound.

"It concerns Granville Leveson Gower," continued the princess. "He is not the paragon of perfection that you believe him to be."

I managed to compose my emotions and find my voice, though it wasn't as steady as I might have wished. "I'm not as naïve as you seem to think. Only a fool would be under the illusion that any mere mortal is perfect. We all have flaws."

"There are flaws," said Princess Caroline slowly, "and then there are selfish indulgences."

Her words made my blood turn cold.

"Forgive me, but I am in no mood for word games. If you have something specific you wish to tell me, just say it."

The princess hesitated, fixing me with a sorrowful look. "Very well." Another sigh. "The two sisters who just left you are *not* your friends. Granville has been intimately involved with Harriet, Lady Bessborough, for years. In fact, she has borne him two children, a fact which she's managed to keep hidden from her husband—not a difficult thing as they so rarely see each other—and the rest of the beau monde."

*No.* I fisted my hands. *No, no, no.*

"I don't believe it." But even as I said the words, I felt a knife-like stab of doubt. "If it's such a well-kept secret, how do *you* know?"

"No secret, however closely guarded, is ever safe in London," she replied. "I have a great many sources who keep me informed on intimate gossip. And Georgiana is not always discreet about what she confides to her closest friends when she is in her cups."

"But . . ." I grasped for some reason to prove the princess was wrong. "Harriet must be at least ten years older than Granville."

"Twelve," she responded. "My sources tell me that the two of them became lovers when he was twenty-one."

"Dear God," I whispered.

"I'm so sorry," replied Princess Caroline. "But I promise you that it's all true."

Dizzy with the shock of such a betrayal, I shook off her hold and steadied myself against the wall.

"Men," muttered Caroline. "They are self-absorbed, selfish creatures. Use them for pleasure, but don't ever, ever entrust them with your heart."

*Too late for that.*

I sucked in a breath. "Even if you are right, he cannot marry Harriet as she is the wife of another. And a gentleman in Granville's political position must have a wife."

"I have heard that Georgiana has broached the idea to her sister of having Granville marry her daughter, Harry-o," replied Caroline. "Might as well keep all the flim-flummery in the family."

"But that's . . ." I searched for a word to express my horror. "That's depraved."

"I imagine that Granville's family might think it unseemly, too. My guess is that they will counsel him to choose a dewy-eyed young virgin fresh from the schoolroom, one who will dutifully play her role without kicking up a dust."

I squeezed my eyes shut, willing myself not to spill a single teardrop. "He would be bored to perdition by an inexperienced schoolgirl."

Princess Caroline allowed an ironic smile. "That's why they have mistresses."

A part of me—the self-confident Pitt side of my family who let no obstacle stand in their way—refused to surrender to despair. Now that I knew the enemy, the battle was just beginning.

"We'll see about what choice Granville Leveson Gower ultimately decides to make."

# Chapter 24

In a surprising show of tact—she seemed to thrive on misery—Princess Caroline retreated, leaving me alone to come to grips with what I had just heard.

Rage warred with self-pity. I wasn't sure whether to curse to the high heavens or wallow in a fit of weeping.

*How could Granville not see all the ways in which we fit together perfectly?* I thought, reining in my emotions to enumerate all the attributes I would bring to a marriage. *I understood the nuances of politics better than any other potential bride . . . I was experienced in running a large and complex household . . . I had the wit and charm to deal with difficult gentlemen . . . I wasn't shocked by his sexual tastes . . .*

There were likely other positives to enumerate, but the one quality he would never get from me was tolerance of his dalliances. I would not turn a blind eye on him having a mistress. It was all very well for a gentleman to sow his wild oats as a young, carefree bachelor. However, I considered marriage vows to be a binding oath.

Lies and deceit were for unprincipled ladies like Harriet and Georgiana. I hated their slyness and their subterfuges. Society made it difficult, but a lady ought to have a code of honor.

And live by it.

Fuming with righteous indignation, I left the ball and returned home, where I took refuge in my study and penned a letter to Granville.

*Fire and ice.* Veering between hot and cold, I poured out my emotions on page after page, making no effort to temper my words, or the anguish and pain his actions had caused me. I didn't stop to think about how I expected him to reply. In the throes of betrayal, all I could think about was my feelings, not his.

It was hardly a surprise when no reply was waiting for me the next morning. It had been late by the time I sent a servant to deliver my missive to his lodgings. There was, I thought rather nastily, the chance that he had been dallying with Harriet and was not yet aware that his perfidy was now known.

After forcing down a cup of tea and a piece of dry toast, I took refuge in my duties to Pitt, reading and sorting through the morning post and writing short summaries of several reports. As I worked, my emotions slowly began to settle and a part of me began to rue letting my temper get the better of me.

Pitt blood, I conceded, was quick to boil. And from my own experience with my family, I knew that reactions made in the heat of the moment were rarely good ones.

My uncle came into the parlor where I had my desk. It was just past breakfast but he was already hunched over, as if he were carrying the weight of the world on his bony shoulders. He paused to wipe his spectacles on the sleeve of his coat, and I saw that the hollows beneath his eyes were getting deeper.

"Has Canning sent his reactions to the speech Fox made to Parliament yesterday?" he queried.

"I'm just finishing writing up an outline of the salient points."

A smile. "What would I do without you, dear Hetty?"

"You would get on just fine," I replied, though his words made me feel better as I returned to organizing my desk.

"What about Granville's financial report for the Privy Council meeting this afternoon?"

I didn't look up. "It doesn't appear to have arrived yet."

Pitt made no comment.

"Shall I send word to his residence, reminding him that you prefer to read over all the reports before the meetings begin?"

He considered the question for a moment before releasing a sigh. "No. I trust that he will explain the nuances to us during the meeting."

A footman interrupted us for a moment as he rushed in to hand me a packet of documents from the Admiralty.

"I fear that all of my council members have been asked to do more than their fair share of work," continued my uncle as I began sorting through the papers. "The king's current mental state is making it deucedly difficult for me to govern."

Negotiating compromises and forging alliances were key to making the wheels of government spin smoothly. The king hated the Whigs as they supported the Prince of Wales's politics, and with his wits in current disarray, there was no reasoning with him. And that put Pitt in a precarious position because it limited his option in choosing senior officials.

As I considered the problem, a thought—granted a self-serving one—came to mind. Even the most honorable men used subtle or oblique manipulation when striving to achieve the result they wanted. Why should I not employ the same methods?

"I fear that I may be guilty of making things a trifle harder for you," I said. I was furious with Granville, but I believed that I could make him see what a good match we were. "I have been taking up more of Granville's time that I should."

"Nonsense. He finds your views on current affairs to be insightful—"

"I'm not speaking of work, Uncle," I cut in. "Granville and I have been enjoying leisure time together, sharing walks in the park and visits to bookshops."

*Along with other unmentionable activities.*

It took a moment for the implication of my meaning to dawn on him. "The two of you have . . ." An embarrassed cough. "The two of you have formed a romantic attachment?"

I flashed my most brilliant smile, reminding myself of the old adage that all is fair in love and war. "It feels so natural. We share so many interests."

My intent was to use my uncle as an unwitting ally. By speaking to Granville with the assumption that the two of us were contemplating marriage, it would put subtle but unmistakable pressure on Granville to declare himself to me.

After all, most ladies of the beau monde used their wiles to wrest a proposal of marriage. Given their druthers, gentlemen were in no hurry to be caught in the parson's mousetrap.

"By Jove," he mumbled. "I . . ."

I had never seen Britain's greatest orator so at a loss for words.

"I, er, yes, I can see that you do," he added.

"There is no formal understanding," I added. "Not yet. But it seems to me that we would have every reason to anticipate a happy future together."

"Indeed," he said softly, looking pensive. "Indeed."

Taking up a sheaf of papers from the Foreign Office that I had organized earlier, I held it out to him. "Have a look at these while I go order you a pot of tea."

I deliberately absented myself from Downing Street before the meeting of the Privy Council was set to convene. I assumed that Granville would arrive early and wish to have a private word with me—a clever move that would limit the amount of time in which I could ring a peal over his head.

My strategy was to let him stew over the coming confrontation throughout his meeting. Then, he would have no choice but to come seek me out. To do otherwise would be admitting that he was a craven coward.

Mean-spirited, perhaps, but to my mind he deserved it.

I returned from an errand to Hatchards bookshop and made a point of sequestering myself in my parlor with the door shut. The mantel clock measured off the passing minutes . . .

And then came a tentative knock.

I waited a long moment. "Come in."

The latch clicked. Granville entered and then shut the door behind him.

My chest clenched, squeezing the air from my lungs. His physical beauty always took my breath away.

"Lady Hester." His voice sounded unruffled as he dipped his chin and gestured at the chair facing mine. "May I be permitted to sit?"

I nodded, glad to have the desk between us.

Granville settled himself in a whisper of well-tailored wool.

Our eyes met and I forced myself not to look away. The silence grew louder, but I was determined to make him break it.

"I sincerely regret the pain you were caused last night by Princess Caroline's revelations."

"Are you going to tell me they are not true?" I demanded.

"Alas, I am not," he replied quietly.

I picked up my pen, taking care not to snap it between my fingers. "How could you lie to me like that?"

"My sins are many, but I never lied to you," said Granville. "That said, I understand your anger."

"Do you?" At the moment, every fiber of my being ached at the unspeakable betrayal.

He bowed his head. "Allow me to explain the circumstances." When I didn't object, he continued. "My affair with Lady Bessborough began when I was quite young, and over the years it became . . . complicated."

His words lit a spark of hope. Aristocratic gentlemen all knew that at some point in their lives, duty demanded that they leave youthful pleasures behind in order to marry and sire an heir.

"And now?" I pressed.

Granville crossed his legs and pinched at the pleat of his trousers. "My position in politics is changing. And so must I."

A flood of relief coursed through me. Perhaps I should have made him grovel, but I was too happy to think of anything other than the fact that my future was not lost.

"It is an untenable situation," I agreed. "A gentleman of your stature and authority must now be very mindful of his reputation. Leaders are always held to a higher standard."

"I am aware of that." He drew in a measured breath. "Just as I am aware of having harmed our relationship."

"Respect, once lost, is not easily found again," I observed.

His gaze moved to the mullioned windows whose panes had turned opaque with the shadows of a passing squall. I thought that I caught a flare of emotion in his eyes but I couldn't tell for sure.

"In the coming days," said Granville, "I hope you will allow me to begin making amends."

Seizing the chance to show both my generosity of spirit and pragmatic understanding the ways of the world, I smiled. "We all make mistakes. It is the lessons we learn from them that matter."

"Wise words, as always, Lady Hester." Granville rose and reached across the desk to clasp my hand. "I shall not intrude on you any longer today. But if I may write to you tomorrow . . . ?"

"You may," I answered, after allowing a deliberate hesitation. "I hope you will not give me cause to regret it."

Shifting his stance, Granville raised my hand to his lips and brushed a kiss to my knuckles. "I shall do my best."

It wasn't until his steps died away in the corridor that my emotions settled enough for me to realize he had, with the consummate skill of a diplomat, soothed me with naught but vague platitudes about responsibilities and the need for change.

There had been no declarations of undying love, no promises about putting an end to his relationship with Harriet.

As I sat back, the flame of hope in my breast wavered, darkness threatening to snuff out the weak light. However, I marshaled my resolve and fisted my hands.

Yes, I had been punched in the gut, but I wasn't about to admit defeat.

Recalling my father's words about my knife-sharp logic, I used my reasoning to form a plan.

Granville could not marry Harriet, and even if he could, she was well past the age to be able to give him a legitimate heir. I, on the other hand, kept reminding myself that I embodied all the attributes of a perfect diplomat's wife. Granted, I didn't bring a large dowry to the marriage, but my illustrious lineage would add to his family's stature. As for his marrying some tongue-tied young lady fresh from the schoolroom, my acknowledged wit and charm along with my practical experience in running a political household made me a far better choice.

And so, as August gave way to September, I began to drop hints at the soirees and entertainments I attended that my relationship with Granville was turning serious. That would, I reflected, put subtle pressure on him to outgrow his youthful indiscretions and do his duty.

My machinations were helped by the fact that he and I were seen together in the glittering mansions of Mayfair, all smiles as we danced and conversed. I felt no guilt over my campaign of whispers, confident that it was all to achieve the Higher Good.

The only fly in the ointment was that pressures of politics prevented us from resuming our frequent trysts. There were two furtive meetings—short carriage rides involving hurried fumblings and rushed intimacy—but other than that, Pitt's needs took precedence over my own. I consoled myself with the thought that I would soon be sharing his bed. As for the fact that his notes had become few and far between, I reasoned that it was because he thought he no longer needed to woo me. Still . . .

"I confess that I am a little cross with you, Uncle," I intoned one morning as Pitt entered my parlor to peruse the first delivery of mail for the day.

His brows shot up. "Heaven forfend that I have unwittingly offended you, Hetty. Please tell me of my transgression and I shall endeavor to remedy it."

"You are working Granville far too hard. I know that things are fraught in Parliament, but he has not a moment to spare for his personal life. Which, I must say, has been a great hardship for both of us, though he is far too devoted to you to complain."

Pitt's face went through a series of odd little contortions. "I did not realize that things had become so serious."

Something in his tone took me aback. "You sound shocked."

"Merely surprised," he replied as he picked up the pile of mail I sorted for him. "Let me think on what can be done."

I smiled. "Thank you."

However, the situation didn't immediately improve. The mood at Downing Street offered some explanation as to why. Even Canning, my uncle's most trusted advisor, was looking concerned. Pitt's leadership was being challenged by a number of factions, including some within his own party.

*Traitors*, I thought angrily, growing more and more concerned over the look of exhaustion etched on every pore of my uncle's face.

My ill feelings were even greater for Harriet and her sister Georgiana, who were working tirelessly within the highest circles of Society to promote Charles Fox and the Whig agenda. In truth, I hated them for their subterfuge and acceptance that betrayals within betrayals were simply a way of life within the aristocracy. I was well aware that ladies had precious few choices. But personal honor was one of them.

One could choose to have principles and adhere to them, no matter how painful the cost.

I fumed quietly for a few more days, receiving naught but several puny excuses from Granville to my increasingly strident notes. Men disliked whining. As did I. However, his behavior was churlish and I felt beholden to tell him so.

Finally, a more substantial missive arrived late one afternoon, written on expensive paper and sealed with his signet ring. My heart fluttered in anticipation as I cracked the wax wafer, but I quickly dismissed the reaction as foolish. Surely he wouldn't be proposing in writing.

I fumbled open the folds and smoothed out the creases . . .

And drew in a ragged breath on reading the words, unsure whether to feel shock or elation.

Dropping the letter on my desk, I quickly rose and went in search of my uncle.

\*   \*   \*

"Ah, I was just about to send for you, my dear." As Pitt looked from the papers he was reading, the smile died on his lips.

"Because you have something important to tell me?" Despite my resolve to maintain my composure, I allowed a bit of acid to sour my tone.

He said nothing.

"You appointed Granville to serve as Ambassador to Russia and didn't feel compelled to tell me?"

His face hardened. "Much as I value your opinion, Hetty, I do not seek your advice—or your approval—on every political decision that I make. The appointment is in the best interest of the country. We desperately need to coax Tsar Alexander into joining with us against France, and to use his influence in the region to help create an alliance with Prussia, Sweden, and Austria."

My throat tightened. "He will need a savvy hostess to help him, and yet he said nothing in his letter to me about . . ." I sucked in a breath. "About our future together."

"Hetty . . ." His eyes flooded with sympathy, along with a more nuanced emotion that I couldn't read. "My dear Hetty. I fear you may have misjudged Granville's intentions. I do not . . ." He paused to remove his spectacles and pinch at the bridge of his nose. "I do not think that he has any intention of marrying at present."

I felt the blood drain from my face. "Th-that can't be true."

"It is," he said firmly. "I broached the subject when I called him in for a private meeting to discuss the government appointment. He admitted that he is not ready to make a decision about his future."

"B-but—" I bit back any further words. *What was there to say?*

"He will be leaving shortly for Russia, and his absence will avoid any unpleasant awkwardness between the two of you. Above all else, we wish to avoid any rumors that you have been jilted. Such gossip would do neither of you any good."

*Jilted.* I refused to believe it. "Many gentlemen get cold feet when facing the surrender of their rakehell ways," I pointed out. "It is my belief that he will come around."

Pitt shook his head, eyeing me with silent pity.

"You'll see," I added.

"Hetty, much as it pains me to say it, you must accept his decision. Even more importantly, in public you must appear unperturbed by his departure, and if anyone presses, you must say that the two of you came to a mutual agreement not to rush into any decision right now." He paused. "My hold on the government is precarious, I cannot afford the scandal of a lovers' quarrel to become grist for the gossip mills."

My breath stuck in my lungs.

"You've seen what the satirical artists did to your father. Can you imagine the glee they would take in having you and the most handsome man in Britain as the subjects of their scurrilous pictures?"

I squeezed my eyes shut, shuddering at the thought.

"This is for the best," assured Pitt. "I like and admire Granville. However, he is not someone I wish to see you marry." A pause. "I'm sending him to Russia because he will do a superb job. But I am also doing it for your reputation—and for mine."

I turned away without further words, determined not to embarrass myself by shedding girlish tears. Pitt would not understand. He had never known the agony of having Cupid's arrow lodged in one heart. Yes, one could pull it out and toss it aside. But that didn't mean the wound would heal.

Once back in my parlor, I went through the motions of work and then excused myself from supper, informing the housekeeper that I had a headache. As Pitt counseled, I had to pretend that nothing was amiss.

However, in the privacy of my own rooms, I allowed my heartache to spill forth. I wept bitter tears, mourning the loss of my elemental innocence. My affair with Camelford had been different.

Love had not been part of our bond.

With Granville, I had given myself body and soul, believing that the acceptance of my love meant it was reciprocated in kind. But men, I now understood, had different thoughts on the meaning of love. For most of them, it was merely a word—a four-letter key to unlock the treasure chest of physical pleasures.

A last sniffle, and then I dried my eyes. *Enough of blubbering.* Granville did not love me now. But that didn't mean he wouldn't come to love me if he had a chance to take in the full measure of how I could enrich his life.

A smile touched my lips. I would leave love for later. At the moment my strategy was to maneuver him into marriage.

Drawing a deep, cleansing breath—one that banished all doubts and self-recriminations—I sat down at my desk and penned an eminently logical appeal to Granville's political pragmatism rather than to his heart.

Logic, however, sparked no magic. Granville's answer to my first letter was more prettily-worded evasions. He claimed to care for me but that the present circumstances—wartime politics, pressure from his family to refrain from making a hasty match, the need to come to terms with his many responsibilities—made it imperative for us to defer any plans for the future until things were more settled.

Coming from a family of legendary orators, I saw it for what it was. A silvery tongue, all flash and no substance.

Acknowledging that Pitt's request was a sensible one—memories of the public savaging of my father by the press were not pleasant ones—I continued to attend the social gathering of the beau monde, taking care to appear in perfect spirits. Perhaps my feverish passion for achieving my goal gave me an added glow, for despite my inner turmoil, I was at the height of my looks.

I danced, I laughed, I garnered praise for the wit and insight of my conversations.

None of it mattered to those whose opinion I was courting.

In particular, Lady Stafford's earlier warmth toward me had turned to a distant coolness. A passing nod, with naught but the briefest of pleasantries, was all I received. I blamed Georgiana and Harriet. No doubt they were reigniting subtle rumors about my past with Camelford to sully my chances.

*What blackguards, considering their own less-than-pristine reputations!*

Even more embarrassing, the leading newspaper in London published the announcement of my engagement to Granville. Pitt was livid, but thank heavens he believed me when I assured him that I had not placed it. I assumed it was a nasty trick by Harriet and her sister to further humiliate me and anger Granville enough to ensure he would not make me an offer.

However, against all odds, I clung to the hope that he might still change his mind and, in a gesture worthy of the grand love stories in history, appear at Downing Street to make a last-minute offer.

But the clock was inexorably ticking . . .

# *Chapter* 25

*October 1804*

*O*ptimism *in the face of great odds . . . What sparks that indefinable resolve in some people, while others see the daunting challenges as too great to conquer?*

I took a seat at my escritoire and leaned back for a swallow of port as I considered the question. It was late, and I was feeling weary in both body and spirit. Adams and I had worked feverishly all day and well into the evening, gathering documents and writing up facts to help Pitt prepare for an important speech in Parliament later in the week.

My hand ached from writing. As for my heart, it hurt with a far more visceral pain.

Which was why I was pondering the question of optimism.

My thoughts immediately went to my great-great-grandfather, the Pitt patriarch from whom our intertwined branches of Pitts, Stanhopes, and Grenvilles had sprouted. Call it optimism, call it hubris—in a world where danger and death lurked in every shadow, Thomas Pitt had dared to leave home and all that was familiar in order to seek his fortune on the far side of the globe.

None of our family ever learned exactly how he came to get his hands on The Diamond. Whatever the story, it made it his fortune.

I slowly twisted my ring, watching the fragment from Pitt's legendary Diamond throw off winks of light. I often used it to summon the strength to stand firm against the tide of conventional expectations.

But tonight, I found my strength flagging. Granville was set to travel by ship to St. Petersburg in just a few days, and it seemed there was little choice but to admit that my dream would sail away with him.

Defeat always tasted bitter. But Granville's casual rejection of me—I felt cast aside like an old shoe that had lost its appeal now that the shine had worn off it—had made me face the terrible truth. I now realized that no rational arguments would likely change his thinking. Empirical evidence didn't matter. The fact was, women were damned from the moment of their birth to walk in the shadows of men.

Tears stung my eyes as the candle flame flickered against the gloom of night.

*What a naïve idealist I have been!* I had scorned Harriet and Georgiana, thinking them weak and cowardly to have accepted living within the strictures of Society. But they had learned all the subtle ways to manipulate the rules, while I had made an utter fool of myself.

I should have known better, of course. Having seen the world of London Society through the lens of Brummell's cynical acceptance of artifice, how could I have failed to understand that the cardinal rule for the aristocracy was never to wear your emotions on your sleeve for everyone to see? That wasn't saluted as honesty—it was ridiculed as naïveté.

Alas, what I desired transcended lies and subterfuge. *Love. Respect. Camaraderie.* The sublime beauty of two hearts beating as one. Was that so absurd?

I rose before dawn the next morning, exhausted from wrestling with my inner demons all night. I packed a valise and left a note for Pitt, informing him that I felt the need for a respite from London and was going to spend several days at our residence in Putney, just outside London. Bowling Green House was a frequent place of refuge for him from the demands of governing, and we often spent several days a week there, so I knew he would understand.

I took a long look around as I paused in the entrance hall of our Downing Street residence, watching the dark-on-dark shadows flit through the deserted citadel of power. Then I eased the front door open and went around to the mews, where I roused the coachman and had him ready a carriage.

Mist from the river swirled through the empty streets, muffling the clatter of the hooves on the cobblestones. With most of London slumbering, the city seemed serene. My rage had burned itself out, leaving a sense of eerie calm, as if I was floating outside of myself.

The smoke-darkened stone and brick soon gave way to woodland and meadows. The carriage turned up a winding lane and through the windowpanes I caught a glimpse of the octagonal house through the flutter of autumn leaves. It was a cozy spot, nestled in a tranquil sylvan setting that felt a world away from the pressures of London. After letting myself out, I dismissed the coachman and opened the door with my key. The housekeeper, I knew, was away for several days visiting family, but I was perfectly capable of seeing to my needs. I had brought everything I needed with me.

My bedchamber was upstairs in the rear of the house, overlooking a small brook that ran through the woods. The sun broke free of the scudding clouds for a moment and I caught a glimmer of light dance over the water.

I stood very still, my palms pressed to the window glass, watching it skitter along with the rippling currents. Woodlarks flitted through the trees, their twittering bringing a smile to my lips. I listened for a moment longer, and then, overcome by a bone-deep weariness, I turned and sank down upon my bed.

It was chilly in the room but I made no move to kindle a fire. Instead, I removed my coat and bonnet, letting them fall to the floor. My shoes and spencer followed, leaving me clad in a thin muslin dress. Repressing a shiver, I slipped under the coverlet and reached for the satchel I had placed on the bedside table.

My hands were trembling as I snapped open its clasp and took out a small wooden box. Nestled within its velvet lining were three stoppered glass vials. One by one, I opened them and poured the contents of each into the empty glass I had brought up from the kitchen.

The liquid swirled with a syrupy heaviness, its color garnet-red from the port I added to mask the unpleasant taste of the laudanum and wolfsbane. Lifting the poison to my lips I swallowed the mixture in a hurried gulp. A strangled cough. And then in one last impulsive gesture I threw the glass at the wall, watching in grim satisfaction as it shattered into diamond-bright shards.

"*Alea iacta est,*" I whispered. "*The die is cast.*"

With that I closed my eyes, but still the tears spilled down my cheeks.

"My heart is at this moment breaking . . ."

# Chapter 26

November–December 1804

Hell was as horrible as the fire and brimstone clerics had warned. Pain sizzled through whatever essence of me was left in the afterlife, the flames burning hot. I writhed, seeking the escape that I knew would not come.

"Lady Hester, Lady Hester!" A familiar voice—it was Elizabeth's—floated through the haze.

*Ah—it seemed that another diabolical torture of the devil was to have me hear my close friends and family calling out to me.*

I felt a stab of remorse for causing them pain.

"Lady Hester!" The voice was now louder, and I felt a shaking sensation.

*How could that be possible when I had given myself to Death?* I twisted in confusion, only to feel a blade of light cut through my consciousness.

"Thank God—she's alive!" cried Elizabeth. "Fetch a physician!"

*No, no—I don't want to live!* I tried to protest but no words came out.

"And send immediate word to Pitt," added Elizabeth. "Tell him what's happened."

I struggled to sit up, but hands held me down. "Don't try to move, milady."

A wet cloth soothed against my burning face, bringing a measure of relief. Fingers then touched my mouth, gently easing it open. Another wet cloth, sweet with sugared water, touched my tongue.

"You're hot as Hades. Suck on this to quench your thirst, milady," coaxed Elizabeth. "Good Lord, what have you done to yourself?"

Before I could conjure up any coherent answer, I slipped back into oblivion.

When I awoke again, I was aware of more voices in the room, pitched low, like the buzzing of bumblebees.

"I came as quickly as I could." Hurried steps crossed the floor. "Move aside, Miss Williams. I need to examine the patient."

"Elizabeth," I surprised myself by managing a whisper. So I wasn't dead after all. "Don't leave me."

Her fingers wrapped around my wrist. "I'm here, milady. But you must allow Dr. Cline to examine you. He has come at Mr. Pitt's urgent request." She smoothed a lock of damp hair off my brow. "Your dear uncle is beside himself with worry over you."

"How—" I began, but Elizabeth silenced me with a squeeze.

"We'll discuss all that later." She stepped back to allow the doctor to take a seat beside the bed.

Clenching my teeth, I submitted to the indignity of his poking and prodding.

After what felt like an eternity, he straightened with a grunt and asked Elizabeth to bring the desk chair over to the side of the bed. Glass clinked against glass—I assumed he was examining the empty medicinal bottles—and another sound rumbled deep in his throat.

"You are damnably lucky to be alive," muttered Dr. Cline under his breath. He touched my belly again, nearly causing me to scream in agony. "How do you feel?"

"Like Hell warmed over," I rasped.

"I fear you have done serious damage to your insides." He turned. "Please bring me my leather satchel, Miss Williams."

I heard him rustle around inside it.

"I am going to leave you with several medicines. You must administer them exactly as I say . . ."

I drifted off again as they fell into hushed conversation, cursing myself for clinging to life.

It was a pattern that would repeat itself over the next few days. Elizabeth and Dr. Cline exerted great effort to tend to me, while I did nothing to help my own cause, as I was still adamant about not wishing to live.

Pain was a constant companion. I found sleep difficult and could stomach no sustenance save for gruel. *What sort of existence is this?* I asked myself, sure that death was preferable to such misery.

It was Pitt's visits that made me ashamed of such thoughts. He came several times when I was hovering in the netherworld of unconsciousness, so it was nearly a week after my drinking the poisonous concoction before we had our first meeting.

My eyes were closed, my shoulders propped up against the bed pillows, and I was taking some earthly solace in the sound of the birdsong outside the window. A small thing, perhaps, but it stirred the black cloud inside my head just enough to allow a few flickers of light.

"My dear, dear Hetty."

At first I thought my uncle's sweet voice was simply another of the tangled dreams that plagued my thoughts. But as I felt a gentle caress touch my cheek, I opened my eyes.

Pitt smiled, and on seeing tears pool in his kindly eyes, I felt like an utter wretch.

"You're awake! Oh, thank the heavens!" He lifted my hand to his lip and pressed a kiss to my palm. "I've been so worried about you."

"I am so sorry," I whispered, knowing even as I said it what a ridiculously inadequate apology it was.

His face tightened in remorse. "Dear girl, it is me who needs to express remorse. This is all my fault—"

"No!"

"Hush," he said, stilling my lips with a touch of his fingertips. "I . . . I should have been more understanding of your heartache." A wince. "I was too wrapped up in my duties to see what was happening. I—I should have known better than to introduce you to Granville. It did not occur to me that he would be so cavalier with your feelings."

"The fault does not lie entirely with him," I admitted. "As you well know, I've always given free rein to my passions, confident that I could guide their galloping over treacherous ground."

I drew in a shaky breath, willing myself not to cry. "I should have known better."

Pitt leaned down, and ever so slowly gathered me in a hug. A small sound—something between a laugh and a moan—caught in my throat. The only other hugs I remembered receiving in my life were from his mother, the dowager Countess Chatham, with whom I had lived at Burton Pynsent.

"How could you have known?" he said, his eyes narrowing. "Your father treated you and your siblings with shameful neglect."

"I . . ." I swallowed hard. "I fear it's my fault that he didn't love me. I wouldn't bend to his will."

"My dear girl, your strength and your passions are part of what makes you such an extraordinary young lady. As are your courage, your curiosity, and your compassion for family and friends."

He pulled me closer. "Be damned with your father for being so selfishly focused on his own desires. Know that you are very much loved and cherished. I can't imagine what I would do without your flame-bright light in my life."

It was at that moment that I decided that I wanted to live.

I slowly started to regain my strength. Elizabeth informed me that Dr. Cline and the household servants had been sworn to secrecy regarding the real cause of my malady. The public explanation was that I had fallen victim to a severe bout of influenza that had left me dangerously weak.

Pitt continued to visit and provide unwavering comfort and support. But there also arose an uncomfortable discussion about my future. His position as prime minister was precarious. His support within the Tory party was razor-thin, and the slightest whiff of scandal could topple his cabinet. So after much hemming and hawing—I could sense that the subject pained him deeply—he informed me that for now it was best that I did not return to residing at Downing Street. And as my current abode, Bowling Green House at Putney Heath, was also a little too close to London for comfort, the solution he suggested was that I return to Walmer Castle.

The offer suited me perfectly. The natural beauty, the sound of the sea, the presence of my militia friends—I couldn't have imagined a better tonic for restoring my joie de vivre. I would rebuild my strength, both mental and physical, through long gallops on horseback through the countryside.

*I will once again be the Amazon in my flame-red frogged tunic,* I vowed.

The thought spurred me to work even harder at rising from my sickbed. The terrible combination of laudanum and wolfsbane had, according to Dr. Cline, damaged my innards. He had warned me that I might be an invalid for the rest of my life.

*Ha!* I was determined to prove him wrong.

My illness and the subsequent forced bedrest had given me a great deal of time to think about my life. And in mulling over my many mistakes, I also came to some interesting realizations. A daunting challenge—be it protecting my brothers from my father's tyranny or running a complicated household like Walmer Castle—seemed to bring out the best in me. I could be petty, I could be arrogant, I could be selfish. But when faced with a dilemma, I somehow found an inner fortitude that allowed me to triumph over adversity.

To be sure, self-reflection was uncomfortable. It was not pleasant to have to admit to my weaknesses and faults. However, the process brought me to an elemental revelation. My father . . .

Camelford . . . Granville Leveson Gower—I had let too many men define my sense of self-worth.

My happiness depended on what they thought of me, rather than how I thought about myself.

I vowed to take more control of my feelings.

My health began to improve. I was able to rise from my bed and take short walks, assisted by Elizabeth and my maid Susan. Bored to perdition, I sent a note to Adams, begging him to come visit and bring some of Pitt's private correspondence for me to read through and organize.

As I had hoped, he appeared the next morning bearing a satchel bulging with portfolio cases.

"Good day, Lady Hester," he announced in the over-cheery voice that was commonly used with invalids. "You are looking well."

"What fustian, Adams," I said dryly. "I should hope we have become good enough friends that you don't feel compelled to lie through your teeth."

He looked a little sheepish.

"There is a looking glass on my dressing room table," I added. "I am aware that my appearance leaves much to be desired." The truth was, I looked like death warmed over, and given my advanced age—I had turned twenty-nine in March—I was likely never to recover the first bloom of youth.

I smiled. "But you are kind to be so gallant."

"Beauty is in the eye of the beholder, milady," replied Adams. "And what I see is a lady who sparkles with wit and intelligence."

A blush spread over my cheeks. I gave a brusque cough to dislodge the lump of emotion caught in my throat. "Come, let us sit down and get to work. I'm afraid that I still tire easily."

We spent a pleasant interlude going through the portfolios he had brought, and I convinced him to leave some of the less urgent correspondence with the understanding that he would return for my finished letters in several days.

Feeling useful raised my spirits another notch, and the arrival of cheerful letters from my brothers Charles and James was further tonic to my soul. I had kept motherly track of them—with Pitt's help, James had left the Navy and joined the same army regiment as Charles—and we corresponded regularly. That they were so happy and thriving in their military careers made me feel that I had done some good in spite of all the egregious mistakes I had made.

By the following week, Dr. Cline agreed that I was far enough along in my recovery to take up residence at Walmer Castle.

I stepped down from the carriage and drew in a lungful of the salt-sharp air, savoring its tang and the happy memories of a place that was the closest thing I had to a real home.

"I will make more good memories here in the coming months," I told myself, looking around at the castle's familiar battlements with a fondness that transcended their being mere hunks of ancient stone. Many a former Warden of the Cinque Ports had held the position for a lifetime. After Pitt retired from politics, there was no reason why he couldn't live out his days here in quiet enjoyment of the gardens and his many friends in the surrounding towns.

"The breeze is picking up, milady." Elizabeth, who was to stay with me until I was settled, hurried over and draped a shawl around my shoulders. "Let us go inside before you catch a chill."

"I won't be wrapped in cotton wool," I responded. "Fresh air and exertion will be better medicine than any of the potions and plasters that Dr. Cline sent along."

Elizabeth appeared skeptical, but as usual, she humored my whims by maintaining a tactful silence.

"But I appreciate your concern." I turned and allowed her to take my arm. "I—I have not yet properly thanked you for saving my life."

Her gaze remained focused straight ahead on the path leading to the main entrance. "I feared that you wished me to perdition for my actions. But Life is too precious to toss away before the Grim Reaper seeks you out."

She slowed her steps. "Besides, I think it would have been the death of Pitt. And I am way too fond of both of you to have suffered such a double loss."

Her words, though said lightly, stirred a spasm of guilt along with a new worry. "I regret having caused him such trouble. Be assured that I have learned an elemental lesson about Life and Love."

I lifted my chin as the gravel crunched beneath our shoes. "Like a phoenix rising from the ashes of its old self, I feel reborn as an older, wiser version of myself."

"Acquiring Wisdom from experience is important," said Elizabeth dryly. "But next time you seek a lesson from Life, please try not to burn yourself to a crisp."

Her gentle humor provoked a laugh as I acknowledged the melodrama of my previous words. "Indeed, I shall try to rein in my penchant for excess," I responded. "What I meant was . . . I am determined to never again let the opinions of others rob me of my sense of self-worth."

Elizabeth turned her head. Our eyes met and she smiled. "I am relieved to hear that, milady. Because you are very much loved, and by people who will never betray you."

I felt tears pearl on my lashes. "I know that now. My uncle . . ." My voice faltered. "My uncle is the very best of men, kind and generous to a fault. And I worry that the strain of all the worries he carries on his shoulders has recently taken a toll on his health."

I swallowed hard. "Does his personal physician . . . ?"

"We are all very concerned," admitted Elizabeth. "Dr. Farquhar says that Mr. Pitt is fatigued from his endless hours of working. Adams has promised to make sure that he pays frequent visits to the Putney Heath house for rest and relaxation."

"Would that he could let himself relax," I muttered. "I fear there is too much fire bubbling through Pitt blood."

"As to that, Adams says that Mr. Pitt has promised to come at Easter for an extended stay at Walmer Castle. I think of all the places he has resided, this one is dearest to his heart."

We walked on in silence, but my last words suddenly sparked

an idea. Pitt had been delighted by my earlier improvements to the gardens at the castle, and I had noted that he always seemed much refreshed by his walks through the trees and ornamental plantings that I had designed. The former chalk mine that he had showed me on the day of my first arrival at Walmer Castle was still untouched and both of us had always thought it would make a lovely sanctuary.

I now had a new challenge, and as I entered the castle, I already felt stronger.

## January 1805

"Burfield, do you not think this a most charming spot?" I had spent several weeks riding and walking the grounds, slowly but surely coaxing my body to recover from its unnatural ordeal. I now felt ready to put my new garden plan into motion.

The head gardener looked around, his grizzled face wrinkling into a frown as he studied the abandoned chalk mine, which was a meandering open pit cut into the craggy rocks, the jagged edges looking sharp as knives.

"Nay, milady," he grumbled. "I think it an ugly hellhole and can't fer the life of me fathom why you dragged us out here."

"Because," I answered firmly, "we are going to transform it into a secluded sanctuary of peace and solitude."

His response was to blow out a very rude sound.

"Oh, come, use your imagination!" I made a grand sweeping gesture encompassing the carved-out area. Granted, the day was chilly and gunpowder gray, giving the rocks a sullen look. But I could already see a footpath winding through it where one could walk and reflect, surrounded by the harmony of Nature.

"I know you have an excellent eye. Envision the rocks softened with furze and creepers. And if we put in shade trees, it would provide an excellent place for Pitt to stroll in summer. You know how much he dislikes the summer heat."

Burfield's scowl gave way to a more thoughtful expression.

I quickly added, "Picture tall grasses, ones that would whisper in harmony with the breezes and add a soothing sound."

"Hmmph." He scratched at his chin as he ventured another look around at the barren stone. "Broom is sturdy and wud give a touch o' color and scent in spring and summer."

I pulled a small notebook and pencil from my cloak pocket. "Yes, yes, broom would be lovely. Let us move around the perimeter and start making a list of possible plantings. Then we can begin drawing up a plan . . ."

# *Chapter* 27

*February–March 1805*

The day was unseasonably mild and I had just finished walking back from the old chalk pit, where work on the garden was progressing nicely. The previous month, Burfield and I had visited Maidstone to order shade trees, and I had once again marshaled the local militia to help with their planting. Though the branches were bare, I could visualize the leafy canopy providing both shade and seclusion for three seasons of the year.

I was proud of what I was accomplishing. I had seen the remains of a ravaged mine, stripped of all its value and abandoned as a useless wreck, and envisioned a way to help it rise from the ashes of its former self and take on new life.

As I turned and headed for my rooms, I suddenly paused. With the sun sparkling over a calm sea, I decided instead to take the stairs up to the tower battlements to savor the vistas and bring a touch more color back to my cheeks. My health was still ragged, my vital organs not yet recovered from the poisons that uncontrollable passion had driven me to drink.

Looking up, I watched the wispy clouds scud across the horizon. I had spent countless hours over the last four months thinking about my actions of the past few years. I had always thought my fire to be my greatest strength. But I had come to realize that it was also my greatest weakness.

Closing my eyes, I listened to the ebb and flow of the waves against the strand, finding its rhythm a reminder that life was constantly in motion. Could I learn to live in harmony with my passions?

The light scuff of steps on the stairs drew me back from my musings. I turned, seeing only shadows at first. But a tiny shape cloaked in forest green wool materialized from the darkness cast by the crenellated stones.

"Forgive me for intruding on you without advance notice." It was Caroline Herschel, the woman astronomer who worked with her brother, William Herschel, the King's Astronomer. "William and I are staying with friends nearby, and I wished to pay you a visit. Miss Williams told me you were up here and said that she thought you wouldn't mind if I joined you."

"I don't mind at all," I replied. "Indeed, it's a great pleasure to see you, Miss Herschel. I have spent many a night stargazing through the marvelous telescope that you and your brother made for Pitt since my return to Walmer Castle."

"The heavens are a source of constant wonder," said Caroline, as she came to join me by the low wall between the crenellations. "I find the vastness always makes me—and my personal worries— feel very small."

I looked back to the sea. The Herschels had many friends within the highest circles of Society. No doubt Caroline had gotten wind of the lurid speculations surrounding my relationship with Granville. Rumors must be spinning like whirling dervishes through the drawing rooms of Mayfair.

"I can't begin to imagine what salacious gossip is being said about me." My throat tightened. "It's true that I've been quite ill, and as you see, I have lost what looks I once had. Other than that, I would take what you've heard with a pinch of salt. Wagging tongues care far more about stirring up malicious rumors than telling the truth."

"I pay no attention to gossipmongers. I know all too well what delight people take in savaging an unconventional woman." Caroline leaned back, and as her cloak flapped open in the breeze, I saw she was holding a cylindrical leather case within its folds. "I took the liberty of bringing you a small gift. It is meant as a reminder to keep your focus on the things that matter."

She unfastened the top and shook out a small telescope beautifully crafted out of brass and rosewood. "William and I designed it like a nautical spyglass." Two quick tugs demonstrated how the retractable barrels pulled out to create an impressive precision instrument.

"Have a look." Caroline held it out to me.

I carefully took the telescope and raised it to my eye, aiming the lens at the ocean's horizon. A lone gull, much magnified, winged into my field of view, soaring higher and higher before disappearing.

"How marvelous!" I exclaimed. "I . . ." I lowered the barrel. "I can't find the words to adequately thank you for such thoughtfulness." A sigh. "If only your skills included grinding the lenses to some magical combination of concave and convex shapes so that they might show me the right path to take in Life."

"Alas, such skills are beyond mere mortals." Caroline hitched herself up to take a seat on the wall. "Finding the right path involves so much more than sight. You must look inward as well as outward."

"But I've been so blind," I whispered.

"There are times when you'll snap the telescope open and see naught but fog and rain obscuring the view," she replied. "The weather is constantly changing, and we don't know how to predict what will happen from day to day. Our own hearts are equally shrouded in mystery."

"Would that I were half as wise as you, Miss Herschel."

"Sometimes resilience is more important than wisdom, Lady Hester." Caroline smiled. "My sense is you have all the qualities you need to discern your own path." A pause. "You just have to trust yourself."

I sat down next to her and slid the telescope shut. "Not an easy thing, given what a fool I've been."

She put her arm around my shoulders and pulled me into a quick but fierce hug. The gesture—ye heavens, she was surprisingly strong for her diminutive size—nearly brought me to tears as I realized how little physical expression of love and support I had received in my life.

It made me feel a little less alone.

"We've all been fools, my dear. But we mustn't let our mistakes crush us." Caroline gestured out at the grounds. "Miss Williams mentioned that you are starting a new garden project. Just remember to keep planting new seeds of hope and optimism in your heart. The elemental cycle of Life is all about barren earth blooming with new growth."

"The earth and the heavens," I mused. "The vastness of the universe is also a source of inspiration. There is so much to explore."

Caroline took the telescope from my hands and slipped it back into its case. "Shall we go enjoy a pot of tea inside while I tell you about some of my latest projects? I have discovered yet another comet . . ."

Caroline Herschel's visit lifted my spirits immeasurably. Kindred souls were so few and far between. I mused a bit sadly about Camelford, and how things might have been different if we had both been a little less wild. But the past was the past, and I was determined not to be trapped any longer in its netherworld of regrets.

I pushed myself harder in my riding, and my strength continued to improve. And as winter turned to spring, the garden in the abandoned chalk mine began to come to life. I worked there most afternoons, digging in the dirt and setting the roots of small shrubberies that would grow for years to come. It was hard but rewarding. I came home each day feeling tired but happy. By lamplight I read through the folders of correspondence that Adams sent down each week and penned the necessary responses, feeling that at least I was able to take some of the tedious tasks off Pitt's desk.

With April fast approaching, greenery began to push up from the earth and the leaves started to unfurl on the tree branches. I found myself counting the days until Easter.

But the date came and went, and Pitt did not arrive at Walmer Castle.

## May–September 1805

"Things are very fraught in London." William Adams moved to the sideboard of Pitt's office at Walmer Castle and poured himself a glass of port. It was the week after Easter and he had decided to bring the dispatch case in person so he could explain the circumstances that were sapping my uncle's strength.

"You had better pour me one as well," I said.

"Aye." The fact that he agreed so readily only served to tighten the knot in my chest.

I took a swallow of the wine before responding. "Surely Pitt's longtime friends—"

"Pitt's longtime friends are like rats scrabbling for a spot close to the gangplank, in case they have to flee a sinking ship."

My eyes widened in disbelief. "You can't mean that!"

"Perhaps I have exaggerated." A scowl. "But not by much. Fox and your uncle's cousin, Lord Grenville, head up a growing Opposition in Parliament. The king and the Prince of Wales refuse to settle their bitter political differences, which makes it impossible for Pitt to broaden his base of support . . ."

I listened in growing dismay as Adams recounted the machinations of the various factions and how Pitt was fighting an exhausting battle in trying to keep his administration from crumbling.

Knowing how his whole life was devoted to politics, I could only imagine the stresses he was feeling in trying to keep the ship of State on an even keel.

"Bad as what I have told you is, I've saved the worst news for last," said Adams, punctuating the announcement with a sigh. "By entering the Spanish conflict, Pitt has broadened Britain's war on the Continent, and it's forced him to raise taxes on a number of things—including salt, horses, and property. His popularity has sunk to a new low, forcing him to try to make an alliance with his former friend Addington."

"Ye gods, he must be desperate," I exclaimed. "There is no love lost between them now."

"Indeed not." Adams grimaced. "Before any deal could be negotiated, the Opposition raised a vote concerning a matter of financial irregularity within the Navy's bureaucracy. Everyone acknowledges that Pitt is incorruptible, but Parliament returned a vote of no confidence in the matter."

He paused to let the gravity of his words sink in. "Even Pitt's loyal followers are beginning to whisper that it may be time for a change in government."

"I must return with you and see what I can do to help!" Much as I dreaded showing myself in London, Pitt's needs were more important than nursing my damaged pride.

Adams eyed me uncertainly. "But your own illness, milady—"

"I am strong enough now that I feel confident I won't suffer a relapse," I assured him. "And my uncle needs people around him in whom he can confide. I am shocked that Grenville has proved so disloyal."

"He may be your uncle's friend and relative, but he is also a politician," replied Adams. "And all politicians have ambition. There is talk that if Pitt falls from power, Lord Grenville will become the next prime minister."

I looked down into the dregs of my wine, knowing that the next few months would be fraught with challenges. "It seems that we have a great deal of work to do. Let us plan to leave at dawn's first light."

The first rays of the day were, however, drowned by leaden skies and a pelting rain, making for a soggy start to the journey. My mood was equally dark. Thankfully, Adams seemed preoccupied with his own thoughts, which allowed me to brood over what lay ahead.

I was sure that Georgiana and her sister Harriet had waged a spiteful war of innuendo to blacken my reputation and turn Granville and his family against me. The thought that I might encounter Lady Stafford, even from afar, made my stomach turn. But I consoled myself with the promise that I would avoid all social engagements. The glitter and gameplaying no longer held any appeal to me. I was there to offer solace and support for my beloved uncle.

Nothing else mattered.

Things were even worse than I imagined when we arrived at Downing Street. Pitt was so weak that he had trouble rising from his chair, even with the aid of a cane.

"My dear Hetty!"

The look that lit up his face made me feel horribly guilty. My selfish histrionics over Granville had harmed not just me. I had caused the person I loved most in life to suffer. I should have been at his side throughout these troubled times within the government.

"I have missed you," added Pitt, his smile turning wistful. "But I am happy to see that Walmer Castle has brought the bloom back to your cheeks."

"Sit!" I commanded, and then came around his desk to press a kiss to his cheek once he had obeyed me. "Walmer Castle would do you a world of good as well, Uncle. You must take a respite from—"

"No time for that right now," he interjected, folding his hands atop a stack of papers waiting to be read. "Perhaps in autumn, when the trees are ablaze with color."

"I shall insist that you come then," I replied. "Burfield and I have made some improvements to the gardens. I think you will be pleased."

"Excellent! I look forward to seeing what you have done."

He forced a jovial tone but I could see that his gaze had drifted back to the work on his desk.

"In the meantime, allow me to take some of those portfolios and read them for you."

Pitt hesitated. "Much as I value your help, my dear, the situation has changed here during your absence. My position is so precarious that I can't afford to give the Opposition any reason to question my actions—"

"You fear that my presence here in Downing Street might stir nasty whispers about my illness, and reflect badly on you?"

He pressed his fingertips to his brow. "It's not that, though I admit unpleasant rumors swirled through Mayfair last October."

"Thanks to that Machiavellian witch, the Duchess of Devonshire," I muttered. "Georgiana is doing it not only for political reasons but also out of pure malice. As for her sister Harriet, she, too, is despicable for choosing to live within such a tangle of lies."

"I don't disagree," responded Pitt in a weary voice. "As I said, the rumors aren't my real worry." He drew in a troubled breath. "When I had a clear majority of support for returning to the office of prime minister, nobody questioned my having a lady as a close advisor. But now . . ."

My uncle shook his head. "The Opposition will pounce on anything to raise questions about my leadership."

"And my mere presence here at Downing Street puts you in danger?"

"I fear the answer is yes," answered Adams, who was now standing in the doorway.

"But my thoughts and analysis are just as sharp as those of your gentlemen advisors." Even as I said it, I knew that had nothing to do with the problem.

"I'm so sorry, Hetty." My uncle slumped back in his chair. "Your loyalty and support is a tonic for my soul. But pragmatism must override all else."

Much as it galled me, I accepted his reasoning. Not for the world would I stir any further trouble for him. "Allow me to stay a little longer, just as a personal companion. I shall avoid any public appearances so as not to provoke any talk. Indeed, perhaps we can go stay in Putney Heath for several days."

"Some fresh air and country walks might be very beneficial for your constitution, sir," added Adams quickly.

I shot him a grateful look.

Pitt cleared his throat. "You would not mind—"

"Not at all," I assured him. The place truly held no awful memories for me. I chose it because of its sylvan setting and air of tranquility, and I wasn't going to let my own foolishness taint its beauty for my uncle.

"Hmmph. Then I suppose it would do no harm to escape the noise and smoke of the city for a brief interlude," mused Pitt.

We left the next morning, and as the carriage crossed Westminster Bridge and made its way to Clapham Road, I saw the taut lines etched around Pitt's eyes begin to relax. I vowed to have a talk with him before I returned to the country about leaving politics behind and retiring to his beloved Walmer Castle. I had no doubt that the king, regardless of his mental state, would allow my uncle to remain Lord Warden of the Cinque Ports for life.

However, I was under no illusion that it would be an easy conversation. Politics was his passion. To give it up would be to lose the essence of who he was. I, of all people, understood that.

But the job was killing him, and so I meant to try.

We passed a very pleasant interlude at Bowling Green House. Pitt could manage only short walks, aided by me or Adams. Still, I could see his shoulders had straightened, as if some weight had been lifted from the frail bones. I did manage to broach the subject of withdrawing from politics, but was quickly silenced by an adamant refusal to consider the idea. If there had been a slight hesitation, I would have pressed him. But I could sense that his mind was made up, and our temperaments were too alike for me to have any hope of wheedling a change of heart.

As for my own position, although I tried to argue my case for remaining in London, both Adams and Pitt insisted that the political situation was such that we couldn't afford to give the Opposition any dirt with which to smear Pitt's name.

And so I dutifully returned to Walmer Castle, where the reimagined chalk pit was now in its first full bloom. I took to walking there every afternoon when the sun was at its zenith, for the leafy shadows of the newly planted trees and the sea breezes provided a secluded sanctuary in which to mull over my private thoughts.

I made myself follow the London newspaper reports on politics—Adams included all the daily copies in the weekly shipment of correspondence—even though the situation seemed to be turning darker with every new delivery.

I made a second short trip to London in September to offer some moral support to Pitt. But he was so distracted by the pressures of governing that I think he barely noticed my presence.

Disheartened, I returned to Walmer, wondering how long things could go on like this.

# Chapter 28

*January 1806*

The answer came in January, when word arrived in Britain that Napoleon had won a momentous victory at the Battle of Austerlitz, smashing the Third Coalition that Britain had formed with Russia, the Holy Roman Empire, Sicily, Naples, and Sweden. News of the defeat was the death-knell for Pitt's leadership. I hurried to Putney Heath to offer my support, knowing that he would seek refuge there from the political turmoil.

I nearly wept on seeing him arrive, so weak and frail that he had to be held up by Adams and one of the footmen as they helped him from the carriage and into the house. Confined by my orders to bedrest for the next several days, Pitt was then able to rise for a few hours and sit in the parlor by the blazing fire—I forbade him to enter his office—so he could gaze out the diamond-paned windows at the wintry woodlands.

I joined him one afternoon as a dusting of snow was falling, turning the dark trees into a spun-sugar scene straight out of a fairie tale. Everything looked so pure and innocent . . .

"My time has passed, Hetty," he said softly. "I haven't long left."

"Nonsense!" I replied. "Rest will soon put you back on your feet and back into the fray."

A sad smile played on his lips. But he tactfully refrained from comment.

"Mr. Pitt, I was just reviewing recent correspondence and your appointment book." Adams entered the parlor and held up an ornate card bearing the royal crest. "The official birthday celebration for Queen Charlotte is taking place tomorrow. I shall send your regrets to the palace—"

"Indeed not!" countered Pitt, his voice suddenly strong and sure. "The king and queen have been longtime friends, and it would be disrespectful to miss the occasion."

"But your strength simply won't permit it, Uncle," I counseled. "They will understand."

He shook his head. "I wish for you to go in my stead."

I blinked in surprise. "I can't—"

"Why not?" demanded Pitt. "The king is exceedingly fond of you, Hetty. He and Queen Charlotte will be delighted to welcome you to the festivities."

"Assuming his wits aren't wandering," observed Adams.

Pitt speared him to silence with a sharp look before continuing. "I remember you sneaking away from Chevening and your father's gimlet gaze to attend Lord Romney's military review in '96. The king was charmed by you. As I recall, he wanted to take you back with him to Windsor Castle and make you part of the court."

"It was a day filled with pomp and pageantry in celebration of raising a formidable militia for Kent. I loved the glitter of the uniforms and fancy gowns—and, of course, the splendid horses." I chuckled at the memory. On spotting me in the crowd, Pitt had invited me to meet the royal family, including the Duke of York and the Duke of Sussex. "The king was so kind to me, and pressed me for stories about my father and his radical ideas, which seemed to amuse him greatly."

Recalling another memory, I added, "Queen Charlotte wasn't quite so enthusiastic about having the daughter of Citizen Stanhope as part of her court, but she, too, has always been pleasant."

"So of course you must go," said Pitt.

That would mean appearing in the very highest circle of Society, a thought that filled me with dread. I wasn't sure that I could bear the whispers and the speculative stares.

"I . . ."

Pitt raised a brow and whispered something, just loud enough for me to hear. "I've never known you to be a coward, Hetty."

I bristled, but my retort died on my lips. Had I become such a coward as to let fear control my actions?

*Let the gossips titter behind their fans and spew their nasty rumors.* Appearing at the gala with my head held high would take the teeth out of their bite.

"Actually, I think that's a splendid idea," I exclaimed. "I have an enchanting new gown that I've not yet had the opportunity to wear."

The gala evening passed in a swirl of glittering gaiety. Toasts rang out and champagne flowed as laughter and good cheer filled reception rooms and grand dining hall. Any anxiety I had about showing myself—vanity had me ruing my lost looks—quickly disappeared as old acquaintances and Pitt's inner circle of advisors sought me out to pay their respects and send their best wishes to my uncle. George Canning was particularly attentive and flattered me by asking my views on various issues.

The next day, Adams appeared in the parlor, holding up a copy of *The Lady's Magazine*. "You made quite an impression, milady." He cleared his throat and read the entry. "'Lady Hester Stanhope was, as usual, dressed with much style and elegance, in black and green velvet, ornamented with embossed gold and studded with rubies, which had a most brilliant effect.'"

I confess, it was pleasing to have drawn such flattering notice. "And here I thought my headdress of feathers and diamonds was the high point of my appearance," I jested.

"I was just about to get to that," replied Adams dryly. "Heaven forfend the editor failed to mention your diamonds."

That made Pitt laugh—a heartening sound that made Adams and me exchange an optimistic smile. Perhaps the rest was restoring his resilience . . .

But optimism proved fleeting. Over the next few days, it was clear that his strength was ebbing. Parliament reconvened on January 21, and Canning sent word that the mood was somber. It was decided to make no formal vote to remove Pitt from office, but to wait for a bit and let Nature take its course.

Two days later, Pitt asked to rewrite his will. I hovered in the shadows, feeling helpless as his funereal-faced personal physician and solicitors filed in and out of my uncle's bedchamber. Dr. Farquhar, a man I disliked for his condescending attitude, earned my eternal loathing by refusing to allow me into the sickroom, saying that Pitt's wits were wandering and my presence might make things worse.

*Be damned with his supercilious orders!* Nothing was going to stop me from saying a final goodbye. I waited until he went down to supper before letting myself into the dimly lit room. Tears threatened to spill down my cheeks as I approached Pitt's bed, though I blotted them away.

"Uncle?" I leaned in and touched my palm to his cheek.

His eyelids fluttered open, and for a moment he gave me a blank look. But then a sweet smile curled on his lips.

"My dear, dear Hetty," he whispered. "I wish . . . I wish you much happiness in the future—"

"Hush," I said as I leaned down to kiss his brow. "What I care about is the present, and what would make me happy beyond measure is to show you the garden that I have created for you at Walmer Castle come spring."

In answer, he groped for my hand. Our fingers twined and I could feel the chill shadow of the Grim Reaper on his frail flesh and bones.

His breathing growing more shallow with each breath, Pitt soon sank into a slumber. I let myself out after pressing another tear-damp kiss to his forehead.

He died later that same day.

# *Chapter* 29

*March 1806*

For the first time in my life, I was completely alone, with no kindly relative to provide shelter and sustenance. *No home, no money, no prospects.* But to my surprise, it turned out that my dear uncle had looked after me in death as well as life. At his bequest, Parliament granted me a yearly pension of £1,200. It was hinted that I could also choose to reside at Windsor Castle—I assumed the oblique offer came from the king himself—and become a courtier. However, I refused.

Now that I had my independence, I wished to keep it.

From this moment on, I would depend on nobody but myself.

After some looking, I found a place to my liking at 4 Montagu Square. It overlooked a lovely central garden and there was a livery stable close by where I could rent a horse for riding in nearby Hyde Park.

While my relations with my oldest brother Mahon had soured over the years—his overweening arrogance had grown insufferable—my bond with Charles and James was growing stronger. Charles had always been my favorite. Now a young man of gentle charm and good cheer, he was quick to write to me and offer moral support. He also sent the happy news that their regiment was soon to be stationed not far from London, so I set about turning my new residence into a home for them whenever they had leave.

I had never been mistress of my own household, and despite the need to be frugal, I found that I enjoyed having the ultimate say over how things ran. Elizabeth Williams had been left homeless on Pitt's death and she accepted my invitation to live with me. Her sister also came to join us, along with my lady's maid, Susan, a cook, and a household maid.

As for my social life, I was not naïve enough to imagine that Pitt's death would not affect my stature in Society. I was no longer the favorite ward of a powerful and influential gentleman but an unmarried lady whose outspoken opinions and unconventional actions had not endeared me to the beau monde.

Still, I was a little stung at how quickly Pitt's inner circle abandoned me. After a few perfunctory visits in the weeks following my uncle's death, they conveniently forgot about my existence. I was of no practical use anymore, which spoke eloquently how little personal regard or respect they had ever had for me.

One old friend did not turn his back completely. Brummell came to offer condolences and express admiration for Pitt's character and command of the English language. I believed that his words were sincere—but I also noted that he came after dark in a public hackney, his scarf pulled up to hide half his face. Ever pragmatic, Brummell wasn't about to risk offending his powerful patron, the Prince of Wales, by being spotted paying a visit to a relative of the prince's old political enemy.

Despite the snubs, I began to find my situation liberating. The fact that I was a single lady living unchaperoned by an older relative—even though I was now thirty years old—was considered outside the bounds of propriety, but I no longer cared about seeking the beau monde's approval.

From now on, I was going to live by my own rules.

*July 1807*

"Ye heavens." Catching sight of the date on the morning newspaper, I paused in straightening up my desk. "Have I really been in charge of my own destiny for over a year now?"

The paper crackled, though I wasn't quite sure whether the sound was meant as applause or disapproval.

I knew what the public would say, but as for myself . . .

As I sat back in my chair to contemplate the question, Elizabeth entered the parlor. "We need to order more port from Berry Brothers—" She stopped abruptly on looking up from the household list in her hands and seeing my expression. "Is that harridan Duchess of Devonshire and her sister stirring more salacious gossip?"

Several months ago, a rumor had begun circulating through the beau monde that I was engaged to my old admirer William Hill, who had been a frequent visitor to my house since returning to London from his diplomatic post abroad. Both Elizabeth and I had speculated that Georgiana and Harriet were the most likely culprits, though it made no sense for them to waste their wiles. I had long ago ceased to be of any interest to the highest circles of Society.

"Not that I know of," I replied. "And as I said, it puzzles me as to why they would bother."

"They do it out of pure spite," muttered Elizabeth.

"Be that as it may, there is nothing in the newspaper that affects us. I was simply reflecting on the fact that we'd been living on our own for over a year." I paused, not quite sure why I was in such a pensive mood. "There have been ups and downs—"

"But no regrets, I trust?" she interjected.

"None at all. These days I only entertain people who I find interesting and engaging, rather than having to toady up to odious oafs because I need their blessing or their help in some project."

I allowed a hint of a smile. "Freedom comes with a price, but I am willing to pay it."

"Ah, getting back to the question of money . . ." Elizabeth gave a tiny wave of her list. "Do our coffers permit me to place an order with the wine store?"

"There are a great many things I will forego," I answered. "Port is not one of them."

We both laughed.

"Then I shall stop and place the order after visiting Paxton and Whitfield for your favorite Stilton cheese."

"Another luxury," I said. "But I do so enjoy port and Stilton. And one must not forego all the pleasures of life."

Elizabeth regarded me thoughtfully. Wondering, no doubt, whether I missed having a gentleman in my life.

*Another good question.* I had long ago realized that passions bubbled like liquid fire through my blood, and that there was nothing I could do about it. *Blame it on Diamond Pitt*, I thought with an inward sigh, glancing down at the glittering gem on my finger.

"Would you also like some cheddar?" asked Elizabeth.

"Not today," I said, resuming the shuffling of papers on my desk.

"Then I shall head off and do my errands."

Shaking off my musings, I took up my pen and began to answer some personal correspondence. The morning clouds were blowing off in the freshening breeze, and as a flickering of sunlight played over the windowpanes I looked up to see the leaves of the trees in the square's central garden come alive with myriad hues of greens.

The cheerful hues reminded me of Walmer Castle, and how happy Pitt and I had been there.

A knock on the front door startled me. We received few visitors these days.

It came again, and I realized that our household maid was upstairs attending to a balky chimney flue. Gathering my skirts, I hurried to the entrance foyer and clicked the latch.

The portal swung open on well-oiled hinges.

The visitor had turned to gaze at the garden. He was clearly a gentleman, though his well-worn navy superfine coat, buff breeches, and well-polished boots looked to have seen better days. Tall and broad-shouldered, he carried himself with a martial grace that was somehow familiar.

I narrowed my eyes as he pivoted, the sunlight setting off sparks of bronze and silver in his wind-ruffled locks.

"Lady Hester." He smiled.

My heart skipped a beat and it took me an instant to catch my breath. "General Moore!"

"Forgive me for appearing with no advance notice," he said after smoothing a hand over his tangled hair, "but I just arrived back in London from abroad and did not wish to delay paying my long-overdue respects to you in person."

"H-how kind of you, sir."

"Mr. Pitt was a great man," said Moore. "And the best of friends. I mourn his loss." The warmth of his gaze echoed the kindness of his words. "I can only imagine how bereft you must feel."

His sensitivity nearly made me come undone. Most people seemed oblivious to the elemental emotional bond that existed between me and my uncle, and the pain that now gripped my heart.

I ducked my head to hide my unshed tears. "I . . . I . . ."

Moore waited patiently for me to continue.

"Good Lord, where are my manners, to keep you standing outside?" Flustered, I hurriedly gestured for him to enter the house.

"I do not wish to intrude," he responded. "No doubt you are very busy—"

"I am never too busy for a friend, sir," I cut in. "And I very much hope that we are friends."

He smiled. "We are indeed, Lady Hester."

"Then I insist that you come in and have some tea." I paused. "Or something stronger."

A glint of amusement flashed in his eyes as he opened the door a little wider and then followed me into the entrance foyer. "A soldier never says no to a wee dram."

"I daresay a soldier never says no to some food to go along with his drink," I responded.

"In the field, one never knows when one's next meal is coming," replied Moore. "So one quickly learns to act on pragmatism rather than politeness."

The general's sense of humor was just as attractive as the rest of him. As I watched the humor dance in his eyes, I suddenly was transported back to the day that I had seen the half-finished painting of Moore in the studio of Thomas Lawrence. Though his face had been naught but oil and pigment on canvas, I had been struck by how the artist had captured his humanity, even without the battle scars that gave him such character.

"Have I a spot of ink on my chin?" inquired Moore.

I quickly looked away. "It's simply nice to see an old friend."

"An old and battered friend, so the view is not particularly edifying," Moore quipped. "But despite the outward scars, my feelings of regard are untouched."

"On the contrary, sir, the years have been kind to you. Your steadfast honor in service to your country has softened all the physical blows," I said. "It is I who have not weathered well in age. I fear that my choices have not been as wise as yours." A sigh. "But perhaps it is our scars that make us know our past was for real."

His expression turned thoughtful.

"Come, have a seat in the parlor, sir, while I go ask our cook to prepare some refreshments," I added before he could compose a reply.

Thankfully, there was a decanter of Scottish malt on the sideboard, a gift from Henry Adams on his last visit. Of all Pitt's friends and colleagues, Adams had not forgotten me after I was no longer useful in achieving their own goals.

I poured a glass for Moore and made a quick visit to the kitchen. He rose when I returned and handed me my own libation.

"*Slàinte mhath*," he said, the mellow clink of our glasses coming together punctuating his words. "That is our traditional toast in Scotland."

The burr of his Glasgow birthplace still lingered despite his world travels. It gave his voice an alluring little rasp.

"*Slàinte mhath*," I repeated. The fire of the whisky warmed my tongue and spread through the rest of me.

"Please sit, sir," I added, and took the chair facing him. "I have been following your exploits in the newspapers." After Pitt's death, Moore's military postings had taken him to Sicily and then Portugal before being dispatched to Sweden. "First of all, allow me to offer my belated congratulations on your knighthood. I must now call you Sir—"

He made a rude sound. "Please don't. I appreciate the honor, but to my way of thinking, a title is merely a frippery."

I nodded, and because I was interested in military affairs and the course of the war against France, I turned the talk to his recent campaign. "Tell me of your recent dealings with King Gustav. Was he truly as mad as a March hare?"

"A hare's unpredictable behavior lasts for only a month," a note of sarcasm edged Moore's voice. "The King of Sweden has taken permanent leave of his wits."

One of the things my uncle had admired in Moore was his forthrightness in criticizing his superior officers or the politicians when he felt that their policies were misguided and had no reasonable military objective.

"My directive was to use my army of ten thousand to guard the Swedish coast from invasion while the Swedish army fought the Russians in Finland," he continued. "I was on no account to use my troops for anything but defensive measures, and I was to stay where we could be easily evacuated by the British fleet cruising the Baltic waters if deemed necessary by our government."

"From the accounts that I read, King Gustav had other ideas," I observed.

A smile touched his lips. "To put it mildly. He wished for me to place myself under his command, and take my men to invade Norway for him—a ludicrous plan, even if I had agreed to ignore my orders, as Sweden was too weak to think of conquering another country . . ."

Moore went on to explain the diplomatic skirmishes that ensued, and how he had been forced to flee on horseback and take refuge on a British ship to avoid being arrested by the Swedish king.

"It must be exceedingly frustrating when politics interferes with sound military tactics," I mused, recalling how Pitt and his colleague Addington had fiercely disagreed on how to fight against Napoleon.

"The politicians have a grand world strategy in mind," answered Moore. "Whether all the elements actually fit together is merely an inconvenient detail." A pause. "If there is a problem, they simply expect fellows like me to hammer the pieces into place."

I wondered how he could be so unflappable. I knew enough of the inner workings of government from serving as Pitt's confidante to be aware of how many asinine orders were issued by politicians who had no knowledge of military strategy or the actual situation in faraway places.

And of how many needless deaths had resulted from such hubris.

"It doesn't bother you when they order you to do the impossible?" I demanded.

"I voice my opinion, and then the decision is theirs." Moore shrugged. "They have their duties, and I have mine. But enough of war stories," he said. "Let us talk of more interesting things." He stretched out his long legs and crossed his booted feet. "Have you a favorite route for riding in Hyde Park?"

"There is nothing so inspiring as the rugged beauty and ocean vistas of the area around Walmer Castle," I answered. "But I can recommend several bridle trails which offer a modicum of challenge."

"I would rather that you show me," replied Moore. "Might I convince you to ride out with me tomorrow?"

"I'm afraid that I am a sluggard these days, and would only ruin your outing," I replied. "My skills are not what they used to be."

"You have a natural gift for riding, Lady Hester. Physical skills may change, but they never go away entirely."

"I appreciate your kindness, but absolutely not," I said firmly. Aware of how much I had changed over the last few years, I couldn't bear for him to see how diminished I was in both body and spirit.

"As for what trails you might enjoy in the park, I suggest you turn north on passing through the Grosvenor Gate . . ."

Moore listened politely to my recommendations, and after another pleasant interlude of exchanging London gossip, he took his leave.

After closing the front door, I hurried back to my study and took a peek through the window to savor the sight of him for another few moments before he turned the corner and disappeared. It was, I knew, an absurdly silly reaction. And yet I felt an unreasonable regret that I was not likely to see him again. Duty done, Lieutenant-General Sir John Moore had far more interesting activities to keep him occupied in London than visiting an old acquaintance who was a mere ghost of her former self.

A glorious blue sky and bright sunlight greeted me the next morning as I took a seat at my escritoire to go over the household accounts. My mood still felt a little clouded, but I quickly uncapped my inkwell and set to work, determined to keep my thoughts on the present, not the past.

I was halfway through the ledger, when Elizabeth interrupted me with a tentative cough. "You have a visitor, milady."

"At this hour?" It was far too early for any social call. "If it's the butcher come to harass us about last month's bill, tell him it will be paid by the end of the week."

"It's not the butcher," answered Elizabeth. "I . . . I think you had better come see for yourself."

Mystified, I rose and followed her out to the corridor. She led the way to the back of the house and out the scullery door to the small courtyard adjoining the cartpath used by the tradesmen for their deliveries.

I stopped short, not quite daring to believe my eyes.

There was Moore in full dress uniform, mounted on a magnificent dappled gray stallion.

"You have precisely five minutes to change your clothing," he announced.

"I-I don't understand," I stammered.

"You hold a cornet's commission in the Queen's Own Hussars from me, do you not?" interrupted Moore.

The memory of his making me a ceremonial officer in the militia so that I might wear breeches while out riding with him made me smile despite my confusion. "Indeed, it is one of my proudest possessions—"

"And seeing as you've never resigned from the ranks, you're still under my command." He waggled a brow. "I shall expect you to be dressed in your magnificent red tunic in"—he pulled out his pocket watch—"exactly four minutes and thirty-nine seconds."

I shouldn't have felt such a rush of elation at the invitation. But pragmatism quickly quashed my excitement. "I can't ride out with you, sir. I don't own a sidesaddle, and even if I did, my livery stable has only nags for hire. None of them could keep up with your mount."

Moore pointed to the left. I turned, and saw a splendid chestnut filly tethered to the iron gate.

"But that's a military saddle—"

"And you possess a pair of military breeches, so I see no impediment."

"You can't mean . . ." I bit at my lower lip. "If I am spotted wearing breeches while riding with you, I fear the scandal might tarnish your spotless reputation."

"Are you afraid of what people might say?"

In truth, the idea of cocking a snoot at Society's rules was awfully appealing. At heart, I was still an unredeemable rebel and I missed the opportunities I'd had in the past to flaunt my refusal to obey its silly strictures.

"Not at all," I replied. "But I don't wish to make you the subject of scurrilous gossip."

"Lady Hester, having faced bullets and blades for most of my life, I assure you that the wagging tongues of some overfed aristocrats don't frighten me in the least." Moore smiled. "Indeed, I say we prick a pin in their pompous arses and chortle over hearing them squeal like stuck pigs."

I couldn't hold back a snort of mirth. "Even though it may get you in trouble?"

"If one isn't willing to make trouble, that means one is afraid to stand for one's principles."

My respect for him rose yet another notch.

"Now, enough fiddle-faddling, Lady Hester." A distinct twinkle in his eye belied the note of steel in his voice. "And that's an order."

I bowed my head to hide my grin. "Yes, sir."

A moment later I was rushing upstairs, feeling as giddy as a dewy-eyed debutante about to attend her first ball. I couldn't explain the lightness of my spirits, save to say that for the first time since my attempt at ending my life—nay, for the first time since Pitt had become prime minister for the second time—I felt a spark of pure happiness.

"A fine day for a gallop!" he called, glancing up at the cloudless sky as I rejoined him and gingerly swung myself up into the saddle.

A short while later, we passed through the Cumberland Gate at the northeast corner of Hyde Park. The area was wilder than the more manicured sections closer to Mayfair and the Rotten Row, the famous bridle path that drew a daily afternoon parade of the beau monde on horseback and in carriages, who all came to see and be seen.

It was still early, and we were the only riders in sight, which drew a wry chuckle from Moore as we turned down one of the bridle paths that led through a copse of elm trees. "It looks like we may have to forego the pleasure of shocking Society." His horse came abreast of mine, so close that our boots were touching.

I tried to ignore the shiver of awareness set off by his touch. Those days were far behind me.

"Are you disappointed?" he added, a mischievous glint in his eyes.

"Not at all," I replied. Up ahead, the trees thinned, allowing a dappling of sunlight to brighten the way. I was familiar with the trail and knew a long swath of meadowland lay ahead, with a cluster of stately trees at the far side, perfect for . . .

On impulse, I fisted my reins and spurred forward. "First one to the oaks wins!" I called, bending low and urging my chestnut filly to a gallop. A rush of wind pulled at my hair and slapped at my cheeks.

*Faster, faster!* I hadn't felt this alive in ages.

Sensing pursuit, my filly responded with a burst of speed. The thud of hooves pounding over the grassy ground filled my ears as I leaned lower. But my rust was showing and I bobbled in the saddle, throwing my mount off stride. Moore flew by me with Centaur-like grace and triumphed with ease.

"I beat you by a length," he called, as I slowed my filly to a walk.

"More like three," I answered. It could have been a mile for all I cared. My heart was racing, my blood was pulsing. My lungs were heaving . . .

It took me an instant to realize that tears were running down my cheeks. "Thank you, Moore."

He merely nodded and looked away to readjust one of his stirrup leathers. Such were his innate sensibilities that I suspected he knew I was thanking him for bringing me back from the dead.

And understood that nothing needed to be said.

I took a moment to tuck the flyaway strands of hair back under my shako and then patted my filly's sweat-sheened neck. "What a magnificent horse. She deserves a better rider."

"You're simply out of practice, Lady Hester. I daresay a few more hell-for-leather gallops will knock the rust off."

"Or land me flat on my derriere," I said dryly.

"Let us try to avoid that." His mouth twitched. "It's a very nice derriere."

*Was he flirting?* The thought made me smile.

"At my age, it's not easy to garner compliments from a handsome gentleman," I responded. "Perhaps I should contemplate wearing breeches more often."

Moore cocked his head, the sunlight setting off amber sparks in his hazel eyes. "Consider it an order. Shall we set the next appearance for the day after tomorrow and rendezvous at the same hour?"

I touched a salute to the brim of my shako. "Far be it for me to disobey my commanding officer."

"Then it's settled." He turned his horse. "Lead the way, milady. I'm looking forward to seeing where the path you have chosen takes us."

# Chapter 30

*Fall–Winter 1807*

The next few months brought a welcome change to the tempo of life at 4 Montagu Square. Moore and I fell into a pattern of riding out together several times a week, and while a few members of the beau monde did see me in breeches, any talk of scandal was quickly squashed by members of Pitt's inner circle, who confirmed that my actions had been approved not only by the general, but also by my late uncle and the militia commanders surrounding Walmer Castle.

Through Moore's influence, I also began to receive invitations to a number of parties, most of which would not pass muster with the highest sticklers of Society. That suited me fine, for they were far more fun. In particular, the Duke of York's mistress was a lively hostess, and always assembled a crowd of interesting guests who were not shy about expressing their views on a variety of subjects. I greatly enjoyed the arguments, often adding my opinion to the cacophony of competing voices.

My brothers Charles and James were eager to make the acquaintance of the general—Moore was much revered throughout the army as a soldier's soldier—and managed to procure leave from their regiment to visit with me in London. The four of us enjoyed several rides together and a quiet dinner at my residence where my brothers were spellbound by Moore's accounts of his various battlefield postings.

I felt a stab of sadness when the boys—I still thought of them as boys—returned to their military duties. The house seemed empty, the echoing silence a reminder of how alone I was in the world.

As if mirroring my mood, the day after their departure was darkened by frequent rain squalls and rumbles of thunder. The gloom deepened by afternoon and unable to concentrate, I couldn't keep myself from thinking about the events of the past three years.

I had reveled in the heady excitement of being in the ultimate center of power at Downing Street, but I hadn't been entirely blind to the shadows lurking just beyond the aureole of brilliant light. The job had taken a terrible toll on my uncle's health, and while we both had seen the warning signs, we chose to tell ourselves that it was only temporary.

Guilt twisted at my damaged innards. My tempestuous affair with Granville had been an extra burden on Pitt's frail shoulders.

Drawing a shaky breath, I moved to the rear windows of the parlor. The view was rather drab—a spindly London plane tree, a gated brick wall and the peaked roofs of the livery stable that stood behind it. Still, watching the flutter of the leaves and ripening seed pods reminded me of the gardens of Walmer Castle and the sense of inner peace I had felt there.

Perhaps my current reaction to Moore was because he had been part of that idyllic interlude . . .

But I sensed it was deeper than that.

Moore was different from all the other men who had touched my life. In contrast to the studied cynicism of Brummell, the unbridled emotions of Camelford and the self-serving charm of Granville, he had an innate steadiness and unruffled sense of calm about him. Within the highest circles of the beau monde, it was au courant to mock old-fashioned values like honor, compassion, and loyalty. And yet, for Moore they were a second skin—not merely words, but an integral essence of who he was.

As for me, passions had ruled my being. But the older, wiser me recognized that they had nearly destroyed me in my pursuit of love. I didn't wish to make that mistake again.

Not that I had any illusions about a romantic entanglement with the dashing general. I was well past the first blush of youth, and had lost whatever looks I still possessed after my attempt to take my own life. I found Moore alluringly attractive and missed the elemental connection of physical intimacy, however, I imagined that he had no lack of . . .

My brooding was interrupted by the arrival of an unexpected note from Moore, and on cracking the wax seal and reading its contents, I felt a flicker of light chase away the shadows.

The top generals at Horse Guards had asked him to review the new shore defenses along the Kentish coast, and so he had been invited by Lord Hawkesbury, who had succeeded my uncle as Lord Warden of the Cinque Ports, to stay at Walmer Castle for the duration of his visit. Pitt had tapped Hawkesbury for his Home Secretary when he became prime minister in 1804, so the two of us were very well acquainted. Moore was aware of that, and had suggested to Hawkesbury that he invite me, along with several of my Pitt and Grenville cousins, to make a country house party of the occasion.

My first inclination was to decline, fearing that the memories and sight of the gardens that my dear uncle had never seen would be too painful to bear. But on reflection, the opportunity to spend a week in constant company with Moore, galloping over the familiar countryside and visiting my militia friends, was too tempting to resist. If I was fated to live life as an aging spinster, with only my memories to keep me company, I wanted to be sure that I had a number of good ones to keep the bad ones at bay.

"Aging spinster," I muttered as I began laying out a wardrobe for Elizabeth to pack into my trunks. "Ha."

Whatever the future held, I vowed to myself that I would never fade quietly into the shadows.

The crunch of steps crossing the graveled courtyard drew my gaze away from the castle battlements. A footman had just handed me down from the carriage and I had paused for a moment to savor every little familiar nook and cranny in the age-old stone.

"Welcome, welcome, Lady Hester!" It was Lord Hawkesbury himself who came to greet me.

I turned, and forced what I hoped was a gracious smile. "Thank you, sir. It was exceedingly kind of you to include me on your guest list for the coming week."

The two of us had often butted heads in the past, as I think he resented my audacity in voicing my opinions in the meetings of my uncle's inner circle of advisors. Today, however, his eyes betrayed a surprising sensitivity as he took my hand between his and gave it a squeeze.

"I imagine it isn't easy to return. But I hope you will make yourself at home," he responded. "Please feel free to explore wherever you wish. I know the gardens were especially dear to you."

"That is very kind of you, sir." I accepted his arm and followed his lead toward the castle's main entrance.

"I think you'll find that very little has changed," said Hawkesbury dryly as the iron-studded oak doors opened at his approach.

*Except for the people*, I thought.

"I've had the housekeeper place you in your old quarters," he continued.

Another kindness.

"I'm sure you would like some time to refresh yourself and rest after your travels. Shall I have a maid bring up some tea and cakes?"

"That would be lovely, sir." I smiled and waved away the footman. "An escort is unnecessary. I know the way."

Hawkesbury nodded in understanding. "But of course." He retreated several steps into the central corridor, leaving me by the stairs. "We shall be gathering in the drawing room for a preprandial glass of sherry at six."

I waited for him to disappear around the corner before starting the climb to my rooms. The way was dimly lit—unlike Pitt, Hawkesbury was using only one candle, not two, in the wall sconces. But I could have found my way up the winding turns in utter darkness. I knew every dip and hollow in the stone treads, which had been worn to the smoothness of silk by centuries of footsteps.

The doorlatch to my quarters clicked with the same little hitch and squeak that I remembered. My hand trembled, but I tightened my fingers, determined to keep a grip on my emotions.

My trunks and a tray of refreshments arrived a few minutes later, accompanied by Susan, who immediately began to unpack and organize my things. After a few sips of tea and a biscuit, I left her to her work and slipped back out to the stairs.

Like a magnet exerting its pull on a bit of metal, the walkway atop the battlements drew me upward. Easing the outer door open, I stepped out into the swirling breeze.

In the distance, sunlight danced over the sea, glittering bright as shards of diamonds on the dark water. The ebb and flow of the surf on the strand—that elemental rhythm of Life, so like an inhale and exhale of breath—reached my ears through the whisper of the wind and I felt a sense of calm come over me. With all the drama between me and my father, which had me flitting from refuge to refuge with various relatives, I had no real sense of home.

Walmer Castle came closest to having a hold on my heart.

I was happy here. Even when my spirits lay grievously wounded—

"Forgive me if I am intruding."

For a large man, Moore moved with a very light step.

"I guessed that you might be up here. But if you would rather be alone with your thoughts . . ."

"You are far better company, Moore." I turned and extended a welcoming hand. "How did you know this was my favorite spot?"

"Pitt talked about how you loved the view." After twining his fingers with mine for an instant, Moore raised his hand to shade his eyes. "I can see why." A pause as he surveyed the surroundings. "It seems to embody the very essence of our sceptered isle and why we hold it so dear to our hearts."

I merely nodded, unable to find the right words to express how perfectly our sentiments aligned.

We stood in companionable silence for an interlude, watching

---

the gulls dip and dart over the sea as the clouds scudded across the cerulean-blue sky.

"Hawkesbury has some decent horseflesh in his stables," announced Moore, turning his gaze to the outbuilding just visible through the gardens. "I took the liberty of arranging a ride for us tomorrow morning, assuming that suits you."

"Nothing would give me greater pleasure," I said sincerely. "If it wouldn't be unconscionably rude to miss supper and socializing with the other guests, I would already be dressed in my breeches."

His eyes dropped to my skirts for a moment. "Duty over pleasure," he said in a husky whisper that raised gooseflesh on my arms. "You are not the only one who finds it a cursed nuisance at times."

I laughed. "Perhaps we should mutiny."

"Don't tempt me."

Banter seemed to come easily between us. With Camelford and Granville, the exchanges had always felt overpowered by the crackling of sexual tension. I was no less physically attracted to Moore, but our primary bond was friendship, not lust.

Strangely enough, that made our relationship even more dear to me. It made me feel that Moore appreciated me for my intellect and ideas rather than my body—something that I had, during my bouts of deepest introspection, admitted was a soul-deep yearning since my childhood.

I cocked my head and regarded Moore with a challenging look. "You do not strike me as a man who allows himself to yield to temptation."

"On the whole, no," he agreed after giving it some thought. "Discipline is part of my nature. However, there have been occasional exceptions."

"Oh?" I raised a brow. "Name one."

He hesitated, and for a moment I wondered whether I had been too bold in my sally. But then a smile touched his lips. "Ha. I gave you an opening and you have pressed your advantage, Lady Hester. Perhaps I should make you a colonel rather than a cornet, and put you on my staff of advisors."

"I daresay I would do the job as well as any man," I replied. "However, you are evading the question, sir."

"A diversionary tactic, but you are too sharp for that." He shifted, his thigh now touching mine.

*Another diversionary tactic?* If so, this one was working. No wonder he was such an excellent general.

However, Moore didn't execute another feint or retreat. "I don't have to think terribly hard for an example, as the latest one occurred just a few days ago. Canning asked for me to put off this trip to inspect the coastal defenses for a week in order to meet with him and other members of Portland's cabinet so as to get my military advice on the situation in Spain and Portugal."

A pause. "I refused, for the chance to spend a week in your company was too tempting to pass up."

He must have caught the spasm of surprise that flitted over my face, for he quickly added, "Don't worry, it was not really a dereliction of duty. They would have listened, nodded—and promptly dismissed whatever I said that didn't agree with their own notions of how to break Napoleon's hold on the Peninsula."

"But . . ." I frowned. "But I know Canning and Castlereagh. They are politicians and know nothing about military strategy."

"Precisely," he said dryly. "In my experience, those are just the sort of pompous bureaucrats who hold the most intractable opinions."

"Then I shall not feel a whit of guilt for enjoying your company."

Our eyes met, and I found it impossible to look away.

"I'm glad to hear it," responded Moore. "It's my understanding that there is to be some informal dancing after supper tonight. You must promise me your hand for the first set."

"I should like that very much." *Very much, indeed.* But before I could say any more, Susan pushed open the stairway door and gave me a tentative look.

"Forgive me for interrupting, milady. But if you don't return to your quarters and begin dressing, you will be late for the supper gathering."

Moore stepped back and inclined a bow. "Until later, Lady Hester."

The next morning I woke with a smile, feeling as if I was still capering on air. The strictures of Polite Society would have forbidden me to dance more than two dances with Moore at any London ball, but as Hawkesbury's house party was an informal private gathering, the rules were far more relaxed. I hadn't kept count, but we were very much hand in hand throughout the aftersupper entertainment.

A blade of sunlight cut across the bedcoverings, auguring well for the coming day's sojourn. Moore had planned for a full day in the saddle, paying a morning visit to our friend, Lieutenant-Colonel Harris, commander of the 2nd East Kent militia, and reviewing his troops before riding farther west to inspect the construction of several new Martello towers. The towers were near and dear to his heart, as he had been instrumental in bringing the concept to Britain after seeing their effectiveness as defensive fortresses in Sicily.

After a blissful stretch and a few more languorous moments reliving the previous evening's festivities, I rose and dressed in my regimental breeches and the scarlet military-style tunic that had served me so well during my former stays at the castle. Moore was already in the breakfast room and we ate quickly, with little conversation, both of us eager to be in the saddle.

He had chosen a magnificent, well-muscled gray hunter for me from Hawkesbury's horses. The groom grinned on seeing me approach and snapped a jaunty salute. "Welcome home, milady."

I smiled and exchanged a few pleasantries, though his words had cut at my heart. Much as I loved it, Walmer Castle would never be my home again.

I was merely an interloper.

"Up you go." Moore recalled me to the moment by leaning down and lacing his fingers together.

My boot touched his hands and in the next instant I was settled atop my mount.

The general's stallion gave a snort, its hooves beating an impatient tattoo on the straw-covered flagging stones. Moore was just as eager for a gallop.

"Stand aside!" he called to the barrow boys sweeping up the dung around the stable entrance.

And suddenly we were naught but a blur of motion and color as we broke free of the shadows and burst into the sunlight. At the sight of the familiar trails leading out to the countryside, I felt a surge of exhilaration and spurred my horse to a neck-and-leather gallop. My heart was pounding, and as the heady thunder of the wind filled my ears, a shout of joy rose in my throat.

A stone wall loomed ahead, forcing the lane to bend to the right. I intuitively knew what Moore intended, and followed his lead as he surged straight ahead. In the next instant, his stallion was airborne, soaring light as a feather over the stones.

"Fly!" I urged as my hunter gathered itself and rose from the ground. We hung for a heartbeat in the air and then landed on *terra firma* in perfect stride.

"*Brava!*" called Moore, who cut back to the lane and slowed his stallion to a walk. I joined him, unable to repress a hoot of laughter.

"Lud, that was fun," I added, after catching my breath and blotting my brow with the sleeve of my coat.

He grinned. "It makes you feel gloriously alive, doesn't it?"

"Aye, the worries of the world seem to fall away for the moment," I mused. "Everything becomes wondrously simple. It's just you and the elements."

"Well said." His expression turned pensive. "And those moments are special for coming so rarely."

I looked around, feeling my heart swell with memories—good memories, as this was a place I had come to love. I had brought gardens to life here, and in turn, it had given me the strength to heal myself during my darkest hours. "All the more reason to cherish them."

Moore smiled at me, and the sunlight seemed to soften to an

ethereal glow. "The older I get, the more I understand that." The wind ruffled his hair as he gazed off into the distance. It was the sudden cry of a gull wheeling overhead that broke the spell.

He gathered his reins. "Come, we mustn't keep Harris and his men waiting."

In response to the note that we were planning to visit him, the colonel had suggested that it would raise the militia's morale to have such a well-known general as Moore make a formal review of his troops. Moore was, of course, happy to be of service and a time had been arranged for the gathering.

The parade ground was just over the hill, and we spurred our horses to an easy canter as the lane wound its way up through the sloping fields. We crested the rise and saw the militia assembled in regimental precision in the meadow below. As we started the descent, a cheer rose up from the ranks.

Moore began to chuckle, and I suddenly realized what they were shouting.

"L'Amazon, l'Amazon!"

"After you, my Warrior Queen." Moore slowed his mount, allowing me to take the lead.

"Moore!" I protested.

"Wave to the troops," he counseled.

I took the white silk handkerchief from my tunic pocket, stood in my stirrups, and gave a jaunty flourish.

The cheers grew even louder.

Lieutenant-Colonel Harris rode up to greet us, and gave me a salute. "The men and I have missed your dash and color, Lady Hester. It's lovely to have you back for a visit."

I stammered a thanks as the men quieted. Harris then introduced Moore, who drew another prolonged cheer.

I hung back as the two of them started down the ranks, taking care to trail well behind them. The cheers had touched me deeply. I knew it was really a tribute to Pitt, in honor of all his efforts to create a defensive force to ward off any French invasion. But the fact that they had remembered me as his companion-in-arms brought the prickle of tears to my eyes. Perhaps in some small way my appearances with my uncle through rain and shine had helped inspire them—

The *bang* of a musket volley, fired in salute to Moore, jarred me from my thoughts. I added my voice to the huzzahs for the general, and then joined him and the colonel as the troops began to disperse.

"Ha! You've put some fire in their bellies," said Harris. "Granted, the threat of invasion is remote these days, given the command our Navy has over the seas. But I don't want them to become too complacent."

He turned to me. "You are looking as magnificent as ever in your dashing red coat, Lady Hester."

"You are far too kind, sir. My warrior days are behind me"—I drew in a deep breath of the salt-scented air—"but my spirit will always be loyal to Walmer Castle and its militias."

"Let us head to my estate, where we shall drink a toast to that sentiment," replied the colonel.

Champagne was soon fizzing, and we raised our glasses in salute to the local troops as well as to king and country.

A sumptuous midday repast was served. I noted that Moore ate sparingly and I did the same, knowing that he was eager to be back in the saddle to inspect the Martello towers west of Kingsdowne.

"Off so soon, Sir John?" asked Harris, seeing Moore push back in his chair. "I have some very fine Scottish malt, if you care to fortify yourself for your afternoon sojourn."

He turned and gave a friendly waggle of his brows at me. "And an excellent vintage of port, milady." A good friend of my uncle and frequent visitor to the castle, he knew of my fondness for the fortified wine.

"I appreciate the offer, but the chance to examine how our craftsmen have handled building the stone towers is even more enticing." Moore glanced at me. "That is, unless Lady Hester wishes to linger for a bit. Then I should be delighted to enjoy a taste of my homeland's whisky."

I quickly rose. "Much as I am grateful for your hospitality, Colonel, the chance to ride through my old haunts is very special to me. I don't wish to waste a moment."

Harris nodded in understanding. "You need not be a stranger, Lady Hester. You are welcome to visit here anytime."

It was a kind offer, but both of us knew it was fraught with both political and social implications. The colonel answered to the current prime minister's cabinet and military advisors, who felt very differently from Pitt about how to fight France. An overt friendship with me would be awkward.

Harris escorted us to the entrance hall but didn't linger over the goodbyes. "Shall you be visiting again soon, sir?" he asked, after shaking hands with Moore.

"Hard to say," came the reply. "Trouble is brewing in Spain and Portugal and how our government means to deal with the situation is uncertain."

The colonel gave a gruff nod and a final wave as we passed through the main portal and turned for the stables.

"You are sure that you feel up to making the sojourn to the towers?" he asked, once we were alone. "You—"

"I'll have you know that I could ride to Hades and back," I cut in.

"And I have your promise that you'll tell me if you're feeling fatigued?"

"But of course," I answered without hesitation. In truth, my body was aching. But I would eat my shako, feather and all, before admitting it.

His gaze held me for an uncomfortably long interlude. "Fine, then let us saddle up, Lady Amazon."

# Chapter 31

The storm clouds blew in without warning. The sun had been pleasantly warm while we reviewed the Martello towers, and Moore had been so engrossed in hearing the officers of the Royal Corps of Engineers explain the challenges of constructing them in the sandy soil that we hadn't rushed our visit. But as afternoon brought a change in the prevailing winds from the sea, a line of sullen gray clouds stole a march on us.

"Damnation," muttered Moore, looking up at the sky once we walked back to our horses. "I should have kept a better eye on the horizon." A frown formed between his brows as he watched how fast they were moving. "With luck, we can outride the rain."

"As you well know, the weather can change in a heartbeat around here." I gestured at the small oblong sack buckled to the back of my saddle. "I've brought an oilskin cloak. I assume you've also come prepared."

Moore flashed a perfunctory smile, but a distant clap of thunder only deepened his look of worry. He quickly untied the reins of my hunter and boosted me into the saddle. "There's a shortcut to the main road," he said after mounting his stallion. "But the first part of the way is steep and rough."

"I'll be fine," I assured him.

He looked about to reply, but another ominous rumble seemed to change his mind, and without further word he spurred forward. The wind was now gusting, bringing with it a knife-edge chill. We rode in silence, our attention focused on the uneven ground. The fast-fading light was making the faint path even more treacherous as the slope steepened and the loose stones grew more slippery in the damp air.

Despite my gloves, my hands were turning cold as ice. Gritting my teeth, I gripped the reins, willing myself to hold steady. Moore would hear no whinging from me.

Mist began to swirl in ghostly pale skeins. The gloom deepened.

As we came to the top of the rocky promontory, he halted to wait for me to catch up. "The worst is over," he said.

As if mocking the pronouncement, rain began to spatter us with fat, frigid drops.

Moore swore and squinted through the fog. "Ahead lies a swath of hardscrabble grazing land for sheep. Beyond that lies the road."

"Then what are we waiting for, sir?"

He hesitated. "Don your cloak."

I fumbled with the fastenings of the bag and managed to pull out the oilskin. Though it offered little warmth, I was grateful for the hooded protection from the wet.

He, too, had covered himself, and was now just a dark-on-dark silhouette against the storm.

I heard rather than saw him start forward, and spurred my horse onward.

We hadn't gone far when the clouds opened up and it started to pour.

The darkness deepened. The wind began to howl. I soon lost all track of time and place. All I could think of was keeping my boots in the stirrups and the reins clenched in my hands—

"Lady Hester . . . Lady Hester."

I was roused from my daze by Moore's voice as he gently pried open my fingers and unwound the sodden leather from around my gloves.

"I've found a herder's hut for us to shelter in until this dratted storm blows over."

I tried to speak but I couldn't seem to move my lips.

Moore pulled me from the saddle into his arms and carried me through a low opening in a primitive stone structure built within the shelter of a rock outcropping. It was cold inside but at least the shingled roof had kept the place dry. He nudged the wooden door shut with his boot and tentatively felt his way through the gloom.

"Ah." He hit up against something solid and poked around at it with his foot. "There seems to be a makeshift wooden bed covered with a blanket." A sniff. "One that reeks of sheep."

He put me down, unfastened my wet cloak, and put it aside. "Let me strike a light," he said as he put a hand inside his own outer garment.

"Ah." I heard a rustling, then a flint struck steel and a weak flame sputtered to life.

"Y-you carry a candle with you?"

"Old habits die hard." He dripped some melted wax onto one of the stones that were embedded in the earthen floor and affixed the candle to it. "When on a military campaign, it's always a good idea to carry some essentials."

He sat down beside me and lifted me back into his lap.

Loath though I was to peel myself away from his warmth, I tried to move away. However, he had my hands trapped within his, as he was busy removing my sodden gloves.

"Really, sir, I'm p-perfectly c-capable of seeing to myself," I stammered through chattering teeth.

His palms began chafing my ice-cold flesh.

A blissful sigh slipped out as heat spread through my fingers.

Moore kept up his gentle massaging. Closing my eyes, I slumped back against his chest.

"Is there a reason that you are so bloody stubborn about accepting help?"

Fatigue must have lowered my guard, for I answered candidly. "Yes, there is. You see, as a lady, I must be twice as competent as a man in an endeavor to win any sort of respect from them."

"You've nothing to prove to me," he said.

"Of course I do. The truth is, like Sisyphus rolling the blasted rock up the hill, I have to prove my mettle over and over again to you, and to all the gentlemen in my life."

Moore didn't reply right away. That he listened—truly listened—and then thought about what he had heard was one of the things that I admired most about him. Another moment passed before he lifted my hands to his lips and feathered a kiss to my knuckles. "Your courage and strength take my breath away."

My heart gave a lurch. "Ye heavens, it is *you* who possess courage and strength, Moore. You face death time after time without flinching."

"I chose to be a soldier," said Moore. "For me, charging into battle is my duty. I understood the risks and accepted them." He removed my shako and smoothed the tangled locks back from my brow. "While you must face countless little skirmishes to stand up for your principles. That takes more than physical courage, it requires moral courage." A pause. "Few people, man or woman, have that sort of bravery."

I sighed and settled more comfortably against his chest. "How is that such a paragon of manly perfection isn't married?" Or perhaps I was mistaken. "That is, I assume you aren't married as I've never heard you mention a wife."

"I am not," he replied.

"You've never been tempted?"

The ensuing silence seemed to thrum against the stones. It was, I acknowledged, a very intimate question, and one I had no earthly right to ask it. But before I could apologize, he responded.

"Once." Another silence.

"Forgive me," I said quickly. "It was impertinent to probe into your personal life."

"I am happy to answer," said Moore softly. "I esteem you too highly to want for there to be any secrets between us."

That he had such faith in me brought a sudden welling of tears to my eyes. *Why had I not had a chance to develop a friendship with this extraordinary man sooner?* He was kind, and courageous, not only on the battlefield, but also in standing up for his principles with the politicians. Pitt had told me about his outspokenness, and how it had affected his career because he refused to back down from expressing his beliefs, no matter the cost.

But perhaps my younger self wouldn't have been wise enough to appreciate his steady flame.

"I fell in love with the daughter of my commanding officer in Sicily, General Fox," he began. "Caroline was seventeen, vivacious, charming, and exceedingly clever."

"I imagine she was also exceedingly beautiful," I mused. "And returned your sentiments?"

Though it was too dark to see it, I sensed his smile. "Yes. And yes."

Moore allowed a moment of silence before continuing. "There was no formal declaration between us. We were simply content to live in the moment—something which is second nature to a soldier. But then Castlereagh was appointed Secretary of War and General Fox was recalled to London, while the accompanying orders turned the command of our forces on the island over to me. I realized that I would have to announce my intentions before he left . . ." He let his words trail off.

"And?" I encouraged.

"And . . . well, I suppose that reason won out over emotion. You see, there were two important issues for me to confront. The first was a pledge that I had made with my brother Graham, a captain in the Royal Navy. We had both come to terms with the fact that the threat of death was a constant in our lives. However, we had seen how the loss of a husband and father caused terrible suffering for wives and young families. So we made a pact with each other not to marry until the war was over."

I found his hand and twined our fingers together. "You, sir, are too honorable for your own good."

That make him chuckle.

"I'm sure your brother would have released you from the agreement. It wasn't as if it was written in blood."

"Perhaps," he acknowledged. "If that had been the only impediment, I might have found a way around it. However, there was an even more important issue. As I said, Caroline was seventeen." A pause. "And I was forty-eight.

"She insisted that the differences in our ages did not matter," he said. "At that moment in time, she might have been right. But as I came to grips with the stark truth, I realized that it would have been unfair of me to marry her. Age and the arc of our life experiences would have soon caught up with us, leaving us both unhappy."

It was a thoughtful, well-reasoned decision. If only I had possessed such discipline, I might have avoided a great deal of pain and suffering.

"Your wisdom does you credit, Moore. I wish . . ." My fingers tightened around his, the connection steadying my emotions. "Never mind what I wish."

He freed his hand, and for a moment I felt adrift. But then, his arms came around me. "What about you, Lady Hester—"

"Oh, please," I blurted out. "Call me Hester. Or Hetty. Formality makes me feel that I have no close family or friends left in the world."

"Then Hetty it shall be," he replied.

The storm raging outside our spartan refuge no longer felt so threatening.

"But only if you will call me John," he added. "I understand what you mean. All the constant bowing and scraping can make one feel very isolated and alone."

"Our thoughts align, John." His given name came so easily to my tongue. "Let us think of ourselves as comrades in arms, and always be here for each other."

"I should like that very much, Hetty," said Moore. "But surely you have had plenty of opportunities to marry in the past."

"Yes, I've had proposals—several, in fact. The trouble is, I am neither fish nor fowl. A traditional marriage, one in which my whole world would be confined to household duties, would bore me to perdition. And the idea of a union in which I am seen as an intellectual equal, and allowed the opportunity to offer advice and counsel, scares most gentlemen."

"Ah." A note of amusement shaded the sound. "Just for the record, I don't frighten easily."

"Indeed, your exploits speak for themselves." But I couldn't refrain from adding a challenge. "However, as a general, you are used to issuing orders and expecting unwavering obedience."

"There are times when a great many lives depend on my orders, and having them obeyed quickly," he said. "For the most part, though, a good general should be happy to have advisors who think for themselves and voice their opinions. Such counsel can help avoid costly mistakes."

"Mistakes," I repeated. "God only knows, I have made more than my share of those."

"Haven't we all?" he said softly.

"I am quite sure that mine have been far more egregious than yours." Intent on matching his candor with unflinching honesty, I forced myself to go on. "My romantic entanglements have not been quite as pure as yours. I have often—too often—allowed my passions to overrule all reason and rules."

"Love is an emotion," responded Moore, "not a mathematical formula or a precise point on a map that can be plotted with a compass or sextant."

"A wild and uncontrollable one at times," I pointed out. *No secrets*, I reminded myself. I wanted him to know the full measure of my true self. "Which is all very well for a man. But heaven forfend when a woman gives way to carnal desire."

Just so there could be no mistake as to my meaning, I added, "In the eyes of Society, I am soiled goods for giving myself to a man without the blessings of a marriage vow."

I took care to say it lightly, but then looked away.

"I have always thought that when it comes to the act of intimacy"—Moore gently cupped my chin and turned me to face him—"it is awfully hypocritical of Society to decree that there is one set of rules for a man and an entirely different set for a woman. After all, it does require two . . ."

His response—that he, too, saw the absurd irony in the rules—surprised a laugh from me. "My transgression doesn't shock you?"

"Alas, I have a confession to make, Hetty." A note of unholy humor resonated in his voice. "I, too, have experienced the act of intimacy without the blessings of a marriage vow."

"What a relief to hear that you are not a saint!" I responded, happy to copy his teasing tone.

"Oh, definitely not a saint." He shifted again, and suddenly I was enfolded in his arms, his lips a mere hairsbreadth from mine. "Indeed, I fear that I would be damned as a sinner for what I'm about to do next."

His kiss was unlike any I had experienced before.

"There is," I said a bit breathlessly, "a great deal to be said for sin."

Neither of us bothered with words for the next little interlude.

As my legs tangled with his, Moore sought to rise—but his knee buckled and banged up hard against the bedstead.

"Damnation." He gave a self-deprecating wince. "Sorry—an old injury from Egypt acts up on occasion."

Finding my footing, I dropped my arms to circle his waist and steady him.

"As you see," he said wryly, "I'm saddled with a number of mementoes from past battles."

"My dear John, be assured that I wouldn't wish for you to be any other way. Your wounds are a badge of honor. They give you character and individuality." I raised a hand to trace the scar around his eye. "While the vast majority of gentlemen within the beau monde are merely pasteboard cutouts, all indistinguishable from one another."

"You are too kind—"

"Be damned with kindness! My acquaintances will assure you that I'm too sharp-tongued and acerbic for comfort. I'm outspoken." My fingertips caressed his cheek. "And opinioned."

"I'm actually quite fond of your opinions."

"No man of my acquaintance has ever said that to me," I replied.

Moore's eyes sparked in the fluttery light. "Then they are all bloody fools."

A gust of wind blew through the cracks in the stone wall and a shiver passed through me.

He drew me to his chest. I could feel our hearts beating as one. "Damnation, you're freezing. I had better get you back to the castle before you catch your death of cold."

My teeth were chattering, but my only thought was that I wished this interlude could last forever.

Cocking an ear, Moore held himself still. "The rain appears to have stopped. We should seize the moment and be on our way."

"It's awfully dark," I pointed out. "And the trail will be treacherous in places from all the rain."

"*Fortes fortuna juvat*," said Moore with a smile. "As we say in the army, 'Fortune favors the bold.'"

Which was why I kissed him again before donning my cloak.

# Chapter 32

*Winter 1808*

My life changed dramatically upon my return to London. Moore's military duties demanded much of his time, and so the opportunity to ride in the park or enjoy a quiet supper together happened only a few times a week. But our bond quickly deepened, and soon not a day passed without us exchanging written notes. The arrival of the morning and afternoon posts caused my pulse to quicken, and the *crack* of the wax seal on his missives and the sight of his looping script brought a fluttery sigh to my lips.

I had not intended to fall in love, still leery of my passion's dark side, which had nearly destroyed me. But Moore, ever the clever and confident general, had quickly outmaneuvered my defenses with his kindness, integrity, and saber-sharp sense of humor.

Until now, I had never truly experienced the sense of being connected heart and soul to a kindred spirit. A platitude, perhaps, but how Moore made me feel defied all attempts to adequately express it in words. He treated me as his equal, which in itself spoke more eloquently than any language.

I also savored the joys of our physical relationship. Mindful of protecting the privacy of our trysts—he never spent the night under my roof—we took great care in choosing our moments. But when they came . . . Moore was an ardent and experienced lover and we both took delight in pleasuring each other.

Our joinings warmed me body and soul. I had never felt so at peace.

But the rumblings of war on the Continent were growing more threatening, and Moore was soon caught up in the political battles as factions within the government fought to come up with a winning strategy.

"Is something worrying you?" After several sidelong glances at Moore's profile, I ventured the question. His normally unruffled composure looked to be on edge.

"Forgive me, Hetty. I fear that I am rotten company for you this morning." The early morning was decidedly chilly, and his breath turned to a swirl of silvery vapor as he huffed an exasperated sigh. "General Gwyn of Horse Guards is a bloody nitwit. I've explained to him all the military reasons as to why the government's strategy concerning the Peninsula is deeply flawed, and asked for his support in presenting the facts to Castlereagh. But he's never commanded a force in the field. I doubt he would know his arse from a hole on the ground if bullets began to fly."

I couldn't repress a snicker, though the subject was a deadly serious one. Horse Guards, the building named for the elite cavalry regiment, housed the command center of the British Army. Moore, for all his accolades and experience in battle, answered to them.

"And you are having no luck in convincing any of the other generals to argue with Castlereagh over the government's proposed campaign to push the French out of Spain?" Lord Castlereagh was a long-time friend and colleague of Pitt's, though they often disagreed about policies. And he was now Secretary of State for War in the present cabinet.

"None of them. They all refuse to listen." His mouth tightened. "Nobody wants to hear me say that corruption and incompetence—the placing of officers who lack experience but are under the patronage of powerful politicians—are threatening our ability to wage war."

"Even if it is true?"

He gave a mirthless laugh. "Most especially if it is true." A sigh. "It's not just that. Our government's overall strategy is fatally flawed. The size of the army they plan to send to the Peninsula is too small to fight Napoleon's by itself. They are counting on the Spanish Army to join our forces, but any military man who has experience with the situation in Spain knows that is highly unlikely."

"I know you are right, both morally and practically, John." There was a laughable irony to what I was about to utter next, but nevertheless, it needed to be said. "But perhaps a better strategy would be to hold your tongue for now and refrain from a full frontal attack against those you know aren't likely to listen. Instead, reconnoiter and find a more likely ally than the generals at Horse Guards and then attack Castlereagh from a different angle."

His expression turned thoughtful.

"The corridors of power are crowded with ambitious men looking to jockey for position so that they may find a way to rise to a higher position. We need to think about who is the strongest rival to Castlereagh, and how we might make him your ally."

Moore chuffed a grunt. "You make it sound very . . . Machiavellian."

"You fight more clear-cut battles, John. You know the enemy, along with his strengths and weaknesses. Politics is far more nebulous. There are shadows within shadows, making it difficult to discern friend from foe."

An oath slipped from his lips. "So you are saying that there is no chance of changing the government's thinking?"

"On the contrary." I smiled. "It will take some maneuvering on the chessboard. But the real game hasn't yet begun."

He raised his brows in question.

"Let me think . . ." I mentally reviewed the list of my uncle's inner circle of politicians. "Now, Sir James Pulteney is a fellow Scotsman and a fellow general, who serves as Secretary at War—which despite its name has very different duties from the Secretary of State for War."

"By Jove," muttered Moore. "I had forgotten that Pulteney had taken on a political position."

"Pulteney is involved in organizational aspects of the army, not its policies, but if I remember correctly, he and my relative Lord Grenville are members of the same club and hunt together in Scotland," I mused. "Now, Grenville has no love lost for the Duke of Portland and his current cabinet. He might be very willing to form an alliance with Pulteney and support your arguments."

"My dear Hetty, I shall hand you my lieutenant-general's commission," he responded. "The war in Portugal and Spain will be over in a fortnight."

Moore's look of admiration brought a flush of pleasure color to my cheeks. "I've had a chance to learn political strategy from one of the masters of the game." I pursed my lips, thinking of the next move. "I happen to know that Lord Grenville is holding a soiree two evenings from now. I will write him and ask if we might attend so that you might tell him some of your thoughts on why Castlereagh's war plan is misjudged."

The elegant drawing room was already crowded, the baritone thrum of masculine voices punctuated by discreet laughter from the ladies and the mellow clink of crystal. My pulse quickened and gooseflesh pebbled on my bare forearms as Moore and I crossed the carpet to greet our host.

Grenville offered a tentative smile. He had always been a little leery of me because I refused to be bound by Society's rules. Nonetheless, it had been kind of him to agree to invite us.

After a kiss to my hand, Grenville looked up at Moore. "It's a pleasure to see you, sir. A number of my colleagues are most interested in hearing your thoughts on the war." He gestured to one of the side salons, where several liveried servants were serving champagne. "Please help yourself to some refreshments and I'll come find you shortly."

I took a sip of the sparkling wine, the bubbles prickling against my tongue as I savored the sight and sounds around me. Honesty compelled me to admit that I missed the excitement of these gatherings, the unseen currents of energy and anticipation as the rich and powerful brokered alliances, both personal and political.

Moore observed the crowd with a polite smile that did not quite reach his eyes.

"You look very handsome in your dress uniform," I said, taking his arm and drawing us to a quiet spot in the shadowed corridor connecting the salon with the main drawing room. I had insisted that he wear his tunic with the gold-threaded embroidery on the black facings, along with the ornate medals he had won for his bravery in battle.

"A real military man shouldn't resemble some pompous opera buffoon," muttered Moore. "I always thought Admiral Nelson looked ridiculous, prancing around covered in gold and glitter." He made a face. "The silly fellow paid for his hubris with his life."

Nelson had insisted in wearing all his medals during the Battle of Trafalgar. A French sharpshooter up in one of the masts of the enemy fleet had spotted the flashes and shot him.

"Pomp and pageantry may be dangerous when bullets and blades are flashing all around you," I replied, "but on this battle-field, it is the appearance of confidence and strength that will win the day. I know Grenville and his friends. Your looks will be just as important as your words in winning their support."

"Are they really that shallow?"

"It's not that simple."

The light from the crystal chandeliers in the main drawing room cast a sparkling light over the guests . . . the ladies swathed in jewel-tone silks and satin, the gentlemen a picture of elegance in their black-and-white evening finery. Moore was the only military offi-cer present, and I noted that his gold-braided scarlet coat was drawing everyone's eyes.

*Like moths to a flame.*

"Negotiations are a complex mix of facts and emotions." I pat-ted his sleeve. "Trust me, first impressions matter. You will have them on your side in an instant."

His gaze drifted back to the festivities. "And then? Battles are rarely won quickly and cleanly."

"Castlereagh is a formidable opponent with powerful support-ers. I'm under no illusion that a victory will be easy—"

"Especially as he resents me for being right about the debacle in Sweden," he interjected.

Moore had warned the government that given the King of Swe-den's irrational behavior and weak army, they were making a grave mistake to send a British military force to help defend the coast. His words had proved prophetic as the mad king had tried to wrest control of the troops. It was only through Moore's quick thinking and clever strategy that the regiments marched to where the British naval force was anchored and were evacuated before any confrontation could take place.

"That's true. Castlereagh was embarrassed in the newspapers. He won't forget it," I replied. "But be that as it may, I think we have a fighting chance. I have some ideas of who else we might ap-proach . . ." I fell silent as I saw Grenville approaching.

"Without your political skills," whispered Moore, "I wouldn't have a snowball's chance in Hell of winning the cabinet over."

"Might I steal the general away from you for an interlude, Hetty?" asked Grenville.

"But of course." I watched them return to the drawing room and exit through a side door that led to the library, then released my breath in a slow exhale, uncertain of what to do with myself.

The swirl of colors and conversations within the crowd sud-denly took on a more brittle edge. I had once reveled in being part of this world—the dealmaking, the compromises, the exerting of subtle pressure through use of both carrot and stick. But now, the manipulations-within-manipulations no longer held the same ap-peal. Perhaps age and adversity had given me more wisdom. Pos-sessing power no longer held such an allure. I had come to value other things.

Turning away from the bright lights and gaiety, I moved to the far wall of the side salon, where a set of gilt-framed botanical prints were on display. *Life.* Planting a seedling and watching it blossom into something that would add to the beauty of Nature. That was more appealing to me than cultivating gossip and innuendo.

I lost myself for a time in studying the details of the hand-colored engravings, taking pleasure in the artistry. But then, a rustling of silk whispered over the carpet and a familiar voice drew me back to the moment.

"My dear Lady Hester, what a surprise! We never see you anymore in Society."

I reluctantly turned to face Georgiana, Duchess of Devonshire, and her sister Harriet, Lady Bessborough.

"I now understand why," added Georgiana. Her brows danced up and down in a suggestive waggle. "I saw you come in with Lieutenant-General Sir John Moore." She fluttered her lashes. "What a handsome devil. I hadn't realized that the two of you were so well-acquainted."

I took a sip of champagne, determined to marshal my emotions and not allow her to provoke me. Georgiana took delight in hurting people. She had caused me immeasurable pain before. I would not allow her to do so again.

"You are looking very well, Lady Hester," interceded Harriet, clearly trying to blunt the sharpness of her sister's claws. "That shade of emerald green is very becoming."

Given her relationship with Granville Leveson Gower, Harriet was the sister I should despise. But I had always found her to be the more sympathetic of the two. She was not intentionally cruel. Still, I paid no heed to her platitudes. Instead, I chose to respond to her sister.

Ignoring Georgiana's mention of Moore, I addressed her first remark. "Yes, I have little interest in mixing with Society these days. Now that my uncle is no longer in need of my support, I choose to socialize with people whom I find truly engaging, rather than with the high and mighty of the beau monde, who are so often more interested in superficialities rather than any meaningful discourse."

For an instant, Georgiana's eyes narrowed in irritation. However, she quickly assumed a condescending smile. "It's not as if you have much of a choice in the company you keep."

Harriet glanced at me, a glimmer of apology pooled in her eyes, as she touched her sister's sleeve. "Come, let us leave Lady Hester to enjoy the art in peace. Shall we go have a look at what's going on in the cardroom?"

"Does the dashing general know of your past?" asked Georgiana, after brushing off her sister.

It was my turn to smile, one that was just as false as hers. "Moore finds tattlemongers and troublemakers just as odious as I do."

Her mouth thinned to a taut line. But before she could form a reply, we were joined by a fourth.

"Forgive me for interrupting, ladies." In the candlelight, the epaulettes, fancy stitching, and ornate medals on Moore's scarlet dress tunic glowed like liquid gold. As for the steel in his eyes as his gaze met mine . . .

I saw the elemental warrior beneath the well-tailored uniform.

"Might I steal Lady Hester away for a private word?" He held out his hand, not waiting for the others to answer. "Come, my dear," he added with a possessive look.

I moved to his side.

"Enjoy your evening, ladies," he added coolly, barely sparing Georgiana and Harriet a glance.

I saw a ripple of envy stir in Georgiana's gaze. *Or was it longing?* Hers was a loveless and cruel marriage. I might have felt sorry for her if she wasn't so heartless in provoking misery for others.

I looked up at Moore as we walked away.

He winked.

"How did you know—"

"That you needed rescuing?" he finished. "I suppose it's become second nature for me to sense when there is trouble." He settled my hand more firmly in the crook of his arm. "And I also recalled you telling me that the sisters had been particularly unkind to you."

It seemed to me that honor and loyalty were woven into the very fiber of his being.

A smile touched my lips. "You are a perfect hero."

Moore made a self-deprecating sound.

"But be forewarned, Georgiana will likely foment some dark

mischief," I added. "She's very skilled at starting malicious rumors. I fear . . ."

I swallowed hard. "I fear she may seek to spread word that we are linked in some scandalous liaison. I will feel terrible if your good deed ends up tainting your reputation."

"I would be proud to have my name linked with yours, Hetty. We are comrades in arms," he replied. "We don't coat our words in spun sugar or let honeyed lies drip from our tongues. We say what we believe, whether other people find it palatable or not."

I nodded. "But it means that we often find ourselves under attack."

"True." His gaze took on a martial gleam. "But I would rather go down fighting for my principles than flee in cowardly retreat."

# Chapter 33

*Spring 1808*

Over the next few months, Moore's principles were under constant attack. He continued to voice his criticism of the government's plans for waging war against the French forces in Portugal and Spain. In reply, the cabinet launched a counteroffensive. Castlereagh, who did indeed harbor a personal grudge against Moore for having been proved right in warning against sending a British force to aid the King of Sweden, stepped up his whispering campaign to brand Moore as a troublemaker who refused to follow the chain of command.

Moore seethed over the veiled insults to his honor and integrity. I tried to explain to him that the battles waged behind closed doors within the various ministries and Parliament were fought with far more subtle weapons than blades and bullets. He hated the intrigue, as well as the inevitable deals and compromises that were made, feeling that right and wrong were quickly lost in the shadows.

I didn't disagree. But that was the way the government worked.

On his arrival in London the previous summer, Moore had been told that he was welcome to a posting in Portugal should he want it, but that he would be serving under General Harry Burrard and

General Hew Dalrymple—known as Dowager Dalrymple. They were both elderly gentlemen, one of whom had grown too heavy to sit upon his horse. Moore had refused the offer, knowing it was a deliberate snub for his outspoken opinions. Now, more than ever, it appeared that his stellar career had come to a standstill. I felt his frustration. But a part of me was glad that he wasn't risking his life on the brutal battlefields of the Peninsula.

However, the spring brought a change in the winds of Fortune. By March, it became clear that Moore would be ordered to serve in Portugal. And as a good soldier, he had no choice but to obey, despite his reservations about the government's strategy.

*September 1808*

"Have you seen my leather valise?" shouted my brother Charles from the top of the stairs.

"It's just where it should be—down here in the entrance foyer next to your trunks," I called back, after casting another look around the jumble of gear piled against the side wall. "Did you remember to add the woolen stockings I purchased yesterday?"

"Yes! And thank you for the extra shaving soap." The rapid-fire thump of bootsteps on the oak treads echoed off the walls as I returned to the drawing room. Charles appeared a moment later and, seizing me in a bear hug, he lifted me off my feet and spun round and round in a whirling-dervish circle.

"Put me down!" I sputtered.

Laughing, he did so and planted a kiss to my brow. "I can't help it. I'm the luckiest man in the world!" he crowed. "I'm off to the war—and as aide-de-camp to Lieutenant-General Sir John Moore!"

I forced a smile, not wanting to cloud his happiness.

"Thank you, dear sister." Charles hugged me again. "For everything. James and I owe our good fortune in life to you and the sacrifices you have made to play both mother and father to us."

Tears welled up in my eyes, but I blinked them away. I had promised myself that I would not weep now that the day of departure was almost here.

"I couldn't be prouder of the two of you. What fine young gentlemen you have become." I leaned back and patted his cheek. "Just promise me that you will be careful and"—I took a heartbeat to steady my voice—"come home safely."

He laughed with the hubris of a young man who believed himself invincible. "Of course I'll come home safely! Moore is a splendid general. We shall march into Spain and give Junot and the Frogs a good thumping. Then we shall celebrate the fruits of our victory with fine wine and luscious . . ." He coughed. "And, er, luscious oranges. From Seville, which is quite famous for its oranges."

"Don't gorge yourself on marmalade," I said dryly.

The clatter of carriage wheels rolling to a halt drew Charles to the front window. "It's my friend Clermont, come to fetch me and my luggage!"

The moment of parting had come.

He whirled around, his eyes bright with excitement. "I shall be staying with him at the barracks tonight, and James will be coming to a farewell celebration."

Thank heavens James was not senior enough in rank to have garnered a spot on Moore's staff. He would not thank me for the thought, but so be it.

"Then we leave at first light for Southampton," continued Charles, "and the ships to transport us to Lisbon."

I forced a smile, though my heart clenched in dread.

He caught me in another quick hug before rushing to answer the knock on the front door. I stood where I was, listening to the hearty laughter punctuating the scrapes and thumps of the luggage being hauled to the waiting vehicle. To Charles, war was a grand adventure, all shiny swords, colorful plumage, and heroic deeds that came with nary a scratch.

I prayed that he would learn the terrible reality—the smashed limbs, the bloody entrails, the gut-wrenching fear—quickly enough to temper his youthful exuberance with a healthy dose of pragmatism.

He looked in through the doorway and blew a kiss. "I'm off, my dear Hetty! Wish me well!"

"With all my heart." I did not seek to touch him again, wishing to part with a show of good cheer, rather than risk betraying my morbid thoughts. Instead I followed him down the front steps and waved until the carriage disappeared around the corner.

"Don't fret, milady." Elizabeth was waiting for me as I trudged back into the house. "The general will keep him safe."

*And who would watch over Moore?*

I merely nodded, not trusting my voice. At least James was not marching off to war. Much to his chagrin, his regiment was remaining in England.

"As you requested, Cook is preparing a special supper for this evening."

"Thank you." I had invited Moore to dine with me. He, too, would be leaving tomorrow at dawn. "Oh, and please take some funds from the household accounts and treat yourself, Susan, and Cook to an evening out after the meal is served." I did not wish for anyone else to intrude on our last night together before he rode off to war.

A flicker of understanding stirred in Elizabeth's gaze. "How kind of you, milady."

The afternoon hours ticked by slowly, though I knew that the evening would pass all too quickly. I straightened up the bed-chamber that Charles used on his visits, carefully folding the clothing left helter-pelter on the floor and putting the items away in the armoire, and then penned some correspondence, though I was barely aware of what I was writing.

My thoughts were elsewhere.

I dressed with care when the time came, choosing a deep claret-colored gown, which I hoped would cast a touch of color to my cheeks.

At last, the rap of the brass knocker signaled that Moore had arrived. I broke away from my pacing in front of the unlit hearth and went to greet him.

"How lovely to see you, Hetty," said Moore as he bowed over my hand.

I flung my arms around him and pulled him close.

"I have been thinking of you all day," he whispered.

"And I you." I leaned back and touched my palm to his cheek.

His lips quirked into that wonderfully crooked wry smile that I had come to hold so dear. "I should think you have better things to occupy your thoughts than a scarred war horse."

"You know how fond I am of horses."

That made him chuckle.

"Come," I said, "let me pour you a drink."

Candlelight added a mellow glow to the nascent gold and pink hues of early twilight as we settled ourselves in the drawing room. Moore and I both chose port in unspoken homage to his coming destination, but tonight its usual velvety sweetness was bitter on my tongue. Still, I took care to keep the conversation light, asking about the logistics for his travel, and whether he had made a decision on final additions to his staff of officers.

After lingering over our preprandial drinks, I rang a small bell on the side table, signaling for supper to be served.

"I thought we would dine informally this evening, with the platters brought here to the table, so that we may serve ourselves," I announced, as Moore helped me into my chair at the head of the table.

"As you well know, I much prefer informality," he answered, taking the seat to my right.

I fixed a plate for him and by unspoken agreement we continued to talk of pleasantries, exchanging fond memories about Pitt and our mutual acquaintances at Walmer Castle. The food was tasteless to me, but Moore appeared to greatly enjoy the offerings. I had ordered his favorite dishes—a creamy chowder of mussels and clams, roasted guinea fowl, new potatoes sautéed with bits of cured ham, and a rich custard studded with sweetmeats.

"What a splendid meal," he said after finishing the last spoonful of his custard and releasing a blissful sigh. "But that is merely sustenance for the body, while your company is sustenance for the soul."

I reached out and placed my hand over his. We sat in companionable silence for an interlude, the soft flickering of the candle-light caressing our flesh.

"Shall we return to the drawing room?" I suggested. Loath as I was to break our connection, I had some gifts waiting there that I wished to give him.

Moore settled on the sofa while I closed the draperies and brought a bottle of Scottish malt and two glasses back with me to further mellow the mood.

A soft splash of liquid sounded as I poured a dram and passed it over. The swirl of amber dark spirits sent a skittering of gold across his face as he lifted the whisky in salute.

"To my Amazon," he murmured.

I regarded him through the cut-crystal facets of my glass. "To my General." Every little scar on his face had come to be inexpressibly dear to me. "The perfect hero."

"Trust me, Hetty, I have my flaws," responded Moore, after quaffing a long swallow of his whisky.

"As do I."

He smiled. "Perhaps that is why we fit together so well."

A laugh tickled in my throat. "What a shockingly risqué thing to say."

"Not nearly as risqué as what I am thinking."

I leaned in to kiss him, savoring the sweetness of the malt lingering on his lips. The crackling fires of passion and lust were all very well, but I loved that the bond between us was something far more elemental.

Fearing that my emotions were about to get the best of me, I quickly turned and reached for the small bag I had placed beside the sofa. "I have several small gifts that I wish to give you for the coming campaign."

Moore put his glass down on the tea table, and moved a little closer.

The rustle of tissue paper rose into the silence. "I-I have heard that the winter in Portugal and Spain can be brutal." I handed him the package, which was wrapped in a striped pattern of gold and cream. "It's hardly a romantic gesture," I added with an apologetic shrug. "But perhaps it will prove practical."

He carefully untied the ribbon around the wrapping and let the paper fall away. "How very thoughtful of you." His fingers traced over the soft buff-colored leather of the shearling-lined riding gloves.

"Hoby himself made them specially to match the exact color of your leather riding breeches," I said, referring to London's most exclusive purveyor of footwear and leather accessories. "He assures me that the tanned sheepskin outer is very tough and the fleece lining very warm."

Moore slipped on the gloves. "They will bring me much comfort," he said. "In so many ways."

"I took the liberty of having him embroider my initials inside the cuff of the right glove," I explained, "so that I may close my eyes and think of holding you close through . . ." I hitched in a breath. "Through whatever ordeals lie ahead."

"My dear Hetty." The gloves came off and he cupped my chin in his palm. "Yes, there will be ordeals. I respect you too much to pretend otherwise. But be assured that your support shall help me weather them."

Ducking my head, I reached into the bag again, hoping to hide the look of fear that suddenly froze on my features. "This gift is more personal."

He accepted the tiny box and smiled at the fancy scarlet bow. "Amazon red." Once the ribbon was undone and the lid was off, he plucked up the small gold ornament and held it up.

"It's a fob in the shape of a seal for your pocket watch," I explained. "To go along with the other three you have on your chain."

Moore turned it over to examine the intaglio design cut into deep red semiprecious stone.

"It's an Amazon riding astride on horseback. I had the jeweler add a wild halo of hair so it is clear that the rider is a lady."

I heard him draw in a breath.

"The stone is carnelian," I continued in a rush. "The ancient

Egyptians believed that it gave courage and strength to their warriors." It was also thought to enhance feelings of love and passion.

"It's beautiful," he whispered, touching his thumb to the carved image before reaching into his waistcoat pocket for his pocket watch. The short gold chain winked in the lamplight as he worked my gift onto the ring that held the other fobs. "It will be a talisman to light up my spirits in times of darkness."

"I wish you didn't have to go, John," I blurted out, pressing my palm to his heart. "If the politicians are half as wrong as we think, it will be a fiasco."

"It's my duty, both to our brave soldiers and our country, to prevent that," answered Moore.

*But at what cost?* I wondered. However, I didn't dare voice that terrible thought aloud.

"I, too, have brought along a gift." He pocketed his watch and pulled out a small folded square of mud-colored oilskin cloth. "Forgive the less than elegant wrapping." An apologetic grimace. "A military barracks is a rather spartan place."

The gesture took me by surprise. I took it but hesitated in opening it, as the realization suddenly hit me that Moore was offering me the first actual gift I had ever received from a gentleman other than a family member.

*Brummell, Camelford, Granville*—they had given me naught but worldly experience. Save for the self-inflicted physical damage caused by Granville's heartbreaking betrayal, I had no tangible token that they had ever been a part of my life.

Moore's expression turned tentative as I made no move to open the oilskin packet. "I have to warn you . . ." He cleared his throat with an uncertain cough. "That is, I hope you do not think it too bizarre . . ."

He fell silent as I lifted the first fold. Intrigued by a fire-gold glimmer, I shook the contents of the cloth into my upturned palm.

It was a small medallion—an eight-pointed star exquisitely crafted in gold, silver and jeweltone enameling. The gold arms were engraved with a wavy starburst pattern that shimmered in the play of lamplight. At its center was an enameled regimental crest rendered in colorful detail. A circular gules of gold, topped by a silver bas relief of a royal crown, surrounded the crest. The word VALOR was centered below the crest, flanked by a location and a date inscribed in a flowery script.

"It is a military medal?" I guessed. My gaze met his. "One of yours?"

Moore looked a little embarrassed. "My first, from some obscure skirmish in the war with our former American colonies."

"Valor," I read aloud. "I imagine you have a box full of these. You should wear them with pride."

He shook his head. "As I have told you, I believe that an officer shouldn't prance around with sparkling baubles pinned to his chest. His actions should speak for themselves."

"Yes, but—"

He silenced me by touching a finger to my lips. "Hetty, no doubt I should have chosen a more ladylike piece of jewelry to express my regard for you. But this just felt right to me because it sums up my feelings for you perfectly. I think you are the bravest person I have ever known, fighting with undaunted courage against all odds for what you believe in, and never surrendering your convictions."

"I wish that I were half as brave as you seem to think. But I cherish your sentiments—and this piece of yourself, which means more to me than words can express." I closed my fingers around the medal. "I shall wear it around my neck on a gold chain as a constant reminder of your faith in me."

After stashing it in a hidden pocket of my gown, I added, "No fancy gem-studded jewelry could ever be as precious to me as this gift."

"Speaking of precious . . ." He drew me into his arms and feathered a caress through my curls. "War is full of uncertainties. I shall not make promises that I can't keep. But if I return—"

"*When* you return," I rasped.

"*Deo volente*," replied Moore.

*God willing.*

"We have both experienced enough in Life to know that Fate

can be fickle, Hetty," he continued. "If—and when—I return from Spain, I hope you will consent to . . ." His hazel eyes took on the glow of molten amber. "To discuss a future together."

*As if that was necessary!* An answer was already etched in my heart.

"Yes," I said simply, knowing that he would understand what it meant. "B-but as you say, Fate can be terribly fickle, John." On impulse, I wrapped him in a fierce hug. "Stay the night with me. Let us create a memory that will last forever, regardless of what the future brings."

"Don't tempt me, Hetty. I am trying to be honorable and not sully your name with gossip." His voice, like mine, was rough with desire.

"Be damned with the strictures of Society." I untied the knot of his cravat and tugged it free. The length of linen slithered through my fingers and fell to the floor.

Moore undid a handful of the tiny buttons running down the back of my gown and slid the silk down to bare my shoulder. I felt a momentary lick of chill air and then his lips were like fire against my flesh.

I worked his jacket off his broad shoulders and tossed it aside. "Take me upstairs."

I awoke to the patter of rain against the windowpanes. The heavens, I reflected, were weeping the tears that I had vowed not to shed.

Moore stirred, the shadowed contours of his muscled torso dark against the tangled bedsheets. I reached out, my fingertips lightly tracing the stubbling of whiskers on his jaw, and wished with all my might that I could stop the march of time and hold onto this moment for a little longer.

But dawn's light was beginning to mizzle through the night mists.

"Good morning," he whispered, after a long and lush embrace.

"Yes and no," I smoothed a hand over his sleep-rumpled hair. "I would prefer that night linger for at least another fortnight."

"Or another eternity," he replied

The bedsheets whispered as our limbs entangled.

But all too soon, Moore lifted my hand to his lips for a fleeting kiss and then released a sigh. "Alas, duty calls, Hetty."

I longed to say *"Be damned with duty!"* But I merely nodded and held him for a heartbeat longer before letting him go.

A seasoned soldier, he dressed quickly and with a minimum of fuss. I pulled on my silk wrapper and moved with him to the door.

"I will say goodbye here, in private," I whispered.

Our eyes met and he nodded in understanding. "I will write as often as I can."

I forced a smile. "Wear your gloves when winter comes. And please make sure that Charles doesn't get into mischief."

He gave my hand a last squeeze before clicking the latch open and letting himself out.

I stood as if frozen in time, my forehead pressed against the grained oak, breathing in the lingering scent of him and our love-making. It was the muffled thud of hooves on the cobblestones that drew me to the window just as Moore rode past my house.

He lifted a hand in salute.

In the next instant he was gone, swallowed in the swirling mist and shadows.

I turned away and moved to my dressing table, where I chose a delicate filigree gold chain from my jewelry case on which to hang Moore's precious gift. My gown lay crumpled on the floor beside the bed. I took the medal from its pocket and hung it around my neck . . .

A touchstone to keep my courage from flagging.

# *Chapter* 34

September–December 1808

Autumn brought a blaze of color to the trees in Hyde Park, but for me, the days passed in a colorless procession of fretful worries. Moore's letters brought an occasional spark of light, and each morning I waited impatiently for the post to arrive. At first they arrived regularly and buoyed my spirits . . .

*I wish you were here,* read one in early October. *The weather is lovely and having you ride out with us in your glorious scarlet tunic à la Amazone would be of great cheer to me and to the troops . . .*

But after some time in Lisbon organizing the logistics, Moore had been ordered to march his army into Spain to support the Spanish military forces in their revolt against French occupation. As he had predicted, the Spanish quickly crumbled when Napoleon himself marched into the country with over 200,000 men to reinforce the French army under the command of Marshal Jean de Dieu Soult.

His letters grew more infrequent. *I fear we shall be beaten,* wrote Moore in early November. *As I predicted, we were deceived into thinking the Spanish army would join with us, and so our forces are very inferior to those of the enemy . . . Thinking of you keeps my resolve from flagging . . .*

Dispatches from Lisbon indicated that Moore's army was badly outmanned and that he was being forced to retreat just as winter took hold of the rugged mountains. I tried to distract myself with the mundane tasks of running my household. But as the reports of the situation on the Peninsula grew grimmer and grimmer, I turned my attention to making sure the politicians did not slither out of the responsibility for creating the military strategy that was proving to be fatally flawed. Already there were hints in the newspapers that they were trying to shift the blame to Moore.

James was now also with Moore, having begged to join Charles in serving as an aide-de-camp. I hadn't had the heart to stop him— I understood passion all too well. So the three men I loved most in the world were in mortal peril. The last missive I received from Moore, which arrived in late November, warned that things had turned dire and I might not hear from him again until the army reached the coast. *The situation had become untenable. Essential supplies are all but gone, forcing me to request that our Navy come extract our remaining men so that they may live to fight another day . . . I hope that our country will feel that I have done my duty as best I could . . .*

Throughout December, the newspapers published reports from the military that Moore and his outnumbered army were clawing their way toward the coastal port of Corunna in order to rendezvous with a British evacuation fleet. It was said that the brutal weather and rugged terrain were taking a terrible toll on the men—discipline was eroding and the French were moving closer and closer . . .

*January 23, 1809*

The quiet of the cold and gray morning was suddenly broken by the rap of the brass knocker on the front door. I put down my pen and shot up from my chair. I had been writing a note to my cousin, Sir Sidney Smith, begging for his public support in defending Moore's reputation against the slanderous whispers that his hapless leadership was the cause of the army's ignominious retreat.

However, the arrival of the morning post always made my heart leap into my throat.

But as I hurried through the drawing room, Elizabeth escorted Pitt's cousin, Lord Grenville, to meet me.

And I knew from his face that my worst fears had come true.

"My dear Hester, it pains me deeply to be the bearer of bad news," he said, not quite daring to meet my eye.

I stood very still, bracing my hands on the back of an armchair.

"But I felt you should hear it from me," he continued, "rather than read about it in the newspapers."

"Moore is dead." My voice was toneless, as if it was not connected to me.

"Yes, I fear so."

"How?" I demanded.

He shook his head. "I'm sorry. I know nothing of the details. The army managed to reach the coastal city of Corunna, and the first ships of the evacuation fleet just landed at Portsmouth late last night. The news reached Whitehall first thing this morning, but the accounts are still too jumbled to piece together." A pause. "Alas, there is no word yet on Charles or James."

"Thank you," I replied mechanically.

Grenville shifted uncomfortably. While he was no longer prime minister, he was still very influential in the government, and I had been constantly haranguing him during the last few months to speak up against the allegations that Moore was solely to blame for the failure of the government's grandiose scheme.

"I am truly sorry, Hester. Moore was a fine man and an exemplary officer. I . . . I know the two of you were good friends."

"Then please defend his honor from the muckworms who will be seeking to sluff off their own guilt by putting the blame on him."

Grenville gazed down at the well-polished tip of his boots. Looking, no doubt, for yet more banal platitudes to utter.

I decided to spare him the effort. "Again, my thanks for coming to inform me." I moved away from the chair. "You may consider your duty done, sir, so please don't feel the need to linger any longer in my company."

A flush of embarrassment tinged his face. His side of the family—the Grenvilles possessed the least fire of Diamond Pitt's descendants—had always thought me too headstrong, and my relationships with Camelford and Granville Leveson Gower had shocked their straitlaced sensibilities. So after Pitt's death, they had made no effort to offer comfort or a helping hand, even though they knew that my estrangement from my father had left me alone in the world.

"I . . ." A cough. "If there is anything I can do . . ."

"How kind of you," I replied coolly, taking the offer for the polite fiction it was. "I shall keep that in mind."

"Well then, if you are sure that you don't wish for me to keep you company while your maid fetches some tea . . ." Grenville had edged back several steps as he spoke.

My chin rose a fraction. "Be assured that I shall manage on my own, milord."

He bowed and withdrew without further words.

I heard Elizabeth let him out. I hurried back to my study and closed the door before she could come and offer condolences.

I gripped Moore's medal through the fabric of my gown, holding on for dear life as I sank into my chair and felt utter blackness wrap around me.

Morning slipped into evening. Another day dawned. *Light . . . Dark*—what did it matter? I had a vague recollection of Elizabeth and Susan fussing over me with broth and blankets, and yet it felt as if I was dead to the world.

But then, later that afternoon a whisper seemed to come out of nowhere.

*Live, Hetty!*

I struggled to sit up. "John?"

Light as air, the voice spoke again.

It was as if the wind was bringing his exhortation from the heavens. I gradually became aware of the everyday sounds of the neighborhood—a barking dog . . . a child's laughter . . . a costermonger bumping his cart across the cobbled square. On opening my eyes, I saw the sparkle of sunlight reflecting off the mullioned windowpanes . . . and knew in my heart that Moore would not want me to surrender. He had faced death on countless occasions and so he had valued Life as precious beyond words.

Summoning my strength, I climbed the stairs to my bedchamber, pausing for a moment to confront the pale, wild-haired specter that stared back at me from the looking glass. Drawing in a deep breath, I slowly unwrapped the black shawl that was wound around me like a shroud and let it fall to the floor.

I rang for hot water, then slowly bathed and dressed—a ritual of emerging from heartache as yet another new self. I had chosen to die once, and in grudgingly coming back to life, I had then experienced the most profound joy of my life. That was the beauty of the future—it offered the possibility of unknown and unexpected surprises.

Most of all, it offered the precious gift of Hope.

A pile of correspondences awaited me in my study when I came down the next morning. I took a seat and after making a mental note of the letters I needed to write to my military friends in Kent informing them of Moore's death, I picked up my pen and set to work.

An hour, or perhaps two, passed as the rhythmic sounds of the nib moving over paper drew me into the task at hand. It was only the sudden knock on the door that caused me to turn in my chair.

"Forgive me, milady." Elizabeth looked in through the half-open door. "But there is a gentleman here wishing to speak with you."

"I am not receiving visitors," I replied, imagining it was one of Grenville's colleagues feeling obliged to pay a courtesy call.

Elizabeth hesitated. "I think you will want to meet with him."

She swallowed hard. "He says his name is Colonel Anderson, and he has just arrived from Corunna."

I had met Anderson several times at parties given by the Duke of York's mistress and knew he was Moore's closest friend and long-time comrade in arms. "Please show him into the drawing room."

"Shall I bring tea, milady?"

"Yes—and do be sure that a bottle of whisky is on the side-board."

"I had better bring pastries as well," said Elizabeth in a low voice. "The poor man looks like naught but skin and bones."

I rose, my body still painfully stiff from my grieving, and went to join my visitor.

"Lady Hester."

Anderson's weather-beaten face was painfully gaunt, the cheek-bones so sharp that they looked on the verge of cutting through his flesh. The purple-dark hollows beneath his eyes looked like mottled bruises and his lips were cracked from the cold.

"Forgive me for appearing before you in such an unsightly state"—he grimaced as he gestured at his ragged uniform—"but I have come straight from the ship to see you."

"Please sit, sir!" I gestured at the sofa. "I am so very grateful that you are here."

His expression clouded at my words. "I must warn you, I come bearing—"

"I know," I assured him. "Lord Grenville brought me the news several days ago."

He looked relieved at not having to be the messenger of Death.

"Sit," I repeated.

His mouth thinned in embarrassment. "I'll likely ruin the lovely damask fabric."

"Be damned with the fabric." I took his arm and gently pulled him down to sit beside me, then I found his bony hand and gave it a squeeze. "I am so glad to see you."

I saw his gaze pool with sadness before he quickly looked

away. "I feel so damned guilty for surviving when . . ." His words trailed off.

"You mustn't." I rose and poured him a glass of whisky from the bottle on the sideboard. "*Slàinte mhath*," I added, placing it in his hands. "John was very fond of that Scottish toast."

"He was, indeed," said Anderson, lifting his drink in salute.

"Charles and James—" I began.

"I'm sorry. Things were so chaotic at the evacuation that I don't know what happened. I saw them both alive during the battle, but . . ." He lifted his shoulders in apology.

I watched him swallow another mouthful of the amber spirits before speaking again. "I have so many questions whirling inside my head—"

"You may ask me whatever you wish," he interrupted. "And I will be honest with you, no matter how painful to both of us." He closed his eyes for an instant. "Moore would want you to know everything."

"Of course he would," I replied. "He never flinched from the truth."

Too terrified to begin with the question that was foremost in my thoughts, I chose another. "The reports in the newspapers over the last two months gave so little information. Was the retreat to Corunna really so terrible as they implied?"

"No words can possibly describe the true horror of it." Anderson blew out a sigh. "We were dependent on Spanish intelligence as to the size and location of the French armies. Alas, the news that Napoleon himself had sensed the peril to his Spanish plans and had marched into the country reached us too late to effect an orderly retreat toward Lisbon. Caught between the Emperor's forces and Soult's army, we had had only two choices—surrender our army or head to the mountains and make our way to the port of Corunna, where the British navy could evacuate us."

"And of course, John would have considered surrender a dereliction of duty."

A mute nod.

We remained silent as Elizabeth brought in the tea tray and a plate of pastries and then quickly withdrew.

Ignoring the refreshments, Anderson continued. "The weather was dreadful. Snow and frigid temperatures made for slow going, and the supply wagons bogged down and the draft horses and oxen began to die, forcing the men to march on without food or extra clothing. Discipline began to crumble. Moore did his best to control what had become a frightened and desperate mob—you know how much he deplored looting and the pillaging of civilians."

"Yes." My throat was too tight to say more.

"Somehow, through sheer force of will, he managed to keep some semblance of order." Anderson blinked. "It was only because the men loved and respected him."

I bit my lower lip to keep my mouth from quivering.

"At last we made it to Corunna, but the ships had not yet made it into the harbor. Soult's army was hot on our heels, so Moore needed to create a rearguard defense to hold them off until the bulk of our surviving army was safely aboard the fleet."

Anderson needed to halt and steady his voice before going on. "Any other commanding general would have decided that his own safety was paramount. But of course Moore chose to lead the defense. Our men fought gallantly, holding ground against the superior French forces. But then a flank looked to be faltering and Moore—along with myself and his senior staff—rode to steady the men and redeploy them. The French cannons were battering our other positions, but there was a lull around us."

He choked back a sob. "And then a cannonball came out of nowhere and suddenly I saw him knocked from his horse. I ran to his aid, and at first I thought he was uninjured. B-but when I turned him over, I saw that his injuries were . . . severe."

"Tell me," I said.

"Milady . . ." His eyes were sheened with tears. "You don't need to know."

"Oh, but I do."

For a moment, I thought he wasn't going to answer.

"Please," I whispered.

With a groan, he did as I asked. "His arm was nearly severed at the shoulder, and the flesh had been shredded around his ribs. We called for a surgeon, but he refused, telling us the surgeons should concentrate on saving the men who have a chance of living. He knew—" A sob tore from his throat. "He knew his wounds were mortal, but he merely smiled at us and told us not to fuss."

Tears pearled on my lashes. "Damn him for being so bloody honorable."

"We made a stretcher for him out of a greatcoat, intent on carrying him back to his quarters." A wry smile. "But he made us turn this way and that for a bit so he could watch the progress of the fighting. It was only when we assured him that the French attack had been driven back that he allowed us to bring him to his bed."

"How long . . . ?"

Anderson looked away. "Several hours. He was lucid throughout, though he dozed off occasionally, and talked with each of us privately, as well as gave instructions for . . . for after he was gone."

Neither of us was now making any effort to stem the flow of tears.

"I . . . I hate to think of him suffering," I said.

"I think it gave him great solace to be able to say goodbye to us." Anderson pressed a hand to his brow. "Your brother James rushed in, having heard the terrible news, and Moore smiled and said . . ."

Another sob welled up in his throat. "He said, 'Stanhope, remember me to your sister'—and those were his last words. He died a few moments later."

Bereft of speech, I leaned in and pressed my cheek to his shoulder. He put his arms around me and pulled me close.

Sharing my grief with him somehow made it more bearable.

It took me some time to master the rush of emotions triggered by the account of Moore's final hours, but finally I felt composed enough to sit up. "It may seem a strange thing to say, but knowing about John's last hours is a great comfort to me, Colonel Anderson. I am profoundly grateful to you."

He nodded and blotted his cheeks with his sleeve.

That he didn't apologize for his tears made me like him all the more.

"I have brought several items that I thought you should have," he said, pulling a pouch from inside his tunic and loosening the strings.

I flinched as he drew out one of the sheepskin gloves that I had given Moore. It was ragged in places, the buff leather now dark with grit—and a bloodstain that nearly made my emotions come undone again.

"I hope you don't think it macabre," explained Anderson, "but I thought that you might like to have it, as he was wearing it when he was shot down."

"Indeed, I am glad to have it," I assured him, carefully wrapping it in one of the napkins from the tea tray. I would keep it in a special box as a treasured reminder of Moore's heroism. But I doubted that I would have the fortitude to look at it often.

A muted jingle drew my gaze back to him. "This, I hope, will be a more welcome memento." Anderson passed over Moore's gold pocket watch, the four fobs still intact and hanging from its gold chain.

Smiling, I cupped it in my hands. "This is precious beyond words."

"I . . . I took the liberty of putting a lock of Moore's hair inside it for you." Like most gentlemen's pocket watches, the timepiece had a locket compartment crafted into the back of the case to hold a miniature painting or keepsake.

"Thank you," I whispered. Not trusting my self-control. I decided to wait until I was alone before opening the locket.

Anderson rose. "Now I should leave you alone with your thoughts," he said. "But I hope you will allow me to call again soon."

"You must come to supper once you are settled!" I exclaimed. "I should very much enjoy your company, sir."

After giving me his address in Town, he tactfully withdrew, leaving me to stare at the starkly simple white enamel watch dial with its elegant black Roman numerals. Warmed by the heat of my hand, the case seemed to pulse with a mellow glow. Like its owner, it had a few dents. Hard-won battle scars, I mused, as I fingered their contours.

On impulse, I took the tiny key hanging next to the fobs and wound the watchspring, wondering if the mechanism had been broken when Moore was hit by the cannonball and knocked to the ground.

For a moment there was silence . . .

And then a steady *tick, tick, tick*.

# Chapter 35

*February 1809*

Alas, I soon suffered another wrenching loss. My uncle Chatham, Pitt's older brother, came to inform me that my brother Charles had died on the battlefield of Corunna at nearly the same time as Moore. His death had been a quick one—a bullet to the heart. By some miracle, James had survived a cannon blast that killed the four friends standing next to him, though he was badly wounded by gunfire.

I had now, within the space of a few years, lost three of the four people I loved most in the world. And when James was finally well enough to return to Montagu Square, it was clear that he was a mere shell of his former self. The mental horrors of war may have left no physical scars, but it was clear that the trauma had affected his mind.

All the joy had died within him. He barely spoke and never smiled, spending most of his hours sequestered in his bedchamber with naught but his inner demons as company. Colonel Anderson, now a frequent visitor to the house, did his best to help me coax James out of his personal Hell, but our efforts met with little success.

"I wonder if perchance a change of scene—somewhere completely new that conjures up no memories from the past—would do James good?" I mused as Anderson and I took a walk through Green Park.

"An interesting idea," he responded. "It's true that the sight of familiar things can trigger old memories. I know that he and Charles were very close, so England may be a fraught place for him right now."

I mumbled an assent. Indeed, I, too, felt bedeviled by ghosts and had been thinking about an escape . . .

"Perhaps somewhere exotic, where nothing is at all familiar, would spark a new interest in Life," I added. "Somewhere warm and sunny, where he could also regain his physical strength."

Anderson frowned in thought. "Are you thinking of the West Indies? Tropical fevers are of concern—"

"Actually I was thinking more of the Levant," I answered, referring to the area in the eastern Mediterranean that encompassed parts of the Ottoman Empire. "I have always wanted to see Jerusalem and the Greek isles."

We walked on in silence for a bit, the longing in me suddenly growing stronger and stronger to leave England behind.

"A splendid idea," said Anderson. "When James has sufficiently recovered, he is due to rejoin his regiment in Gibraltar, so a Mediterranean trip makes logistical sense. And I have heard the Greek isles provide an idyllic retreat for Westerners in need of peace and quiet."

*March–July 1809*

The first thing I did was to move from 4 Montagu Square to a smaller house at 14 Green Street, with the idea of finding an even cheaper residence for the summer months somewhere in the countryside. The previous year, I had visited Bath just after Moore had left for Portugal, and during a trip to the Wye Valley in nearby Wales I had fallen in love with its wild splendor. And so I wrote to inquire whether a cottage was available, as it appeared that putting together the details—and the finances—for a prolonged journey to the Levant would take some time.

An offer came back for a farmhouse nestled by the Irfon River, which I promptly accepted.

It turned out that an old acquaintance of Pitt's—a dashing and colorful South American revolutionary general by the name of Francisco de Miranda—reappeared in my life as I was packing to leave for the summer. A darling of the London intellectuals because of his support for the high-minded principles of liberty and equality, the charismatic Miranda was welcome throughout the drawing rooms of Mayfair for he kept the beau monde entertained with his storytelling.

James had met the general through a military friend and appeared to enjoy his company, so I encouraged Miranda to visit us in Wales. I think he took it as an amorous invitation, for when he arrived in the valley, he pursued me with shameless flirtations.

In the past, I might have found him irresistible. He had the sort of devil-may-care disregard for the rules of Society that had always appealed to me. However, I also knew he was a bon vivant with more than one mistress and several illegitimate children. The superficial games of passion and seduction no longer held any allure for me. I enjoyed riding out with him through the countryside, as well as debating politics and military strategy. But my heart was safe from the wiles of his silvery tongue.

I did appreciate that his company seemed to be helping James recover from his black moods. Hearing his occasional laughter at Miranda's outrageous stories made me grateful for the general's company.

His frequent presence at the farmhouse prompted my brother to bring up the subject of my relationship with the general during one of our daily walks along the river.

"Miranda says that you would make a perfect partner for his upcoming expedition to South America, where he is looking to free his country from the shackles of Spanish rule," observed James. "I would think that might appeal to your adventurous nature."

His last words were more of a question than a statement.

"He is a charming rogue, full of grand ideas and lofty goals," I answered. "I like him—very much, in fact. But I'm under no illusion that his effusive compliments are anything but playful flatteries," I replied. "I don't take them seriously."

"Do you—"

I didn't wish to focus on my feelings and so quickly cut him off. "But I'm delighted that you find him such good company. The stories of his exploits are entertaining. And I admire his fortitude in not letting his setbacks quench his enthusiasm for pursuing his dreams."

James gave me a searching stare, which I pretended not to notice.

Our boots crunched over the pebbles of the footpath.

"So, you won't be sailing to the New World with him?"

I looped my arm through his and gave it a sisterly pat. "Indeed not! I am very much looking forward to traveling with you and discovering the wonders of the East."

James looked a little relieved. He smiled and began chatting about all the things he wished to see in the Greek isles, and yet shadows remained pooled in the depth of his eyes.

*Fall–Winter, 1809*

As the riot of summer colors began to fade, we returned to London, where to my frustration I encountered yet more complications in trying to arrange passage aboard a naval ship headed to the Mediterranean. Given the war raging on the Continent and surrounding seas, there were no other viable options for travel, so I set to work in asking favors from our relatives in the government.

While I waited, I turned my attention to the task of finding a physician to accompany us. James's wounds were not quite healed, and my health wasn't perfect, so it had been deemed a necessity to have a man skilled in the healing arts to be part of our party, no matter the extra cost that I could ill afford. A family friend recommended the son of an acquaintance, a young man who was studying medicine at St. Thomas's Hospital under Henry Cline but had not yet finished his requirements. Apparently a personal tragedy had made Charles Meryon eager to escape from England for a time, and so he eagerly agreed to all my terms, including a modest salary. He would accompany us for a year, visiting Sicily and other lands to the east.

With that settled, all we needed was for the Admiralty to approve our travel request.

And yet the days dragged on without any word.

Riding in Hyde Park had become a luxury I couldn't afford, and so I began taking walks in the small park near Green Street every morning, hoping that the fresh air and exercise would help quell my impatience. A graveled footpath ran along the perimeter of the grounds, and my daily routine was to circle around it three times before heading home.

I was just passing through the gated entrance one morning in mid-September to begin when a sudden hail caught me by surprise.

"Lady Hester?"

Puzzled, I stopped and looked around. I knew nobody in the neighborhood.

A feminine figure dressed in a forest-green cloak and matching bonnet stepped out from the shadows of the boxwood hedge. As she came closer I was shocked to recognize Harriet, Lady Bessborough, one of my sworn enemies.

"Why, what a coincidence to encounter you here." I made no attempt to keep the sarcasm out of my voice. "This humble part of Town is not one of your usual haunts."

"No, it's not," she replied. "But I was hoping to have a word with you."

"Whatever for?"

"I . . ." Harriet took a moment to adjust the silk cording of the elegant reticule looped around her wrist. "I have been wanting to tell you how sorry I was to hear of General Moore's death. But as I didn't feel a letter was the right way to do so—"

"You thought I would rip it up without reading it?"

She allowed a wry smile. "It seemed a distinct possibility."

"Thank you for the courtesy." I turned away. "Consider your duty done."

"Wait!"

I hesitated.

"Might I accompany you for a bit? There is more that I wish to say."

Curiosity won out over pique. I nodded brusquely and resumed walking.

Harriet hurried to catch up. But strangely enough, we continued on in silence until the path led into a glade of coppery beech trees.

"Moore was an exemplary man and admirable hero," she began. "I imagine that you feel his loss deeply—"

"What are you hoping to accomplish?" I snapped. "Are you trying to provoke me into breaking down into tears and baring my soul so that you may run back to tell your sister and chortle over my misery?" I quickened my pace. "Go to the devil. Your wicked games no longer have any power to wound me."

Harriet matched my stride. "I don't blame you for thinking the worst of me. You were hurt immeasurably by being caught up in a web of intrigue that was not of your own making."

She paused by one of the trees and looked down at the fallen leaves on the ground. "There was never an intent to cause you pain. Things . . ." A sigh. "Things were exceedingly complicated."

I made a rude sound. "That's one way of putting it."

To her credit, she gave a self-deprecating laugh. "No matter how I describe it, words cannot disguise the fact that you suffered, and for that I am truly sorry."

Honesty deserved honesty, I decided. "I never blamed you. I'm aware that life within the beau monde is full of complexities and contradictions, especially for ladies."

"Indeed. Society does not look kindly on those who refuse to conform to the rules and lead lives of quiet desperation." Harriet looked up. "I make no excuses for Georgiana. She can be cruel. But I think it is because her own heart has been battered and broken so many times in the past."

"Hearts are fragile," I conceded. "And once broken, they are not easily mended."

"True."

Our eyes met with a flicker of mutual understanding.

She drew in a shaky breath before speaking again. "Granville . . ."

"Your kindness does you credit," I interrupted. "But you need not speak for him."

"I was merely going to make an observation." Harriet paused, and when I made no objection she continued. "Perhaps it is human nature that we fool ourselves into thinking that the things we desire can be had without consequences. However, I think men are more prone to such delusions than women. They are taught to expect that they can have what they want, while the lessons we learn are more pragmatic."

I found myself regretting that we had never had the chance to become friends.

"I know that Granville deeply regretted the hurt he caused you," she added. "Gentlemen can also feel trapped by Society's expectations. He made choices that he came to regret."

"Choices under such circumstances are rarely simple or easy." Forgiveness felt easier than clinging to painful grudges. "We all make mistakes."

Harriet gave me a grateful look, and then quickly changed the subject. "I heard from Lord Chatham that you are soon to be traveling to the East with your brother James and expect to be gone for at least a year."

"We are planning to explore Greece and the Levant," I replied. "I am very much looking forward to broadening my horizons."

"It sounds marvelous." A dappling of sunlight softened the shadows within the glade. "I wish you a fair wind and cloudless skies as you navigate what lies ahead."

"Thank you." On impulse, I held out my hand. "May you find happiness in your future."

Harriet hesitated, and then smiled as our palms touched together. "Write to me on occasion. I should like to hear how you are faring."

"I shall," I promised, and realized that I meant it.

The breeze freshened, tangling the ribbons of her bonnet in the fastening of her cloak. She gave my hand a squeeze before releasing it and smoothing her collar. "Godspeed, Lady Hester."

As I watched Harriet walk away, I felt oddly happy to have her support. Perhaps making peace with my past augured well for my upcoming journey.

But I would just have to wait and see.

Finally, just before the end of the year, I received word that we had been granted permission to join a naval frigate headed to Gibraltar, and from there we would be given official papers to continue our journey east.

And so it was that on January 13, 1810, I locked the front door of my rented house on Green Street and quitted London for the Royal Dockyards of Portsmouth, ready for whatever new adventures lay ahead.

# *Chapter* 36

*February 10, 1810*

Grunts punctuated the shrieks of the circling gulls as a group of sailors threw their weight against the capstan and the massive anchor chain began to rise from the depth of the harbor waters.

*At last we are underway*, I thought in silent exultation, lifting my face to the sun's rays. Our ship—HMS *Jason*, a fifth-rate frigate— had been scheduled to depart five days ago, but the winds had been fickle, dying to a mere whisper that left all but the smallest vessel of the Portsmouth fleet becalmed at their moorings.

"All hands aloft!" bellowed the lieutenant of the port watch, sending a swarm of men scrambling up the masts and onto the yardarms. More orders and then canvas cracked loud as cannon fire as sails unfurled and the frigate ghosted down the channel leading out to the open sea.

I turned to watch the bustling wharves recede in the distance, and felt no regrets over all that I was leaving behind.

The wind freshened as we rounded the last spit of land and picked up speed as more sails unfurled. Making my way through the shrouds and spars, I headed to the bow of the ship, where I found a quiet spot near the base of the bowsprit. Spray flew up as the hull sliced through the waves, white flecks of foam against the gray-green water.

I snapped open the telescope that Caroline Herschel had given me—I considered it one of my most precious possessions—and lifted it to my eye, following the diamond-bright winks of sunlight on the waves to the far-away horizon. And at that moment, I truly understood her excitement of exploring the heavens, where the vastness and wonder of the unknown put all our petty worries and fears into perspective—

"What are you expecting to see?" Wrapped in a thick wool cloak, James shuffled up to join me in the lee of the foresail. He shaded his eyes and grimaced as the sting of the cold wind hit his cheeks. "There is naught but an endless expanse of unfathomable ocean."

"On the contrary, take a look for yourself!" I replied, offering him the glass.

He took it and squinted through the lens.

"Follow the ripples of sunlight," I said. "They are drawing us ever forward to the horizon."

"Which is just an amorphous blur of gray," muttered James. He lowered the telescope and turned to regard the fast receding coast.

"Don't look back." I placed the telescope in my cloak pocket and put my arms around him, drawing him close. "Keep your focus on the path ahead. There is Hope out there, just past the line between sea and sky."

"I can't see it, Hetty." James blinked, the salt spray pearling on his lashes as he stared out at the waves. "I-I miss Charles, and that seems to cast a black shadow over everything."

I held him tighter. "Over the last few years, I have had my heart broken by betrayal, I have lost Pitt, who was more of a father to me than my own flesh and blood, as well as dear Charles and John Moore, the love of my life. So believe me, I truly understand your pain."

"Y-you loved Moore?"

"I did. With all my heart. We planned to be married when he returned from the war."

He fumbled for my hand and gave it a tender squeeze. "I'm so sorry, Hetty." We stood for an interlude in silence looking out at the sea. "I-I don't understand . . . How do you manage to be so optimistic?"

"Because I choose to be," I answered. "You mustn't let adversity crush you."

He swallowed hard.

For all their so-called strength, I mused, men were not nearly as resilient as women. Perhaps it was because they were told from the moment of birth that Life would be kind and give them whatever they wanted. While women were tougher. We had been taught that however unfair it was, we must learn to survive the slings and arrows that came our way.

"Alas, pain is part of Life. But don't let it close your eyes to the possibilities of the future."

"I shall try, Hetty." His voice was nearly lost in the sounds of the ship, but perhaps I had planted a seed of Hope. After another moment of silence, he shivered. "It's awfully chilly up here. I'm going down below to my cabin."

The frigate tacked, the sails thundering as the hull swung around to a new direction.

Alone again, I smiled as a thought suddenly came to mind. Like the captain who orders the set of the sails and the course of the ship, I was the commander of my soul. I had learned that I was strong enough to weather the storms of life. *Ridicule, rejection, heartache, grief*—let all the elemental crosscurrents and waves slam against my tiny speck of being.

I would not sink.

I thought back to telling Moore that it was our scars which reminded us that our past was real. I wouldn't give up my memories of the all-too-short joy with him in order to expunge all pain I had suffered.

It was the journey that mattered, I reminded myself. Darkness or Light, Heaven or Hell, Joy or Sorrow—it was all a reminder that we were alive.

And that was a celebration in itself.

I took up the telescope again and twisted the dial to bring the lens into focus.

My blood began to pulse. Just over the horizon lay an unexplored world with the promise of new adventures, new opportunities.

I looked up to the sun and once again the wind seemed to bring me a whisper from Moore.

*Fortune favors the bold.*

"I will be bold, John," I promised. "I will be brave."

Up ahead, the future beckoned . . .

And I was ready to embrace it.

# *Epilogue*

I never returned to Britain.

I sit here now, old and wrinkled, in the courtyard garden of Djoumi, my desert fortress in the Levant. It's been twenty-eight years—nearly half my lifetime—since I sailed away from Portsmouth. The salty scent of the wintry sea has long since faded. These days, I inhale the heady fragrance of the exotic gardens I've created within my courtyards, their perfume edged with the darker spice of incense and memories.

*Oh, such richly nuanced memories.*

James and I explored the Greek islands and the splendors of Athens. My brother grew stronger in body and mind, and returned to his regiment in Gibraltar, while I and the rest of my party continued on to the fabled city of Constantinople, capital of the Ottoman Empire, and then headed to Egypt. Shipwrecked off the island of Malta, I was forced to wear borrowed men's clothing fashioned in the colorful Turkish style, with flowing robes and embroidered trousers. It was a style I came to love and never relinquished. My travels also took me to the Ionian Islands, Palestine, Lebanon, Syria . . .

*Over the years, I partied with pashas and princes . . . rode unveiled through the gates of Damascus as the crowds welcomed me as the Queen of the Desert . . . raised my own army . . . brokered peace between the power-*

*ful warlords of the region . . . excavated ancient ruins in search of answers to the past . . .*

A second lifetime of stories.

I smile, paper crackling as I look up from the letter in my hands. Harriet and I had kept up a regular correspondence, and both of us have been greatly amused by the many tales about my life that have swirled through the drawing rooms of London and beyond.

It seems that I have become famous.

*My dear Hetty,* she wrote in this latest missive, *you would chuckle to see the grand banner that hangs over the entrance of the British Museum, announcing the current exhibition of artifacts discovered by the intrepid explorer and renowned archaeologist, Lady Hester Stanhope.*

During my early years in the Levant, I came into possession of a medieval Italian manuscript that hinted at hidden treasure buried in the city of Ashkelon. Intrigued, I badgered the Ottoman authorities for permission to excavate. I found no horde of ancient gold but, fascinated by the layers of civilization that were uncovered in the digging, I insisted on doing a careful job of preserving what we found and methodically recording the details in an excavation journal. The logic of it seemed obvious to me, but apparently I am now hailed as leader in the field for seeking to understand the past.

*The newspapers frequently mention you as a political force in the Levant,* continued Harriet. *The beau monde is greatly impressed by the published engravings that show you riding astride in your turban and robes at the head of your private army.*

Indeed, the irony often makes me laugh. It's here, half a world away from Britain among the tribal fiefdoms of the desert, that I have finally found what I always yearned for. I am recognized and respected as an equal among men. I have power and influence. I sit at the negotiating table, a force to be reckoned with.

That, in turn, has made me a celebrity, not only in Britain but throughout the rest of the world. I am courted by international travelers to the region, who call me the most celebrated adventurer of the era and beg for the privilege of a private audience. British diplomats seek my advice on how to deal with the various rulers. I entertain kings and queens from the Continent in the splendor of my mountain citadel.

I put aside Harriet's letter and slip my hand beneath my robes to touch Moore's medal, which has been my constant companion—and confidant—since that fateful morning he had ridden away. I like to think that he is smiling at what I have made of myself.

*Fortes fortuna juva.*

My time is growing short. Cicadas serenade the fading light. The sun is setting over Mount Lebanon, the shadows deepening, swirling like *afreets* and *djinns* in the purpling twilight. I will soon be gone, mortal flesh turning to dust.

But oh . . . what a life I have had.

# *Author's Note*

When my editor and I first began discussing the idea of this book, I had some reservations. A *fictional biography?* That seemed like such an oxymoron, and coming from the world of fiction, where I could happily scribble away, making things up as I went along, the thought of trying to piece together Truth and Imagination in one story seemed a little daunting . . .

And then there was Lady Hester Stanhope herself. I've written a number of books set in Regency England, so I'm fairly knowledgeable about the history and notable people of the era. Her name was familiar to me, but only for the later part of her life, when she was the most famous—and eccentric—adventurer of the early nineteenth century. From what little I had read, Lady Hester was considered opinionated, abrasive, headstrong, and emotionally unstable. That certainly gave me pause for thought. To write a book about her meant that the two of us would be spending a lot of "up close and personal" time together. Was it a commitment I was willing to make? What if we didn't get along?

Still, her story was intriguing enough that I decided to do a little more research. One of the first things that caught my eye was the tale of The Diamond—the "origin story" of the Pitt family's rise to become one of the most powerful and influential aristocratic families in Britain. Intermarriage over several generations with the equally impressive Stanhope and Grenville families added yet more luster to the family tree.

The more I read, the more I became fascinated, not only by the clan's position within the highest circles of Society but also by the amazing range of their individual talents and achievements—three prime ministers, a foreign secretary, and First Lord of the Admiralty, a famous scientist, a dashing war hero, to name just a few.

So how did Lady Hester fit into this blazing array of luminaries?

With her own fiery spark, I quickly discovered. As soon as I delved into her life, it became clear that she had inherited the same fierce intellect and ambition that so many of her male relatives possessed. The trouble was, she was born into a world that permitted women— especially aristocratic women—no role in life save to produce an heir and a spare, ensure the smooth running of a household, and smile prettily at parties while keeping any opinions to themselves. And yet, that didn't deter Lady Hester.

As I read on, I was captivated by what a strong sense of self she had, even as a child, and how determined she was to have a voice and be heard. Showing the same grit and daring as her great-great-grandfather, "Diamond" Pitt, and wielding her own considerable wit and charm, Lady Hester rebelled against the rules. And against all odds—though not without disasters to go along with her triumphs—she earned a place for herself in the highest echelon of government, working with her uncle as his private secretary and hostess, where she was included in the debates on the great issues facing Britain. Her personal life was just as colorful, as she was intimately involved with some of the leading men of her era.

And yet, I had never heard of Lady Hester's extraordinary achievements during her life in England . . .

However, one of the things I love about history is that it is not etched in stone. Our view of the past is constantly evolving. Present-day scholarship is looking at what's come before us with a broader perspective. More and more stories are coming to light of extraordinary people—like Lady Hester Stanhope—whose important achievements in so many fields of endeavors have been marginalized or left out of the traditional narratives because of

prejudice—gender, race, ethnicity, sexual orientation . . . Their
deeds enrich our understanding of history and give us a truer picture of the past—and offer inspiration for the future.

And that's why this book became a labor of love for me. I came
to admire and applaud Lady Hester. Yes, she had plenty of faults.
She could be hot-tempered, impetuous, and reckless. Her judgment was sometimes flawed. But her courage, her compassion, her
refusal to surrender her dreams won me over. Her story, and her
achievements, deserves to be known.

Now, on to the actual process of combining fact and fiction!
In the middle of writing this book, I was asked to give a talk
about writing a novel based on the life of a real person. As my
title I chose *The Intersection of History, Fiction, and Imagination: A
Re-imagining of the Extraordinary Life of Lady Hester Stanhope*—
which captures the essence of what I set out to do.

First of all I had to gather the historical facts. I was fortunate in
finding a wonderful scholarly biography of Lady Hester Stanhope,
*Star of the Morning: The Extraordinary Life of Lady Hester Stanhope* by
Kirsten Ellis, published by Harper Press (UK) in 2008. (See my
Acknowledgments for a list of resources.) Its meticulous account
of Lady Hester's life not only gave me a good overview of her and
her extended family, but also provided detailed dates from which I
could build an accurate timeline for the part of Lady Hester's life
that I had chosen to write about. (Trying to cover her whole life in
one novel struck me as impossible, so I decided to concentrate on
her life in England, which interested me even more than her later
exploits in the Levant.)

The timeline gave me a skeleton. Now I had to flesh it out by
learning enough about the real people involved to make them
come alive in my head. And then I had to shape all the bits and
pieces in to a plot, for a novel needs to have pacing and dramatic
moments to keep readers engaged.

That Lady Hester came from such a prominent family meant
that much of her personal correspondence was preserved, so I
learned a lot about her from her own words. She was a great letter
writer and kept in frequent touch with friends and family about

what was happening in her daily life, as well as her opinions on issues of the day. (Lady Hester's niece, the Duchess of Cleveland, published a collection of such letters in book form, along with her own annotations, which I found extremely interesting.) I came to really appreciate Lady Hester's pithy humor, her intelligence, her sharply cynical yet pragmatic views. The letters also gave hints of her disappointments and her strength of character in not letting her ambitions be squashed by a world ruled by men.

Then, of course, there was the famous three-volume *Memoirs of the Lady Hester Stanhope, As Related By Herself in Conversations With Her Physician*. Later in life, Lady Hester dictated recollections of her life to her personal physician, Charles Meryon, which he published after her death. It's a fascinating account, though it's clear that her memory—and her own desire to edit her experiences—along with the fact that Dr. Meryon might have had his own ax to grind, make it a less than totally reliable source.

I also read biographies and articles on George Brummell, Lord Camelford, Granville Leveson Gower, William Pitt the Younger, and Lieutenant-General Sir John Moore, which helped me to understand them as individuals, which in turn allowed me to create a more nuanced portrait of Lady Hester. My research also involved reviewing material on the secondary characters, including the Duchess of Devonshire, Lady Bessborough, Sir Sidney Smith, Sir Thomas Lawrence, and Princess Caroline of Brunswick.

Most of the other people who appear briefly in the book are also historical figures—Lord Chatham, Hester's beloved grandmother Hester Pitt, George Canning, William Dacres Adams, Colonel Paul Anderson, Elizabeth Williams, the maid Susan . . . even Burfield, the gardener at Walmer Castle.

So how did I put this all together?

As someone who believes that actual history is often more interesting and provocative than fiction, I decided from the beginning that I wanted to stay as accurate as possible in telling Lady Hester's story. So I've tried to stay true to the known facts in depicting her relationships with her family and the four men with whom she was emotionally involved. Whenever I found a notable detail in my research, I would work it into my fictional narrative—for example, the night her father put a knife to her throat; helping her half brother Mahon escape from Chevening by climbing out an upper window using bedsheets tied together; creating the gardens at Walmer Castle by marshaling the local militia to dig and plant; the house party in Weymouth hosted by Lady Hester's dashing cousin, Sir Sidney Smith, which included Princess Caroline, the Duchess of Devonshire, and Lady Bessborough; Colonel Anderson meeting with Lady Hester to give her Moore's bloody glove (here I took the artistic liberty of adding the pocket watch, which is on display at the National Army Museum in London) after the Battle of Corunna—are all true.

Using these vignettes, and a myriad of others like them, I then would use my imagination to write a scene with Lady Hester as the narrator. I chose to tell her story in first person because she was such a forceful, magnetic, and emotionally complex individual it seemed the best way to capture the nuanced facets of her personality.

When it came to the four important men in her life, I also wanted to portray those relationships as accurately as I could.

Lady Hester arrived in London with little experience in the world of the beau monde due to her eccentric upbringing. Through her uncle, William Pitt the Younger, she soon met the cynical, self-assured George "Beau" Brummell, who by all accounts taught her elemental lessons about the intricate rules-within-rules that governed the highest circles of Society. They shared a sardonic sense of humor but both of them seemed to recognize that their temperaments and aspirations were not well matched.

Lord Camelford, known as the "Half-Mad Lord," appealed to Lady Hester's rebellious nature. She found his devil-may-care recklessness exciting and alluring, while he, in turn, sensed a kindred soul who chafed at the idea of leading a boring conventional life. I discovered that Camelford was, in fact, a great fan of the rough-and-tumble world of prizefights, happily rubbing shoulders with the working class and funding events from his considerable fortune. Thus I wrote a scene of him taking Lady Hester to a boxing match. He visited her often while she was staying with her grandmother at Burton Pynsent. The dowager allowed Lady Hester a great deal of freedom, and my research shows that they did indeed travel together to Cornwall and stay at Boconnoc, Camelford's ancestral estate, where Lady Hester lost her virginity.

His behavior did become increasingly erratic, and she was smart enough—and pragmatic enough—to realize they would both likely burn each other to a crisp.

Granville Leveson Gower was the exact opposite. Handsome, charming, skilled in the art of diplomacy, he appeared a paragon of perfection, and Lady Hester was smitten. But as described, he was entangled in a longtime affair with Lady Bessborough—though that didn't stop him from seducing a willing Lady Hester. He did possess a collection of erotic books, and the two of them did tryst on Primrose Hill and during carriage rides. Lady Hester did set out to win a marriage proposal from him, and was devastated when she realized that despite all her efforts her hopes were in vain. The rejection did, in fact, cause her to try to take her own life.

The historical record is less forthcoming concerning her relationship with Lieutenant-General Sir John Moore. They did become friends during her early days at Walmer Castle and often rode out together—Lady Hester was a superb equestrian and was known to ride astride—before his military duties sent him abroad. And the friendship was rekindled when he returned to England and came to give her his belated condolences on Pitt's death. Lady Hester did help him navigate the complex factions of government as he tried to advise the cabinet on the military situation on the Peninsula.

As for their personal relationship . . . historians disagree on whether they had a love affair and were secretly engaged to be married. But I'm a romantic at heart, and on reading their letters to each other, I chose to believe that they were indeed soulmates and lovers who respected each other's intellect and opinions.

*Fact and Fiction.*

As I have said, I've tried to be historically accurate as to the time and place of each scene. I've also done as much research as I can to postulate what Lady Hester may have been feeling at the time. But as for the actual conversations and expressions of emotion . . . that's all my creative speculation. Yes, I've taken some artistic liberties with the characters as I've shaped my research into a novel. Some historians may take issue with my decisions, but that's the beauty of writing fiction. Imagination is an integral part of the process. That said, I've tried to be true to the essence of all the incredibly interesting people who played a part in this story. As for Lady Hester . . .

If she were to read this book, I hope she would smile and feel that I've done her justice.

# Notable Resources

*Star of the Morning: The Extraordinary Life of Lady Hester Stanhope*, by Kirsten Ellis; Harper Press (UK), 2008

*Memoirs of the Lady Hester Stanhope, As Related By Herself in Conversations With Her Physician*, by Charles Lewis Meryon; originally published in 1845

*The Life and Letters of Lady Hester Stanhope*, by her niece the Duchess of Cleveland; John Murray, London, 1914

*Lady Hester Stanhope*, by Martin Armstrong; Viking Press, New York, 1928

*Lady Hester Stanhope*, by Mrs. Charles Roundell; John Murray, London, 1909

*Lady Hester Lucy Stanhope: a new light on her life and love affairs*, by Frank Hamel; Cassell and Company, Ltd., 1913

*William Pitt the Younger*, by William Hague; Harper Perennial, London, 2005

*The Life of Lieutenant-General Sir John Moore, KB*, by his brother James Carrick Moore; John Murray, London, 1834

*The Life and Letters of Sir John Moore,* by Beatrice Brownrigg; Basil Blackwell, Oxford, 1823

*The Life of Sir John Moore: Not a Drum was Heard,* by Roger William Day; Leo Cooper, 2001

*The Life of George Brummell, ESQ.,* by Captain Jesse; Saunders and Otley, London, 1845

*The Half-Mad Lord,* by Nikolai Tolstoy; Holt, Rinehart and Winston, New York, 1978

*Granville Leveson Gower: Private Correspondence, 1781 to 1821,* edited by his daughter-in-law Castalia, Countess Granville; E. P. Dutton, New York, 1916

## Websites Related to the People and Places in This Book

English Heritage.org is a fabulous site, rich with fascinating resources on the country's history. The site features wonderful images and details about Walmer Castle and Lady Hester's time there:

https://www.english-heritage.org.uk/visit/places/walmer-castle-and-gardens/history-and-stories/history/

https://www.english-heritage.org.uk/visit/places/walmer-castle-and-gardens/history-and-stories/hester-stanhope/

The National Army Museum in London has a terrific website that showcases a section on Lieutenant-General Sir John Moore. (You can see a photo of his pocket watch, which I describe in this book.)

https://www.nam.ac.uk/explore/john-moore

Two of the grand estates described in this book have websites—and if you are as plump in the pocket as Diamond Pitt and the Half-Mad Lord, you can actually rent their legendary Boconnoc for a private stay or wedding:

https://www.boconnoc.com/

https://cheveninghouse.com/history.htm

# Acknowledgments

Writing itself is a very solitary endeavor, but creating a book takes, as they say, a village. I am so profoundly grateful to my village—I couldn't have done this without all of you!

From the very beginning, my wonderful agent, Kevan Lyon, encouraged me to take on this project and patiently read through the sample chapters and first draft, providing key suggestions that helped to shape the story. I'm incredibly fortunate to have her guidance.

My amazing editor, Wendy McCurdy, then took my manuscript and whipped it into final shape. I use that verb deliberately. Yes, she made me cry at times during the revision process—a profusion of dead adjectives and overwrought prose are buried in the margins of track changes, but their demise was all for the higher good! She made the book better and I'm truly indebted to her expert editing!

And kudos to Kensington and its fabulous PR and Art departments. I'm really grateful for their support of Lady Hester. Special thanks go to Alex Nicolajsen, who first raised the idea of my doing a historical novel. Vida Engstrand and Michelle Addo are always wonderful at working their magic in promotion. As for art director Seth Lerner, he deserves a gold medal! I have an MFA in graphic design, and admit that I am likely a Holy Terror when it comes to reviewing cover designs. However, he handled my suggestions with great grace and patience, and the final result is stunning.

Friends are key to survival during the endless months that drag on between that first blank page and "The End." The Word Wenches, my fabulous blogmates and writer pals—Nicola Cornick, Christina Courtenay, Anne Gracie, Susan Fraser King, Mary Jo Putney, and Pat Rice—have been cheerleaders of this project from the get-go. Not only did they provide crucial Beta Reads, but as we're spread out around the globe, there was *always* someone awake to offer sympathy and cyber chocolate when I started sniveling and feeling sorry for myself. I love you guys!

Profound thanks also go to the inimitable John R. Ettinger, whose myriad talents include an expertise in British history. No author could have a more perfect comrade-in-brainstorming! He provided invaluable counsel while helping me sort through all the facts and shape them into a story . . . as well as coming to the rescue when I tied myself in plot knots! (I owe you a *really* good bottle of single malt whisky!)

My dear college roommates—Rachel Hockett, Lawrie Mifflin, Keri Keating Ricci, and Margy Wiener—all avid booklovers, patiently listened without complaint (and only an occasional eye-roll) when I rattled on about British history during our regular Zoom meetings. Their enthusiasm was a real balm for the spirit when The Muse was feeling cranky.

And, as always, heartfelt hugs go to my family for their unflagging encouragement and support, which means more to me than words can express.

# THE DIAMOND
# OF LONDON

## Andrea Penrose

## ABOUT THIS GUIDE

The suggested questions are included to enhance
your group's reading of Andrea Penrose's *The Diamond of London*.

# DISCUSSION QUESTIONS

1. Lady Hester came to London knowing that the traditional expectation of her aristocratic world was that she would quickly accept a proposal and get married. Why do you think she had no interest in doing so?

2. What attracted her to George Brummell? What made her uneasy? Would they have been happy as a couple?

3. Why did Lady Hester find Camelford so alluring? What was the main reason for her attraction to him? How were they alike and how were they different?

4. Lady Hester saw Granville Leveson Gower as the perfect match for her. Do you agree?

5. What do you think she would have had to sacrifice in order to make a marriage with Granville work?

6. Why do you think she tried to take her own life?

7. Did Lady Hester make a wise decision in refusing to accept the traditional role of a woman in her era? Should she have followed the example of the Duchess of Devonshire and played by the unwritten rules of Society in order to have some freedoms? Or do you applaud her for refusing to give up her principles?

8. What do you think was most important to her—Love? Freedom? Something else?

9. Lady Hester's extended family—the Stanhopes, the Pitts, and the Grenvilles—included some of the most powerful and influential gentlemen of the era. Was that a blessing or a curse? Did any of them understand her as a person?

10. Lady Hester had no close women friends or role models in her life. Why do you think that was? And how did it affect her?

11. Lady Hester was steadfastly loyal to those she loved. Did that hurt her? How?

12. What do you think were Lady Hester's greatest strengths? Her greatest weaknesses?

13. Would you call Lady Hester courageous? Reckless? Or something more nuanced?

14. Do you think the heartaches and pain that Lady Hester suffered were worth the triumphs she won? What choices would you have made?

15. What do you think Lady Hester wanted most in life?

16. Of all the men she knew, who do you think was the love of her life?

17. If you were casting a movie of Lady Hester's life, who would you choose to play her?